MURDER ON THE FARM

KATE WELLS

Boldwood

First published in Great Britain in 2023 by Boldwood Books Ltd.

Cover Design by Nick Castle

Cover Photography: Shutterstock

A CIP catalogue record for this book is available from the British Library.

Paperback ISBN 978-1-78513-421-0

Large Print ISBN 9978-1-78513-417-3

Hardback ISBN 978-1-78513-416-6

Ebook ISBN 978-1-78513-414-2

Kindle ISBN 978-1-78513-415-9

Audio CD ISBN 978-1-78513-422-7

MP3 CD ISBN 978-1-78513-419-7

Digital audio download ISBN 978-1-78513-413-5

Boldwood Books Ltd
23 Bowerdean Street
London SW6 3TN
www.boldwoodbooks.com

For the Malvern Hills, my constant home wherever I find myself.

1

As Jude Gray tore down the driveway of Malvern Farm, she glanced at the clock on the dashboard.

'Bugger it,' she cursed.

Ben's wedding was due to begin in twelve minutes and the church was a fifteen-minute drive away. She put her foot down a little harder on the accelerator and prayed that there would be no tractors around when she pulled out onto the country lane leading out of Malvern End. Jude hated being late for anything. She'd always taken pride in her punctuality and yet she knew that it would take a small miracle for her to arrive at the wedding on time.

It had all started so well. Noah, her shepherd, had recruited a couple of extra pairs of hands to help with the lambing whilst she was at the wedding to allow her to enjoy a proper afternoon and evening off. Frank, Noah's dad, had arrived just as Jude was washing off her blood-stained hands in the sink at the back of the lambing shed.

'Everything all right here?' Frank asked Noah.

Frank was old farming stock and still not quite sure what to make of a young female farmer. He'd worked on Malvern Farm for all his adult life, introducing Noah to its ways from the day he could walk. Frank had taken over the tenancy of another local sheep farm when Noah was ready to take his place as the Grays' chief shepherd, but he still came to help out when needed, as long as the ties of his own farm allowed.

Adam's mother had kept to the more traditional role of *farmer's wife*, making cups of tea and hearty meals whilst the men laboured on the land. Frank hadn't quite known what to make of Jude's more immersive, hands-on approach, so she was used to him directing his questions and thoughts to his son instead. Frank stood, stroking his bushy grey beard and peering expectantly at Noah through thick glasses.

'Busy,' said Jude. 'There's a ewe in pen eighteen who had a bit of an issue with ringwomb but, with a bit of a cervical massage, she birthed okay in the end.'

'I've no doubt she did,' said Frank. 'Noah's a safe pair of hands for any ewe.'

'All Jude's work, Dad,' said Noah.

'Right,' said Frank, not bothering to hide his obvious surprise. 'Well done, then, Jude. You'll be wanting to go in now and get ready for this wedding, I suppose, so go on, I'll pick it up from here and Spud will be along soon too.'

It was a little later than Jude would have liked but she still had plenty of time to scrub the smell of sheep and hay from her body, wash, dry and even style her hair before pulling on the satin slip dress she'd bought in the post-Christmas sale. When she had checked the full-length mirror, it was almost like catching sight of a previous version of herself. For once, she looked her actual age rather than the haggard old woman she'd got used to greeting in her reflection, generally wearing a uniform of checked lumberjack shirts and old jeans. Jude couldn't help thinking about how things might have been if life had played her a different hand, been kinder and fairer. She should now be helping Adam to knot his tie and going through the best man's speech with him one last time, perhaps with a baby chuckling happily at them from the bed. She turned away from the mirror. There was no time for melancholic thoughts. A little mascara and her favourite lipstick and she felt ready to tackle the world. Shrugging a shaggy mohair cardigan over the top of the dress to try to keep the February chill at bay, Jude was ready to go twenty minutes before her planned ETD.

Looking back, she wished she'd just jumped in the car then, given herself plenty of time to drive out to Great Malvern and arrive in a cloud of calm serenity. But she hadn't. She'd decided to pull her wellies on and cross the yard to check in one last time with Noah and the ewes in the lambing shed.

Noah was the third generation of shepherd to have been employed by Malvern Farm and Jude was sure he knew more about sheep husbandry than most shepherds twice his age. Lambing was a tough season and this was her second one without Adam. If it hadn't been for Noah's easy company, vast experience and constant support, Jude knew she'd have had no chance of keeping the place afloat. She found him busy with a ewe who'd already birthed one lamb and was trying to deliver its trickier twin, so Jude left him to it. With Pip, her collie-cross, trotting at her heel, she walked along the line of lambing pens, each containing either a mother and her new baby, or a pregnant ewe about to give birth.

Jude's heart sank when she looked into one of the pens. A new mum had clearly rolled over on top of her poor baby and, with Noah already up to his elbows, Jude knew she had no choice. Her experience told her that the lamb's chances of survival were not good, but this one was clinging on, its eyes shut but its squashed chest rising and falling steadily. If Jude left it, waited for Frank or Spud to get back from the fields or Noah to finish with the difficult birth, the lamb would die. She looked down at her dress and flinched. Going back to change into something more appropriate would waste time that this little mite didn't have. She took an old fleece from a hook on the wall and jammed it over her outfit to save as much of it as possible. Then she climbed into the pen to scoop up the partially flattened newborn.

Five minutes later, Jude was back in the farmhouse kitchen preparing the first colostrum feed for the lamb, who was wrapped in the old fleece and lying in a box in front of the ancient Aga.

'Here we go,' Jude whispered when the feed was ready. She held the lamb against her and measured the tube to make sure it would reach the stomach. Then she gently clamped the lamb between her legs and put the end of the tube in its mouth. As she pushed it down the lamb's throat, it began to make tiny chewing movements.

'That's it,' Jude said, delighted at this positive sign.

Once the tube was in place, she poured the warm first milk through a syringe and watched gravity draw it into the lamb's stomach. The tiny mew of annoyance as Jude pulled the tube out at the end of the feed made her smile.

'You might just be okay,' Jude said.

She'd given the lamb a fighting chance but at the cost of her careful wedding preparations. Standing in the kitchen in her knickers and bra, Jude ironed out the crumples of her damp dress. Her tights were beyond redemption, laddered and covered in muck, so she tossed them in the kitchen bin. There was no time to try to find another pair in the tangle that was her underwear drawer, so she hoped the church would be warm.

* * *

Jude's knackered old Land Rover County 110 pulled up outside Great Malvern Priory precisely twenty seconds after the beautiful vintage Rolls Royce that contained the bride and her father.

'Sorry,' Jude said as she ran past them. 'Tilda, you look absolutely beautiful.'

The bride gave her a stiff look, the harsh features of her face pulling taut in un-camouflaged annoyance. Jude always had the feeling that Tilda had never particularly warmed to her. Still, if Tilda was about to marry Ben, one of Adam's closest friends, then she'd just have to keep making an effort.

'Blimey,' Sarah said as Jude slid into the seat next to her. 'What do you smell of?'

'Possibly sheep placenta,' Jude whispered back. 'Is it really bad?'

'Not a total disaster,' Sarah replied, producing a bottle and spritzing Jude with a little Estée Lauder before leaning across and pulling a stray piece of hay from her hair.

Sarah flicked her phone to camera, turned the screen to selfie mode and held it up for Jude to see.

The camera flashed.

'Hey!' said Jude. 'What was that for?'

Sarah looked at the screen. 'Sorry.' She frowned. 'Didn't mean to do that, I got it out for you to use as a mirror. But it is a fabulous shot!'

Jude winced at the picture on the screen. She put her hand up and tried to tame the tangle of hair that had been so elegant just a short time ago.

'God, I look a mess,' she said.

'I've got a brush in my bag,' Sarah said. 'And a lippy.'

'I don't suppose you have any spare tights in there too, do you?'

'I'm afraid not.'

'Shh,' Sarah's boyfriend, Nate, hissed sharply.

As the organ struck up and the congregation stood, Jude glanced at her friend. It had been ages since she'd seen Sarah and she was shocked to notice how tired and stressed she looked. She'd definitely lost far too much weight and there was something unsettling about her eyes. Usually so expressive and full of life, they seemed to have lost their spark completely. Jude had been so wrapped up in the farm and the lambs recently that she'd barely had any time for Sarah. In fact, when she thought about it, she hadn't seen her at all since New Year's Eve, and that was almost two months ago.

'She does look lovely, doesn't she?' Sarah sighed as Tilda glided past them, her tall, curvy frame encased perfectly in an expensive-looking ivory gown and her immaculate honey-coloured hair piled up in an elaborate do, studded with tiny flowers. Jude looked down the aisle towards Ben, who was standing at the front with Charlie, the best man and final member of their friendship group. Both tall and broad-shouldered, as Adam had been. The three amigos, with matching haircuts, Ben's dark, Charlie's sandy and Adam's mousy, thanks to Bev in the village who'd seen to their hair for a fiver ever since they were boys. Jude imagined Adam standing there next to them, the ever-calming presence, and felt his absence stab her yet again.

She looked at Sarah and saw that her eyes were glued to the groom. For a long time, Jude had assumed that if Ben Wilkinson ever got married it would be to Sarah Lloyd, as did pretty much everyone else in the village. Theirs had been a complicated relationship, on again, off again but always simmering away, so it was a huge surprise when Ben announced his engagement to a girl none of them had even met before. Although Sarah had never said as much, Jude knew she'd taken the whole thing very badly. And Nate, the boyfriend who had appeared on the scene just a couple of weeks after Ben announced his engagement, was clearly a rebound. Jude's eyes moved across to Nate. He'd been with Sarah for almost a year and yet Jude hardly knew him. He baulked from company, especially that of Sarah's friends, it seemed. Nate glanced up and caught Jude watching him. He glowered at her before returning his attention to the service sheet.

After the service had ended, the Malvern Hills watched as the guests stood outside the old Benedictine monastery waiting for the endless photos to be over so everyone could get on with the business of making their way to the reception. Although Jude had lived her entire life in the shadow of the hills, the sheer size and magnificence of the granite peaks never failed to impress her. They rose up from the pretty Victorian town like a row of old friends and their very presence had a way of calming her and making her feel safe. Though right now she was more impatient for the warmth – and toilet facilities – of Eastnor Castle.

'Your legs are turning blue,' Sarah said.

'Thanks,' Jude replied. 'I'm bloody freezing. Fancy picking February for a wedding.'

Jude could see that Sarah was also shivering, despite being bundled up in a fake fur coat with a ridiculously long, silky scarf wrapped several times around her neck.

A sudden angry shout caught the attention of all those gathered and Jude turned to see Charlie holding his hands up to fend off a torrent of anger from a tall brunette in a garishly bright fuchsia-pink jacket.

'Oh dear,' said Sarah. 'What do you suppose he's done now?'

Whatever it was, the brunette was clearly not happy. She slapped him hard across the face before storming off down the path that led out of the bottom of the churchyard.

'Youch.' Jude winced. 'We'd better go and see if he's all right.'

Charlie, Ben, Sarah and Adam had been a tight group ever since they'd attended Malvern End Primary School together.

Meeting them much later in life, Jude might have found it difficult being a newcomer to such a close group, but she had been accepted into the fold immediately. She'd been brought up by her mother in Malvern Link, a larger and busier district of the Malverns, on the other side of the hills. It was Ben, her friend from university, who'd introduced her to the gang originally when they met up one summer when they were back home for the holidays. Jude had fallen for Adam instantly and, luckily for her, the feelings had been returned and it hadn't been long before she was fully entwined in his life.

Sarah too had welcomed her with open arms, saying over and again how nice it was to have another girl to help disperse the testosterone. Since Adam's death, his friends had rallied around and helped in whatever ways they could, and it was a source of lingering guilt that Jude had drifted away a little as the ties of the farm had made her permanently either busy or tired.

'Everything all right?' Jude said when they reached a sheepish Charlie.

'You saw that?' he asked.

'Everybody here saw that,' said Sarah.

'Ah,' he said. 'That's embarrassing.'

'Whatever did you do to that poor woman?' Sarah asked.

'I just mentioned that she looked a lot older in real life than she did in her profile picture.'

'Her profile?' said Jude. 'Oh, Charlie, please don't tell me you brought a girl you found on the internet to your best friend's wedding?'

'What's the problem?' said Charlie. 'Tilda told me I had to bring someone or it would mess with the table plans.'

Before Jude could comment further on Charlie's dubious decision to bring a woman he'd never met before to a wedding where he was the best man, Ben came over to join them.

'My favourite people,' he said, clapping Charlie on the back and kissing Jude and Sarah on both cheeks.

'Congratulations, mate,' said Charlie. 'Lovely service.'

'Nothing to do with me.' Ben grinned. 'Tilda and her mother have been planning this thing for years.'

'But you only got engaged about a year ago,' Jude pointed out.

'Exactly!' said Ben. 'I don't think it really mattered to her who she married. Today is not about me, it's about flowers and dresses and impressive guest lists and smoked duck sodding canapés.'

Jude had never been exactly sure what had attracted Ben to Tilda. He was one of those magnetic men, steeped in charisma and charm, who'd never been short of female attention. At uni, Jude had watched in permanent amusement as girls lined up to try to be the one to win him over. Even if things with Sarah hadn't made it past the finishing post, he could have had his choice of partners and yet he'd chosen prickly Tilda.

'Sorry, ladies, but I need to borrow Charlie for a moment,' Ben said. 'Bloody photo schedule.'

Jude squeezed Sarah's hand as the two men walked away to be carefully positioned by the photographer in a pseudo-carefree tableau. The chilly wind chose that moment to catch Sarah's fringe, lifting it and revealing just for a moment the clear outline of a bruise.

'What the hell's that?' Jude asked, pushing Sarah's hair aside to get a better look at the shiner that was partly hidden under her hairline. It looked old and had started to fade but no amount of carefully applied concealer could disguise how enormous it was.

'It's nothing,' Sarah said, pulling her head away. 'I slipped and caught the edge of the table the other day. Silly, really.'

'Sarah?' Jude didn't believe a word. 'Is there something going on? Are you all right?'

Sarah bit her bottom lip and tears sprang into the corners of her eyes. Jude went to put her arm around her friend but Sarah pushed her away.

'I can't do this now,' she said. She glanced nervously behind her and Jude saw Nate returning from the sneaky trip he'd made to Café Nero on Church Street, noticeably with just the one takeaway cup for himself.

Jude had always found Nate Sanchez to be a selfish and difficult man but now she wondered if there was an even bigger reason why she should feel uneasy about his relationship with her friend.

2

Eastnor Castle was a grand Victorian take on what a medieval castle should look like. The building was large and imposing and it was set in the most incredible grounds, all in all the perfect venue for an impressive wedding. Most of the guests had stuck to the bride's request to *enjoy champagne and canapés on the lawn* whilst she and Ben were whisked off by the photographer to make the most of the opportunities the gardens and lake offered. Jude, Charlie and Sarah, with a reluctant Nate in tow, had taken their champagne flutes and ducked inside to get away from the cold. Jude looked around the room decked out for the reception meal in awe, with its wood panelling, enormous chandeliers and heavy gilded frames containing ancestral paintings. She was extremely grateful to see a fire crackling in the stone fireplace and felt herself warm up just at the sight of it.

'Bollocks,' said Charlie, looking at the table plan. 'I'm not sitting with you guys.'

'No,' said Sarah, with an edge of the utterly-pissed-off. 'You've made the top table, unlike us who will be lurking at the very back on table thirteen with all the other bottom-tiered wedding dregs.'

'Why do you care?' Nate asked.

'Ben's one of my best friends,' said Sarah. 'I've known him my whole life and then Tilda bowls in. It's like she's always trying to keep us apart.'

She looked at Nate's red face.

'All of us, I mean,' she added.

'Look!' said Jude, pointing to the other side of the room, glad of the excuse to break the atmosphere. 'Granny Margot made it after all.'

Sarah's face lit up at the sight of her beloved grandmother, garishly yet perfectly bedecked in a bright floral two-piece outfit with a huge hat sitting on her silver bobbed hair. A man Jude recognised from the care home where Granny Margot was a resident was holding her arm and with her free hand, she clutched a walking stick. Jude adored Granny Margot almost as much as Sarah did. She was a remarkable lady who'd been a women's rights activist, a farm worker, a key member of the local WI and an early advocator for the environment. She'd raised a child on her own before fate had played her a cruel hand, stealing her own daughter away during childbirth and leaving her with a granddaughter to take care of, but she'd taken on the role with love and gumption.

'I thought I might find you in here,' said Granny Margot. 'I told Gerwain that you'd have found a cosy spot. Who on earth would throw a February wedding and then insist all the guests stand around outside, freezing their bits and bobs off?'

Sarah gave her a big kiss and took her arm from the carer.

'I didn't think you could make it,' she said. 'If you'd told me, I would have come and picked you up myself.'

'I didn't think I could either,' said Granny Margot. 'But this wonderful man knew how much I wanted to be here for Ben and for you too, my love. He made it happen.'

'Anything for my favourite resident.' Gerwain smiled. 'But

we've only been allowed to do this if I stick around and we have you back at Perrins House by nine.'

'You make me feel like Cinderella.' Granny Margot grinned.

'Just call me your fairy godmother!'

Tilda bristled at the sight of Granny Margot who had, she pointed out, declined the invitation and had therefore not been included in the table planning. Charlie suggested that, as the seat next to him was no longer needed for his poor choice of date, Granny Margot could sit there with him at the top table and, much to Tilda's annoyance, Ben agreed heartily. He also ensured an extra chair was found for Gerwain, which was added to table thirteen.

'Why are my friends stuck right at the back?' Ben asked his new wife.

'You said you didn't want anything to do with the wedding plans,' Tilda said before sashaying up to her place centre stage.

The meal was suitably delicious and the wine generously supplied but Jude felt uncomfortable on table thirteen as she watched Sarah down a bottle of chianti pretty much on her own. Nate was obviously not impressed by her swift transition from tipsy to drunk and was making it embarrassingly obvious to everyone else sitting around them.

Speeches are rarely the most anticipated part of a wedding, and Tilda's father's was particularly long, dull and predictable. Ben's was much lighter and shorter too, delivered with the usual helping of charm, but the best came at the end when Charlie gave his very comical, well-pitched account of Ben's childhood.

'As we all know, our good friend Ben is one of life's achievers,' he said. 'Always seems to fall on his feet somehow... however, it wasn't always that way. When we were kids, he used to land in all sorts of trouble, but he really excelled himself in Year 5 when he watched Ray Mears's *Tracks* programme and thought he'd have a go at survival foraging in the school playground. He should have paid closer attention to Mr Mears, though, as he ended up in hospital having his stomach pumped after eating a whole load of ivy berries. It took him a very, *very* long time to shake the nickname Ivy!'

Sarah snorted at the memory, much to Nate's obvious disgust.

Jude was glad when the speeches were over, the cake cut and Charlie and Granny Margot had swapped the top table for table thirteen.

'Great speech,' Jude congratulated Charlie. 'I've heard you all call him Ivy a few times but I didn't know that's where it came from.'

'I remember it very well,' said Granny Margot. 'You were so upset, Sarah.'

'I still think it was his way of getting off school for a few days,' Sarah said.

'I thought you were the leader in that, Charlie,' Jude said. 'Adam told me you were quite the entrepreneur when it came to faking sick notes from everyone's parents.'

'Ah, yes.' Charlie grinned. 'There can be benefits of having a nerdy friend.'

'How's everyone getting on?' asked Ben, joining them at the table.

'We were just talking about Charlie's brilliant speech,' said Jude. 'Adam would have chuckled at the sheep joke.'

'Not sure all of Tilda's family got it,' said Ben.

'To be fair,' slurred Sarah, 'Tilda herself probably didn't either.'

'Of course she didn't!' Ben snorted.

There was an awkward silence around the table, broken by a giggle from Sarah. Despite herself, Jude felt a little sorry for Ben's new bride. She hadn't slotted into the friendship group quite as well as Jude herself had. Mind you, she made it difficult at every opportunity and it was very clear she thought herself far too good for small-town life.

'So, Nate,' said Gerwain, 'Margot tells me you had something to do with that word game everyone is raving about.'

'Lexigle,' said Nate, reluctantly joining the conversation. 'Yes, that's right.'

'Sarah's idea, really,' said Ben. 'She's brilliant at making up word puzzles. We all used to get very competitive over her annual Christmas quiz so it's no wonder Nate saw her talent as a great opportunity.'

Nate scowled, his jaw tightening, and began to rip his place card into tiny bits of confetti.

'Not really,' said Sarah. 'I just like playing with words but I know nothing about technology. That's totally Nate. Have you played it, Gerwain?'

'Not yet,' he replied. 'But I keep meaning to have a go.'

'Oh, you should,' said Sarah. 'It comes out every day and it's loads of fun. Nate's so clever really.'

Nate was obviously not in the mood to be centre of attention.

'I'm not feeling well,' he said. 'I'm going to call a taxi to take me home.'

He stood up to leave and Sarah looked horrified.

'Don't go,' she pleaded.

As though he hadn't heard her, Nate threw his starched white napkin onto the matching tablecloth and walked quickly towards the exit. Sarah scrabbled to her feet and wobbled a little before rushing out after him.

'That man!' said Granny Margot. 'I don't trust him and I can't for the life of me see why Sarah is with him.'

'I agree,' said Ben. 'She could do so much better.'

'But Mr So-Much-Better has just got married,' said Margot

dryly. 'Now, Jude, my love, would you go and check on her please? I'd do it myself, but I worry I might hit him with my walking stick.'

Jude found Sarah in the ladies' washroom, sitting on the floor, crying into a ball of toilet paper.

'He told me to fuck off,' she sobbed.

Jude sat on the floor next to her.

'Are you ready to tell me exactly what's been going on?' she said. 'Because I'd bet this year's prize ram you didn't give yourself that bruise on the corner of a table.'

Sarah gathered herself and stared wild-eyed at Jude before making her decision.

'I've got myself into a bit of trouble,' Sarah confessed. 'It all started with a few gambling games when I was on my own and bored one evening.'

Jude's heart sank as she realised what was coming next.

'I won a little money and it felt so good that I used it to play a few more games. One thing led to another and... the internet makes it really easy. You can do it whilst you're sitting at home in your pyjamas these days.'

'Oh, Sarah,' said Jude. 'How much did you lose?'

Sarah looked her straight in the eye.

'Thousands,' she whispered. 'But that isn't the worst of it. I ran out of money, so I got a loan. Then I couldn't pay my debts so now the loan has a loan. The interest has grown like you wouldn't believe and I owe over seventy thousand pounds.'

Jude gasped involuntarily.

'Holy shit!' she said.

'I know,' said Sarah. 'Like I said, I'm in a bit of trouble.'

'What about Nate?' Jude asked. 'Have you spoken to him?'

'No!' said Sarah. 'Nobody knows and you have to promise not to tell a soul.'

'But he's made a fortune from Lexigle, from *your* puzzles – surely he can bail you out?'

'No!' said Sarah, a haunted look burning in her eyes. 'I have to do this on my own. If I tell Nate, he'll think I'm only with him for his cash.'

'Then talk to Charlie?'

'Jude, you promised,' she said desperately. 'You can't tell anyone.'

Jude sighed deeply and wrapped her arms around her friend.

'Try and forget about it tonight,' she said. 'I'll help you figure out a plan tomorrow.'

At 5 a.m., Jude's alarm told her to pull her exhausted self out of bed and go and relieve Frank from his night shift. She'd woken up thinking about her conversation with Sarah at the wedding. Some things appeared better in the light of day but this was not one of those things. It was all well and good telling Sarah that she would help her sort this mess out, but how on earth could she deliver on this promise? The farm accounts were always teetering danger-ously near the red and everything seemed to be getting more expensive by the week. Fertiliser, fuel, energy, feed, the list was endless. And she'd need to think about some bigger investments on Malvern Farm soon if they were going to creep towards the Net Zero goal. It was far too early to phone Sarah, so Jude went to message her instead. There were two unopened photo attachments sent from the wedding. The first was a selfie of them both, a sad smile on Sarah's face that didn't quite make it to her eyes. The second photo was the one she'd taken in error – of Jude, looking startled with straw sticking out of her hair. She smiled before sending her friend a quick message telling her she'd call her later.

The chilly February rain was showing no sign of relenting as

Jude headed back out into the yard. Noah was already in the lambing shed, his own dog, Floss, lying loyally at his feet. Unlike Pip, Floss was a well-trained sheepdog, vital to the farm team when it came to herding the flock.

'How was the wedding?' said Noah.

'Eventful,' said Jude. 'I think I'd rather have been here helping with the ewes.'

'Sarah there with that Lexigiggle bloke of hers, was she?'

Jude knew that Noah had a very large crush on Sarah, even though he'd never admitted it outright to her. They'd both grown up in the village together, although he was slightly older and, according to Adam, Noah had never had a serious girlfriend. This was something Jude couldn't understand as he was one of the gentlest men she'd ever met, attractive too in an earthy, rugged way. She also knew that he had no time for Nate.

'I know you know it's called Lexigle,' she teased. 'Don't think I haven't caught you playing it more than once when you think nobody's looking.'

'Yeah, well...' Noah blushed slightly.

'I take it our flattened friend didn't make it?' Jude asked, letting him off the hook.

Noah smiled and opened the wooden warm-box where any lambs with mild hypothermia were put to try to bring their temperature up. Jude peeked inside and recognised the lamb she'd rescued the day before.

'She looks all right,' she said in delight.

'Her mother clearly didn't think so,' said Noah. 'I thought she might take to her but no. Bloody useless ewe.'

'Any possible surrogates?'

'There were a couple, but we gave them to stronger lambs than this 'un. I'm afraid she's not really top of the viable list.'

'Then I'll raise her myself.'

'Thought you'd say that.' Noah grinned.

Jude prepared a milk feed before taking the lamb out of the warm-box.

'Come on then, Pancake,' she said, sitting down on a bale of straw.

'Oh, no,' said Noah.

'What?'

'You know not to name the livestock, Jude.'

She smiled. She did know that. It made it harder when the time came to send them for slaughter. But what Noah didn't know was that little Pancake was not going to be joining the rest of the lambs when their fateful day came. This tiny fighter was a sign of hope and tenacity and Jude had every intention of keeping her. The lamb sucked enthusiastically at the offered teat.

The local radio was on in the background but Jude's mind was elsewhere as the newsreader reported on politics, more train strikes and the divorce of a minor celebrity. It wasn't until they focused on the county news that her ears pricked up.

'Did she just say there's been a break-in at Great Malvern Priory?'

'That's right,' said Noah. 'I don't know what the place is coming to. First the theatre had a sculpture stolen, then someone went off with some old coins from the museum, in broad daylight that was too. A couple of weeks ago it was the statues from the park and now the Priory. Where are people's scruples these days?'

As the sun tried to break through the mizzle, filling the cloudy sky with yellowish hues, Jude loaded the quad's trailer up with feed pellets and forage ready for the field rounds. She whistled for Pip, who came tearing across the yard, eager at the thought of a run. Although she wasn't a trained sheepdog, Pip still had her uses and was excellent at keeping the hungry flock at bay whilst Jude tipped the feed into the troughs and spread the hay forage.

'Good girl, Pip,' she called when the job was done.

She drove the quad slowly around the field, checking the flock for any sign of a problem. Everything seemed in order, so she turned the bike and headed towards the second field. Driving towards the gate, her eye was suddenly caught by something near the oaks lining the edge of the field and she drove a little closer to see what it was.

Beneath the tree was a pile of logs that had been chopped down a couple of years previously and were still waiting to be cut into manageable sizes for the wood burner. Behind the logs, something white was just visible, covered in fur, and she hoped it wasn't one of her ewes in trouble. As she drew nearer, she realised that the white bulk was not that of a sheep. Most of it was hidden by the logs, but there was something dreadfully familiar about the part she could see. Her skin tingled and her insides lurched as she began to imagine the very worst scenario and prayed that it was just her over-tired, over-worried mind playing tricks on her.

Jude put her foot on the accelerator and tore towards the trees, fear rising as the shape of a body became clearer and clearer. And then she knew without a doubt that her initial panic had been brutally warranted. She stumbled and fell onto the rain-sodden ground as she jumped off the quad. Scrambling to her feet, she ran towards the trees where a human body lay broken in the mud. A body dressed in a white fake-fur coat and a wedding outfit that Jude recognised with a sickening wrench.

'Sarah!' she cried, rushing over to her friend's lifeless form. Under the thick branch of an oak tree, her friend lay face-first in the mud, the long silk scarf she'd worn to the wedding looped tightly around her neck. It had ripped in two, Jude noticed, the other half still tied to the branch above, flapping innocently in the breeze like a flag of surrender.

Jude screamed.

She heaved Sarah's body over and wiped the mud from her face, instinctively checking for any sign of life. A breath, a pulse, any indication that she could be saved. But she knew there was no point. The purple hue of her body and the icy feel of her skin told her all she needed to know.

* * *

Jude propped herself against the Aga and shivered as a deep chill radiated throughout her body. Watching her farm become a hive of flashing blue lights and people in uniform had been both horrifying and surreal. It had left her with a numbness that made her feel oddly detached from everything that was happening around her.

'Shall I put the kettle on?' Detective Sergeant Binita Khatri asked. 'Make us both a cuppa?'

DS Khatri's accent was a soft West Midlands burr and her manner matched it perfectly. Gentle and earnest. She'd been the one to take Jude's arm and steer her away from Sarah's broken body, talking quietly to her as she led her back through the fields and into the farmhouse. She gave Jude a moment to gather herself whilst she threw teabags into two mugs and waited for the kettle to boil.

'I really hate to do this to you when you're still in such shock,' she said, placing a mug of tea on the pile of *Farmers Guardian*s in front of Jude. 'But it would be great if you could help me out with a few details.'

Jude clung to the mug, allowing the heat to scald the skin of her hands, and stared into the brown liquid, two shades paler than she'd have made herself.

'What do you want to know?'

'Why don't we start with an account of what happened this morning?'

Jude blew into her tea and took a sip. It was too hot to drink but the sting on her lips was somehow cathartic. With the help of the hot tea and gentle encouragement from DS Khatri, she managed to describe how she'd come to find the body of her friend. It wasn't hard to remember the details; the hard part was going to be forgetting them.

'You knew Miss Lloyd, Sarah, well,' DS Khatri said gently. 'Can I ask if there was anything you noticed that struck you as odd when you last saw her?'

Jude thought back to the wedding. Plenty had been odd about her, yet it seemed disloyal somehow to even be contemplating sharing all she knew about Sarah's money troubles with the police.

The DS saw the hesitation.

'Anything you can tell us might help piece together what went wrong here,' she said.

Jude considered what DS Khatri meant and a wave of nausea gurgled in her stomach. Whichever way she looked at it seemed unthinkable. Either Sarah had chosen to end her own life or someone else had decided to do it for her. It was too late to save Sarah, but DS Khatri was right, Jude needed to help them find the truth.

'She had money worries,' she said eventually.

'What sort of money worries?'

'The sort that begins with a few online games and ends up with visits from loan sharks.'

'I see,' said DS Khatri. Jude saw no trace of judgement behind her kind brown eyes. Only understanding and empathy. She noted something in her little book before looking up again. 'Can you give me the name of the loan shark?'

Jude shook her head. 'Sarah only told me about it yesterday

when we were at our friend's wedding. I knew there was something wrong because she looked awful, like I'd never seen her before.'

Jude stopped and willed time to rewind to the previous night. If only she'd insisted that Sarah come in and stay the night at the farmhouse instead of letting Charlie take her back to her own cottage. Sarah had been drunk. Very drunk. During the taxi ride back from Eastnor Castle, she'd alternated between teary remorse and fierce resolve until she fell asleep on Jude's shoulder.

'What's going on?' Charlie had mouthed at Jude.

Jude had been desperate to share Sarah's predicament with him. She knew they were as close as any siblings might have been and he would certainly have wanted to help but it wasn't Jude's place to make that call. And now it was too late. She scrunched her eyes tight against the memory and the suffocating fingers of guilt. DS Khatri gave her a moment before asking her next question.

'Can you tell me what you meant by *she looked awful*?'

'She'd lost weight,' she replied. 'She looked exhausted and she drank a lot too, which she only ever does...'

Jude stopped and gulped back a large clot of fresh nausea as she realised her mistake. She took a deep breath before starting again.

'She only ever *did* when she was stressed. Oh, and there was a bruise.'

She lifted her fringe out of the way and indicated to the DS where the bruise had been.

'It was huge. She told me she'd slipped and caught it on the table, but...'

'You didn't believe her?'

Jude shook her head.

'Was she in a relationship?'

'Yes,' said Jude. 'Nate Sanchez.'

The DS snapped her head up.

'The Lexigle guy?' she asked.

'Yes, they'd been together for nearly a year.'

'Wow!' said the DS. 'I love that game – try and play it every day. What's he like?'

Jude wondered how to answer the question. Sarah had seemed to love him despite the fact that he wanted to keep his life with her separate from everyone else. Jude had her suspicions about the bruise, but that's all they were.

'I don't really know him,' she said truthfully. 'He was never all that keen to get involved in Sarah's life.'

'We'll need to speak to him. Do you have an address?'

'No,' said Jude. 'I think he lives somewhere on Avenue Road, near the station.'

'Not to worry. We'll find him. Is there anything else you can think of that might be useful to our enquiries? Or anything you'd like to ask?'

Jude shook her head.

'Then I'll leave you in peace for now. You've been very helpful, Mrs Gray.' She handed Jude a card with the West Mercia badge printed on it alongside her details. 'Please call if you think of anything else or you have any questions yourself. I'm afraid there will be some activity around the site for a while. But we'll try to cause you as little disruption as we can.'

4

There was so much that needed doing on the farm, but Jude couldn't bring herself to get on with things, move on with her life when Sarah's had been rubbed out so deftly.

Suicide?

It just felt all wrong. Why hadn't she turned to her friends? Asked for help?

Jude felt stifled and needed to get away from the farm, so she grabbed her coat and walked down the farm's driveway, lined on one side by a field and on the other by woodland. An old milk churn stood at the end of the drive below a wooden sign that told anyone passing this was the entrance to Malvern Farm. There was also an honesty stall where Jude put boxes of eggs from the bantam hens for folk from the village to buy. Jude sat on the churn and stared up towards the hills, thinking of Adam. Being on the farm made her feel that much closer to him but she still ached from the loss every day and, right then, she'd have given almost anything to feel his strong, comforting arms around her. There were plenty who had told her to sell the farm when he died. What did she know about farming, after all? But Malvern Farm was her home. Adam had taught her so much over the years they'd shared and she'd loved learning and working alongside him. When two tears dripped from the end of her nose, she scrubbed them away roughly. Crying had never helped her deal with anything. She took her phone from her pocket and called Charlie.

'Jude,' he said, his voice distracted. 'Not a great time.'

'I have to tell you something,' she said. 'It's important. Can you come over?'

She could hear shouting, though it was muffled, as if Charlie had covered the mouthpiece.

'Not easy at the moment,' he said when he'd finished yelling. 'Problems at work. Meet up for a pint at The Lamb later? I'll text you.'

'It can't wait,' said Jude.

But the phone line had already gone dead.

She tried again but it went straight to answerphone. She thought about calling Ben but he would be in Marrakesh now, enjoying the beginning of his honeymoon. Should she disturb him or let him have a bit of peace before he returned home to discover this awful tragedy that would no doubt tear his very soul apart? Out of all of them, perhaps he had been the one who'd loved Sarah the most.

'Garrh!' She exhaled through gritted teeth, closing her eyes and pushing her palms into her sockets to try to dispel the image of Sarah's fragile body lying in the mud. She knew there was work to be done at the farm, but she couldn't face going back there just yet.

She turned right, out of the farm drive and towards the village. Spring was trying to fight the February chill with little buds studding the hedgerows and signs of bulbed flowers sprouting from the grass verges. Usually this would lift Jude's spirits but she barely noticed them. In a trance, she walked the familiar route, past The Lamb pub and the village green, Mrs James's shop and the tiny school where Adam and the others had gone as children and where Ben now worked. Jude had even done a few supply teaching shifts there herself. She and Ben had graduated together with matching teaching degrees, and that first summer, she'd made the trip over the hills to see him almost every day, as well as the friends who had visited him so often at uni, most especially a young farmer called Adam. It had been the happiest, sunniest summer she'd known and had ended with an engagement ring and plans of running a sheep farm. It now seemed such a long time ago, and how cruel time had been to that happy, carefree group with their futures laid out in front of them. First the hideous cancer that claimed Adam so bloody fast. And now poor Sarah.

Jude kept walking. Right to the far edge of the village where she found herself drawn to Sarah's little stone cottage. She opened the gate and walked up the path to the front door. A huge wave of grief welled up inside her as the numbness of shock began to wear off and the reality of the morning took over. An enormous, guttural sob erupted from deep within, another close behind.

'Everything all right, my dear?' asked Janet Timms, local busy-body and Sarah's next-door neighbour.

Jude knew that the news of Sarah's death would be all around the village soon enough but she didn't want Janet Timms, massive gossip and egocentric dramatist, to start the grapevine off just yet.

'Fine, thank you,' she said. 'If you'll excuse me.'

Without waiting for an answer, she walked around to the back of the cottage to the neglected greenhouse where she found the key always kept in a seed tray, and then she let herself into Sarah's cottage.

* * *

Once inside, Jude allowed her grief to properly take hold. She sat on the floor of the tiny kitchen, her back against the 1960s Formica cupboards which Granny Margot had fitted new. When the tears came, they came in force and Jude had no choice but to let them fall. She stayed where she was, with her arms wrapped tightly around her knees, until her back ached and her tears ran dry. The tiny cottage resonated with the essence of Sarah, and Jude wasn't ready to leave it just yet. Deep down she knew that she should probably leave the cottage for the police to go through, but she felt connected to Sarah there and she wanted to hold off the reality of the horror outside these safe four walls for just a little longer so she walked across to Sarah's bedroom. Everything about it was utterly Sarah. A little untidy and chaotic but pretty, well-loved and friendly.

Jude picked up the paperback that lay unfinished on the bedside table. A Botticelli cherub stuck out of the pages, a little over halfway through, marking the last page Sarah had read, which seemed so sad that Jude decided to take the book home and read it herself. An old, slightly yellowed photo of the four friends as teenagers also sat next to the bed. The boys were dressed in poorly fitting dinner suits and Sarah was wearing a figure-hugging, full-length dress made from some sort of glittering jersey fabric. They had their arms around each other and stood beneath an arch of balloons, faces flushed and eyes shiny. Jude traced the outline of Sarah's face and then of Adam's. So much hope for the future in those happy, carefree eyes.

The more she thought about it, the less it made sense. The debts she could just about understand. They were an easy thing to accumulate. She herself had played the lottery online after Adam had died, hoping that a cash injection would make things so much easier for her at that point, and once she had an account set up it was ridiculously easy to be tempted – just one more online scratch card or instant win until she'd spent nearly fifty quid in one week without even blinking.

No, it wasn't the gambling that shocked Jude, nor the loans – Sarah had always been so trusting, sometimes to the point of naivety – it was the suicide itself that Jude just could not come to terms with. Sarah had been one of life's optimists. There was always hope in her world, so surely she would have tried everything before she gave up.

'What happened?' Jude whispered to the empty room.

Sitting on the edge of the bed, in a room that smacked of innocence, Jude was more and more certain that Sarah had not been capable of suicide. And the ramifications of this fact were even more frightening. If Sarah hadn't wanted to end her own life, that could only mean someone else had made that decision for her.

Jude stood up, putting the paperback and photo in the overly deep pockets of her waxed farm coat. She looked around the room, searching for something but unsure what. Answers, maybe? Something that either proved or disproved her doubts about Sarah's apparent suicide?

Sarah's chest of drawers was covered in bottles, sprays, brushes and hair elastics – the fundamentals of life but nothing that gave Jude any more idea of what had happened to her friend after the wedding. She opened the top drawer. Peeking at Sarah's underwear felt wrong, as if she was spying on her in the bathroom, and Jude was about to close it when she caught sight of the corner of a little book. She knew, before she pulled it out, that it was her diary. Jude had given it to her for Christmas, personalised with a photo of them both on the cover. After Adam died, Jude had found keeping a diary to be incredibly therapeutic, so she'd given this to Sarah in the hope it might bring her some solace from the obvious dip in her mental health. At the time, Jude had assumed this was a result of Ben's engagement. She'd had no idea how much graver her problems had actually been. She wondered if Sarah had been using the diary to record her thoughts but, when she opened it, she saw that it was full of coded appointments and to-do lists. Ironic, as Sarah was one of the scattiest, least organised people she knew.

Jude traced the letters of the familiar, scrawling handwriting on the first page. The primary school teacher in her had always despaired at Sarah's poor letter formation. It had been an affectionate, ongoing joke between them.

'I can't even tell what some of your letters are,' Jude had teased. 'I mean, where the hell is Walvern? It says on your address it's in a county I've never heard of before called Morcestershire!'

'Some of us are born for more important things than perfect handwriting, you know,' Sarah had retorted.

A loud knock on the door shattered the peace of the cottage and made Jude jump. She wedged the diary into her pocket and peered through a crack in the curtains. A particularly bullish-looking man who looked well over six feet tall and had a weaselly face made up of sharp, mean features stood on the doorstep. He knocked again and Jude held her breath, waiting for him to give up and leave. But he didn't. He bent down and started to fiddle with the lock which, in less than half a minute, clicked open.

Jude had heard of the flight or fight response but her traitorous body decided to go for a third option. The *freeze and stare at the bedroom door, waiting to see what would happen next* response. Through the half open door, Jude could see the man who was now in the hallway – rough, big and completely at odds with the pretty cottage. Jude had no idea what his game was, but she knew she would not be a welcome addition to his mission if she was discovered, so she crept over to the window and tried – unsuccessfully – to open it.

The cottage was still as Jude peered round the edge of Sarah's bedroom door but the rustling and scraping noises that were coming from the sitting room indicated that the intruder was in there, snooping around, imagining he had the place to himself.

Jude's fear only just outweighed her anger at the thought of this brutish man going through Sarah's private things. With her blood pounding, she stepped out into the hallway. The front door was only a few steps away and she crossed the carpet silently. The door was still unlocked and opened, thankfully creak-free.

'Oh, my goodness,' declared a voice loudly from the other side of the opening. 'You did make me jump.'

Janet Timms! Damnit!

'Go,' said Jude, angry at the cursed woman whose presence meant any chance of a sneaky getaway had been lost completely.

'Well, I never,' said Janet. 'Is that the thanks I get for being a concerned neighbour?'

Jude stepped over the threshold and tried to push Janet back down the garden path. Janet was a small woman who seemed to live on nothing more than cigarettes and Scotch whisky. She was also very light, Jude discovered, when she shoved a little too harshly and Janet stumbled backwards, falling into the lavender bushes. Before Jude was able to offer her a hand up, she felt herself pushed forwards with such vehemence that she also ended up in the lavender.

'Sorry, ladies,' the man said, striding over Jude. 'I missed my step there. I do hope you're all right.'

His coarse face was at odds with the sentiment and Jude saw he was carrying a laptop and iPad under his arm.

'Give those back,' she said, pulling herself up.

'Just collecting what's rightfully mine,' he said. 'Totally legal. Debt collectors are allowed to enter a property to seize goods as long as it isn't locked.'

Jude didn't believe this was the case any more than she

believed the door had been unlocked or that this thug had missed his step.

'If you're behaving within the law then you won't mind me taking your details,' she said, hoping her voice sounded braver than she felt.

'I don't think that will be necessary. Besides, Miss Lloyd will know who I am. I sent her a letter informing her I would be paying a visit.'

He smiled the smile of a coyote who'd fought off all competition for a rotting animal corpse. 'Sticking to the law,' he added.

Jude felt ridiculously helpless as she watched him walk back down the path and out through the gate. He got into an expensive white Range Rover with a striking red roof, which quickly roared into life. Jude managed to pull her phone out and catch the back of it on camera as it sped off away from the cottage and out of the village.

5

Jude put out a hand to help Janet out of the lavender bush.

'Well,' said Janet. 'What do you suppose that was all about?'

'A chancer,' said Jude.

'Could be,' Janet mused. 'There have been a couple of break-ins in the village of late. Poor Selma Howard had all her jewellery stolen the other week and the Taylors' son left his bike chained to his garden fence two nights ago and it was gone in the morning.'

'There you go then.'

'He seemed to know Sarah, though,' Janet Timms continued. 'It sounded as though she's in some sort of debt.'

'Utter rubbish,' said Jude. 'Are you all right? No cuts or bruises?'

'A little shocked.' Janet seemed to be as happy for the spotlight to be swung her way as Jude was to swing it. 'Now how about I put the kettle on?'

For such a feeble-looking woman, Janet seemed utterly unfazed by her encounter with the lavender bush. In fact, she seemed a little too excited by the entire unfolding of events and it irked Jude. This was not a TV drama or juicy fodder that would make for a good bit of gossip at the next village coffee morning – which was something Jude felt sure Janet Timms would be organising very soon.

'Please don't feel as though you need to stay,' she said.

'Nonsense,' said Janet. 'You need the company after that awful ordeal. Besides, I'm sure the police will want to talk to me when they get here. I am a key witness, after all. You give them a ring whilst I make the tea.'

As Janet pushed past her and bustled into the kitchen, it appeared Jude didn't actually have a choice. Jude left her to it, locked and bolted the front door and went back into Sarah's bedroom. She took the phone from the back pocket of her jeans and pulled out the card DS Khatri had given her.

Her call was answered quickly.

'Hello. DS Binita Khatri.'

'It's Jude Gray. We met this morning...'

'Of course,' said DS Khatri. 'How can I help?'

'I'm at Sarah Lloyd's cottage,' she explained. 'I didn't really mean to be, I just needed to get away from the farm and I somehow ended up here.'

'Okay,' said the DS. 'You beat us to it. We were sending a team over later this afternoon. Did you find anything?'

'I wasn't here long before someone broke in saying he had a right to be here as he was collecting payment for a debt,' she explained. 'He said he was acting lawfully as the door was unlocked so he didn't have to break in but he was lying. I'm pretty sure he picked the lock.'

'Either way, it would still be illegal,' said DS Khatri. 'Did he take anything?'

'He took Sarah's laptop and iPad. I'm not sure what else.'

'Damnit!' said DS Khatri. 'Sorry. I'll bring a team round straight away.'

Ten minutes after her phone call, DS Binita Khatri's car pulled up outside and Janet Timms leapt to her feet to let her in.

'Such a shock this all is,' she said to the detective sergeant.

'It must be,' said DS Khatri. 'Did you know Sarah Lloyd well?'

Janet started and looked at Jude in surprise.

'You make it sound as though she's no longer with us,' she said.

Jude blanched. Of course there was no reason why Janet would have known this. She herself had only discovered the body a few short hours earlier and it wasn't something she'd wanted to talk about with the biggest gossip in Malvern End. DS Khatri looked taken aback.

'I'm so sorry,' she said. 'I assumed you knew.'

'No,' said Janet. 'What happened?'

'An accident,' Jude snapped.

'Heavens!' said Janet. 'What kind of an accident?'

'Thank you for the tea,' said Jude. 'We wouldn't want to keep you any longer than necessary.'

'But the detective will want to speak to me,' said Janet. 'I was here when that awful man broke in.'

'You were not,' Jude pointed out. 'You saw him come out of the house and were headfirst in a lavender bush when he left with Sarah's laptop.'

'But I...' stuttered Janet.

DS Khatri was quick to read the situation.

'Right now, I have things I need to do at the cottage and some initial questions for Mrs Gray. If you could let me have your name and address, I'll make sure one of our officers comes to take a statement very soon.'

She flipped open her casebook and looked at Janet expectantly. The lady gave a small sigh before giving her details.

'Thank you,' said DS Khatri as she showed Janet Timms to the door – and purposefully out of it.

'There's one in every neighbourhood.' She smiled. 'Now, how about you tell me everything that happened. In your own time.'

There was little to tell. Jude gave her account of the break-in as well as a description of the man – although it was a description that probably matched thousands of people living in Hereford-shire and Worcestershire alone.

'I did manage to take a photo of the car he was driving,' she said. But when they looked at it, most of the number plate was hidden by the garden hedge, only the last three letters visible.

Watching the uniformed police move around Sarah's cottage was the final straw for Jude. It had been one hell of a day and she was utterly spent. As soon as DS Khatri had finished taking her statement, Jude stood up to leave.

'Can I drive you home?' DS Khatri asked.

'Thanks, but I'll walk. It's not far.'

'Are you sure?'

Jude stopped for a second. It wasn't far, that was true, but she didn't fancy walking back through the village. God forbid Janet Timms or another gossipmonger would be just waiting to pounce, desperate for more information. It would be quicker to walk directly to Malvern Farm up the track that led from behind the row of cottages past the fields. She could avoid the village busybodies that way. But that would mean walking past the oak trees and this was definitely not an option.

'Actually, DS Khatri,' she said. 'If you're sure it wouldn't be putting you out...'

'Not at all,' the detective sergeant said. 'And please call me Binnie.'

Jude nodded. 'Thank you.'

During the short journey back to the farm, it was as though both women had made a silent pact not to talk about Sarah. Binnie made comments about the beautiful countryside and Jude was grateful not to feel the need for a two-way conversation.

'Thanks for the lift,' Jude said when they pulled up in the farmyard.

'No problem,' Binnie replied. 'We'll speak again soon. But please shout if you need anything in the meantime.'

Jude nodded. 'Thanks. Will do.'

As Binnie's car drove off, Pip came bounding out of the lambing shed to greet her.

'Hello there.' Jude bent down to rub the dog's ears.

She looked towards the shed, knowing that Noah would still be in there. He had adored Sarah and would be taking this very badly too but, as awful as everything was, the ewes weren't going to stop lambing because their farmer and shepherd were going through hell. It was time to get back to work.

'Come on,' she said. 'Let's go and give Noah a break, shall we?'

The shepherd was lying on the straw of one of the lambing pens, dealing with a prolapse, when Jude walked in. It didn't seem to be going too well.

'You're here,' he said gruffly. 'There's one in pen five could use your help.'

Jude was a little taken aback. She wasn't sure what she'd expected. Noah wasn't the sort for tears or shows of emotion but she'd expected something more than this.

'Are you all right?' she asked gently.

'I am,' Noah replied curtly. 'She's not, though.' He indicated the ewe making a terrible noise in pen five.

'Right,' said Jude.

She took her waxed coat off and hung it on a peg. Then she rolled her sleeves up and got to work. It took everything she had to carry on with life, but she was so busy it was almost certainly better than having nothing to do, allowing her mind to revisit the awfulness of that morning. Eventually, Frank and Spud Simons came back to relieve them from duty.

Spud lived in the village and was one of those men who was built like an ox but had the gentle nature of a much smaller creature. He was ruddy faced from being outside for so much of the time and his voice was soft with a thick Herefordshire accent. Frank greeted Jude with a nod and a rhetorical 'How's things?' before going over to get the rundown of the day from Noah. Spud hung back, though, shifting uneasily from one foot to the other.

'I heard things happened here whilst I was gone,' he said. 'That right?'

'You could say that.'

'Was it Sarah they found?'

'It was.'

'I'm right sorry to hear that,' Spud said, patting her arm. 'She were a lovely girl.'

Jude wondered how many more times she would have to explain. How many more people would need to pat her arm and say nice things about Sarah?

'Thanks, Spud. Now that you and Frank are here I'll head inside now if you're okay,' she said before leaving him to the lambs and retreating to the sanctuary of the farmhouse.

* * *

Jude's phone showed a long list of missed calls, several of which were from the same contact.

Charlie Watson's mobile.

She opened the answer phone and listened to both messages he'd left. The first one, around lunchtime.

'Hey, sorry I couldn't chat earlier. Everything okay? I'm in meetings this afternoon but we'll talk this evening?'

The second left just fifteen minutes ago.

'Bloody hell, Jude! Just got home from work and there's all sorts of crazy things going round the village about Sarah. What the hell? I'm coming round.'

Right on cue, the doorbell rang and Pip jumped up from her spot by the Aga, barking a warning to any potential intruder.

'Quiet,' Jude said.

Pip quietened and sat by the door expectantly, her hackles raised, ready for action, only relaxing when the door was open and she recognised Charlie as a friend. She rolled over, hopeful of a belly rub from one of her biggest fans, but was disappointed as Charlie went straight to Jude and caught her in an enormous hug. Jude rested her head against his collarbone and allowed his presence and warmth to comfort her.

'Is it true?' he whispered into her hair.

Jude couldn't find words. Not even a simple *yes*. She just nodded and clung to Charlie as though, if they shared their grief, perhaps somehow it would ache a little less.

6

Charlie stayed with Jude that night. They sat up drinking from bottles of Westons cider. At some point they cooked oven chips in the Aga and let most of them go cold on the coffee table, neither one having much of an appetite.

They didn't talk much. They just sat as close to each other as they could and watched whatever the TV threw at them until their minds were numb and their eyelids heavy.

Thanks to the wood burner and Charlie's diligence at keeping it stoked, the sitting room was warm. Jude fell asleep on the sofa, wrapped in a blanket, the cider allowing her a few precious hours of respite.

She woke with a groggy head, unsure of where she was. The disorientation was unsettling but it took just a second for reality to kick in with a vengeance. She sat up. The fire had gone out and the room was chilly. Charlie was still asleep on the other sofa, his blanket lying on the floor next to him with Pip, ever the opportunist, curled up on top. Jude took her own blanket and used it to cover Charlie. He slept on.

The kitchen clock told her it was a little past five. Jude's stomach growled – partly due to the number of empty cider bottles lined up by the sink and partly to the fact that she'd hardly eaten anything since breakfast the day before. Not even twenty-four hours ago but in a different life where she didn't yet know what was waiting under the oak trees for her to discover.

She set the kettle to boil and heaped a large spoon of instant coffee into a mug. She looked in the bread bin where half a loaf of bread sat next to her supply of chocolate chip brioche. Taking two slices she checked them for mould, and when satisfied with the lack of green or blue, she put the bread between the two wire grills of the Aga toasting rack and went to the fridge to find butter and milk.

It was still night dark outside and would be for a good hour and a half yet, but Jude knew she couldn't avoid the day. She had no choice but to carry on with life, just as she'd had to do when Adam died. She still didn't have much of an appetite, but she forced down the heavily buttered toast before filling her thermos with more strong coffee.

Left foot, right foot, she told herself.

Things were going to be difficult, she knew that, but she could get through this, she'd done it before. She just had to keep going, one step at a time.

Left foot, right foot.

Charlie was still asleep when Jude poked her head around the door and whistled gently for Pip. She pulled her waxed coat from the peg and put it on, feeling the heaviness of the pockets and remembering the things she'd taken from Sarah's cottage. Had this been a mistake? The book and the photo surely wouldn't be missed but what if there was something of importance in the diary? She placed the framed picture on the dresser then opened a drawer below and dropped the paperback and diary inside. She'd call DS Khatri later, but not before she'd found the time to have a proper look at Sarah's diary herself.

It was with a hideous sense of déjà vu that Jude crossed the farmyard. Everything seemed just as it had the previous morning, except now she knew how that had ended.

Noah was bottle feeding Pancake when Jude entered the lambing shed. Floss was lying on a pile of hay and Pip bounded over to say good morning, her tail wagging as though someone had injected it with speed.

'You can take over now you're here,' Noah said.

Pancake mewed with objection when the bottle was taken from her mouth. Jude took both lamb and bottle and sat on a bale of hay. Watching the tiny mouth knead away at the teat was calming somehow and Jude was grateful for the job.

'Frank gone home?' she asked.

'He was fair done in,' said Noah. 'Not long to go now, though. I think we might only need him for a couple more nights.'

'Almost done for another year then.'

'Yeah. Glad we got on with tupping early last year.'

Jude nodded. It had been Noah's idea to get the ewes pregnant earlier in the autumn in order to have an early lambing season. They'd just about managed an April lambing the previous year but it was harder to find shepherds with time to come and take shifts and, without Adam, the work had been too much for her. It had almost broken her. This year they were almost finished with a healthy new flock of February lambs before many other farms had even begun. Frank taking on the night shifts had been a godsend.

'Yes,' Jude said. 'Good call. Thanks.'

Both fell silent, aware of the banality of their chat.

'Jude,' said Noah, awkwardly pushing his thick fringe from his eyes. 'I wanted to say sorry for yesterday. I was gruff with you and you didn't need that on top of... well, you know.'

'I do,' she said. 'And thank you. It was a shitty day for all of us.'

Noah nodded. Then he stood and stretched his back out before picking up his shepherd's crook.

'I'll do the field checks this morning if you like,' he said.

Jude was glad to let him. She would have to go back to the top field and see those oak trees again at some point. But not just yet.

She kept herself busy which wasn't hard. It may have been coming up to the end of the lambing season for Malvern Farm, but there was always still plenty to do.

It was whilst Jude had her hand inside a ewe's vagina to feel for the stubborn foreleg of the lamb inside that DS Binnie Khatri came into the lambing shed later that morning.

'Sorry,' she said. 'Bad timing?'

Jude twisted to look up.

'There's never a good time during lambing,' she said, immediately ashamed of the gruffness in her voice. 'Sorry. Give me a moment?'

'Of course.'

With great relief, Jude felt the leg that had been hindering the birth finally join the other, meaning she was able to pull with the ewe's contractions until a slimy bundle slithered out onto the hay. She cleaned it off, used a piece of hay to open the nostrils and was rewarded for her efforts with a little bleat. Jude carefully clipped the cord and sprayed the stump with iodine before standing back. Once the lamb had got shakily to its feet and successfully latched onto its mum for that first colostrum feed, Jude climbed out of the pen and left them to it.

'Let me just wash my hands,' she said, waving her bloodied forearms unnecessarily.

Binnie followed Jude to the stainless-steel sink.

'We've arrested the man who broke into Sarah's cottage yesterday,' she said.

'That's great news,' said Jude. 'And so quick too.'

'It wasn't hard,' Binnie admitted. 'Your description was very helpful, as was the picture you took of his car with the partial licence plate. He was already on our records as there've been other reports of him and his less than ethical debt collecting techniques.'

'How does he keep getting away with it?' An angry knot tightened in her stomach.

'Keeps himself just within the limits of the law,' said Binnie. 'Usually.'

'Not this time?'

'Possibly not. We do need your help, though, to get a conviction. He's a worm and has a decent lawyer. Is it all right if I ask you a few more questions?'

'Of course,' Jude said.

This did not sound like a conversation she wanted to be having in the middle of the lambing barn and she was sure she wouldn't be missed if she ducked off just for a short while.

'Noah,' she called. 'Will you be all right for a bit?'

'Yep,' he replied. 'Take as long as you need.'

'I'll be in the house if you need anything.'

Jude and Binnie crossed the yard, with Pip, as always, at Jude's heel, and went through the little porch that led into the kitchen. There they found Charlie, dressed in a pair of boxer shorts and a vest, scrambling some eggs on the Aga.

'Oh, shit,' he said, clearly embarrassed at his state of undress. 'Sorry. I was just making myself some breakfast before I headed off.'

'This is DS Binita Khatri,' said Jude. 'My friend, Charlie Watson.'

'Nice to meet you,' Charlie said, grabbing an apron from a hook and putting it on as though this somehow offered him more dignity than just being in his underwear.

'Did you know Sarah Lloyd?' Binnie asked.

Charlie nodded. 'We went to school together,' he said. 'Friends ever since.'

Jude's heart crumpled even more as she looked at the familiar face etched with lines of grief. Sarah had been important to many people and her death would be felt by them all for a long time to come. Jude just hoped she'd realised that in life.

'When was the last time you saw her?' Binnie asked, flicking open her notebook.

'At the wedding,' said Charlie. 'We shared a taxi back.'

'You and Sarah?'

'Yes. Well, Jude too really, although we dropped her off first at the farm and then went on to Sarah's cottage. I wanted to make sure she got home safely before I walked to my own house.'

'You were worried about her?'

Charlie's haggard face fell further. 'Something was wrong,' he said. 'She was in a terrible way that night. Although she had been for a while. Since that new boyfriend of hers landed in our lives...'

'Nate Sanchez?'

'Yeah,' said Charlie. 'Not a nice guy in my opinion.'

'In what way?'

'I never felt as though Sarah was able to be herself when he was around. It was like he always wanted to control her.'

'Do you think he was violent with her?'

'In all truthfulness, I couldn't say.'

'I'm sorry to ask you,' said Binnie. 'But was there anything Sarah did or said that you think might go some way to explaining why she could have taken her own life?'

Charlie sucked in a deep breath through his teeth.

'I don't know,' he said. 'All I can tell you is that she changed a lot in the past few months. Something big was up but I don't know what that was.'

'Did you know about her debts?'

'Debts?' Charlie looked at Jude in surprise and she felt a little pinch of guilt. 'No, nothing. Are you sure?'

'She told me at the wedding,' Jude admitted. 'Things had got pretty bad.'

'How bad?'

'Loan shark bad.'

'Christ.' Charlie rubbed his temple. 'Why didn't she tell me? I would have helped her out. I could have done something. She didn't need to go and...'

His face was a contorted mix of anguish and frustration.

'How was she when you left her?' Binnie asked.

'Fine!' Charlie said, desperately. 'Or at least I thought she was. Not fine exactly... She was obviously going through hell. But I thought she was just going to go to bed. If I'd thought she'd be...'

He stopped talking, put his hands over his face and scrubbed as though trying to scratch out his thoughts.

Jude watched as Binnie wrote something else in her little book.

'I don't think she would have done it,' Jude said in a small voice, only just daring to speak the words aloud, knowing the implications they held.

'What do you mean?' Binnie asked.

'I mean, I don't think Sarah would have killed herself,' she said, a little more weight behind her statement this time.

Charlie took his hands away from his face.

'Right,' said Binnie. 'Well, we are still waiting for pathology to confirm cause of death. I shouldn't really tell you, but the initial coroner's inquest says that this is almost certainly a case of suicide. We've found no sign that there was anyone else up in the woods and no external signs on the body of a struggle. With the evidence of money troubles and poor mental health, Sarah had clear reasons to do it, so it's all pointing to one thing at this stage. We would need something really solid to elevate this to a murder enquiry.'

The word hung viscerally, each person in the room allowing it to sink in as a possibility. Jude felt sick. But she also felt a wash of determination. If Sarah had been murdered, then there would be evidence somewhere. And if the police were going to drag their heels, assuming no foul play, well then, Jude would have to investigate herself.

7

Whilst Charlie left the kitchen to get dressed, the DS had a list of questions for Jude about the break-in and the man she'd seen: Les Turner, a ruthless debt collector who lived in relative luxury on the outskirts of Worcester.

'He's claiming that you let him into the cottage and he legally took assets owed. There are no signs of a break-in, which he claims backs up his side of the story.'

Jude thought back to the previous day.

'He must have picked the lock somehow,' she said. 'There's no way I would have let him in. Have you asked Janet Timms?'

Binnie raised an eyebrow. 'Oh, yes,' she said. 'She had plenty to say. But nothing very helpful. She didn't see the man enter and assumed you let him in as she saw you in the cottage first.'

Bitch, thought Jude. She knew it was unfair because Janet Timms had only spoken the truth. But would it have killed her to have twisted it a little? After all, it would have been obvious to anyone what had happened.

'Surely he can't just get away with this? Have you at least got Sarah's things back?'

'I'm afraid not. He says he's already sold them on.'

Jude was fuming. Not just because it sounded as though this man was going to get away with robbery, but also because she felt he must somehow be as tangled up in Sarah's death as he had been in her debts. Huge debts that she couldn't pay back. Money owed to this Les Turner who was obviously a very nasty piece of work. How nasty, though? Nasty enough to kill?

'Do you think he could be involved in her death?' Jude asked.

'I couldn't possibly make that connection at this point.'

But there was something about the way she looked at her. Something in her deep brown eyes told her she *had* already made the link and *wasn't* going to let it lie.

'Please don't let him get away with this.'

'I will do my very best.'

Jude opened the kitchen door to let her out. They both had work to do and Jude had the reassuring feeling that Detective Sergeant Khatri was exactly the right person to have on her side.

The postman was pulling up as Binnie got into her car.

'Morning, Jude,' he said, passing her a bundle of letters, almost certainly made up of bills and junk mail. 'Police here again, are they? Nasty business that. I was very sorry to hear about Sarah.'

'Thanks, Sid,' she said. This was definitely something she was going to have to get used to. It came with the territory of a rural village lifestyle.

Back in the house, she returned to Charlie who'd finished his breakfast and was standing next to the dresser with the framed photo in his hand.

'This was our school leavers' ball,' he said. 'I didn't know you had it.'

'I didn't. I found it in Sarah's cottage yesterday.'

'It's like that Agatha Christie film. We're losing them one by one.'

'Have you told Ben yet?' Jude asked.

Charlie shook his head. 'I thought about it. But what can he actually do? It might be better to let him enjoy what's left of his honeymoon before he comes home to face this mess. What do you think?'

Jude nodded. 'I guess you're right.'

Charlie leant in to give her another of his big hugs and, for a moment, it felt as though he might never let go. And then she realised he was crying. Silently and still, but she could feel his tears damp just above her ear.

'I wish we could go back to before,' he whispered. 'When you'd just married Adam and moved over to our side of the hills. Just the five of us, with everything to look forward to.'

Jude couldn't find the words. Her own pain mirrored Charlie's so violently.

'We'll figure this out,' she said. 'Whatever happened to Sarah. We will work it out.'

Charlie pulled away and wiped his eyes on the sleeve of his hoodie.

'I'd better get going,' he said.

'Come whenever you like.'

He nodded and then he was gone.

And Jude had to find the strength to step back out into the yard and tend to her farm.

Right foot, left foot, right foot, left foot.

* * *

Well-practised, Jude poured her energy and her mind power into her farm tasks. Not allowing thoughts of suicide, murder, break-ins or coroner reports to infiltrate.

When there were no lambs or ewes to tend to, she tidied the pens and prepared them for the next batch of pregnant ewes. There were plenty of other jobs to keep her occupied too, and she took comfort from Pancake, who was already developing bags of character and had learnt that humans, especially Jude, came with milk, mewing happily whenever Jude approached her pen. Noah had clearly adopted the same form of self-preservation and Jude noticed him talking to the lambs more as he put the docking rubber rings on their tails to lessen the risk of flystrike later in the spring. This was something that welfare campaigners had an increasing issue with but it was a painless way of keeping the lambs safe from the hideous agony caused by fly maggots burrowing deep into the skin, so Jude and Noah were adamant they kept the practice going to protect their livestock.

'Lunch time,' Noah called across the barn.

'You go ahead,' Jude called back. 'I'm going to do a supplies check.'

'You need a break,' Noah insisted. 'Come and eat something. You'll be no good for anything if you're skin and bone and passing out every two minutes. Look, I made a bite for you when I made my own this morning.'

He waved a tinfoil package at her and Jude found herself smiling. Adam would certainly have approved and she could almost hear him telling her to listen to Noah and have a proper lunch. She set down her pad of paper and joined the shepherd on the bale of hay.

'Will ham and cheese do you?'

'Perfect,' said Jude, taking the package and peeling back the tinfoil.

'Blimey,' she said, taking a big bite. 'This is a bit of a superior sandwich, Noah.'

'It's fresh bread, not that plastic stuff you get from the supermarket. And I added some of my own home-made chutney.'

'It's delicious. Thank you.'

It was good to take a break and Jude definitely felt a little better after the exceptionally good sandwich.

* * *

That evening, Charlie messaged to see how she was. It wasn't the sort of question she could reply to truthfully via text, so she gave a thumbs up and a cursory *U?* to which Charlie replied with a thumbs up of his own.

Jude threw a frozen chicken curry in the Aga and went upstairs for a shower. She and Adam hadn't done much in the way of home improvements since his parents had moved to be with his mum's infirm sister in Canada soon after the wedding, leaving the farm to Adam and Jude. But the one luxury Jude had insisted on was a power shower.

'I'm not going to come in every day covered in farm crap just to try and wash it off under that pathetic trickle you call a shower,' she'd said after a particularly mucky day of work.

'Oh, really?' Adam had teased, pulling her close. 'You smell all right to me.'

'It took me half an hour to shower and even then I'm sure I've missed quite a few bits.'

Adam undid the belt of her dressing gown and she allowed it to slip to the floor.

'Exactly where are these dirty bits?' he teased. 'Or do I have to check every part? Just in case?'

As Jude stood in the heavy jets, the memory of his lips on her skin made her shiver. She stood under the powerful stream until her skin was red from the heat and her head began to feel giddy. Then she wrapped a towel around her hair and Adam's robe around her body and she went downstairs to kill another evening alone with her thoughts.

The curry was piping hot when she took it from the Aga. The smell of it made her mouth water, even though she knew it wouldn't taste as good as it smelled – ready meals never did – but she was hungry and that was a good sign. She left it to cool whilst she went through the sitting room and up a step into the old music room at the front of the house to retrieve her laptop. A piano stood against one wall, a dusty remnant of Adam's childhood now covered in piles of paper and stacks of files. This room had a great view over the yard and Jude had quickly purloined it as the farm office when she'd first moved in and found herself in charge of the reams of paperwork.

Jude picked the laptop up from the desk and took it back to the kitchen table. She put the radio on for background noise and caught the end of a news bulletin about one of the big supermarkets set to harvest their biggest annual profits to date.

'You'd never think it,' Jude told Pip. 'Considering how much they squeeze us at farm level. It'd be nice to see some of those fat profits filter down to those of us that actually produce the food in the first place.'

Frank was constantly telling her that the supermarkets were going to be the death of British farming if big changes weren't made, and Jude had to say she was inclined to agree.

Jude opened her laptop. Stirring her bowl of curry with one hand to release some of the heat, she typed in her password with the other.

Phone reception had improved immeasurably during her time on the farm, but broadband was still frustratingly slow. Jude watched the little blue spiral spin around and around.

'If I'm going to find out what happened to Sarah,' she said to Pip, 'then I think Les Turner is a good place to begin.'

Once the search engine had fired up, she typed in *Les Turner Worcester loan* and a string of results appeared. There was a professional website that promised *competitive loans for bad credit*, *soft credit checks* and *instant funding of up to £10,000*.

The website made it sound risk free, appealing and even friendly which was nothing like the experience of poor, gullible Sarah.

Angrily, Jude left the website and read a couple of local articles about court cases against Mr Lester Turner of Cleeves Road, Worcester. It was clear that Sarah wasn't alone in falling foul of the loan shark. Just as Binnie had said, there were others who'd reported him but he'd always managed to wriggle out of trouble.

'Not this time,' Jude growled.

The phone vibrated on the table, making her jump. When she looked at the screen, she saw that it was her younger half-sister, Lucy. Their shared father had left Jude and her mother behind in Malvern when Lucy was born and he'd moved to Maidenhead to be with his new family. Despite the geographical distance between them and the best efforts of Lucy's mother, the two sisters had always been close.

'Hey, Lou-Lou,' she said. 'How are you?'

'Hi, Judy. I'm all right.' Her sister paused. 'Well, actually no, not all right. Sebbie is driving me up the wall.'

Sebbie was Lucy's two-year-old, born out of wedlock, which had been a point of great concern for their father. Both girls considered this to be rich, seeing as he himself had left Jude's mother when his affair with Lucy's mother had led to pregnancy.

'What's that scamp been up to now?' Jude asked, glad of the modicum of normality.

'He peed on the carpet, not once but three times today. Honestly, I think he does it on purpose sometimes.'

Jude chuckled. 'Maybe he's not quite ready to ditch the nappies yet?'

'He's twenty-seven months old,' Lucy said as though this explained everything.

'So?'

'My new mum's handbook says that potty training should take place between eighteen and twenty-four months. We're already late as it is.'

'I'm sure he'll master it in the end,' Jude said gently. 'Look what happened with food. You couldn't get him to eat anything solid for ages and now he'd trough down a steak and chips if you'd let him.'

'Jude, I'd never give Sebbie red meat. The handbook says a vegetarian diet rich in pulses is the best thing for infants.'

Jude wasn't sure that was entirely true, but she knew better than to question her sister, or *The New Mum's Handbook*.

'How's Dad?' she asked instead.

Despite him swapping his old family for a newer version when she was only five, Jude felt no anger or animosity towards her father. After he moved to Maidenhead to be with Lucy and her mother, Jude didn't see him that often. He'd never really seen any reason for the sisters to meet up so the only time they did was for two weeks every summer when Jude's mother went on the annual *girls' holiday* with her friends. Jude didn't really enjoy the company of her father, and Lucy's mum made it perfectly clear she didn't enjoy Jude's, but the two girls adored each other and that relationship had never faltered.

'He's been a total nightmare since Mum died,' Lucy said. 'Although he only has himself to blame, of course.'

'Poor Dad.'

'Poor me. I'm the one getting it in the neck from him on a daily basis. You're so lucky living far enough away from him.'

Jude sighed. How typical of Lucy to think of things in this light.

'Anyway,' Lucy went on, 'I've decided Sebbie and I need a break so we're coming to stay with you for a week or two. I hope that's okay.'

Jude almost choked on her curry.

'What?'

'Oh, don't be like that. It'll be fun. Sebbie loves his Aunty Judy and it'll be lovely for you both to have some bonding time together.'

'Lou, I have the farm to deal with. We're in the middle of lambing.'

'Perfect! Sebbie and I can help.'

'I'm not sure either of you are ready for sticking your hands up a ewe's fanny,' Jude said.

'You don't really do that, do you?'

'Every day at the moment.'

'You can keep that job. Leave us with the feeding or grooming or something.'

A picture of Lucy and Sebbie busy in the lambing shed trying to brush the lambs' fleeces and put bows around their ears made Jude laugh.

'Not much grooming to be done, to be honest,' she said.

'Well, whatever. We're happy to muck in.'

Before Jude had the chance to object further, or tell Lucy about Sarah, the other pretty big reason why it wasn't a great time for a visit, Lucy cut her off.

'Must go, Judy. Sebbie's screaming his head off and last time it was because he'd got his willy caught in the toilet seat, so I'd better go and check on him. We'll see you tomorrow. Much love.'

'Tomorrow?' Jude exclaimed.

But the phone was already dead.

Jude rang back but Lucy didn't answer. She sent a text asking her to call back, explaining that it really wasn't a great time for a visit but that she'd love to see them both later in the year. But even as she sent it, she knew it was pointless.

Bugger it. She'd have to dig out some clean sheets for the spare rooms. No, sod that. Lucy could do it herself when she arrived.

Jude went to fill the kettle for a cup of camomile tea, in the vain hope it might help her sleep. As she picked it up, she knocked the pile of letters she'd propped there that morning and they skittered to the flag-stoned floor.

'Crap,' she said, bending down to pick them up.

Then she saw something that made the skin all over her body prickle and her pulse thump loudly in her ears.

Amongst the bills and clothing catalogues was an envelope bordered with tiny roses. The stationery was familiar. Jude had seen it before, just as she had the distinct, messy handwriting on the front. Both belonged to Sarah.

8

Jude's fingers shook as she opened the envelope. By the time she'd taken the single piece of rose-bordered writing paper out, her entire body was shaking and she had to sit down at the table to read it.

Dearest Jude,

I am so sorry to do this to you. To all of you.

It has just got too much for me. I made some very bad choices and I ended up with a lot of debt that I won't ever be able to pay off. I am so embarrassed.

This way I can make it all just go away. I hope you understand.

Your best friend Sarah. xxx

Jude read the note twice. The writing was clearly Sarah's, although even more messy and frenetic than usual. Hardly surprising considering the state she must have been in when she wrote it. Jude imagined her friend sitting at the tiny table in the cottage, still in the outfit she'd worn to the wedding. She'd been so drunk and must have been an emotional wreck, almost certainly crying as she formed the terrible words.

'Oh, Sarah,' Jude whispered. 'What happened?'

She knew she should take the note to the police but Jude couldn't bring herself to call DS Khatri. Surely this note would be the evidence they needed to close the case. Suicide – easy, job done – onto the next thing.

And yet, despite the overwhelming evidence, Jude couldn't shake her doubts. She read the note again. It seemed so stark. Was there room for doubt? Could she have been talking about something else? She didn't actually mention her intentions specifically.

The more Jude tried to find an explanation, the further away one seemed.

* * *

The following day was the beginning of a new month. March brought the sun with it, quickly seeing off the early frost and warming the lambing shed. Frank had worked his last night at Malvern Farm, lambing over for another year, and had left to prepare his own flock, which had been tupped six weeks later than the ewes of Malvern Farm so would be starting to birth any day.

Noah was preparing the John Deere tractor for fertiliser spraying, leaving Jude and Pip to watch the lambing pens when she heard someone enter the shed.

'Knock, knock,' Janet Timms called.

Jude's heart plummeted into her wellies. She was crouched on the hay, just about out of sight and wondered if she stayed quiet enough the irritating woman would leave. But Pip had other ideas, barking a greeting at the unwanted visitor.

'Ah, there you are,' Janet said. 'I brought you some banana loaf.

I thought you might not be eating properly after all you've been through.'

'Hello,' Jude said, standing up. 'Thank you for the thought.'

She had little choice but to wash her hands and accept the wicker basket, covered in a tea towel commemorating the funeral of Queen Elizabeth. Jude peeked under the cloth.

'It looks delicious,' she said. 'Noah and I will enjoy it when we have time to break for lunch.'

She placed the basket on the empty oil drum they used as a table, next to her flask of coffee and Noah's box of sandwiches.

'How are you coping?' Janet asked, fake sincerity poorly disguising her thirst for first-hand gossip. That woman was worse than a tabloid journalist.

'We're pretty busy,' Jude said. 'Lambing always keeps us on our toes but we're actually coping well. Thanks.'

'I'm glad to hear it,' said Janet. 'But it must be so difficult to keep going after what happened to poor Sarah. And right here too, on this farm.'

She looked around as though hopeful she might find another body swinging from the rafters. The grapevine had obviously been busy and this particular gossip wanted to know what was true so she could confidently pass it on to the rest of the village.

'I'm doing my best not to think about it,' said Jude.

'Of course.' Janet patted her arm. 'Of course. I heard it was you who found her body. Must have been awful for you.'

'I'm sorry,' Jude said, trying hard not to grit her teeth. 'I really don't have time to chat. As I said, it's such a busy time here at the moment and I must get on.'

'How about I keep you company?' Janet Timms suggested. 'We can have a bit of a natter whilst you work.'

Jude couldn't stop her eyebrows rising. Was this woman for real? If she were a dog, she'd be some sort of terrier. Permanently yapping around people's ankles, demanding attention and sinking her teeth in relentlessly.

At that moment, Noah returned.

'Ah, there you are,' Jude said with relief. 'The sprayer all ready for me, is it?'

'Ey?' said Noah, failing to hide his confusion.

'I'm sorry, Mrs Timms,' Jude continued, 'but I need to get out and fertilise the pasture fields or my growing flock won't have enough grass to eat when we stop feeding them forage. No time for a natter now.'

She stared hard at Noah, willing him to understand.

'Yep,' Noah replied. 'She's ready and waiting for you. Floss and I've moved the flock to the far field so you can spray the front two today and we'll move them over at the end of the week.'

Jude hadn't wanted to take the tractor out to spray the pasture because it meant she'd be driving up past the oaks. She hoped Janet might take her leave, allowing Noah to jump in the tractor and do the job for her, but she didn't. She watched as Jude climbed into the cab, fired up her trusty old John Deere and drove across the yard into the first of the grazing fields.

The first time she'd been in a tractor had been at the end of the summer she and Adam had met. She'd been sitting on the arm rest as Adam drove them around the bean fields. She watched him chisel plough the spent earth and then he'd swapped seats and given her the controls, guiding her as she used the heavy machinery to cut into the baked post-harvest ground. She'd felt empowered and capable as she looked behind and saw the straight rows of broken soil left behind. At the end, she'd lifted the plough, turned the tractor... and snapped a branch off a tree as she misjudged the width of the plough swinging in the air behind her.

'Bollocks,' she'd cursed.

'Bollocks for the tree,' Adam laughed, jumping out of the cab to check the plough and to push the branch out of the way.

'No harm done,' he said. 'Not a bad job either. Apart from the tree, that is.'

Under his guidance, she'd ploughed the rest of the field. By the following autumn, she'd learned to drive both of the farm's tractors with confidence and she loved it. The lofty feeling of being up high, the view of the land it gave her and the knowledge that she was doing something useful. The ancient Massey Furguson was loud and dusty, the fabric of the seat held together with duct tape and the door kept shut with a length of baling twine. Jude named her Maz and together they'd covered many acres. The John Deere was newer and had the luxury of air-con but Jude always said it lacked Maz's character. Something that both Adam and Noah teased her about.

Generally, Jude loved driving the tractors but right then, she wanted to abandon the cab and let Noah get on with it.

She'd have to face the fields again at some point, she knew that well enough. And the pull to get away from Janet Timms was strong so she did what she had to do. She knocked the tractor into gear and headed out towards the field. Letting down the spraying arms after driving through the gates, she drove the tractor up and down the length of the biggest of the four grazing fields until every inch had been covered with the organic fertiliser to bring on good-quality grass feed for her flock.

When she'd finished, she folded the spraying arms back up. Without stopping to think, she drove through the gate into the next field where it was impossible to miss the yellow and black tape cordoning off a large area by the oak trees.

Jude put the tractor in neutral and allowed herself a minute to take in the scene. She'd expected to be taken straight back to the moment she'd found Sarah in the mud but the reality was not as violent as she'd thought it would be. The place was the same and yet very different. Then, the sky had been ominous and cloud filled with mizzle hanging thickly all around her, but the presence of the sun now transformed the field to something different – enough for it to hold no memories for Jude, at least none that were any more difficult to bear than the ones already etched in her mind.

The throb of the powerful tractor engine and the warmth of the sun flooding in through the glass of the cab went some way to calming her. Being there again strengthened something deep inside Jude. Moping had never helped anyone achieve anything. She'd made a resolution to do all she could to find out what had happened to Sarah and she was going to make good on that promise.

9

At lunch time, Jude checked her phone for any updates on Lucy's planned visit.

There were none.

She called her sister to try again to persuade her not to come.

Lucy didn't answer.

She sent a WhatsApp message, which returned two blue ticks almost instantly.

Lucy didn't send any reply.

Jude called again, and again there was no answer. This time she left a voicemail.

At teatime, Lucy's car pulled into the yard.

Jude had just taken delivery of the lamb tags for that year's flock when she heard the car door slam. She was at the kitchen table sorting through the paperwork to make sure the tags' numbers matched and everything was in order.

'Shit,' she said to Pip, who woofed a note of agreement.

'Judy!' Lucy exclaimed, walking straight into the kitchen without knocking.

A grumpy-looking Sebbie was stuck to her hip, his strawberry-blond hair clinging to his head and his face red and shiny as though he'd just been woken from sleep. He reminded Jude of Lucy as a toddler. They'd both inherited the red-head gene from their father but whereas Lucy's had come out pale and wavy, Jude's was thick, straight and the colour of conkers. In all other ways, the two sisters looked almost like twins, although Jude was always pleased to see that the height gap hadn't shrunk since Lucy's eleventh birthday and Jude was still taller by a good few inches.

'Hi, Lou-Lou,' she said. 'I guess you didn't get any of my messages then?'

'I thought you were just being a spoil sport. We won't be any trouble and we *really* needed to get away from Dad for a bit.'

Lucy thrust her child towards Jude.

'Take Sebbie for me, will you? I'll just go and unpack the car.'

Sebbie didn't want to be passed from mother to aunt and as soon as Lucy stepped outside, he scrunched his face up and started to cry.

'I know how you feel, little guy,' said Jude. 'But hey, you're here now so let's make the most of it. Are you hungry?'

She went to the cupboard and found a packet of Tony's miniature chocolates.

'There you go,' she said, peeling one and offering the chocolate to Sebbie, who stopped crying instantly and stared at it.

'Grape?' he said.

'No,' said Jude. 'It's a chocolate.'

'Clocklet,' he said reverently.

'Close enough.'

Lucy returned, her arms loaded with a plastic riot of toys, seats, potties, and God only knew what else.

'What the hell is that?' Lucy said as she dumped the lot on the kitchen table.

'What?'

'In Sebbie's hand, and round his mouth. In fact, all down his jumper too.'

She grabbed a pack of wipes from an enormous changing bag and started to scrub at Sebbie's face. Sebbie, of course, objected heavily to this.

'You haven't given him chocolate?'

'Um,' said Jude. 'It was only a small bit of Tony's. It's all fair-trade and ethical. Not all right?'

'*Not* all right!' said Lucy. 'Sebbie does not eat refined sugar.'

Poor kid, thought Jude.

'Sorry,' she said.

By the time Lucy had moved all their things in, the house looked more like a nursery than a farm. Jude relented and made up the bed in the main spare room. Sebbie had a travel cot which was set up in the little box room and was accompanied by a rather large bag of clothes. Lucy suckered a blackout blind across the window and plugged a baby camera into the socket. A booster seat with five-point harness was strapped to one of the kitchen chairs and a huge variety of toys were soon strewn around the sitting room.

'There are loads of Adam's old toys in the playroom at the back of the house,' Jude said. 'Sebbie's probably not ready for the Hornby trains yet but there's a big box of Lego. Everything's in the big cupboard so help yourself.'

'Thanks,' said Lucy. 'I think it's probably safer if we stick with what we've brought.'

Jude wasn't exactly sure what this meant but she didn't say anything.

'I'll let you settle in,' she said. 'I need to get back out to help Noah for a couple of hours. Make yourself at home. You know where everything is.'

'We'll come with you,' said Lucy. 'Sebbie could do with some fresh air after the journey.'

'Great!' There was no point in saying anything else. Lucy had clearly made up her mind and was already stripping Sebbie of his inside shoes and stuffing his feet into a bright red pair of wellies with elephants printed up the sides. A large R was stamped on the toe of one and an L on the other.

'This is your *left* foot, Sebbie. *Left.* Can you say *left*?'

'Lellie,' said Sebbie.

'Yes, they are your wellies,' said Lucy. 'But can you say *left* wellie?'

'Lellie,' Sebbie repeated and then took the one with the R on and flung it across the kitchen.

'I'll meet you out there.' Jude smiled. Despite her misgivings, having her sister and nephew to stay for a little while might be just the distraction she needed. As long as that was what it remained. A *little* while.

'We're all done,' said Noah, who was standing by the sink drying his hands.

He nodded proudly at the pens.

'They've all lambed?' Jude asked.

'They have. That's it for another year.'

It was a good feeling. They had a little over eight hundred new members of the Malvern Farm family, many of whom had already been let out into the fields to roam and graze. The remainder were either in the pens still or the larger barn next door where they moved the young lambs with their mums after they'd successfully bonded. Lambing over, things would quieten down for a bit and Jude was more than ready for that.

'Still got this one to tend,' Noah said, pointing at Pancake's pen. 'She'll be needing you for a month or so before she leaves the bottle.'

Jude lifted the lamb and rubbed the top of her head.

'Doggie,' said Sebbie as he ran across the shed. He had both wellies on the correct feet, a thick coat zipped right up, bobble hat tied under his chin and a warm pair of mittens.

Noah knelt down to the same height as the child.

'Nope,' he said. 'Not a dog. That's a lamb.'

'Lamb,' repeated Sebbie.

'That's right,' said Noah. 'Might make a farmer out of you yet.'

'You remember my sister, Lucy?' said Jude. 'And little Sebbie?'

'I do. Nice to see you both. Come to stay for a bit, have you?'

'Yes,' said Lucy. 'We've come for some country air to recharge the batteries.'

'Plenty of that round here.' Noah smiled.

'I'm about to give Pancake her milk,' said Jude. 'Do you want to help, Sebbie?'

Noah went to mix and warm the feed whilst Jude sat Sebbie down on a hay bale.

'Is it safe?' Lucy asked.

Noah raised an eyebrow and Jude sighed.

'Of course it is. Unless Sebbie has suddenly developed a severe allergy to lambs.'

Lucy looked stricken. 'Is that possible?'

'He'll be fine.'

She passed the warm bottle to Sebbie, who giggled as Pancake nudged his arm, eager for the milk. Jude helped Sebbie angle the bottle so that Pancake could suckle properly. The toddler didn't stop chuckling and even Lucy started to relax a little.

'Lamb dink,' Sebbie laughed. 'Lamb dink milk.'

'S'right,' said Noah. 'She'll need lots of it too if she's going to grow up big and strong like you.'

Jude looked at Noah gratefully. He'd got her through another lambing season and his gentle, stoic nature had been exactly what she'd needed. Despite everything hanging over her, in that moment Jude found a quiet contentment.

A quiet contentment that was soon broken by the sound of a car driving over the yard.

'I'll go and see who it is,' said Noah.

He was back just moments later.

'It's that policewoman again,' he said. 'Wants to talk to you.'

'The police?' Lucy said, her eyebrows shooting through her hairline.

'I did try to tell you,' said Jude, untangling herself from the jungle of gangly lamb and toddler limbs. She passed Pancake to Noah, much to the annoyance of both lamb and child.

'I need to go but I'll tell you everything as soon as we're done.'

'Visitors?' DS Binnie Khatri asked, looking around at Sebbie's paraphernalia.

'My sister's come to stay for a few days,' Jude explained as she cleared a space at the kitchen table to allow them to sit down.

'Sorry,' said Binnie. 'I could have just called but I wanted to come and see you.'

'Don't worry,' said Jude. 'I do love my sister but she does seem to have completely taken over around here. Do you have any younger siblings?'

Binnie's eyes darted away and Jude thought she'd overstepped the mark, asking too-personal questions.

'Sorry,' said Jude. 'Any news?'

'We had no choice but to release Les Turner.'

'Seriously?' Jude's heart started to hammer loudly beneath her ribs.

'We had no grounds to keep him in for longer than twenty-four hours.'

'But he robbed Sarah's cottage. And he may well be involved in Sarah's death.'

She thought about the note that had arrived the previous day and was glad now that she'd kept this to herself – for the moment at least.

'He's claiming he had her permission and that the appointment had been previously arranged. He has an email trail confirming this.'

'That doesn't mean he couldn't have killed her, though.'

'As far as the evidence goes, it was suicide,' said the DS, gently. 'We've currently got no reason to look any further into Les Turner.'

'No!' said Jude. 'It doesn't add up.'

'What do you mean?'

'It's just not Sarah,' said Jude, feeling the truth of her conviction deeply. 'None of it makes any sense to me. Why go out in the rain wearing her wedding outfit, climb the path behind her cottage to the trees and hang herself using a scarf? She'd have hated the thought of being discovered like that, filthy and ruined. I knew Sarah and I'm telling you this wasn't her.'

Binnie thought carefully before she answered.

'I'm not ruling anything out at this stage of the proceedings,' she said. 'But I have to be careful not to step on my boss's toes. Look, I'll chase the post-mortem results and see what they turn up but, in the meantime, I want you to know that I'm not going to let this lie. And anything you can think of that might be helpful, let me have it. However small. If it can help me build a case, then I need to know.'

Jude thought about the suicide note and the diary. She knew she ought to give them up and yet she stayed silent. The suicide note would only help prove that nobody else had been involved, and Jude wanted time to go through the diary herself before she passed it on.

10

Lucy wanted Sebbie to go to bed at 6.30 p.m.

Sebbie did not agree.

Fed, bathed and pyjamaed, he was still full of excited energy and a mile away from settling down when he was zipped into his sleep suit and put in the travel cot.

Lucy and Jude watched him on the little screen of the baby monitor as he chatted to his soft toys for a while before throwing his favourite knitted teddy across the room and then screaming angrily when he realised he couldn't get it back.

Eventually, after several stories with his mum, several more with Aunty Judy and around half an hour of standing in his cot alternating between singing a song about a turtle, shouting for attention and finally beginning a bout of angry crying, Lucy relented and allowed Jude to put the television on.

It took two and a half episodes of *In the Night Garden* for Sebbie to finally succumb and fall asleep on Jude's lap.

'I'll take him up,' said Lucy.

'No,' said Jude. 'Leave him a little longer.'

She was winding her finger through his soft curls and enjoying the feel of his little body, heavy on her legs. It was something she'd thought would come to her one day and yet, when Adam died, so did her hope of becoming a mother. It wasn't that she was too old, but she was married to the farm now and couldn't begin to think about finding someone new.

'You haven't told Dad I'm here, have you?' Lucy asked suddenly.

'I rarely speak to him,' Jude answered. 'Why? What's up?'

'Nothing, really,' she said, though Jude found herself not quite believing her. 'I just don't want him to know I'm here, that's all. Now, are you going to tell me what's been going on and why the police have been visiting?'

Jude gave a big sigh. Where to begin?

For once, Lucy listened with few interruptions as Jude unravelled everything that had happened over just a few short days. Starting at the wedding and bringing them all the way up to the moment Lucy and Sebbie had arrived at the farm.

'Jesus Christ,' Lucy said when she'd finished. 'You should have called me, I'd have come here straight away.'

Jude smiled. 'You're here now,' she said. And she was surprised to realise that she was actually very glad about it.

'So, what now?'

'Now we wait for the post-mortem,' said Jude.

'You don't think it was suicide?'

Jude shook her head. 'I just can't see it.'

'And you've told the police?'

'Of course,' said Jude. 'The detective sergeant on the case is brilliant but her boss seems to have written Sarah off. He's in no hurry to look beyond the easy.'

'What about this loan guy, though? Surely that can't be a coincidence?'

'No, but if anything, it just strengthens the case for suicide.

They see Sarah as a stupid girl who got herself into money trouble and couldn't see any other way out.'

'Then we need to find something to prove differently, don't we?'

Jude was grateful for her sister's support but she was also grateful when Lucy's fatigue kicked in.

'Sleep well,' Jude whispered to them both as Lucy carefully scooped Sebbie up and took him upstairs.

Although she herself was utterly exhausted, Jude relished the first peaceful moment of the day. She took the opportunity to pour herself a glass of cider, throw another log on the burner and retrieve Sarah's diary from the dresser.

Sitting curled up on the sofa with Pip stretched out over her, Jude opened the diary. The pages were filled with scrawled notes in Sarah's scruffy handwriting, reminders and meetings, but nothing of much interest, partly down to the shorthand she used. There were a lot of mentions of N, presumably Nate, and Jude was surprised to see hearts drawn around some of them.

Dinner with N (heart)
N – 3.30 @ AH (heart)
Weekend with N (heart)

This one on the weekend of Sarah's birthday, which made Jude wonder if she, and the others, had actually been wrong about Nate.

There were other, less romantic mentions of him too in her to-do lists.

Book N dentist. Get N new pillow. Take N's shoes to be fixed.

'Why didn't you make him run his own bloody chores?' she said to herself.

Jude recognised herself in the diary in a couple of places.

Call J, it said, the week after New Year, on the anniversary of Adam's cancer diagnosis. Sarah had always remembered things like that, either calling or popping round to check on Jude when the difficult anniversaries arose.

LX was clearly something of great importance to Sarah as this was written every day for a period of two weeks, before and after Ben's wedding: the night she died. Each one was followed by a number: LX1, LX2... but nothing more. No clue as to what these might be referencing.

Other initials appeared several times too: LT, CB and GM, the last of which was obviously Granny Margot. There were several phone calls flagged with LT and Jude felt nauseous as she realised these must mean Les Turner – Sarah's efforts to try to come to an agreement over a payment plan or to beg for more time to sort herself out. Having met the revolting man, Jude had no doubt that these phone calls would not have been pleasant for Sarah to manage.

CB was the only person she couldn't place and it bothered her for two reasons. Firstly, because Sarah had met this person several times in the weeks leading up to her death, and secondly, because at the top of one page there was a scribble that appeared to link LT and CB together. Both sets of initials set next to each other joined by a thick arrow made from many layers of heavily scratched pencil, with a large question mark stamped next to it. If LT, Les Turner, had indeed been linked to this CB, as Sarah seemed to have suspected, then this was someone Jude wanted to investigate further.

11

Despite there being no ewes left to birth, Jude's body clock was still tuned into lambing time and she woke at 5 a.m., around eight minutes before Sebbie.

She heard him chattering to himself to start with before the chattering turned into song and the singing finally gave way to hollering.

She figured that she may as well go and get him up as she was awake anyway. Give Lucy a break, maybe even a bit of a lie-in. She pushed her feet into an ancient pair of slippers and pulled a hoodie on over her thick winter pyjamas.

'Morning, sweet boy,' she said, as she pushed the door of Sebbie's room open and was greeted by a huge grin and two outstretched arms.

'Aundy Chewdy!' he exclaimed. 'Get Sebbie up.'

'Come on then,' she said, scooping him up and nuzzling her nose into his warm neck.

Sebbie laughed at her and then wriggled to be put down.

'Let's go downstairs first,' Jude said. 'If you're really quiet and we don't wake Mummy, we can watch some cartoons.'

With Sebbie engrossed in a chain of *Peppa Pig* episodes and happily sucking on a sippy cup of warm milk, Jude looked at Sarah's diary still lying on the coffee table where she'd left it the night before. She picked it up and read every entry again carefully in case there was some clue she'd missed. The more she looked, the less she saw. So much was hinted at in the notes and scribbles, and yet nothing laid bare. Threads that became more tangled the more she tried to smooth them out. And the questions they threw up – so many questions.

Jude took the diary up the step into the old music room, switched on the printer and photocopied all the pages. She knew she'd have to give the diary to Binnie but she wanted to have the chance to think more about what it contained. There must be *something* she was missing, hidden in the sketchy entries.

'Aundy Chewdy,' Sebbie shouted from the sofa. 'Peppa stop.'

Jude could see that the television had stalled and was displaying a frozen image of the small pig dressed in red, a blue swirl circling over her snout. The infernal sign of buffering, possibly the most irritating symbol of the modern world.

'Just a minute, poppet,' she said.

She took the key for the filing cabinet from a little hook that a safety-conscious Adam had screwed to the back of a heavy wooden table lamp, just in case the farm was broken into and someone wanted to steal all the bank details and passwords. His theory had always made Jude chuckle. The coffers were consistently near empty so any robber who managed to find and use their bank details would have been sorely out of luck. But now it was just another of those comforting little nuggets of her husband's life that Jude liked to hold on to.

She opened the filing cabinet and dropped the photocopied pages into one of the hanging files. Then she locked the drawer and put the key back on its hidden hook, before returning the diary itself to the drawer of the dresser.

The time immediately after lambing was always fairly quiet at Malvern Farm. Especially this year, as they'd finished so early the crops didn't need much tending yet. There'd be slurry spreading and top dressing to be getting on with soon enough but that could wait.

After the first proper breakfast Jude had sat down to eat that year, Lucy bundled Sebbie upstairs to get him ready for his day. Jude tidied up the breakfast things and did the washing up and then put the diary in her oversized handbag, planning to drop it in to DS Khatri at the police station later that day.

Jude fed Pancake her morning milk, filled the troughs with forage and feed pellets for the ewes and lambs still being kept in the big barn and then checked them over. She let the hens out of their coops, fed them and collected their eggs, boxing them up ready to put in the honesty box at the end of the drive. Back in the house, she put on fresh jeans, brushed her hair out and cleaned her teeth. She put her coat on, added her phone and purse to her handbag and picked up her car keys.

In the time it had taken Jude to do all of that, Lucy and Sebbie had just about managed to have breakfast. They were still a very long way from being ready. Jude hated wasting time when each minute on the farm could be filled ten times over, so she decided to pop into the village in the meantime. She'd bought herself a pair of jeans online but they gave her a massive wedgy and needed to be returned. She also had a couple of cheques to pay in that had been sitting in the office for weeks from a couple of local shops who bought eggs from her and still insisted on paying their bills this way.

Mrs James, who ran the joint post office and shop, was clad in her usual work uniform of polo neck sweater, tweed skirt, and floral-printed wraparound apron with big pockets. She always reminded Jude of Mrs Overall from Victoria Wood's *Acorn Antiques* series and the fact that her gentle voice had a Birmingham lilt to it only added to the effect.

'Good morning, Jude,' she said. 'I was so sorry to hear about Sarah.'

Jude liked Mrs James a lot – she'd been working at the post office since Adam was a child when he used to pop in for his weekly sweet allowance every Sunday – but, like a few others in the village, she loved to pass on juicy titbits and, right then, there was nothing juicer than the tragic death at Malvern Farm.

'Thank you,' said Jude. 'Can I return this, please? I've got the slip here.'

'Of course,' said Mrs James, taking the parcel from her.

'Can I have a book of stamps too?' she asked. 'Second class.'

Once the parcel was dealt with and stowed in the postal bag, Mrs James took a book of stamps from the till. Jude peeled one off and stuck it on the envelope containing her cheques.

'You might want to leave that here. I'll stick it in the bag,' said Mrs James. 'There's robins nesting in the post box in the village, so you'd have to go up to the one on Croft Bank.'

When she got back to the farm, Sebbie was strapped in his car seat in the back of Lucy's car.

'Where have you been?' said Lucy as she tapped the car key impatiently against her thigh. 'We've been waiting for you.'

Jude rolled her eyes and got into the passenger seat.

And, finally, they set off.

'Pink house,' said Sebbie, waving a chubby fist at the old stone cottage where Noah lived. The cottage had indeed been painted pink whilst in the hands of the previous owner, a lady named Old Leah, who had apparently lived there her entire life and refused all offers by Adam's family to introduce electric or gas. Noah had modernised the inside of the cottage somewhat, but the outside remained the colour of cooked prawns.

They were soon down the drive, where they pulled over to put the eggs in the honesty box. Then they turned into the lanes, which had high hedges and poor visibility.

'Sing song,' Sebbie demanded from the back.

'Not today,' said Lucy. 'Mummy and Aunty Judy want to hear each other talk.'

'*Sing song!*' Sebbie said again with more authority than Jude thought was right for a two-year-old.

Lucy clicked a button on the steering wheel and the car was suddenly filled with the sound of a jolly woman singing a song about a dog who went to the seaside.

'Sorry.' Lucy grimaced.

The seaside dog song took them out of the lanes and onto Croft Bank, a steep road that climbed the side of the hills. Large houses sprouted on either side as gradually they came into a more inhabited part of the Malverns. At the top of Croft Bank, Lucy had to pull the hand brake on to stop the car from rolling back down the hill. She craned her neck to look round the side of the huge stone building that had once been an exclusive boarding school.

'I hate hill starts,' she said as she revved the engine. There was a slight smell of burning clutch.

'Mum always said that if you learn to drive in Malvern, you can drive anywhere.' Jude smiled.

'I suppose you've got an automatic then?' said Lucy, choosing her moment and wheel-skidding out onto the West Malvern Road.

'Are you kidding me?' Jude said. 'Have you seen my car? I think it only just post-dates a manual choke!'

The West Malvern Road led further up around the side of the hills before a gap known as the Wyche Cutting took them through to the east side and down into the main town of Great Malvern.

Here the Priory stood, taking up the entire side of the still steep main road. They drove past and turned at the bottom of the hill to find the supermarket.

Neatly, Lucy nipped into a mother and baby space and Jude got out to fetch a trolley. It was the first time she'd been out in the town since lambing had started, except for the day of the wedding, and it would be nice to choose her own food rather than relying on whatever she'd managed to throw into the basket of her fortnightly online delivery shop.

With Sebbie safely contained in the seat of the trolley, Lucy and Jude navigated the aisles, collecting fresh vegetables, cooked meats, fancy cheeses, even a tub of hummus. Not a single ready meal or chocolate chip brioche made it in. For a little while, life felt something like it should do. A little hint at normality in Jude's otherwise topsy-turvy existence.

They'd just paid for the shopping when Jude caught sight of a familiar face, queuing at the self-checkout, with a basket load that screamed *cooking-for-one*.

'Charlie!' she said, rushing over to give her friend a hug.

Charlie hugged her back tightly.

'Hey,' he said. 'Sorry I haven't called. It's just been...'

He didn't need to finish because Jude knew exactly what he meant. He looked awful. Still handsome in his own way but a wash of sadness and lack of sleep taking the shine away.

'Hello,' said Lucy, joining them.

'Hi, Lucy,' said Charlie. 'Gosh, it's been ages since we last met. This little feller was nothing more than a babe in arms.'

'It's good to see you,' Lucy replied. 'We were just thinking about stopping for a coffee if you want to join us?'

'Were we?' Jude noticed a look on her sister's face that she hadn't seen for a while. Not since before Sebbie had come along, at least. She wasn't sure why she felt so irritated by the fact Lucy was flirting with Charlie, nor that she had taken over completely without thinking. But nonetheless, she wasn't really up for a forced chat over a very public coffee.

Lucy ignored her and started to push the trolley towards the café at the back of the supermarket, Charlie following in her wake.

'Look, there's one table over there by the window,' said Lucy. 'Charlie, why don't you and I go and nab it whilst Jude gets the drinks.'

She whipped Sebbie from the seat of the trolley and marched towards the table.

'Mine's a soya latte,' she called over her shoulder.

Charlie looked at Jude as though not entirely sure what he should do.

'Americano?' Jude asked.

'Yes, please,' he said. 'Do you want a hand?'

'Thanks,' said Jude. 'Grab that highchair for Sebbie and I'll see you over there.'

Jude ordered the drinks at the counter and added a juice box and snack-sized bar of Tony's chocolate for Sebbie to annoy her sister as much as to pacify her nephew. She took out her credit card to tap the machine.

'I'll bring the hot drinks over to you,' the man behind the counter said.

As she neared the table, she unwrapped the chocolate.

'Do you want this, Sebbie?'

'Clocklet,' said Sebbie, with a grin so wide Jude took it to mean *hell yes!*

'We'd better ask Mummy first,' she said, staring into her sister's eyes defiantly.

Touche! If Lucy wanted to avoid a full-on melt-down in front of everyone, she'd have to relent and let Sebbie eat the chocolate.

Lucy visibly clenched her teeth before turning to her child.

'Maybe just a couple of chunks...'

Jude took the wrapper off and broke the whole bar onto the tray of the highchair.

Lucy was clearly enjoying Charlie's company and, once Jude had thawed a little, she decided that it was actually a very nice thing to see Charlie so animated and enjoying himself too. It also gave her the perfect opportunity to go and do the things she had really come into town for without feeling guilty about leaving Lucy on her own.

'I have things to do,' she said. 'Will you be okay if I nip off for a bit?'

'How long will you be?' Lucy asked.

'Meet you back at the car in a couple of hours?'

'A couple of hours? What on earth do you need to do in this tiny town that will take you that long?'

'I've got a few errands. And I need to go and see someone.'

'Who?'

'Actually, I want to go and see Sarah's Granny Margot. I haven't seen her since...' she tailed off.

'Do you want company?' Charlie asked. 'I've been meaning to go myself.'

'No, actually. I'd like to go on my own if you don't mind. But if you're not busy, you could always show Lucy and Sebbie where the Winter Gardens are. I'm sure Sebbie would love to see the ducks and have a play in the park.'

'Sure,' said Charlie. 'Happy to. Why don't we meet you there when you've finished?'

'Perfect,' said Jude.

* * *

Great Malvern police station was on the same road as the Perrins Care Home where Granny Margot lived so Jude called in on the way past.

Jude went up to the front door expecting to walk in and find a reception desk where she could ring a bell and ask for DS Binitra Khatri, but the door was shut and locked.

'I'm sorry but there's no longer a walk-in service here,' said a voice behind her and she turned to see a uniformed officer. 'Cutbacks.' He shrugged.

'Could you see if DS Khatri is in?' Jude asked. 'I need to speak to her about something.'

'Can't help, I'm afraid. If it's a non-emergency then you can go to Worcester. Or you could give her a ring.'

Jude toyed with the idea of leaving the diary with the constable but something stopped her. She felt as though Binnie was possibly the only person who saw Sarah's death as something more than the face-value suicide it appeared to be. It seemed vital that the diary made it to her hands safely and not just ended up in some evidence box waiting for however long it took for someone to get around to looking at it. To be fair, this was based on nothing more than a gut instinct, but then Jude Gray had always been one to trust her gut.

'Thanks, I'll give her a ring later,' she said.

'Can I say who was looking for her?'

'It's Jude Gray.'

Jude left the police station and turned out onto Victoria Road, feeling a little deflated.

It was just a short walk to the nursing home and as she approached, Jude felt her insides tense. She'd been there several times to visit Granny Margot, having got on like a house on fire when she was still able to live at the cottage with Sarah. Having no relatives of her own living nearby, since the death of her mother,

Jude had adopted Margot as a kind of surrogate granny of her own. She'd been there to help her move out of the cottage and into the home – a decision that had been entirely Margot's own, claiming she felt stuck in the cottage on her own all day and wanted to be in the company of others her age. Jude suspected there was an element of wanting to give Sarah her own space too, but she knew she'd never have admitted it.

Granny Margot and Sarah had been a pair. Devoted to each other. Jude now had to go in and try to comfort the old lady, and she didn't have any idea how to begin.

12

Granny Margot was sitting in the day room of Perrins Care Home, looking out of the large bay window that offered a wonderful view of the gardens.

'Hello, Margot,' said Jude, sitting down next to her.

The old woman turned at the sound of Jude's voice. Her papery skin was thinner than ever and glowed in its paleness thanks to the sun streaming through the window. She had a lace handkerchief clasped in one hand and a glass of what looked like sherry in the other.

'Jude!' said Margot, resting the handkerchief on her lap and taking Jude's hand. 'Thank you for coming to see me. How are you?'

'I'm all right, thanks,' she said. 'And you? I would have come sooner but we've been so busy at the farm with the lambing.'

'Was it a good season?'

'It was,' said Jude. 'Eight hundred healthy little ones.'

'That *is* good to hear,' said Margot. 'I miss the days of walking through the fields up at Malvern Farm in the spring. Nothing quite like the sound of lambs in the sunshine, is there?'

'Margot, I am so sorry about Sarah,' Jude said, unable to keep up the chatter without saying what she'd come to say.

Granny Margot's hand tightened around hers. There were tears in her wrinkle-framed eyes but they didn't overspill.

'She didn't do that to herself,' Margot said with so much determination that Jude was sure nobody would be able to doubt her for even a second. 'Not my Sarah. Not for any reason.'

'I know,' said Jude. 'I know she didn't.'

'Did you know about her debts?' Granny Margot asked.

The question floored Jude as Sarah had told her nobody else knew.

'She told you?'

'No,' Margot admitted. 'She didn't need to. I knew my grand-daughter well enough. She asked me to sell the cottage, which was the first sign something was amiss. Sarah loved that place as much as I did; there would only be one reason for wanting to sell. So, I asked her outright.'

'What did she say?'

'She didn't say anything,' said Margot. 'But she didn't need to. Her face told me all I needed to know. She was in trouble and it was big enough trouble to want to sell the house.'

Jude noticed that the old woman's hands had started to tremble.

'I said no. I told her if she was in trouble then there were other ways of dealing with it and of course she smiled and told me there was nothing to worry about. If I could only go back in time...'

'There's nothing you could have done differently,' said Jude, gently. 'Nothing at all. I've had that same conversation with myself plenty of times. What if I'd been a better friend and noticed what was happening earlier? What if I'd gone back to the cottage with her and stayed the night to make sure she was all right?'

'What ifs are a dangerous trap to fall into,' said Granny Margot.

'You're right. What we need to do now is look forward. We need to find out the truth about what happened to our beautiful girl.'

Jude nodded. She thought about taking the diary out to show Margot. Perhaps there was something hidden in there that the old lady would be able to find more meaning in than she'd managed? But then maybe it would just cause her more pain and Jude didn't want to be responsible for that.

'Do you know anyone with the initials CB?' she asked instead.

'Why do you ask?'

'I'm doing a little investigating of my own.'

'That's my girl,' said Margot, some of the old twinkle returning to her tired eyes. 'Now then, CB. There's Chris Barnett from the village, but I don't think he's of much interest to you.'

'The old head teacher at the primary school?'

'That's him. He lives in the house right on the edge of the village, you know, the one with the beautiful wisteria over the door.'

Jude nodded.

'He tends to keep himself to himself,' Margot expanded. 'Has a flock of racing pigeons he flies competitively whilst his wife, Cynth, makes cakes and jam for the WI.'

He didn't sound much of a likely suspect, but Jude logged his name anyway.

'Then there's that Bradfield girl,' said Margot, in full detective flow now. 'Crystal-May-Rose her parents named her.' She shook her head to show just what she thought about a triple-barrelled first name.

'Who's that?' Jude asked.

'Her mother was great friends with my Lizzie,' she said. 'They had their babies at the same time. They were both very young mums, so I made an effort to take Sarah around there to play with

Crystal. I thought it was what Lizzie would have done herself. As a toddler, Crystal turned into a real princess and it got worse as she grew up. Spoilt rotten and spiteful with it. They went to the same primary school and Crystal tried to make sure Sarah's life was miserable, but she hadn't banked on Sarah chumming up with the boys. Sarah was far happier in a pair of jeans, climbing trees and dipping for tadpoles in the pond than she would have been hosting tea parties in a posh pink frock. Crystal-May-Rose teased her relentlessly, expecting to break her at some point, but I think the only person she made miserable in the end was herself. It was a good thing all around when they moved out to Worcester.'

Granny Margot allowed herself a little smile.

'That sounds like Sarah,' said Jude. 'But I'm not sure we can add this Crystal to our investigation if they only knew each other as children.'

'That's the thing,' said Margot. 'She turned up in Sarah's life again at the end of last year.'

'Really?'

'Oh, yes,' said Margot, leaning forward just a little bit. 'Got a job at the spa where Sarah worked. Crystal-May-Rose worked as beautician, or whatever the proper name for it is these days, and I have to say that, even after all these years, I think Sarah quite enjoyed the irony of being her boss.'

'Interesting,' said Jude, making a mental note to look this Crystal-May-Rose up. 'Any other people with the same initials that you can think of?'

Granny Margot tapped the centre of her forehead with an age-marked finger and then took a large swig of sherry.

'Well, there's always Cedric Beaufort.' She grinned.

'Who?'

Margot pointed to a man slumped in a recliner chair on the

other side of the room. He was fast asleep, his face melting into the cushion behind his head.

'Shall I let you question him?' Jude smiled.

'I haven't heard him speak more than three words in the entire time I've been here,' said Margot. 'So, it shouldn't take long.'

It was nice to see Granny Margot smiling. Jude thought she looked just a little less broken than when she'd arrived.

'Anything else you think of that might be helpful, let me know,' she said, realising that she was sounding more than a little like DS Khatri.

Granny Margot nodded and grabbed her hand, suddenly a picture of pure drive and determination.

'Find the truth,' she said.

Jude felt her own resolve strengthen. What had been a fairly flimsy plan to unpick some of the loose threads surrounding Sarah's death had now become a solid promise. To Granny Margot. To Sarah. To herself.

'I'd better go,' she said. 'My sister's visiting and she's killing time at the Winter Gardens. She's not the most patient of people so if I'm too long then I'll be hearing about it for the rest of the day.'

'I won't keep you,' said Margot.

'I'll come again soon,' said Jude and leaned in to give her a hug.

Jude was walking across the highly patterned carpet, perfect for disguising any number of little accidents or spillages, when Granny Margot's voice called her back.

'Nate,' she whispered to Jude. 'I don't know if I trust him. Sarah seemed to think he was wonderful but there was something not right about him. He didn't come to see me very often but, when he did, he said very little. In my day he would have been called *brooding*. And Sarah never seemed to relax in his company either. I couldn't put my finger on it, but I never warmed to him. Am I being unkind?'

'No,' said Jude, 'I'm not completely sure I trust him either.'

'He had a row with Charlie at the wedding too,' Granny Margot said. 'Gerwain and I heard them.'

This didn't really surprise Jude. She knew that tensions had always been high amongst Nate and the boys. Neither Ben nor Charlie trusted him and the animosity between them had been threatening to boil over for ages. Jude wondered what exactly had been the trigger to finally push Charlie over the edge.

'What was it about?'

'I don't know for sure. But it was something to do with Sarah because I picked out her name.'

Jude nodded and made a note to ask Charlie about it when she got the chance.

* * *

Jude marched up Victoria Road, past the granite stone council offices and turned into the bottom of the Victorian gardens behind the theatre. She knew Lucy would be watching the time impatiently and Jude fully expected to be berated by her sister when she found her.

Jude had always loved spending time in the Winter Gardens. It had been renamed Priory Park before she'd been born but her mum and many of the locals had continued to use the original name. As a child, she'd splashed in the old paddling pool, now long gone. She'd run backwards and forwards over the rickety, hump-backed wooden bridge and thrown crusts at the ducks in the pond below. The bandstand sometimes hosted musicians but, more often than not, it was just another place for children to play. There was even a brick with her initials on somewhere around the base, laid when the bandstand had been refurbished, her parents celebrating her birth by paying for a commemorative inscription.

It was a place for lazy summer days and gentle strolls, but today was a day for speed: Jude power-walked along the path next to the pond, puffing slightly as she made it to the playground.

As it happened, she needn't have worried.

'You were quick,' said Lucy.

'I've been gone almost two hours!'

'Really?' said Lucy. 'Well, we've had a lovely time, haven't we, Sebbie?'

Sebbie, who was popping in and out of a giant bauble made from wicker, shrieked with laughter as Charlie pretended to chase him in character as a large bear. It looked as though he was indeed having the time of his life.

'Charlie took us for a walk through the hidden paths and Sebbie had a play on the bandstand.'

'Look at Sebbie,' the small boy shouted in delight as he ran out of the bauble and down the wooden ramp at high speed. 'No catch me.'

'We'll see about that,' said Charlie, charging around the side of the bauble and catching him up in a whirling spin that made him shriek again from the excitement.

'You're good with him,' said Lucy, smiling broadly as Charlie deposited Sebbie on the ground next to her.

'Again,' said Sebbie, holding his arms up for another twirl but Charlie shook his head.

'Not this time, little man,' he said. 'I'd better get going. Things to do and all that.'

Lucy touched him lightly on the arm. 'Thank you for looking after us,' she said, giving him a kiss on the cheek.

Charlie blushed and Jude felt oddly maternal – to both the adults standing in front of her.

'Why don't you come for dinner this evening?' she asked.

'Are you sure?' he replied. 'I don't want to gate crash.'

'Of course. But just to warn you, I'm not cooking.'

'I'll pick up a takeaway,' said Charlie.

13

That afternoon, whilst Sebbie was having his nap, Jude decided to show Lucy the diary. Two minds were often better than one and Lucy had always been fantastic at solving riddles.

'What do you make of this?' she asked.

'What is it?'

'It's Sarah's diary. I found it in her cottage and I think there are things in it that could be helpful, if only I could figure out what the hell they mean.'

'Interesting,' said Lucy. 'Let's have a look.'

Jude passed the diary over, realising how good it felt to have someone on her side, someone who didn't even question the fact she'd taken the diary or ask why she hadn't given it straight to the police. Perhaps the old cliché was right: perhaps by sharing her problems with Lucy, she was halving them – or shrinking them at least.

'She had terrible handwriting, didn't she?' said Lucy. 'And she did love a code.'

'I think LT has to be Les Turner, the loan shark.'

'And N is obviously Nate,' said Lucy. 'But who are LX and CB?'

'That's just it,' said Jude. 'I have no idea but look at this doodle here. She's obviously making some sort of connection between CB and Les Turner.'

'You're right. And judging by the way she's gone through the paper, she pushed so hard with the pencil, she was pretty angry about it too.'

Lucy fanned through the pages and then stopped and flicked to the very back.

'There's something else here,' she said, passing the book over to Jude. 'Did you see these? They look a little bit like Lexigle clues.'

Jude looked at the page covered in scribbled notes. Most of them had been crossed through but three had been ringed to stand out.

'She was always playing with words and puzzles,' she said. 'Maybe this was her putting clues together for one of our birthdays? Can you work this one out? *Achieve for the season.*'

Lucy picked up a pencil and tapped it on the table. 'No,' she said after a while. 'I got nothing. What's the next one?'

'Beware of a muddled Mr Goose,' read out Jude.

'That one's pretty easy.'

'Is it?'

'Yes. Muddled, that's puzzle talk for an anagram. Mr Goose – well, that has to be gander so we are looking for another word that uses the same letters as gander, probably something to do with being wary.'

'Wow,' said Jude. 'You are good.'

Lucy wrote all the letters down in a ring and stared at them for no more than twenty seconds before she sat back and exclaimed, '*Danger!* Odd word for a birthday card.'

'What about this one?' said Jude. 'An oil platform within the beat of an unborn child. No idea what that means.'

'You need to split it up,' said Lucy. 'The first bit could be a rig, and the fact it is *within* means that these letters could come in the middle of the word.'

'Okay,' said Jude. 'What about the rest of it?'

'Not sure,' said Lucy. 'If it was a Lexigle word then we'd know it was six letters long and we'd be able to click for an extra clue.'

Lucy wrote the clue on a scrap of paper. 'Leave it with me,' she said.

'Gah!' Jude expelled. 'Why did she have to be so bloody cryptic? There has to be something hidden here and yet the more I look, the more it seems to just run away from me.'

At that moment, Sebbie started howling through the baby monitor and Jude recognised the budding of a tension headache. She needed to be alone, truly alone.

'Do you mind if I leave you to it for just an hour or so?' she asked.

'Of course not,' said Lucy. 'Do what you need to do and we'll be here with a cup of tea when you get back.'

Jude kissed her sister gratefully, called for Pip and jumped into the Land Rover.

The hills were always like a magnet to Jude, and in less than ten minutes, she'd driven through West Malvern and out along Jubilee Drive where the very tips of spring bluebell shoots were just starting to make their presence known. In six weeks or so, the side of the hill would be a riot of blue and green.

Jude crunched over the gravel of one of the many car parks that ran along the side of the hills. She jumped out of the car and could already feel the healing power the hills always lent her. With Pip running ahead, she marched straight up the side of the hill and stood on the ridge where she could see the flat farmlands of Herefordshire spanning out all the way to Wales.

The wind was cold yet the sun warm and Jude breathed deeply, allowing her brain to still. Pip busied herself, sniffing every rock and springy patch of moss, searching for signs of rabbits.

Jude's phone rang, breaking the peace. She looked at the screen and swiped to dismiss Charlie's call. He would just have to wait. In fact, *everything* would have to wait. She needed a moment of her own to regroup. Gather herself for what lay ahead. She switched her phone off completely and thrust it into the depths of her waxed coat.

Ignoring the paths and choosing to clamber over the rocks in the way she had as a child, Jude made her way along the ridge of the hills for a while. The hills were much busier now than they had been in her youth, with too many people running, cycling and walking – cluttering the place too much for her liking.

Jude needed to be away from them all, so she dropped down into a patch of woodland that not many people knew about. The hills were veined with paths like this one that criss-crossed their way through less well-trodden routes, away from the growing hordes of tourists.

Stray thoughts kept clawing at her mind. The note was a planned element in a death that otherwise seemed so impulsive. Using a flimsy scarf to hang herself in a tree was surely not the action of someone who had considered all her options. Why would Sarah write a note then walk through the village to post it, only to retrace her steps back to the cottage, up the path behind and through into the fields; all the while dressed in her wedding outfit?

Something else was bothering her about the note and then she realised exactly what it was. The post box in the village was out of use; Mrs James had told her that birds were nesting in it. So, for Sarah to have posted her note, she'd have had to walk all the way up to the next box on Croft Bank, which just made the whole thing seem even less likely.

Jude sat on the remains of a forgotten wall that had been

partially claimed by ivy. There, listening to the birdsong and
finding pattern in the tree bark and fir cones around her, Jude
found her peace. She sat until her bottom became numb but her
mind at least was calmer.

Only then did she retrace her steps back to the car park.

A little nugget of guilt nibbled at her; as she sat in the driving
seat, she flicked her phone back on.

Another missed call from Charlie and one from Ben too,
accompanied by a voicemail. Ben was still on his honeymoon in
Morocco for another week. What was he ringing about? Unless...
no. Surely there was no way he could have heard about Sarah
whilst he was living it up on the north coast of Africa?

She clicked on the message and put her phone onto speaker.

'Jude, what the hell? I've been trying to get hold of you and
Charlie but nobody will sodding well answer. Is Sarah all right? I
saw something on Instagram. It's freaked me out so I would very
much appreciate you calling me back.'

Shit!

Jude wondered how she'd have felt if she'd been on holiday
when Sarah died and nobody had let her know. They'd done it for
Ben's sake but, in hindsight, had it been the right decision to keep
this information from him? He'd been every bit as much Sarah's
friend as she or Charlie had.

She steeled herself and pressed the call back button. It went
straight to answer phone, so she tried Charlie, whose phone also
went unanswered. All the peace she'd managed to find on the top
of the Malvern Hills seemed to shrivel away. She would have to
drive back to the farm and try them both again from there.

* * *

The smell of curry permeated through the kitchen that evening when Charlie arrived with two bags full of foil containers.

'Anupam's finest,' he said, setting them down on the counter. 'I wasn't sure what you'd both want so I bought a variety.'

'Did they manage to get an earlier flight?' Jude asked, less interested in the curry and more interested in Ben. 'He was so angry when I spoke to him this afternoon. We should have told him, shouldn't we?'

'Perhaps,' said Charlie. 'I feel terrible. He texted whilst I was waiting for the curry. They're at the airport on standby.'

'Christ,' said Jude. 'What a mess.'

'I know. There's nothing we can do about it now, though.'

Jude took two bottles of Westons from the fridge, passed one to Charlie and took a deep slug from her own.

'I found Sarah's diary,' she said.

'Oh?' Charlie tipped the poppadoms out onto a plate.

'I thought it might help work out what happened to her,' said Jude. 'But she was very sketchy with the details.'

'Did you get anything useful?' Charlie asked as he offered her a poppadom.

Jude snapped off the edge and dipped it in mango chutney. 'It's just a bunch of initials and some mentions of meetings and phone calls. Les Turner is in there quite a bit.'

'Who?'

'The guy she borrowed money from. And I think he's somehow linked to someone with the initials CB. Any idea who that could be?'

Charlie thought for a bit. 'Not off the top of my head.'

'Granny Margot mentioned someone called Crystal-May something-or-other.'

'Crystal-May-Rose Bradfield?'

'That's her.'

Charlie laughed. 'She might have been a prize cow,' he said. 'But that was years ago, when we were all still at primary school. I can't see how she would have anything to do with Sarah's suicide.'

'You think it's suicide then?' she said.

'You don't?'

'I can't,' said Jude. 'It's just not like Sarah.'

'I'd have agreed with you,' said Charlie, 'but then I wouldn't have thought getting mixed up with loan sharks was Sarah either.'

Jude took another sip of cider. Charlie was right, of course, but she had the very strong feeling that there was a lot more to this than was evident on the surface.

'Maybe,' she said. 'But I still intend to do some digging. Even if it turns out I'm wrong about this, at least I'll know I did everything I could.'

'Jude, be careful,' said Charlie.

'What do you mean?'

'I mean, I don't want to see you getting hurt by dragging this thing out longer than you need to. Maybe it's best to leave well alone. Let the police do the digging.'

Jude felt her temper inexplicably rise. It was a sensible enough suggestion, after all, and said with the very best intentions.

'That's just it, though,' she said. 'They're not digging. DS Khatri as good as told me they're happy to put it down to suicide, closed book, nothing more to see here.'

'Well then, maybe that's what we should all be doing,' said Charlie.

Jude glowered at him. But his face was full of his own pain as well as concern for her. She soon melted.

'Come on,' she sighed. 'Let's get some plates out.'

* * *

Lucy was in very good spirits. Her constant babble and brightness went a long way to lift the mood over dinner and it also meant there was no opportunity for Jude and Charlie to continue their debate further. This, Jude thought on reflection, was almost certainly a good thing.

'Tell me more about this mysterious Nate,' Lucy said. 'I can't believe you all know the man behind Lexigle.'

'He's an idiot,' said Charlie, through a mouthful of lamb biryani.

'Not a fan?' Lucy laughed. 'I take it you don't play Lexigle then?'

'No, I don't,' Charlie retorted. 'He ripped it completely from Sarah and I'm not going to give him a penny of my money for doing so.'

'It's free to play,' said Lucy. 'All the money comes from the adverts that pop up, but he won't see any of that now it's been sold.'

'Please don't tell me you play,' said Charlie.

Lucy threw her hands up in mock submission.

'What can I say? It's addictive.'

'Go on then,' said Jude. 'Show me what the fascination is.'

Lucy took out her phone and flicked open the Lexigle app. The home screen had her profile with a cute avatar she'd created for herself under the username *LuceWoman*. The app held a record of all her scores as well as her participation run and her global rating. There was a tab for her friendship group which she proudly opened to show that she was at the top of the table.

'Most of the girls have dropped a day or two here and there but I haven't missed a single challenge so far this year.'

'What exactly do you have to do?' Jude asked.

'Look, I haven't done today's challenge yet. It's usually the last thing I do when I go to bed, let me show you.'

She clicked on the daily challenge button and a grid appeared on the screen along with a clue.

'All the words are six letters long,' she explained. 'If you get it right with just one clue, you get ten points but if you get it wrong, they give you another clue and a random letter from the word. You get fewer points the more clues it takes you. Ready?'

'Go on then,' said Charlie.

'A sapphire scream.'

'Load of rubbish,' said Charlie.

'No,' said Lucy. 'You just have to look at it logically. Sapphire could be something to do with the colour or the jewel. And a scream could be a call, shout, anything like that.'

'Or maybe something to do with that painting,' said Jude. 'By Edvard Munch.'

'Ooh, yes,' said Lucy. 'Munch is a good one, perhaps there's a link to eating? Gem and eat? Is there such a thing as gemeat?'

'No,' said Jude, searching on her phone. 'But there's gamete.'

'Could work,' said Lucy. 'Anagrams are not uncommon.'

She typed the word into the grid and it shimmered. The line with the word on it lit up red. A second clue appeared on the screen along with the first letter – M.

'What happens now?' said Jude.

'We get another guess. If we get it this time, we get eight points. Clue two. Too many crows spoil the day.'

'How about we play Uno instead,' Charlie suggested.

'I've started now,' said Lucy. 'And I don't want to break my streak. Too many crows. Black birds or something to do with the Tower of London?'

'Lou!' said Jude. 'Those are ravens.'

'All right,' said Lucy. 'Too many must be a clue, a large group.'

'The collective noun for crows is a murder,' said Jude.

Lucy counted the letters off on her fingers.

'Yes!' she said. 'That fits. And it works for the first clue too because you scream blue – or sapphire – murder. And let's face it, murder would certainly spoil the day, wouldn't it?'

Jude said nothing about the crassness of her sister's comment but it took the edge off her mood nonetheless. She watched as Lucy entered MURDER onto the grid and the screen turned green with a little shower of stars and confetti.

Lucy gave a whoop. 'Did it in two.'

'I still think it's rubbish,' said Charlie. 'Nowhere near as good as the original puzzles Sarah did for us.'

Lucy threw a chunk of naan bread at him and Charlie retaliated with a poppadom frisbee which shattered when it hit a bottle of cider. Jude saw the bottle wobble and she leant across to stabilise it, instead knocking it over and spilling the remainder of its contents all over the table.

'Bugger,' said Charlie, jumping to his feet. 'I'm so sorry. I'll get a cloth.' He ran to the sideboard and opened the drawer.

'Not that one,' said Jude, pushing her chair back in her haste to stop the inevitable.

But Charlie had already pulled the suicide note from the drawer and was reading it, his face ashen.

'Jude?' he said, holding it up.

14

Jude stared at Charlie, willing something sensible to come out of her mouth.

'You hid this?' he said.

'I didn't want to show the police,' she replied, hating how feeble her voice sounded.

'But you hid it from me too.' He looked like a wounded dog and Jude felt like shit.

'I'm sorry,' she said.

'Why?'

'I didn't know how to deal with it. I suppose I thought you'd make me take it to the police and that they'd stop looking for the killer.'

'There is no killer,' Charlie said. His voice was calm but in a way that felt as though it was on a knife edge, ready to snap. 'I know you want to think the best of Sarah. Don't you think we all do? But maybe it's time we listened to the facts.'

He waved the note at her. 'Maybe it's time we listened to Sarah.'

'What are you going to do with that?' she asked.

'I'm going to do what you should have done as soon as you got it. I'm going to take it to the police.'

'Please don't,' said Jude. 'They'll stop the investigation if you do.'

'Jude, I want it not to be real too,' he said, his voice cracking. 'I want so much to go back to last week and to stop all this from happening, but I can't. None of us can.'

His body was shaking and tears were rolling down his face. Jude could see how broken and vulnerable he looked and she felt guilty for keeping the note from him. Sarah had been one of his oldest friends, part of his life since childhood, just as Adam had. And now both were gone and it wasn't just Jude who was finding it difficult to process.

* * *

Ben and Tilda arrived back from Morocco the following morning. Ben called Jude from Birmingham Airport.

'I'm sorry I was awful to you on the phone yesterday,' he said. 'It was just such a shock.'

'Charlie or I should have called you,' said Jude. 'We talked about it, but what could you have done? We thought it would be better to let you enjoy your honeymoon and then deal with all this when you got home.'

'That's pretty much what Tilda said.'

Jude felt herself warm a little to Ben's new bride.

'She was seriously annoyed I brought her home early actually,' he continued.

Jude's warmth disappeared instantly as she imagined the conversation that had ensued, with Ben insisting they cut short their all inclusive stay in the fancy hotel she'd been boasting about for months.

'Do you want to come round later?' she said.

'Is Charlie with you?' Ben asked. 'I've been trying to get hold of him but he's not answering his phone.'

'He was here last night. He said he's absolutely snowed under with work at the moment so he's probably just in meetings.'

'Why don't we meet up at The Lamb this evening?' said Ben.

* * *

The Lamb was the epicentre of Malvern End and fairly busy when Jude walked in. It was early still but half of the tables were already filled with an assortment of folk from the village. Two retired couples were playing dominoes at one table, the men drinking pints and the women halves, almost certainly as they had done for their entire married lives. They nodded to Jude as she walked past and Jude smiled back.

There was no sign of either Charlie or Ben, so she sat on a stool at the bar.

'Half a pint of Dorothy's please, Ted,' she asked the landlord. Dorothy Goodbody had been Adam's favourite bitter and she'd quickly developed a taste for the same.

'That sister of yours not with you?' Ted asked.

Bloody hell, you really couldn't sneeze in the village without everyone knowing about it.

'She's looking after her little one,' she replied.

'Sorry to hear about Sarah, love,' said Barbara, Ted's wife. 'She's left a hole in the village, she has. Such a lovely girl, wasn't she, Ted?'

'She was indeed,' said Ted. 'Lovely girl.'

'We all miss her,' Jude agreed.

Ted put the glass down in front of Jude and she handed over a tenner.

'No, no,' said Ted. 'It's on the house.'

'That's very kind of you,' said Jude, slipping the note back into her pocket. 'Now, did I hear that congratulations are in order?'

Jude had become something of an expert in moving conversations along when people had asked her about Adam. Her self-preservation strategy had been to change the subject and she could see that this particular talent was coming in useful again.

Barbara beamed and took out her phone.

'She had four in the end,' she said, showing Jude a picture of four scrunched-up little puppies lying in a box with a border collie. 'Can't tempt you to take one for the farm? It would be wonderful to keep at least one in the village.'

'I'm afraid not,' said Jude. 'Pip's enough of a handful for me.'

She chatted to Ted and Barbara for a while, dodging any mention of Sarah, until Tilda's sharp voice cut through the atmosphere as she and Ben made their entrance.

'Why did we have to come to this ghastly pub?' she said, loud enough for everyone in The Lamb to hear.

'You didn't have to come,' said Ben. 'I told you to stay at home.'

'This is supposed to be our honeymoon,' said Tilda. 'You've dragged me away from Marrakesh, so I don't think it's too much to ask that we spend time together at least. God, I can't wait for you to get another job so we can leave this backwater behind us.'

This was not a revelation for Jude. For as long as Tilda had been in their lives, she'd been mentioning whenever she could that Malvern End was a short-term arrangement until Ben found a job in a private school, preferably in the city. This was a conversation that Ben had always kept noticeably quiet about but Jude knew his heart belonged to Malvern and he'd never leave it. For some reason, though, he obviously still hadn't mentioned that to his new wife.

'Hello,' Jude said, thinking that if she made her presence

known she might at least give Ben a break. 'My round. What can I get you?'

Ben's eyes were red raw, as though he'd been crying very recently, and his face crumpled even more when he saw her.

'Jude!' he said, rushing to give her a hug. 'I can't believe it. I just can't bear the thought of Sarah not being here.'

'Sorry you had to cut your holiday short.'

'I'm not sure why we had to if I'm honest,' said Tilda. 'There's nothing much we can do here to help, is there?'

'No,' said Jude for want of a better answer.

'Can I get you another?' Ben nodded at Jude's empty glass.

She shook her head. 'Thanks, but I'm driving.'

'I'll have a double gin and tonic,' said Tilda.

'Let me get these,' said Charlie as he arrived, planting a kiss on Jude's cheek before turning to Ben. 'Mate, how was the honeymoon?'

'Bit shit, actually.'

Jude noticed Tilda bridle, but Ted had just placed a glass of gin and tonic in front of her, distracting her enough for the conversation to move on without her commenting on her new husband's summary of their first trip as a married couple.

'I'm sorry we kept it from you,' said Charlie. 'We didn't want to ruin your honeymoon.'

'Yeah, well, I'm here now. And I want to know everything.'

Jude glanced at Charlie.

'Let's go and sit over there,' she said.

They collected their drinks and moved to a table in a quiet corner, beneath a cluster of old horse brasses nailed to the wall. Then Jude and Charlie told Ben everything they knew about Sarah's debts, her death and the break-in at the cottage. Ben was unusually quiet as they talked. He sipped his pint steadily, giving Jude the feeling that it was so his hands and mouth had something to do. As he took in what they were telling him, the severity of the debts and Sarah's struggle with the loan shark, he turned ghostly pale before his cheeks took on a red blush.

'Who gets themselves into those sorts of loans nowadays?' said Tilda and then tipped her head back to down the rest of her drink. She set the glass on the table with a jingle of ice cubes.

Ben turned on his wife instantly and delivered a filthy glare, which she appeared to be oblivious of.

'What exactly do you mean by that?' he said. Jude could tell he was trying hard to keep his voice level.

'I would have thought it was obvious to everyone that if you can't pay a loan back then getting another one is only going to make things worse,' said Tilda.

'It's not that simple,' snapped Ben. 'You have no idea what Sarah was going through, none of us did. She was a brilliant person who clearly found herself in trouble and couldn't see a way out. I for one feel absolutely shite that we weren't able to stop this happening. And I think that if you can't say anything useful then you should bloody well keep your thoughts on this to yourself.'

Jude inwardly cheered.

Tilda looked as though Ben had physically slapped her.

'I'll meet you back at the house,' she said stiffly. Ben barely looked up as she picked up her coat and bag and stormed out of the pub.

It made Jude wonder for the umpteenth time what had attracted the unlikely pair to each other, and so quickly too. In just over a year they'd met, dated, become engaged and were now married. She kept lambs on the farm for longer than Ben and Tilda had been together.

'Sorry,' said Ben. 'She can be an absolute pain in the arse sometimes.'

'Don't worry about it, mate,' said Charlie. 'I'm sure she's just pissed off being dragged away from her honeymoon.'

'Yeah, well, some things are more important than sitting around on a beach all day. I knew something was up with Sarah. But suicide? It just seems so unlike her. How can they be sure?'

'Jude got a note,' said Charlie. 'It was awful to read. Our lovely girl in such a terrible way.'

'Shit,' said Ben. 'Poor Sarah.'

He closed his eyes and rubbed his hands across his head. Jude recognised the pained expression on his face. It was one she'd sported a lot recently. It was one of frustration and despair at the utter waste of a life. Regret and anger that they hadn't worked harder to find out what was at the core of Sarah's problems and perhaps helped make it better.

'Anyone seen Nate?' Ben asked.

'No,' said Charlie. 'Why?'

'Just wondered if he was feeling as shit about Sarah as he should be. I mean, he may not have been the one to tie that scarf around her neck, but he certainly had a big part in making it happen.'

'Bit harsh isn't it, mate?' said Charlie. 'I mean, I know he's a prick but Sarah clearly loved him.'

'You obviously didn't see the bruise he gave her,' said Ben.

'He hit her?'

'We don't know that for sure,' said Jude. 'And that reminds me, Charlie, what were you two arguing about at the reception?'

'What?' Charlie was blushing again. 'I didn't know anyone heard us. It was really weird: he had a go at me for trying to steal Sarah away from him. Convinced I had a thing for her. He's a proper nutter.'

'Bastard,' said Ben. Jude noticed that the knuckles of his hand, wrapped around the pint glass, had turned white.

'He can't be all that bad,' said Jude.

She pulled Sarah's diary from her bag where it had been since her wasted trip to the police station, opened it up and found the entries she was looking for.

'They were off having dinner here and for a romantic weekend away.'

'Let me see,' said Ben.

Jude passed the diary over and Ben took it with shaking hands. He flicked through the pages, skimming what Sarah had written.

'Have the police seen this?'

'No,' Jude confessed. 'I haven't had the chance to drop it round yet. But look at this, there are so many calls with LT, which must be Les Turner, the loan shark. He was a really nasty piece of work and she owed him a really big stash of money. What if—'

'Stop it, Jude,' said Charlie. 'Put the bloody thing away. You're just torturing yourself and I really don't know what you're hoping to achieve, dragging this pain out for longer than necessary. This Turner bloke sounds like a nasty piece of work but don't you see that this just makes it easier to understand why Sarah killed herself?'

'But—' Jude began.

'Charlie's right,' said Ben. 'You need to let this go. I know it's hard but it's hard on all of us. None of us want this to be real but it is and you've got the note to prove it.'

Jude sighed. She didn't have the note; Charlie had given it to the DI the day after he'd found it in her dresser. What her friends were saying made perfect sense. It's what any sane person would tell her. It's what Adam would have told her and in all probability it was what Sarah would have said too. But something kept telling her that it wasn't right. And if she didn't chase that feeling and carry on pushing for answers then who would?

'Stop picking at things that are only going to end up hurting more,' said Charlie.

'Fine,' she snapped, realising she was playing a game that she would never be able to win.

'I need to go to the loo,' she said, putting the diary back in her bag.

In the solitude of the ladies' toilets, Jude splashed some water into her face and thought about what Charlie and Ben had said. Were they right? Was she just prolonging the pain and anguish by trying to find alternative explanations where there just weren't any?

One thing was certain: if there were secrets to be found in the diary, then a little help from the police in extracting them might be very useful. And perhaps there would be just enough within the pages to encourage them to look at the suicide note differently. Show them that there was more to Sarah, and her death, than the assumptions they'd surely made. And if not, then she still had other threads that she could investigate on her own.

15

Lying in bed that night, Jude found herself thinking about Nate Sanchez. Charlie's words bothered her. *I know he's a prick, but Sarah clearly loved him.*

And she had. Despite his bad temper and reluctance to get to know her friends, Sarah had definitely loved Nate. Granny Margot had her doubts, but they were also founded on his aloofness and disconnect to the rest of her world, rather than any outright nastiness on his part. He'd taken her out for a romantic meal and a weekend away and, to be fair to Nate, the few times Jude had been out with them he'd been very attentive to Sarah, albeit in his own stiff and awkward way.

Had they judged him harshly?

But then there was the possessive argument he'd had with Charlie at the wedding and the fact that he'd as good as ripped the idea for Lexigle from Sarah and apparently hadn't paid her a single penny for it. Jude had Googled it and he'd made three million pounds when he'd sold it, plenty to help out his sister and still have change for bailing Sarah out. And what about the bruise? There was still a niggling suspicion that he could have been behind that. He was a man with two very different sides and those sorts of people were the kind that Jude was naturally wary of. Still, if she was going to investigate this thing further then she had no choice, really. She would have to go and pay a visit to Nate Sanchez.

* * *

Jude was woken by a loud scream, followed by a crash. Within seconds, she was out of bed and tearing down the wonky bare-wood stairs. Lucy's raised voice was coming from the kitchen but she sounded angry rather than frightened.

Noah was standing by the door with one hand up, the other on Pip's collar, trying to gently placate Jude's angry sister. On the flag stones between them, a white puddle was spreading quickly, running through the network of joins in the stonework like a miniature, milky version of the canals of Venice. Shards of glass were catching the light of the sun that had recently risen and was streaming through the kitchen window.

Pip seemed very keen to investigate further but glass-studded milk was no breakfast for a dog. Thankfully, Noah was holding her back.

'What the hell happened here?' Jude asked.

'I was delivering the milk,' said Noah.

'Why don't you just leave it outside like any other milkman?' said Lucy. She had pulled her dressing gown together tightly as though protecting herself from the indignity of being seen in her pyjamas. She turned to Jude. 'Or better yet, why don't you just get it from the supermarket?'

'Sorry, Noah,' Jude said. 'Thanks for the milk.'

They both looked at the mess on the kitchen floor.

'Perhaps you could take Pip out with you until I've got this cleared up?'

'Of course,' said Noah, looking very glad of the chance to get out of the house. 'Come on Pip, let's go and feed those hungry sheep.'

Pip looked back longingly at the spilt milk, which was now seeping into the edge of the rug by the Aga, but she padded obediently after Noah.

'What was he doing in your house?' asked Lucy.

'Noah has a key,' Jude explained. 'It's easier that way as he often does little jobs for me and I'm not always in. Twice a week we get milk delivered from Max Brewster's farm on the other side of the village. Depends who's delivering. Sometimes Jonno makes two stops, one at the pink house for Noah and then he comes on up to the farm. But if it's Eddie then he tends to drop mine off at the pink house too. Noah brings it up for me and puts it straight in my fridge.'

'I don't think I like people letting themselves into your house in the middle of the night.'

'It's not the middle of the night. It's almost seven. I can't believe I slept in this long actually. Is Sebbie not up?'

'Oh, God,' said Lucy. 'It's really late for him. I hope nothing's wrong.'

Lucy ran off to check on her precious boy whilst Jude went to the porch to grab an old dog towel. She threw it down onto the pool of milk to soak the worst of it up before using the dustpan and brush to sweep up the shattered glass. The rug would need a wash or it would smell like baby vomit in a few days.

The kitchen floor mopped, and the milk-sodden towels and rug dealt with, Jude set about getting breakfast ready.

Her mind turned to DS Khatri. It had been two days since she'd been to the police station to unsuccessfully drop off the diary and she still hadn't got round to calling the DS to tell her about it. Once it was a reasonable hour, she'd give her a ring.

After breakfast, Jude was left in charge of Sebbie whilst Lucy took the opportunity to grab a quick shower. She was surprised just how quickly the small boy could move when she thought he was safely occupied. Jude swept the ash from the wood burner and started to lay the fire, ready to be lit that evening and, when she turned around, Sebbie was no longer parked in front of the television where she'd left him.

'Sebbie?' she called.

'For you,' Sebbie said, excitedly running in waving a piece of paper at her. On the paper were a lot of swirls and stripes in black marker pen. There were more all over Sebbie's pyjama top too.

'Oh, Sebbie!' Jude said. 'Your mummy is going to be a little bit cross with us if she sees that. Let's get that top off and into the machine, shall we?'

Once she'd changed Sebbie into a new top and zipped him into his coat, Jude took him out to feed Pancake. She was growing stronger every day and she seemed to love being in human company much more than the other lambs. Jude knew this would be down to the fact that to Pancake, humans equalled food, but it was still wonderful to be greeted each morning by the little woolly bundle as she skipped across the floor of the shed.

'Canpake,' said Sebbie in delight.

Pancake did the wonderful little dance she always did when she saw Jude: front legs off the ground, then back legs, then all four legs. Her tail could only be described as frisky as it jerked and twitched jauntily.

'Sorry about the milk,' said Noah, who was in the shed, treating a ewe with a case of mastitis. Her udders looked red and sore and Jude noticed how gently Noah was handling her.

'Not a problem,' she said. 'Lucy isn't used to the comings and goings around the farm yet.'

'How long'll she be staying, do you s'pose?'

It was a fair question but one to which Jude realised she had no idea of the answer.

'I guess it depends on how much time she's taken off work.'

Sebbie had already become quite the natural with Pancake and knew exactly what to do when Jude passed him the warmed bottle of milk. She was almost envious of the small boy who was able to absorb himself completely in what he was doing, utterly oblivious of everything else around him. When did children lose that basic joy of the small things in life? She knew she never grinned or giggled quite so wildly when she bottle fed a lamb.

'Noah,' said Jude. 'You've lived in the village longer than me.'

'Been here my whole life,' he said.

'What do you know about Chris Barnett or Crystal-May-Rose Bradfield?'

Noah raised his eyebrows. 'Interesting couple to put together,' he said. 'Mr Barnett used to be my headmaster. He never seemed to have what it took to be a good teacher, though. Too quiet and he always struggled to keep us young 'uns under control.'

'I can't imagine you were ever too much of a bother.' Jude smiled.

'Not me, of course,' said Noah. 'But there were plenty who took their chances with poor Mr Barnett. Everyone liked him, though. He had a fair-sized retirement do at The Lamb when he left the school. Now he keeps himself to himself, racing those pigeons of his.'

'Did he know Sarah?' asked Jude.

'Course,' Noah replied. 'He'd have taught her too.'

'No other connection?'

'Not that I know of. Why d'you ask?'

'I'm trying to track down someone with the initials CB who knew Sarah.'

Noah looked at Jude thoughtfully for a moment. 'What are you up to?'

'I just want to find out what happened to her. There was more going on in Sarah's life before she died than we know about. I'm sure of it.'

'And you think Mr Barnett is involved?'

'Someone with the initials CB was. And I'm struggling to think of many around here.'

'Well, I don't think it can be Mr Barnett,' said Noah.

'Because he was so quiet and nice?'

'No,' said Noah. 'Because he's been away on one of those fancy cruises with his wife since the middle of January.'

'Are you sure?'

'I am. He asked my friend Bodge to look after the pigeons whilst he's away.'

Jude hadn't really thought there was much chance of the old headteacher being the CB in Sarah's diaries and now she felt it was safe to strike him from her investigation altogether.

'What about Crystal-May-Rose?'

Noah chuckled. 'She was a couple of years behind me at school, with Sarah and Adam and them lot. But that didn't matter. *Everyone* knew who Crystal-May-Rose was. She made damn sure of that.'

'Was she popular?'

'I guess so,' said Noah. 'Always had a gaggle of other girls round her. Didn't get on with Sarah, though, but then Sarah was never one to try and fit in with the frills and dolls gang. She was always happier with the boys.'

Jude noticed the way the corner of Noah's lips turned up slightly on one side in a crooked half-smile. She thought again about the unrequited love he'd carried around all those years and wondered if it had started as puppy love in the school playground.

'Mind you,' Noah went on, 'that Crystal-May-Whatsit left the village when she was still a child.'

But she was back. This girl, who had obviously hated Sarah so much, was now a woman who had been working with Sarah and Sarah hadn't mentioned it to anyone except Granny Margot. Jude decided to add Crystal-May-Rose to the list of people she wanted to pay a visit.

16

As Jude stripped off her jeans and jumper and stuffed them into her old swimming duffle bag, she sniffed at her skin, wondering if it smelled of fertiliser or whether farm smells had invaded her nostrils so much they'd set up camp in there. She thought it might be a very good idea to shower off before she went for her treatment with Crystal-May-Rose.

It had been a very long time since Jude had donned a swimming costume. She stood, observing her body in the mirror of the spa changing room cubicle. The physical work of the farm kept her in pretty good nick but her skin was winter white and she was mortified when she realised that she hadn't shaved her legs in a very long time. She was lucky that her leg hair grew pale and downy but there was a fair coverage of it nonetheless. Lucy would definitely have something to say about that.

Once she'd made up her mind to pay Crystal-May-Rose a visit, Jude had phoned the Malvern Spa to check the beauty therapist's availability. She pretended that Crystal had been personally recommended to her by a friend so she would wait until she had a gap in her schedule.

The receptionist checked the diary and discovered a cancellation for that afternoon so, without thinking of the logistics, Jude booked it and then added a second appointment with the only other available therapist for Lucy.

'I can't just go swanning off to a spa,' Lucy said. 'What about Sebbie?'

'I'll look after him,' Noah offered.

'Oh,' said Lucy, her brow furrowed. 'I'm not sure. He hates to be away from me.'

'Rubbish,' said Jude. 'A break would do you good. And I'm sure Sebbie will have a blast with Noah.'

'He can help me feed the lambs,' said Noah. 'And then he can sit up in the tractor whilst we go and spray the potato fields.'

Lucy didn't look enamoured with the idea of Sebbie going on a tractor ride, but she agreed to leave him with Noah if he promised they would stay off farm machinery and that he'd make sure Sebbie got his afternoon nap.

Jude had spent the morning spraying the potato fields with liquid fertiliser. It took longer than she expected due to a clog in the spraying arm which meant she had no time for anything other than a change of clothes and quick hair brush before she drove Lucy over the hills to the spa.

As fate had it, a fire alarm had been triggered a short while before Jude and Lucy arrived and, although everything was up and running again, it had pushed all the appointments back by half an hour. This gave the two sisters a little time to investigate the spa before their treatments.

The spa pool was housed in a room bright with copious amounts of glass and sunlight. It was sectioned off into little enclaves so that groups could sit and enjoy the jet bubbles together. A row of long plastic flaps dangled from an opening that cut the pool in half, taking those who wanted outside.

'Wow,' said Lucy. 'That's so pretty.'

'It is,' said Jude. 'But have you seen the bucket of cold water up there?'

Lucy looked to where Jude was pointing. A wooden bucket stood ready for someone brave to stand below and pull the cord, which would tip the freezing contents over them in a cold-water douche.

'It's based on the old Victorian water treatments that made the town famous,' said Jude. 'Are you up for it?'

Lucy shook her head vigorously. 'Um, not today.'

'Fancy a dip instead?' Jude peeled off her robe a little self-consciously and put it on one of the loungers that stood next to the pool.

'God almighty,' said Lucy. 'What the hell are you wearing?'

Jude looked down at the ancient one-piece she'd owned since sixth form. It was definitely of an era, asymmetric and highly patterned with a ruff over one shoulder. The elastic was pretty old and Jude was a little nervous that when she got in the water it might give up altogether. Hopefully the one ruffed shoulder strap would keep it in place and spare her blushes.

'Not my first choice, I admit,' she said. 'But then I gave that to you.'

Lucy de-robed, revealing the more flattering costume that Jude had bought herself before her honeymoon. It was plain but elegant. Black with a white band across the stomach and another that acted as a halter-neck.

'Thanks,' said Lucy. 'Although to be fair, there's no way I would have come with you if you'd made me wear that monstrosity you've got on.'

'You're very welcome to it,' Jude said. 'It's just nice to be able to be here spending some precious time with you.'

Perhaps the level of saccharine was a little too much because

Lucy punched her playfully on the arm and then ran over to the steps that led down into the pool.

'Last one in is a slime bogey,' she called over her shoulder.

Jude smiled at the term they'd coined as children. Although there were five years between them, their camaraderie had breached the age gap, and the annual two-week summer sleep-overs they spent together were filled with fun and games. This had spilled over into the letters they'd written to each other, before Lucy had caught up with Jude technologically and then texts became their preferred methods of communication.

The water was heaven to Jude's muscles and bones, which were aching far more then she'd realised. It wasn't really a pool for swimming in, so Jude and Lucy waded through, ducking under the plastic flaps that took them outside. They found an empty enclave and sunk down onto the moulded seats at the edge.

'Bubbles?' Jude asked.

'Of course,' Lucy replied.

She hit the button on the side of the pool and a stream of jets pushed into Jude's skin, massaging it and kneading at the knots and tired aches of the muscles beneath.

She shut her eyes for a moment and breathed deep. In another life, this could be a regular thing. In a life where there was no farm to look after, no sheep that needed her constant care and attention, no crops and fields that needed treatment throughout the year, no accounts that required endless juggling, and no to-do lists longer than she could begin to make a dent in. Jude knew she'd made the right decision keeping Malvern Farm going after Adam died and she'd never really considered throwing in the towel for an easier life, but it would perhaps be nice to try to carve out just a little time for things like this. And not just because she needed the opportunity to suss out a player in the mystery of her best friend's death.

Her mind wandered back to Sarah, as it did so much of the

time. Then to Crystal-May-Rose. What would she say when she got her chance to speak to her? What was she expecting to hear back? What the hell was she doing?

A sudden splash of water in her face snapped her from her ponderings.

'Hey!' she said, wiping the water from her eyes.

'I thought you wanted some quality sister time,' Lucy said. 'And there you are, nodding off at the first opportunity.'

'Sorry,' said Jude. 'I was just...'

'It's all right,' said Lucy, suddenly gentle. 'You've got so much on your plate. It must be really hard.'

She brushed the dripping tendrils of hair from Jude's face and stared at her with eyes full of compassion.

'I've been watching you,' she said. 'My bubbly, strong sister. You look so tired. I know I'm always wrapped up with Sebbie and my own life dramas, but I want to help. If I can.'

The unusual show of empathy took Jude a little by surprise. It had always been her job to support Lucy. She was the strong one. She was the able one who kept her shit together, whatever else was going on around her, and yet in the spa pool, it felt as though the tables had been turned. Her strength and determination slipped into the churning water and she found herself suddenly drowning in the enormity of the situation she was in.

The back of her nose began to tingle and then clog, which was her body's warning sign that tears were imminent, and a second or two later, there they were. Jude, who made a point of never crying in public, was weeping into the pool.

Lucy's arms were instantly around her, drawing her in and holding her tight. It felt strange to be on the receiving end of this sibling support system. And yet it was exactly what Jude needed. She allowed herself a few moments of tears before she gave herself a metaphorical slap around the face and forced her breathing to regain a deep regularity until she was calm again. Only then did she untangle herself from her sister's embrace.

'Sorry, Lou-Lou,' she said.

'Why?'

'You don't need to be dealing with this.'

'I want to,' said Lucy.

'Really? I thought you had enough of your own stuff to deal with. Dad called this morning wanting to know if I'd seen you, by the way.'

Lucy whipped her head up.

'What did you say?' she asked.

'I told him that I had no idea where you were, of course. I guess this has something to do with why you came to visit so urgently?'

'Not at all. I just wanted to come and see you.' Lucy caught Jude's eye and smiled a heavy smile laden with worries. 'Who am I kidding?' she said. 'I came because my own life almost broke me and I wanted the one person who can always scoop me up to, well... scoop me up, I guess.'

'And you ended up with this instead.' Jude grinned. 'A snotty mess in the most hideous swimsuit ever created, who can't even manage to keep her legs shaved or her eyebrows plucked and who lives on a diet of chocolate chip brioche and strong coffee!'

'Just being with you makes me feel better,' said Lucy. 'Although I would like to take you shopping for a new swimming cozzie.'

'Tell me what's bothering you,' said Jude.

'I will,' said Lucy. 'But I want you to go first. Talk to me properly. You've been there for me so many times. I know I was rubbish when Adam died but let me help you now instead.'

Jude saw an earnestness in her sister's face that she'd never seen before and it triggered something inside her.

'I still don't think Sarah killed herself,' she said. 'I know there was a note and I know Charlie and Ben buy it. I mean, it is the most obvious explanation, but it just doesn't add up – for so many reasons. And now Charlie has taken the note to the police they'll stop investigating altogether. I want to find the truth but all I have is a poxy diary with a few scribbled notes in code form, and a real sense that I'm missing something.'

Lucy took both of Jude's hands and stared at her with a steely look of determination.

'If this is what you think, then I trust you completely and if an investigation is what needs to happen, then I'm in,' she said.

17

Jude and Lucy got out of the pool and walked past the Victorian bucket therapy to the steam room. Inside was like a magical grotto, dark with thousands of the tiny lights studding the mosaic tiled walls. The steam seeped into every pore, unblocking Jude's sinuses and warming her throughout.

'Can't find a quieter place than this,' said Lucy. 'Now, let's go through what we already know. LX is important. Could be a person, although I think the way it was used in Sarah's diary makes that unlikely. The key players from the diary are LT, N and CB. We know who the first two are, but we need to find out the identity of the third, especially as we suspect them to be linked to Les Turner.'

Jude suddenly felt a little sheepish at her espionage.

'In fact, that's actually why we're here,' she said.

'Here at the spa?'

'Yes. The woman doing my facial is called Crystal-May-Rose Bradfield. She went to school with Sarah and bullied her for years. She left Malvern for a while but is now back and working here. Sarah was her boss. I know it's a long shot, but this CB character is clearly an important piece of the jigsaw and there were very few people in Sarah's life with those initials.'

'This Crystal-May-Rose is definitely worth investigating,' agreed Lucy. 'But why didn't you tell me that was the reason for our little outing?'

'You'd seen the suicide note,' said Jude. 'I thought you'd be like the boys and assume that was the end of it, no point in looking for other answers. But it just doesn't fit. There's something very odd about the way Sarah walked halfway up Croft Bank, still in her wedding clothes, to post the note before doubling back to the farm. Why not just leave it somewhere obvious in the cottage where someone would find it? Also, the more I think about it, the more I can't understand why she didn't send one to Granny Margot too. They were so close; if Sarah was going to say goodbye and sorry to anyone, surely it would have been Margot, not me.'

'You're right,' said Lucy. 'It doesn't make sense. Writing a letter takes thought and a certain level of process but using the scarf you happen to already be wearing to hang yourself from a tree whilst still in a pair of high-heeled shoes? That is the act of someone who hasn't thought things through properly.'

'I keep thinking about the wording of the note too. I wish I'd thought to photocopy it before Charlie took it to the police. I want to have another read to see what else it could have meant.'

'Can you ask this DS Khatri of yours?'

'Maybe,' said Jude, making a mental note to do just that. She'd call her first thing in the morning.

'And then there's Nate,' Jude said.

'You don't trust him?'

'I don't really know him to be fair,' said Jude. 'But I think that's part of the problem. He didn't make an effort to get to know any of us, not even Granny Margot.'

Lucy chewed her lip for a second.

'Maybe he's shy?' she said. 'I mean, you are quite a formidable gang to break into.'

'I'd have thought he'd have made an effort for Sarah's sake, though.'

'He's an IT guy, right?' said Lucy.

'What's that got to do with anything?'

'He's used to sitting in front of a computer on his own all day. There was a girl like that in my post-natal group. I thought she was a really snooty bitch when I first met her but I stuck with it and kept talking to her every session – there were only three others in the group and they all knew each other already... Eventually, when she got to know me a bit more, she came out of herself. Turns out she's really nice, just finds talking to people such a struggle that she clams up and comes across as pretty rude.'

'You might be right.'

'I had another look at those clues she wrote in the diary,' Lucy continued. 'The first one I think is *fright*. The oil platform being the rig within the initials FHT which stand for Foetal Heart Tones – or the beat of an unborn child. And I think the second one is possibly winter because win means achieve and winter is obviously a season.'

'Winter, Fright and Danger,' said Jude. 'Not very happy words, are they?'

'No,' said Lucy. 'That's what I thought.'

* * *

Jude had only ever had one massage before and that was a brutal attempt by someone Adam had recommended when she put her back out lifting hay bales.

That massage had been carried out in a stark white room, on an easy-wipe bed covered with a layer of blue tissue paper. The room Jude stepped into for her facial with Crystal-May-Rose couldn't have been more different. It smelled of expensive oils and luxury. Prints of lotus flowers hung from the walls and the lighting was soft and welcoming. Wave sounds and the gentle dinging of peace bells filled the room in an unobtrusive, blend-into-the-background sort of way.

'Hello,' said Crystal-May-Rose, 'my name's Crystal, what would you like me to call you?'

'Jude is fine.'

'Lovely. If you'd like to make yourself comfortable under the blanket there, I'll go and get you a glass of water.'

As soon as Crystal left the room, Jude was swift to pull the ruffled strap of her hideous costume down and hide it, and her hairy legs, under the soft blanket. The heat of the treatment bed and the softness of the blankets felt amazing against her skin.

Whilst she waited for Crystal to return, Jude closed her eyes and breathed in deep, allowing her body to sink into the bed.

'I'll put your water there for you,' said Crystal, reappearing. 'You're here for a facial today, I see. Lovely. I'm going to start by asking you what oils you prefer.'

A small bottle was waved under Jude's nose. It smelled earthy and deep, not really Jude's sort of thing. She had enough of that on the farm. A second bottle replaced the first, this one citrussy and fresh.

'The first was sandalwood,' said Crystal. 'The second was geranium and lemongrass. Do you have a preference?'

Jude picked the geranium oil and watched as Crystal poured a little into her palms.

The feel of someone else's hands on her skin was a little strange and not altogether relaxing to begin with. But it didn't take long, as Crystal's oily, warm fingers started to massage her neck and arms, before Jude felt the tension begin to seep out of her body and sink through the treatment bed and under the door. When Crystal turned her attention to Jude's scalp, Jude was so relaxed she almost forgot the reason for her visit. As her mind began to swim and wander, Sarah's face appeared, reminding Jude of her mission.

'Have you worked here for long?' she asked.

'Only a few months,' said Crystal, still using her soft voice with the calming cadence. 'But I love it already.'

'I can see why,' said Jude. 'It is very lovely. And the people seem great.'

'Yes, they are. I'm very lucky. It's a brilliant team.'

'You must all have been devastated by Sarah Lloyd's death.'

Crystal's fingers caught in Jude's hair and pulled back with a sharp movement, stinging her scalp slightly.

'Sorry,' said Crystal, adding a little more oil to her fingers and moving from Jude's hair to her forehead. 'Yes, of course. It was very sad.'

'Very sad,' said Jude. 'Did you know her well?'

'She was my boss,' said Crystal, her calmness slightly more forced now and her fingers a little more tense.

'I'm sorry to hear that. It sounds as though she was much loved around here.'

'I suppose she was,' said Crystal, her voice sharp now.

'It's always so sad when these things happen,' Jude continued. 'Someone so well liked with it all to live for. It makes me wonder what else had been going on in her life to make her end it that way.'

To Jude, the statement sounded clunky and fake, as it obviously did to Crystal, who decided a break was needed.

Without answering, she laid a warm, damp flannel over Jude's eyes.

'I will leave you to relax for a while and then I'll come back to apply some of our lovely moisturiser.'

The soft, gentle voice was back but Jude wasn't fooled. She'd paid for a forty-five-minute treatment and she knew this hadn't taken more than about twenty minutes. She was losing her chance, and she wouldn't get another one, so she took the flannel off her eyes and sat up. Crystal was washing her hands in the tiniest sink, just behind the treatment bed.

'I'm so sorry,' said Jude. 'I've offended you, Crystal-May-Rose.'

'Who are you?' Crystal snapped. Any effort at faking the super-calming voice now gone completely.

'I'm just someone who should learn to filter what she says better. It's always been a problem of mine.'

'No. You called me Crystal-May-Rose. Not a name I've used in years and not one that anyone here knows me by. What do you want?'

Bugger it. Jude had blown it totally and Crystal was about to leave the room, possibly to talk to someone about getting Jude thrown out altogether. She had no choice but to have a go at a little honesty and see if she could find anything more out that way instead.

She held her hands up.

'Fair enough,' she said. 'Although I am sorry for my bluntness, I just wanted to talk to you.'

'About what exactly?' Crystal folded her arms over her purple asymmetric tunic.

'About Sarah Lloyd,' said Jude. 'She was my best friend and I know she thought a lot about you. I find it helps, talking to other people who were important to her. She was so excited when she found out you'd be working together.'

'That's utter shit,' said Crystal. 'Sarah hated me and the feeling was mutual. If she told you anything different, then she was obviously just as good at lying as she was when she was a kid.'

Jude was taken aback by Crystal's vehemence.

'What do you mean?'

'Your precious friend obviously never told you about what things were like between us at school then.'

'No,' said Jude. 'No, she didn't.'

This was technically true, even though she had an idea from what Granny Margot and the boys had said.

'Sarah was a bitch, even then. She thought she was so much better than me. Especially with those boys in tow.'

'Really?' said Jude, unable to keep the doubt from her voice.

Crystal glared at her, her perfect mouth a tight pinch and her groomed eyebrows almost meeting in an angry V.

'Yes, really. But she had a way of making everyone else think it was never her fault. She treated people like shit and always came up smelling like roses. I hated school and it was all down to her. She had everyone calling me Princess Poofy just because I liked wearing dresses and playing with Barbies. Pretty much the whole school joined in. It was really nasty and, in the end, Mum had to move me away.'

Jude found it impossible to link the girl Crystal was talking about to her own sweet-natured Sarah. And yet the rawness in Crystal as she spoke was very real. Was it possible for two people to have such a different view about the same period of time?

'Sorry,' said Crystal. 'I know she was your friend and everything, but she was a total cow. I couldn't believe it when I started working here and she turned up in my life again. I thought a beauty spa was the last place she'd want to work.'

'I guess she changed.'

Crystal snorted but offered nothing else.

'Do you know someone called Les Turner?' Jude asked.

'No,' Crystal-May-Rose said. 'And I think it's best we leave this now. Feel free to use the room. It's yours for another fifteen minutes.'

With that, Crystal stalked over to the door and left Jude sitting on the treatment bed, slightly bemused.

* * *

Lucy was keen to hear every detail of Jude's conversation with Crystal but Jude just wanted to get changed and out of the spa as quickly as possible. In the airy reception, she set her handbag on the counter and took her purse out to pay the bill. In her hurry to pull her card from its nest, her arm slipped, knocking the bag to the ground and sending years' worth of handbag detritus skittering across the floor.

'Bollocks,' muttered Jude, who'd been hoping for a quick, quiet getaway. She abandoned her place at the desk and ran after a tube of lip balm that had picked up speed on the sandstone.

A couple of members of the spa team had also collected up bits that had been flung in other directions and Lucy was stuffing everything back into Jude's handbag.

'Christ, Judy,' she said, waving a Vick's Vapostick and an insect bite pen at her. 'I think there might be a kitchen sink possibly under one of those sofas we haven't found yet.'

Jude was mortified to see a tampon, popping out of its ancient packaging, lying on the floor a little way away. She bent down to pick it up and was even more mortified to see who reached it first. Crystal-May-Rose Bradfield. She passed it back to Jude, who stuffed it into the pocket of her cardigan.

'Look,' said Crystal. 'I'm glad I saw you again. I think I was a bit rude earlier. Just because I wasn't Sarah's biggest fan doesn't mean

I should have been a cow like that. She was your friend, after all, and we shouldn't speak ill of the dead.'

'Thanks,' said Jude. 'I shouldn't have sprung it on you like that either.'

The two women smiled tentatively at each other and parted ways.

In the old Land Rover, Jude sat with even more of a knot of uncertainty than she had before their trip to the spa.

Taking into account the very weird way Jude had acted, Crystal hadn't seemed all that bad. But she clearly hated Sarah, and Jude couldn't help thinking there was a lot more to their relationship than she'd uncovered. She was still Jude's prime suspect to take the role of CB. And if she was CB, what was the connection Sarah had made between her and Les Turner?

18

Lucy felt invigorated after the spa. Jude, less so.

There were so many things clamouring around her crowded mind that she found it very difficult to focus on Lucy's constant chattering as they drove out of the spa car park.

'Judy!' said Lucy in clear exasperation.

'What?' she said. 'Sorry, Lou, I was miles away.'

'I can see that, but can you please start talking. Tell me what happened. Did you find anything out with Crystal-May-What-sername?'

Jude sighed. 'I found out she hated Sarah. Apparently, she reckons it was Sarah who did the bullying at school.'

'Not the other way around?'

'Not according to Crystal, no.'

'Either way, though,' said Lucy, 'it's a long time for either of them to hold on to a childhood grudge, isn't it?'

'Maybe. But we don't know what happened when they met up again. If Crystal *is* this CB from Sarah's diary, it's possible there's something else going on.'

'Then we need to find out,' said Lucy.

Jude smiled. Despite Lucy's tendency to be full-on, Jude was glad she'd involved her sister. She was more detached from everything than either Charlie or Ben and it would be good to have someone to bounce ideas off.

Jude's phone rang.

'Can you get that?' she said.

'Haven't you got Bluetooth?' Lucy asked, digging around in Jude's bag. 'God, even my crappy car has phone connection.'

'She way pre-dates Bluetooth,' said Jude, giving the steering wheel a loving pat.

'It's DS Khatri.'

'Answer it then!' said Jude. 'And put it on speaker. Hello?'

'Ah, Jude,' said Binnie. 'Sorry I haven't been in touch sooner, I had a few days off sick. I heard you came to the station looking for me, is everything okay?

'Oh dear,' said Jude. 'I hope you're feeling better.'

'Much. Thank you. I wondered if you were in, actually. I have a few things I'd like to discuss with you.'

'My sister and I are just heading back to the farm now,' said Jude. 'We're on West Malvern Road so should be home in ten minutes or so.'

'Right. I'll see you then.'

The phone clicked and Lucy tossed it back into the cavern of Jude's handbag. 'What do you suppose she wants?' she asked.

'We'll find out soon enough, I suppose.'

The farm was quiet when the old Land Rover pulled into the yard. Jude poked her head into the lambing shed but there was no sign of Noah or Sebbie.

In the house, Pip greeted them in her usual overexcited way. They dumped their bags in the kitchen, but the rest of the house was silent.

'Where are they?' said Lucy, looking anxious, already straight back into *Mum mode.*

'They won't have gone far without Pip,' said Jude. 'Perhaps they're in the garden.'

As they moved through the kitchen into the sitting room beyond, Jude noticed the wood burner had been lit. The gentle sound of quiet voices could be heard from the back of the house. One low mumbling, the second much higher. Jude put her finger on her lips and beckoned to Lucy to follow her quietly, up the step to the music room/office and down again into Adam's old playroom.

There, sitting on the floor in the middle of an enormous pile of Lego bricks, were Sebbie and Noah, chattering away together as though they were old friends.

In between them stood a rather wonderful house with multi-coloured walls, four big windows and a red tiled roof. They were in the process of decorating a green base sheet with flowers, a low wall and even a little gate.

'Now then, young Sebbie,' Noah was saying, 'I think perhaps we've got enough flowers on that side. Why not put that one over here?'

'Flo'er here?' asked Sebbie, pointing to a little space in the garden.

'Just the spot,' said Noah. 'Now what about this one?'

He passed the boy another flower and Sebbie looked thoughtfully at the garden before sticking it on the dimple right next to the other one.

Jude looked back at Lucy, half expecting her to be panicking about the fact her precious boy was playing with the Lego she'd been so adamant was not for him. But instead, her face was full of pride and joy as she watched Sebbie play.

'Mummy!' said Sebbie, catching sight of her and waving frantically. 'Look. I made a house.'

'So you did. It looks like you've been having lots of fun with Noah.' She looked at Noah. 'Thank you for watching him whilst I was out. It was so kind of you.'

'We've had lots of fun,' he replied. 'He loved the quad bike best, though, especially when we took it over the ditches at top speed. Nothing like off-roading on a farm vehicle.'

Lucy's face fell. 'You took him out on a quad bike?' she said, incredulously.

'You didn't say not to...' He laughed. 'We stayed away from the tractors, though.'

Jude chuckled inwardly. She knew Noah well enough to know when he was joking. Lucy, though, did not.

'I can't believe it,' she said. 'I hope you at least put a helmet on him.'

'Helmets?' said Noah. 'No need for helmets on the farm. Besides, we don't have one small enough for him.'

Lucy's eyes grew wide and her mouth opened and closed at least three times before she spoke. Jude was trying so hard not to laugh out loud that she had to chew the side of her cheek.

'Really!' puffed Lucy. 'How irresponsible can you be? He's only two years old. Anything could have happened to him and I'd have —' She stopped as Noah's face crinkled into a big smile. Then she turned and saw Jude's face.

'Very funny,' she said. 'The neurotic parent. I get it.'

But she had the grace to smile along with them as she bent down to gather Sebbie into a hug.

'I'd ask you to stay for dinner,' said Jude. 'But I'm afraid the DS looking after Sarah's case is due round any moment.'

At Sarah's name, Noah's face fell and he nodded.

'No problem,' he said. 'I'd better do the rounds before we lose the sun anyway. See you in the morning.'

Jude walked him to the kitchen door and waved him off. 'Thanks again,' she said. 'You're a star.'

'Not much difference between lambs and children to be fair,' he said. 'Give them food and a bit of attention and they're easy. I'll see you in the morning.'

Jude gave him a hug then opened the door to let him out. DS Binnie Khatri had just arrived.

'How are you feeling?' Jude asked, surprised to see her in a pair of jeans and thick knit jumper. Her hair, usually tied up in a bun, hung loosely around her shoulders.

'I'm fine, thanks.'

'Come in,' Jude said. 'I was just about to put the kettle on. Would you like a cup?'

'I'd love one, please,' said Binnie. 'Been swimming?'

She pointed to the two bags on the floor. Jude touched her wet hair. Perhaps a good detective was always noticing clues and making connections.

'I took my sister to the spa,' she said.

'Nice,' said Binnie. 'Was that the one Sarah worked at?'

Jude nodded and threw two teabags into the pot.

Lucy joined them in the kitchen. 'Sebbie's shattered so I've just put *Peppa Pig* on for him. I've got about ten minutes before he starts squawking and a cuppa is exactly what I fancy.'

She turned to the detective.

'Hi, I'm Lucy. Jude's sister.'

'DS Binita Khatri.' Binnie held her hand out. 'Binnie.'

'I hear you're trying to solve this awful murder,' said Lucy.

Binnie coughed. 'Perhaps we could sit down? That's part of the reason I'm here. I have to inform you that the pathology report has come back. It states hanging as the cause of death with no other injuries sustained other than those expected. There is nothing to suspect that anyone else was directly involved and that, linked with the suicide note your friend Charlie gave the DI... well, it's enough to satisfy him that this is a case of suicide.'

Jude's heart sank. It was the news she'd been expecting but it was not the news she'd been hoping for.

'But I know there's more to it than that,' she said. 'There are too many other things to think about. The business with the loan shark for a starter and then the way that night must have panned out, if it really was suicide. I just can't imagine why she'd have walked through the village to post the note, then back again, up to the path behind the cottage and into the fields to hang herself with a scarf. To me, it's like forcing bits of a jigsaw together that just don't want to go.'

'I agree,' said Binnie.

'Pardon?'

'I said I agree with you. There are other things that don't make sense. Her shoes, for example.'

'Shoes?' said Lucy.

'Yes. Shoes like that are not made for walking in. Killer heels with soft rubber pads. To get from the cottage to the post box in the village would be about a ten-minute walk.'

'It would be,' said Jude, 'if it was working, but it's closed at the moment because there's a family of birds nesting in it. She'd have had to go up to the box on Croft Bank.'

'So, what's that? Another twenty minutes by foot?' said Binnie. 'Probably more like half an hour in heels like that.'

'Nobody would be able to walk down country lanes that far in a pair of heels,' said Lucy.

'And even if they did,' said Binnie, 'the rubber on the heels would be ground down. I looked at the shoes. The heels weren't too bad. Covered in mud from walking over the fields, of course. But the rubber itself didn't show much sign of wear.'

'They were new for the wedding,' said Jude. 'Nate took Sarah shopping for a new outfit, shoes included. She wore them in the church, of course, and a little bit outside on the tarmac. Then we went straight to the reception where she ended up kicking them off before the dancing started. They were already hurting her feet.'

'Then she definitely wouldn't have kept them on,' said Binnie.

'Did you tell the DI about your suspicions?' said Jude.

'I did. But he wasn't very interested. To be honest, he's involved in tracking down a big organised crime racket at the moment. It will be a huge feather in his cap if he breaks the case, so he's not all that interested in anything smaller.'

Binnie looked at Jude then Lucy. 'Between you and me, of course,' she said quickly.

'Of course,' both sisters agreed.

'Anyway, I decided to do a little digging of my own,' Binnie continued. 'Seeing as I'm not expected to work on this – now the pathology report has come through – I decided a couple of sick days wouldn't go amiss.'

Jude looked at the Detective Sergeant with a fresh layer of respect.

'Did you find anything?' she asked.

'I really shouldn't be telling you this,' the DS said. 'In fact, I could get into so much trouble if anyone ever found out...'

She stopped and looked at Lucy. Lucy drew her fingers across her lips as though doing up a zip.

'I won't say a word,' she said.

'I went to Les Turner's house,' said Binnie.

'Wow!' said Jude. 'You went there on your own?'

Jude had seen Les Turner. She'd been knocked flying by him and she'd caught the ruthlessness in his voice and the cockiness in his swagger. If he'd found Binnie in his house, snooping around, then Jude didn't think he'd have any issue in dealing with her however he thought fit.

Binnie leant down and pulled something instantly recognisable from her bag.

'Sarah's laptop!' exclaimed Jude. 'Bingo!'

19

The laptop was unmistakably Sarah's, covered in self-adhesive Scrabble letters that she'd arranged to form a grid of meaningful words and names, including Jude's.

'Illegally got, I'm afraid, so I can't take it to the tech team to look at. That's why I brought it to you. I wondered if you might be able to guess her PIN.'

'I don't need to guess,' said Jude. 'I used it enough times when I was round at her house.'

She took the laptop and keyed in the number. It was the same one that unlocked Sarah's phone and the same as her iPad.

'It's code for GRAN. G, the seventh letter of the alphabet. R – 18, A – 1 and N – 14.'

A sudden rush of little footsteps and Sebbie was there, flinging himself dramatically at Lucy's knee as though his very world was ending.

'Sebbie hungry,' he said. 'Clocklet?' he added hopefully.

'No chocolate,' said Lucy, giving Jude a sideways glance. 'I'll make you some couscous for supper, come on.' With Sebbie clinging to her leg, she got up.

Jude stared at the home screen of Sarah's laptop. It was a picture of her sitting in the garden of the retirement home with Granny Margot. Both women had joy etched into every part of their faces as they squinted slightly into the sun. Light caught their hair and made it illuminate around their heads, one halo silver-grey and one honey coloured. Sarah had her arms tightly around her grandmother and Margot's hands rested over the top. Bound together in that one captured moment with total love for each other.

'Where do we start?' Jude said, desperately hoping for anything that might be useful to their investigation. Anything that would shine a better light on what had been happening in Sarah's life in the run up to her death.

'Documents,' said Binnie. 'Then web searches, photos and whatever else we can find. We could be here for a while!'

Jude watched as Binnie opened the documents drop-down and they were given a list of options.

'Start at the top?' suggested Jude.

The first folder was titled *Attic* and contained architectural plans for what was clearly an attic conversion of the cottage. There were builders' quotes too, all dated around two years ago. Jude vaguely remembered Sarah talking about building work to give her and Granny Margot more space. It was at a time when Jude was coping with Adam's cancer, then his death, whilst simultaneously trying to keep the farm ticking over. She'd had no time to think about attic conversions and she now assumed that Granny Margot's move to the retirement home had put a stop to any building ideas. If it hadn't, then Sarah's debts certainly would have.

'On to *Finances* then,' Binnie said.

With a sense of unease, Jude watched as Binnie clicked the tab and opened another drop-down. She expected to see a horrific account of just how enormous the hole was that Sarah had dug for

herself. But there was nothing there linked to the debts or to Les
Turner's loan agency. In fact, the folder was very sparse. Just a
couple of spreadsheets that outlined Granny Margot's savings and
pension alongside the fees she was paying for the nursing home.

The next file was *Granny* which, as expected, contained all of
Granny Margot's paperwork. Details of the retirement home, life
insurance policies, will, even funeral wishes.

'She was so organised,' said Jude in wonder. She'd always
considered her friend to nudge more onto the scatty side, but she'd
obviously underestimated her.

'It might be worth having a look at the will,' said Binnie. 'You
never know what these things kick up. For example, with Sarah
out of the picture, who would Margot's money and house go to?'

But there was nothing of note there; Margot had no next of kin
other than Sarah. As thorough as ever, she'd noted that if Sarah's
death preceded her own, everything she owned would be given to
the West Mercia Women's Aid charity.

'I think we're in for the evening,' said Jude. If she was right,
they were going to be searching through the computer for a fair
while to come. And her stomach was telling her that it was time for
refuelling. 'Are you hungry?'

'Well, I wouldn't want to put you out,' said Binnie.

'In other words,' Jude said, 'yes, you are. Good, so am I. Would
Welsh rarebit do you?'

'I'm not sure I've ever had that before.'

'It's just Jude's fancy way of saying cheese on toast,' said Lucy,
shovelling the couscous she'd cooked into Sebbie's mouth.

'It's a little more than cheese on toast,' said Jude.

'Sounds good,' said Binnie. 'Can I help?'

'You can get some glasses out of the cupboard over there if you
don't mind.'

Jude was glad they'd managed a trip to the supermarket the

previous day so she wasn't embarrassed by any stale bread or cheese that needed the mould scraping off. She flicked the little electric grill on and threw three pieces of bread under it. Whilst it was toasting, she took the new block of Red Leicester cheese from the fridge and cut thick slices. Then she retrieved the half-toasted bread from the grill and spread the uncooked sides with butter and an onion chutney that Noah had made last autumn. She laid the cheese slices on top and sprinkled them with Lea and Perrins Worcester Sauce before putting them back under the grill.

Thanks to Lucy, there were cherry tomatoes and salad in the fridge and even avocados in a bowl on the unit.

By the time the rarebits were grilled, Jude had arranged a healthy-looking mix of fresh salad on three plates and Binnie had organised glasses of water and cutlery for the table.

Jude felt a warmth she hadn't for a while. Perhaps it was due to the simple rarebits, which was actually the most cooking she'd done in a long time. Maybe it was down to the fact that she was enjoying some female company or perhaps it was because, for the first time since she'd vowed to find out what had happened to Sarah, she felt as though there was a real chance of making headway.

They returned to the files, whilst eating their hot, cheesy toast.

Many contained nothing of interest but when they opened one labelled *Marple* they discovered a host of little thumbnail pictures.

'This could be interesting,' said Binnie, clicking to open a slideshow of the photos.

Jude looked at them as Binnie started scrolling through. They were all clearly taken through a dirty window, probably as the photographer – Sarah in her investigative Miss Marplesque role? – stood outside, spying on the contents of the building. It was a filthy building, by the look of it, concrete floor and whitewashed walls with the paint peeling off in large chunks.

The first few photos showed wide views of the room which was full of a very strange mix of stuff. Furniture, electrical devices, paintings, boxes, even clothes. It looked a little like the flea markets Jude and Adam had enjoyed visiting at the Three Counties Showground once upon a time but in the photos, there was no order. Stuff was piled high with no apparent reason for their placing.

'Do you think it's the spoils of the loan shark business?' Jude asked.

Close-ups followed of some of the items, slightly blurry, indicating that the camera phone had probably been on highest magnification to take the pictures. The smeary glass of the window didn't help either, but the photos were clear enough to see what each one was of.

'What the hell?' Jude said, staring at the screen. 'Go back, Binnie. Yes, that one.'

'What the 'ell, Aundy Chewdy,' said Sebbie, innocently.

'Curb your language if you can,' said Lucy. 'You know he copies everything you say.'

'Sorry,' said Jude. 'But come and look at this.'

She'd asked Binnie to pause on a picture that clearly showed bronze heads of a man with a handsome moustache and a woman with a serene face.

Lucy left Sebbie in charge of his plastic spoon and came to see what Jude and Binnie were looking at.

'What is this?' she said.

'Hang on a minute,' said Jude. She went into the sitting room and over to the newspapers that were piled up by the log burner, waiting for their turn to be used as a fire starter. Jude leafed through until she found the copy of the *Malvern Gazette* she was looking for.

'I thought so,' she said, placing it on the table in front of them. There on the front page was the headline:

BRONZE BUSTS OF LOCAL HISTORICAL HEROES STOLEN FROM PRIORY PARK

Beneath the headline was a picture of two empty stone plinths. And next to that was another of the same plinths, this time holding large busts of the composer, Edward Elgar, and opera singer, Jenny Lind. The very same busts that were now showing on the computer screen in front of them.

'Stolen goods then,' said Lucy, an edge of excitement in her voice.

'And I'd be willing to bet all the lambs on the farm that whoever stole them would be very keen to keep this fact quiet,' said Jude.

They continued to scroll through the photos. Most of them were of goods, almost certainly ill-gotten. The last few pictures were the most interesting as they contained something more than just objects. They were of a second room, and this one contained people.

20

The photographer had managed to capture the back of a man, bending over a box, although it was impossible to see anything that might help them identify him. The next picture was slightly clearer as the man stood up, although it was still only a back shot.

'Can you zoom in?' Lucy asked.

Binnie did just that, but the picture became blurrier and there were no striking features that could be made out. The man looked average height, average build, white, any age between mid-twenties and fifty, hair hidden under a woollen hat. The only thing they could say for sure was that it wasn't Les Turner.

'Go on,' said Jude. 'Are there any more?'

The next photo showed the man again, this time facing the camera.

'Zoom in?' Jude asked.

Still not clear, but there was a blurry face visible now.

The next shot was much clearer and, when Binnie zoomed in on his face, the features could be made out with ease.

'Do you recognise him?' Binnie asked.

Jude shook her head. 'Not someone from the village,' she said.

The next photo showed the man from a slightly different angle and the following one introduced a new character. A woman this time. Tall and slim with brown hair tied in a high ponytail, she seemed to be having an argument with someone just out of sight. Binnie zoomed in as much as she could on the woman's face. It wasn't terribly clear but it didn't need to be to see that she was obviously very angry about something.

'Do you recognise her?' Binnie asked.

'It's difficult to say for sure,' said Jude. 'But I don't think so.'

Binnie scrolled onto the next picture and Jude heard herself gasp reflexively as a face filled the screen. It was the same woman, but this time she was right up by the window and looking directly into the camera. Whoever had been taking the photos had clearly been caught out.

'I know her,' said Jude as she took in the beautiful but harsh features of the furious face. 'I'm sure I do. I just can't think where from.'

'Local?'

'Not from the village,' Jude replied. 'But there's definitely something familiar about her.'

The more Jude racked her brains to find the link between the woman in the picture and the nugget of something her memory was trying to spit up, the more the link evaded her. She stared at the face, but it refused to give up its secrets.

'That's it,' said Binnie.

'I'm not surprised,' said Lucy. 'I'm pretty sure I'd have scarpered too if that woman caught me snooping where I wasn't wanted.'

'Is there anything else in the folder?' Jude asked.

'Nothing.'

'Can I print a copy?'

'Go ahead,' said Binnie.

Jude plugged the laptop into the printer and printed a copy of the clearest photo of the man and the woman in the hope it might jog her memory.

'I need to get Sebbie to bed,' said Lucy. 'You carry on without me.'

Jude kissed the top of Sebbie's head as he flung himself at her for a goodnight hug, covering her jumper with little bits of couscous from his hands and smears of yoghurt from his mouth. He smelled biscuity and warm and his downy hair felt wonderful against Jude's cheek. She'd been so worried about their arrival but already she'd grown to love having the two of them around. She wasn't looking forward to the day they'd be heading back to Maidenhead.

'I need a cup of tea,' said Jude, setting the laptop back down on the table in front of Binnie. 'Can I get you one?'

'I'd love one. Thanks.'

Jude went over to the sink to fill the kettle, thinking about the new thread they'd just uncovered. Sarah had obviously discovered a pretty big theft organisation, but why had she been there in the first place, hanging around somewhere so dodgy taking photos of criminals? What had she been hoping to achieve?

'If Sarah had taken these photos to the police,' Jude said, 'would there have been a reward? Something that might have helped her pay back the loan?'

'Not unless one of the individuals had set up a reward fund privately,' said Binnie. 'I can have a poke around at work but it would have had to have been some hefty reward to cover Sarah's debts. And something like that would have been well promoted by the person offering it. I was wondering more about Sarah using her evidence as blackmail?'

Jude took two teabags from the box and threw them into the teapot, noting how many she'd got through of late and making a mental note to buy more before she ran out.

Blackmail? Was there any way she could see Sarah dabbling in something so terribly underhand?

'No,' she decided. 'I know things were rock bottom for her and she was desperate, but she had the strongest morals and I just don't see her resorting to blackmail.'

She took a bottle of milk from the fridge and put it on a tray together with the teapot and three mugs. She set it on the table as Lucy rejoined them.

'He's out like a light again,' she said. 'What did I miss?'

'I didn't realise Sarah had written clues for Lexigle,' said Binnie, looking at the laptop screen.

'She always played around making puzzles and quizzes up for us; it was Nate's inspiration for the game and I think she wrote a lot of the early clues, but as soon as it started making any money, she stopped. Nate said work and pleasure should never be mixed.'

This had been another sting point for the friends, who couldn't understand how he could rip off Sarah's idea so unscrupulously and yet not allow her to remain a part of it.

'Well, he changed his mind at some point,' said Binnie. 'There's a contract on here for a trial period of two weeks' worth of clues with the potential to build more if Lexigle uses the ones she delivers.'

'Really?' said Jude.

'Yes. It's dated halfway through January, so it's possible some of her clues have already been used.'

'I wonder why she didn't say anything,' said Jude. 'Does the contract mention pay?'

Binnie continued to read. 'Yes,' she said. 'She was paid pretty well for the trial period and there was another instalment due if the words were used.'

Lucy had gone very quiet and was tapping her fingers on the

table, staring at a spot on the wall halfway between the floor and the ceiling.

'Got something?' asked Jude.

'Maybe,' said Lucy. 'Two of those three clues we found, *Winter* and *Danger*, were Lexigle words recently, although the clues were different.'

'Could they still have been hers?' Jude asked.

'Definitely,' said Lucy. 'I remember I got *Danger* in one so there were still four other clues to go. I think it took me three attempts to solve *Winter* but the clue we found in the diary wasn't very good, so it's possible it had to be replaced. Also, do you think this could explain the LX notes in Sarah's diary? If I remember correctly, there were fourteen numbered inclusions on consecutive days which could be the days her clues were going to be used.'

'Yes,' said Jude. 'That would make perfect sense and it would be really nice somehow to know that Sarah had been included in her game after all. She'd have loved that.'

'Diary?' asked Binnie.

'Oh, God,' said Jude. 'I totally forgot, you haven't seen the diary yet. I found it at Sarah's cottage when I was there. It was the reason I came to see you at the station the other day, to drop it off. I almost left it with the officer I saw but I wanted to make sure it definitely got to you.'

'I'm glad you didn't hand it in,' said Binnie. 'It'll be much easier to go through if it isn't locked in the evidence room.'

'Surely you could get into serious trouble with the DI if you were caught helping us,' Lucy said. 'Why are you doing this?'

Jude kicked her under the table. She'd wondered herself why the DS would be going to all this effort, potentially risking her career for a case she wasn't even supposed to be working on. But without her help, Jude would have a far larger mountain ahead to climb, and it felt as though she'd be trying to do it in flip-flops too.

'Of course, we are incredibly grateful,' said Lucy. 'But you could lose your job. What's in it for you?'

Binnie looked at Lucy and then at Jude. 'It's a fair question,' she said. 'So, I suppose it deserves a fair answer.'

She took a deep breath before beginning.

'The very first case I worked on as a freshly qualified DS was a suspected suicide of a woman called Ashani. It looked cut and dry, or at least that was what my DI thought.'

'But not you?'

'No,' said Binnie, sombrely. 'Not me. But I was new to the job, right down at the bottom of the ladder, so my voice didn't count for anything.'

Binnie stopped and took a long sip of water. Jude saw that her hands were visibly shaking.

'It's all right,' she said. 'You don't have to explain anything to us.'

But Binnie continued as though she hadn't heard.

'Ashani had also been the victim of a stalker for many months before she died. I was sure the stalker had a hand in her death, but I had nothing that could prove it.'

'Did he get done for stalking her at least?' asked Lucy.

'Nothing more than a caution and an injunction to stop him going near her. He was questioned after she died but they were just going through the motions. He wasn't even detained but I knew, I *knew* he was guilty. If I'd pushed deeper, looked harder for concrete evidence...'

She tailed off and let out a deep sigh.

'If I'd gone with my gut instinct then maybe we'd have locked him up before he did it again.'

'No!' said Lucy.

'Two bodies instead of one,' Binnie confirmed. 'He was more careless with the second girl, Bhavna. Not even the DI could ignore the facts, so the arsehole was convicted of murder. He's in prison now but he was never officially linked to Ashani's death. I didn't do enough for her and if I had, I could have saved Bhavna.'

Binnie's voice caught and Jude laid her hand silently on her arm.

'Perhaps if I find out who's behind Sarah's death it will help set things right just a little bit.'

Jude nodded. 'That's sort of what we're all doing,' she said. 'Trying to set things right a little bit.'

The three women gazed at the table, all lost in their own thoughts and private troubles.

'Let me get the diary,' said Jude. 'I can't make much sense of it but who knows, you might have better luck.'

She reached for her bag and rummaged through it.

'She uses a lot of codes and shorthand,' she warned. 'LT, who I think we can safely assume is Les Turner, crops up a lot, as does someone with the initials CB, who I think is somehow linked to Les.'

'That in itself is interesting,' said Binnie.

'Where the hell is it?' said Jude, digging right down to the bottom.

'Give it here,' said Lucy. She grabbed it and tipped the contents all over the table. For the second time that day, everything that resided in the depths of the bag was free to roll and slide wherever it fancied.

'It's not here,' said Jude.

'Are you sure that's where you put it?' Lucy asked.

'Pretty sure,' said Jude, thinking back to the last time she'd held the diary in her hands. She knew she'd had it when she'd been at The Lamb and she'd definitely put it back in her bag. Since then, there had been no reason to remove it.

'Bugger,' she said. 'It must have fallen out with everything else at the spa. How did we miss it?'

'Unless it wasn't *missed*,' said Lucy.

'Oh, God,' said Jude, realisation dawning on her. 'Crystal-May-Rose!'

* * *

Jude showed Binnie the photocopied pages of the diary, grateful she'd had the foresight to take them when she thought she'd have to give the diary up. They looked through the pages again but nothing new jumped out at them, even with a fresh pair of eyes looking for something.

'I'll take a copy of these,' said Binnie. 'But I don't think it will change anything as far as the official investigation goes as there's still so little to go by.'

When Binnie went home, leaving the laptop at the farm for safe keeping, Jude and Lucy tidied away the supper things.

'What are you going to do about Crystal-May-Rose?' asked Lucy.

'I don't know,' said Jude. 'I can hardly march up to her and ask if she stole the diary, can I?'

'No, but you could ask her about Les Turner and see what she says, or at least how she reacts.'

'Maybe,' said Jude. 'I need to go and see Nate too. I've got plenty of questions for him.'

'You don't trust him, do you?'

'I just don't know what to make of him,' said Jude. 'He didn't help Sarah when she really needed it, but then Sarah was absolutely adamant he didn't know about the debts. There's no denying he's a difficult character, even Granny Margot thinks so and there are very few people she doesn't like. But then we know from the diary that he took Sarah out for romantic meals and away for her birthday weekend, and she loved him enough to put hearts next to their dates.'

'Hang on,' said Lucy. 'Are you sure the diary said he took her away for her birthday?'

'Yes,' said Jude, the penny dropping straight away as she understood Lucy's confusion. 'Except he didn't, did he?'

'No,' said Lucy. 'I remember you telling me how annoyed you were on Sarah's behalf because he buggered off to see his sister that weekend. Booked the plane ticket without even clocking the date.'

'You're right,' said Jude, angry at herself for not spotting this sooner. 'I suggested that Charlie, Ben and I took her out for a meal instead but she said she just wanted a quiet one on her own.'

She picked up the copied diary pages and leafed through to the date she was looking for.

'And yet here it is. That's definitely her birthday and she clearly had plans to go away with someone called N.'

'So, if she wasn't having a romantic weekend with her boyfriend,' said Lucy, 'who is the N in the heart that she was meeting instead?'

21

Jude had once thought she knew pretty much everything there was to know about Sarah. They'd shared so much over the years and yet Jude was quickly realising just how many secrets Sarah had been keeping. The debts, the amateur sleuthing into a gang of robbers, her role in putting together Lexigle clues... Now did she need to add an affair to this list?

She racked her brain to think of who the mysterious N could be, but her mind drew a blank. Lucy had suggested Noah as the obvious candidate, but Jude was very quick to point out that Sarah's birthday this year had been the week before lambing began so he had not left the farm. They would just have to keep thinking.

* * *

Pancake the lamb was thriving. Despite her fairly shocking start in life, she'd put on weight well and was fit, healthy and apparently always happy. Not bad for someone who'd been flattened by a mother who went on to reject her within the first few hours of life.

'How's she been doing with the creep feed?' Noah asked. 'I noticed you started her on it.'

Jude had just warmed the morning bottle and was taking it over to Pancake's pen, where she was skipping and bouncing at the prospect of what was about to come her way.

'She was a week old yesterday,' said Jude. 'So, I thought it was about time to see what she made of the pellets.'

Marking time with Pancake was easy as the date of her first day in the world was also the date of Sarah's last.

'You're doing a good job with her,' said Noah. 'Well, you and your young helper, of course. He still in bed, is he?'

'He was when I came out,' said Jude. 'I think the Malvern air is doing him good. He's sleeping really well, which is something I don't think Lucy is used to.'

'Giving her time to get some extra rest too, I should think.'

'I suppose so,' said Jude, noting the care in Noah's voice.

'Well, I guess I'd better get this day started,' said Noah.

'What have we got going on today?' she asked. 'Did you get the sheep shifted into the front fields yesterday?'

''Fraid not,' said Noah, a little smile curving at one side of his mouth. 'Bit busy building a house.'

'Ah, yes, of course. How could I have forgotten? The budding architect and his able accomplice. Thank you again for looking after Sebbie for us.'

'I s'posed you both needed a bit of a break. After everything that's been going on,' Noah said. 'Did you have fun?'

'Yes,' said Jude. 'Not exactly what I was expecting, but it was really nice to spend some time with Lucy.'

Pancake started to nudge Jude's hand, alerting her to the fact she'd let the bottle slip and there was no milk in the teat. She tilted the bottle back and watched the lamb as she went happily back to her task of emptying it as fast as she could. The little tray of creep feed Jude had put down for her yesterday was empty. This one had a good enough appetite and a lust for life.

'I'll go and get those sheep moved out of the top field,' said Noah, picking up his hooked shepherd's crook. 'Then we can think about getting the rest of the lambs out.'

He looked around for his trusty dog, who was never too far away and always ready to be called to action.

'Here, Floss!'

Floss instantly stopped rolling around the floor of the shed and was by Noah's side in seconds, much to the annoyance of Pip, who looked on dejectedly as her playmate was led out through the door.

Jude set Pancake back in her pen. There were still eighty pens set up, although most were now empty, only ten or so of them housing mothers and lambs who needed a little more care for various reasons. They'd been very fortunate not to have too many surplus lambs this year, only a handful who'd been left mother- less, and Frank had bought all except Pancake to rear on his own farm.

With Pancake and the rest of the pens in check, Jude pulled open the rickety shed door and stepped out into the yard, where she found Noah talking to Lucy and Sebbie. Noah was bent low, investigating something that Sebbie had in his hand.

'Aundy Chewdy!' said Sebbie, catching sight of his favourite aunt. 'Look, Sebbie found a egg.'

He rushed over and opened his tight little fist to reveal a smooth pebble.

'That's a very nice egg,' said Jude. 'Where did you find it?'

'There!' said Sebbie, pointing over his shoulder to the path where a million other little pebbles sat. Jude wondered what had made this particular one stand out so delightfully for her nephew.

'Canpake?' Sebbie asked, trying to pull Jude to the lambing shed.

Jude looked over to Lucy and Noah, who were deep in conversation. Noah chuckled deeply at something Lucy said and Jude saw how soft his face was when he looked at her. It was almost the same way he'd looked at Sarah.

Jude shook the thought away. She was being ridiculous. Lucy was almost certainly flirting, but then she always did – always had. And Noah was just being nice back, enjoying the company of her vivacious sister.

The sound of a car approaching caused Jude to turn around. She was surprised to see Charlie's little green Fiat so early on a Saturday.

'Well, I'd best be getting on,' said Noah.

He gave one sharp whistle between his teeth and Floss was instantly at his heels again as they strode across the yard towards the pasture fields.

'You're early,' said Jude, kissing Charlie on each cheek. 'What got you out of bed at this hour?'

'It's the best time of the day. And what a day it is too.' He pointed upwards at the blue sky and the crisp light of the new sun. 'Too nice to be anywhere other than on the river.'

'What?' said Jude.

'I thought you could do with a break,' he continued. 'I've rented a boat for the day from Tewkesbury. We can pootle down the Avon, look out for kingfishers. Maybe stop for fish and chips at Pershore?'

'Are there life jackets?' said Lucy. 'Don't look at me like that, Judy. Sebbie can't swim so of course I would think about his safety first. Same as any mother would.'

Jude held her hands up. 'I didn't say a thing.'

'There are life jackets for everyone,' said Charlie. 'I promise.'

'Perfect,' said Lucy. 'Sounds like a lovely idea.'

'Not for me, I'm afraid,' said Jude. 'Busy day on the farm.'

Lucy pouted at her like a spoilt toddler who hadn't got her way. 'You said lambing was over,' she pointed out. 'And it is Saturday.'

'Lambing *is* over,' said Jude. 'But there are still a million things to do on the farm.'

'I thought that's why you employed one man and his dog,' Charlie said, nodding towards Noah's retreating back.

'Be fair,' said Jude. 'I'm not sure what you have against Noah, but you know I couldn't manage the farm without him.'

'Sorry. I just find him a bit creepy. Maybe it's the way he was always pining after Sarah.'

'You noticed that too?' said Jude. 'I thought he kept it pretty well hidden.'

'Not at all. Did Sarah never show you the crap he used to give her?'

'No...' Jude was finding there were more and more things Sarah hadn't trusted her with.

'I suppose it was quite sad really. He couldn't take no for an answer.'

'I think he's sweet,' said Lucy. 'And I'm sure he can spare you for just one day, couldn't he?'

'Sorry,' said Jude. 'I had the afternoon off yesterday and it wouldn't be fair to ask him again. You guys go, though. Bring me back some fish and chips.'

The farm felt quiet without Lucy and Sebbie there, even though they'd only filled it for a few days.

Once Noah and Floss had moved the flock out of the big top field, Jude was able to take the tractor in with the sprayer so she could fertilise the pasture. It would be good when the grass was growing again, providing fresh food so that there was no longer any need for last year's dried hay. The supply they'd harvested themselves at the end of the previous summer was running very low, so she'd have to order some in from elsewhere, which meant further expense to drain the seriously depleted coffers. More of this glorious spring sunshine would be very welcome to continue to dry out the winter-saturated ground and warm it up to encourage the grass to wake up again.

Jude and Noah spent the rest of the morning moving the lambs old and strong enough to leave the big shed, along with their mothers, to the fields where they were welcomed by a chorus of bleating from those already out there. New friendships in the waiting.

It was hard work and, by lunch time, they were both ready for a break.

Jude went back inside to make a couple of calls that had been playing on her mind. She got nothing useful from the spa. Nobody had handed the diary in, which was not a surprise and when she asked if she could speak to Crystal, she was told she wasn't working that day. It was probably for the best as Jude didn't really know what she'd have said anyway.

Detective Sergeant Khatri, though, picked up her phone after just a couple of rings.

'Hi, Binnie,' said Jude. 'Can you talk?'

'Oh, hello,' said Binnie. 'If you could just give me a moment, I'll move somewhere a little easier to hear you.'

There was a series of scrapes and the sound of background voices until Binnie was on the line again.

'Sorry,' she said. 'I wanted to step out of the office. Easier to chat when there are no ears listening in. How can I help you?'

'I think Sarah may have been having an affair.'

'Right,' said Binnie. 'Do you know who with?'

Jude explained the chain of realisation that had led her and Lucy to the obvious conclusion, although she felt incredibly disloyal for doing so.

'Might be worth making a list of anyone whose name begins with N who Sarah knew and we can go from there,' said Binnie. 'Do you think Nate knew about it? As I mentioned, I did go and talk to him as part of the initial enquiry, but he was aloof and very unresponsive to questioning.'

'That sounds about right,' said Jude. 'I hope he didn't know, although I can't help thinking about Sarah's bruise and the argument he had with Charlie on the night of the wedding.'

'That's all circumstantial,' said Binnie. 'But I do think he's worth keeping in our minds. I can't really go and talk to him again. If it got back to my DI somehow that I was questioning suspects for a case that is as good as shut, and on my own too, I would be in serious trouble.'

'Maybe I should pay him a visit?'

'Be careful if you do. And let me know how it goes.'

'Will do,' said Jude. 'Thanks.'

'Whilst I've got you on the phone... I do have a little bit of information about Les Turner.'

'Okay,' said Jude, her pulse quickening slightly at this potential lead. 'Something that can help pin this on him?'

'The opposite, I'm afraid,' said Binnie. 'Les Turner was in Birmingham on the night Sarah died so it's very unlikely he had a direct hand in her death.'

'Really?' She'd felt so completely sure he was the one who'd killed her and the disappointment she felt at this brick wall was hard to swallow.

'But he's one of a very few suspects we have,' she said. 'And he's also big enough and strong enough to have got her into the tree. Not many people fit that profile.'

'Jude, I think we have to face facts,' said Binnie. 'Realistically, not even someone as strong as Les Turner could have managed to tie Sarah in the tree without leaving signs of a struggle. And pathology would have picked anything like that up straight away.'

'That can't be true,' said Jude, refusing to believe that Sarah had willingly done this to herself. 'Could she have been drugged first?'

'Toxicology came back clear for everything other than alcohol.'

'But did they do a full analysis?' Jude asked. 'If they'd already put this down as suicide, would they still be thorough?'

'I can't see it slipping the net.'

'There has to be another explanation!' said Jude in frustration. 'We just need to think.'

'I'm just being honest with you,' said Binnie. 'But it doesn't change anything. I can't find a logical explanation as to why Sarah ended up as she did, but I promise I'm doing everything I can to help.'

Jude swallowed; her mouth had gone dry at this new revelation. Were they both being blinkered? She because she didn't want to see the truth that Sarah really had chosen to end her own life, and Binnie to try to put right the terrible wrongs from her early career?

22

Jude felt despondent as she went through the lambing shed, methodically taking down all the pens that were no longer needed. Noah had already made a start and the barn was quickly emptying. Each time a pen was dismantled, they carried the aluminium sections out to the trailer Noah had set up ready to transport them to the storage shed on the other side of the yard.

'You all right, Jude?' Noah asked.

'Just thinking about Sarah.'

He nodded. 'Thought so. You know I'm not all that good with words but I'm not too bad with listening.'

He seemed to become embarrassed then, pushing his hand through his thick hair and looking down at the ground. 'I mean, you have lots of people for that, I suppose. But, well, I'm here if you need me.'

She gave him a kiss on the cheek, which surprised her as much as it did him.

'Thanks,' she said.

'Yes, well,' said Noah. 'I mean it. Floss and me will help in any way we can.'

Jude was warmed by the earnestness of his kind face and the heartfelt sentiment.

'Come on,' Jude said, snapping out of her melancholy somewhat. 'These pens won't shift themselves.'

'Barn disco?'

'Can't think why we left it so late,' said Jude. 'Shall I do the honours?'

'Please do.' Noah grinned.

Barn discoes were something that Jude and Noah had invented when he'd caught her the previous lambing season with the radio turned up. It had been a particularly gruelling day and Jude was near breaking point when Gloria Gaynor's 'I Will Survive' came on. It was just the song she needed and she began dancing around the barn like a mad thing, flinging her arms around and singing at the top of her voice. Noah had found it as amusing as Jude had found it embarrassing when he caught her mid-spin, using a lambing aid, recently used for pulling a tricky lamb successfully from its mother, as a microphone.

'Barn disco,' said Noah. 'Might just catch on.'

And it had. The sheep didn't seem to mind the music and it helped lift the spirits on the toughest of days. Jude tuned into Absolute Radio 90s just as Blur's 'Country House' was firing up.

'Perfect choice,' she said.

Her heart was not really in it at all, but when Noah got Floss and Pip spinning and jumping in excitement, she couldn't help laughing at their classic canine comedy. She was soon bobbing along with Noah and the dogs, her head jerking, and feeling much better for it. It was amazing how a bit of music could lift even the gloomiest spirits.

With the music to help them along, the second half of pen clearing went much faster and soon the pens were all stacked into the trailer.

'Want a hand unloading?' she asked.

'You're all right,' said Noah. 'If you get the shed ready for the new inmates, we can have them in today.'

He jumped into the cab of the tractor and Floss followed him up.

Jude took a yard broom and started to sweep out all the old hay, straw and sheep droppings from the lambing shed. It looked so empty now that there were only ten of the eighty pens left standing. The muck would have to be scooped up and taken over to the compost pile at the far side of the farm where it would ferment, with a little bit of help, until it had become brilliant fertiliser to go back on the land.

Once clear, Jude mixed three large buckets of disinfectant and sluiced the concrete floor, careful to brush all the liquid away from the pens still being used. When this was done and the ground was left to dry, Noah was back with the trailer.

'Grab a shovel,' said Jude. 'We've got a load of shit to shift.'

'Right you are, boss.'

Physical exertion was a great way of numbing the mind from pain and, by the time the muck heap had been shifted and the remaining lambs and ewes moved from the big barn into the newly prepared large pen of the lambing shed, Jude had sweat dripping down her spine.

'Coffee?' she suggested.

Noah picked up the flask. 'Empty,' he said. 'Why don't you come down to the pink house for a fresh brew?'

'I'll follow you down,' she said. 'I need to give Pancake her last feed of the day before I shut the shed up for the night.'

'Bring her with you. Not the first time that cottage has seen a lamb.'

'All right. I'll do that.'

She gathered up a bottle and measured out the correct amount of powder into the bottom. Then she wrote a quick note to Lucy which she pinned on the door of the shed. She scooped a wriggling Pancake up, whistled for Pip and followed Noah, who was waiting for her in the yard.

The inside of the pink house was always warm. The original range still stood in the tiny kitchen, which Noah kept stoked throughout the winter. Like the Aga was to Jude, the range was his source of heating, as well as his means of cooking. It had been there since the days of Old Leah's childhood. The cottage had been almost like a living museum whilst she'd been alive and Jude could remember visiting her when the floor was still packed earth and the whole place smelled of a mixture of damp and coal.

When Leah had died, Jude had helped Adam and Noah finally bring the cottage into the twenty-first century, fitting it with electricity, running water, an inside toilet and a hot water tank so that it was fit for Noah to move into. There was not much need for electric heaters, though, as the cottage was small, the heat from the range was more than enough to permeate it and the thick Malvern granite walls insulated it all year around.

'Take that chair,' said Noah, indicating the one closest to the range.

Jude sat down with Pancake between her legs. Floss had flopped into a big cushion on the red-tiled floor and Pip had rudely joined her without hesitation. Floss didn't seem to mind, though.

'Busy day,' said Noah as he handed her a jug of warm water for mixing Pancake's feed.

'Always is.'

'That's true enough.'

Pancake bleated with impatience as Jude clamped her firmly between her calves and added the warm water to the bottle before shaking it vigorously to mix the powder in properly.

'You've done well with that one,' said Noah.

'She's made of strong stuff.'

'Like you,' he added.

'Oh, I don't know about that,' said Jude. She'd felt a lot of things since Adam had died, and then Sarah, but strong was not often near the top of the list.

'Most in your shoes would have given up on this place,' Noah continued. 'But not you.'

'No,' said Jude. 'I suppose not.'

Being in Noah's kitchen had a soothing effect. He was a kind and gentle person and very uncomplicated company. How different Sarah's life might have been if she'd loved him back and he'd been allowed the chance to look after her as he'd so clearly wanted. The letter N from the diary drifted into her mind.

Jude knew she was right, though: Noah hadn't left the farm during lambing. But was there a chance that he hadn't needed to?

'Did Sarah ever visit you here?' she asked.

Noah looked up in surprise. 'Now and again,' he said. 'Why do you ask?'

'I know how much you cared for her. I was just daydreaming about how different things might have been. I don't suppose she came here on her birthday, did she?'

'Now, why would she do that?'

'I don't know,' said Jude. 'Just a thought.'

'Well, it's a wrong thought,' said Noah. 'She hadn't been here for months.'

When Jude saw Charlie's car drive past the window of the pink house, she knew it was time to go, though she wasn't quite ready to leave the snugness of Noah's kitchen and the gentleness of his company. Even Pancake had lain down next to the dogs' cushion with her head resting on Pip's back paw.

It was like a haven, somehow detached from the rest of the world and all its madness.

'I'd best be getting back,' she said, reluctantly draining her coffee mug and pulling herself from the chair.

Pancake and Pip lifted their heads, neither looking all that keen to leave the warmth of the range either.

'Come on, guys,' Jude said, picking up a sleepy Pancake. 'See you in the morning, Noah, and thanks for the coffee.'

It was a short walk back up the drive, past the pond and across the yard to put Pancake safely to bed in her pen. Jude shut the lambing shed up for the night and went back to the farmhouse, just as the back end of Charlie's car disappeared down the drive.

'Aundy Chewdy!' Sebbie said, rushing over to give her legs a hug. 'I go'ed on a boat.'

'You did?' said Jude. 'Lucky you!'

'Your legs stink,' he said, pushing away and pinching his nose.

'Sebbie!' said Lucy.

'To be fair, he's right,' said Jude. 'In fact, I think it's likely not just my legs that stink. I'm going to head up for a shower.'

* * *

Feeling refreshed, if not totally revitalised, after a hot shower, Jude sat on her bed for a little while, bundled up in her thick pyjamas and bathrobe. She brushed out her wet hair and thought about the conversation she'd had earlier with Binnie. The DS clearly thought there was no way anyone else would have been able to put Sarah in the tree, a view shared by her boss, who had seen this as proof no further foul play had been involved.

If that was the case, then the only logical explanation was that Sarah had done it herself. Logical, perhaps, but believable? Jude just couldn't see it. But if it was neither of these things then what was the third, hidden option that nobody had thought about? There must be one if Jude was to cling to the belief that Sarah hadn't killed herself, but there was nothing that could explain how else it might have happened.

The revelation about Sarah's affair made her skin prickle the more she thought about it. What if Les Turner really didn't have anything to do with Sarah's death and it was the other N who did? Or what if Nate had found out about the affair and his temper had taken over? And then there was the familiar woman in the photo they'd found on Sarah's laptop, if only Jude could remember where she'd seen her before.

As Jude sat there puzzling over the possible answers and not finding even a dash of certainty in any of them, Lucy burst in.

'Lou!' exclaimed Jude. 'You frightened the life out of me. Haven't you ever heard of knocking?'

'I thought you'd want to see this,' said Lucy.

She pushed her phone so close to Jude's face that any sort of focus was impossible. Jude took the phone, wanting to see what Lucy was so excited about. On the screen was the first clue for that day's Lexigle word.

An oil platform within the beat of an unborn child.

'Fright,' said Jude, straight away recognising the clue as the very same at the back of Sarah's diary. 'So, her words definitely were used.'

'Yes,' said Lucy. 'And I think she used them to try and tell us something.'

Jude looked up in surprise.

'What do you mean?'

'*DANGER* and *FRIGHT* were two of her clues and it can't be a coincidence that she chose two such punchy words, not when

MURDER was also used a couple of days ago. Well, I didn't think so anyway, so I used the dates from the diary, assuming that LX stands for Lexigle and the fourteen dates were the ones Sarah's clues came out on. Here,' she said, handing Jude a piece of paper. 'I wrote them down.'

Jude looked at the list.

DANGER

DEBTOR

STOLEN

BRONZE

WINTER

GARDEN

OPIATE

POLICE

MURDER

GRANGE

BARLEY

FRIGHT

'Blimey,' she said. 'When you set them out like that, can this be anything other than a list of clues?'

'I know,' said Lucy. '*STOLEN BRONZE* from the *WINTER GARDEN* can only mean one thing, but it's nothing we didn't already know. *DANGER* and *FRIGHT* are clearly telling us how worried Sarah was and *DEBTOR* suggests that this could easily still be linked to Les Turner in some way. As for *OPIATE*, *MURDER* and *POLICE*, they escalate this up a level as far as I'm concerned.'

Jude shivered at the thought of what this could mean. Robbery was one thing, but if Sarah's investigation had uncovered something even more sinister then it was no wonder she was frightened.

'What about *BARLEY* and *GRANGE*?' Jude asked.

'No idea,' said Lucy. 'But it is something we can work on, isn't it?'

'Definitely,' said Jude. 'There are only twelve words here, though.'

'That's because the last two haven't been set yet. We'll have to wait until tomorrow for the next one.'

23

Sundays were traditionally a little quieter on the farm than the rest of the week. Adam's parents had been religious and liked to hold a day of rest when possible. Each week, they'd eat a big Sunday lunch before walking on the hills to allow batteries to be recharged and the family to spend time together. The Sunday lunches had been dropped when Adam's parents moved to Canada, but Jude and Adam carried on the weekly walks on the hills, taking Ollie, and then Pip too, along the lesser-known paths. Over the years, they'd walked all sections from Eastnor to West Malvern and Jude felt she knew the hills so well she could have mapped them out blindfolded.

That Sunday in particular, Jude craved the stoic immovability of the hills. The weather had heated up further, offering them an unseasonably warm morning and, once Pancake was fed and the other barn lambs and mums seen to, Jude could feel the rest of the day calling her to make the most of it.

Lucy had played Lexigle as soon as she woke up but the word, *FATHER*, meant nothing to her. They'd called Binnie and left a message on her answerphone, but Jude had no idea if the police would take them seriously over a bunch of words set on a game app. And, even if they did, what would they gain? Would it even be too far-fetched for Binnie? Jude didn't think so, but she was keen to speak with her and talk the theory through.

Jude mulled the three words over, trying to unlock their secrets as she sat in the Land Rover waiting for Lucy and Sebbie.

FATHER, GRANGE, BARLEY.

BARLEY, GRANGE, FATHER.

It was frustrating knowing that she held the key to Sarah's mystery but having no idea how to use it. Jude needed the head-space the hills offered and she tried not to be too impatient with her sister as the minutes ticked on. It had been Lucy who'd insisted on joining Jude, which dashed her hopes of a long stride-out around the North Hill and up to the top of the Worcestershire Beacon before the rest of the world woke up and this popular part of the hills became too busy. The Beacon was the highest point of the Malverns, just a few feet short of mountain status, despite the extra rocks the Victorians had heaped on top to try, unsuccessfully, to tip it into the grander category. It offered stunning views across the three counties and into Wales, which was why Jude loved it, but it was also why more and more people had started to flock there in far greater numbers than they ever had before. For Jude it was a route best walked as the sun was still young.

It was also not the sort of walk that could be done with a two-year-old in tow who wanted to stop and examine every stone, weed, feather and puddle they came across on the way.

'Sorry,' said Lucy as she bundled Sebbie into the car seat Jude had put there ready. 'Sebbie needed to go on the potty but we couldn't find the potty because someone moved it out of the bathroom.'

Why did Jude get the feeling she was being blamed for something?

'Didn't find it in time so he peed on the floor instead but don't worry, I've mopped it up. He splashed his dungarees, though, so I had to get him changed. Anyway, we're here now.'

Jude pulled into her favourite parking space next to a little-known path that led up to the hills. It was the part her mother had taken her to each year when it snowed as there was a flat patch perfect for making snowmen, and a long, straight sledge run that shot down the side of the hill, ending safely in a large cushion of bracken scrub.

It was a steep climb to begin with, up behind a row of houses. They took it slowly, with Sebbie pointing out the primroses and snowdrops that studded the grassy bank. He'd rejected Lucy's hand, thrusting his mittened fingers into Jude's instead.

'Aundy Chewdy, look!' he said as he spotted first the flowers, then a gate with a picture of a dog on it and a garden with a blue slide. He pointed at everything. All was new to him and he soaked it all up with wonder.

Far from wishing she'd left her little extended family at home so she could have marched up to the top of the Beacon, Jude found she was happy going at Sebbie's pace, covering hardly any ground but seeing the very familiar through new eyes.

At the top of the path there was a little spring. One of the many that spouted from the hills, channelling off the famous water that had attracted the Victorians to Malvern, turning it into a spa town.

'Wotter,' said Sebbie, picking up a pebble and throwing it into the spring with a satisfying *splosh*.

Pip ran over and stuck her nose deep into the rivulet of clear water.

Sebbie laughed as Pip smacked her nose backwards and forwards in the water, making little arcs of droplets in the air.

'Pip, no!' he giggled as he stepped a little too close and a fine spray caught him in the face.

'That's enough now,' said Lucy. She pulled a tissue from her bag and wiped Sebbie's face with it. 'Let's go and see what's up here, shall we, Sebbie?'

'No,' said Sebbie. 'Wotter.'

He pointed at the spring and scowled at his mother.

'There might be cows this way,' said Jude. 'Let's go and have a look.'

'Cows!' said Sebbie. His fickle attention easily won, the small boy strode on up the path towards the promised cows.

'Are there really cows?' whispered Lucy.

'There really are cows grazing the hills,' said Jude. 'I'm just not promising where.'

Sebbie slept in the car on the way back. They'd walked for over an hour and a half, right to the very northern tip of the ridge where, to Sebbie's delight, they did come across a small herd of soft black and white belted Galloway cattle.

'He's such a sweetie,' she said, glancing in her rear-view mirror at the little boy. 'You should be so proud of him, Lou-Lou.'

To her horrified amazement, Lucy burst into tears.

'Whatever's the matter?'

She pulled into the gateway of a field and switched the engine off so she could face her stricken sister.

'I'm sorry. I wasn't going to do this,' said Lucy. 'Well, that's not true actually. I did come here to talk to you but then all this business with Sarah, and you being so busy with the farm. I just thought you had enough on your plate to worry about me.'

Jude stretched awkwardly across the arm rest to hug her. 'Don't be silly,' she said. 'Whatever else is going on in my life, you are always important to me, and I would like to think you could tell me anything.'

Lucy blew her nose and looked up at her with red eyes.

'Paul wants to go for custody,' she said.

'I didn't think he wanted anything to do with Sebbie,' said Jude.

'He didn't. He was a total prick about the whole thing when I told him I was pregnant. Made out as if I'd planned the pregnancy just to trap him, which is beyond ridiculous. What we had was fun to begin with. He made me laugh and I enjoyed being with him but it wasn't a relationship, not a proper one, anyway, and definitely not one I was so desperate to cling onto that I'd deliberately get myself pregnant. He turned into a complete dick overnight.'

'Of course, I remember,' said Jude. 'It was around the same time we found out Adam was sick. He was more furious about Paul than he was about the cancer!'

'So was Dad,' said Lucy darkly. 'Only he was furious with me for not wanting to force Paul to step up to his responsibilities.'

'Like *he* did, you mean,' said Jude sharply. 'When he left me and Mum behind.'

'Exactly!' said Lucy. 'Bloody hypocrite. I tried telling him that I'd asked Paul for help but he cut me off completely. Paul was vile, Jude. Really nasty, in the end. He said some awful things about me, and about Sebbie too. But that didn't make any difference to Dad. He was so angry about the whole thing and was all up for marching round there and demanding that Paul married me. He probably would have too, if I'd told him where to find him. Can you imagine that? Dad had never even met him and I'd never talked to Dad about him, as far as he knew it was just a one-night stand and yet Dad thought that should be the basis for a lifelong union.'

Jude shook her head, her teeth clenching at the double standards her ever pious father constantly exerted.

'So why has Paul changed his mind now?'

'I think it may have something to do with Dad,' said Lucy. 'He was banging on about my poor choices and basically told me that if I was going to go waltzing off to strange men's bedrooms in the middle of the night, then I should have expected things to end badly.'

'Bastard,' said Jude. She knew her father had archaic notions, but this was far beyond belief, even for him.

'I told him that Paul wasn't a stranger and that I'd seen him every day when I went to get my morning coffee on the way to work.'

'Oh, Lou,' said Jude, realising how her father could have used this information.

'Yep,' she replied. 'I may as well have just given him the address. He went straight round to the coffee shop and then, next thing I know, Paul is ringing me up saying he wants to share custody. He's never even met him, for God's sake!'

'So, what now?' asked Jude. 'What can I do?'

'You can let us stay on at the farm for a bit.' She looked half apologetic and half pleading but they both knew there was no question about Jude's instant agreement.

'You and Sebbie can stay as long as you like. I've kind of got used to having you around now anyway.'

She hugged Lucy again, trying to soak up some of her pain. Jude had never been so furious with her father in her life. What he had done, trying to force her sister into a relationship with such a rubbish example of manhood, was equally as unforgivable as what Paul had done. And Jude understood in that moment the neuroses her sister displayed when it came to her son. With their dad and Paul behaving as they were, of course she wanted to protect Sebbie in every way she could.

* * *

DS Binnie Khatri was excited about the discovery of the previous words and there was no doubt in any of their minds that Sarah had been deliberately laying a breadcrumb trail.

'Why would she do that?' Jude asked when they'd spoken on the phone. 'Why not just tell someone what she knew?'

'It could be for several reasons,' said Binnie. 'Perhaps she was using them to blackmail someone in order to pay off her debts, or Les Turner himself in the hope he would drop them altogether.'

The idea that her warm-hearted friend would be capable of blackmail was unpalatable.

'Could she have been leaving them as an insurance policy?' she asked. 'If she was scared for her life and wanted to leave behind a way of pointing us towards the truth, should anything happen to her?'

'It's possible,' said Binnie. 'The order of the words is certainly important. Let's see what the last one is and go from there.'

'Will you pass our thoughts onto your DI?' Jude asked, hopeful that this might be the piece of evidence necessary for them to take her theories of foul play surrounding Sarah's death seriously.

'I will,' said Binnie, 'but in all honesty, I'm not sure he'll do much as he's so busy with the organised crime case. But the diary pages were enough for him to allow me to officially work on Sarah's case again; he confirmed that this morning.'

'That's great news!'

'We *will* get to the bottom of this, Jude.'

Jude wondered at the vehemence in Binnie's words. The DS was every bit as desperate as Jude was to solve the mystery of Sarah's case despite the risks to her career. Jude wasn't entirely sure she understood why, but it didn't matter. With Binnie on their side, perhaps they would be able to get to the bottom of it all.

* * *

Over an early breakfast the next morning, Lucy and Jude opened the Lexigle app and looked at the first clue for that day's word, the final one that Sarah had set.

'Craftsman of oak and ash,' Lucy read out.

'Trees,' said Jude. 'Or wood. What's another name for a carpenter that only has six letters? Whittle? No, that's seven.'

'Joiner?' suggested Lucy, counting the letters off on her fingers.

'Try it.'

The line lit up red when Lucy typed it into the grid.

The letter U appeared in the second box, indicating its place in the hidden word.

'A walk around the gardens with Tina,' Jude read out.

'Tina,' said Lucy slowly.

She and Jude looked at each other as the answer hit them simultaneously.

'Turner,' they said together.

Sarah's last breadcrumb could not be clearer. Jude had been right all along: whatever had happened to Sarah, Les Turner had the starring role.

After breakfast, Jude, Lucy and Sebbie collected the eggs from the bantam hens and boxed them up. Lucy bundled Sebbie into his buggy and Jude loaded the egg boxes carefully underneath before they set off down the farm's drive to stock the honesty box.

As they walked, Lucy and Jude talked about the Lexigle clues, most of which were clearly understandable, though three were still a mystery – the possible keys to working out exactly what had happened to Sarah.

'*GRANGE, BARLEY* and *FATHER*,' said Lucy. 'Are there any barley farms around here?'

'Plenty of farms that grow barley, but I'm not sure how that helps. And what about father. Whose father?'

Before they could delve into the meanings of these final three clues, their attentions were caught by a sound disturbing the serenity of the woodland.

'Oh, thank goodness it's you,' said Janet Timms, bursting out of the trees in front of them.

Jude felt her entire body clench at the sight of her. She was always popping up when she wasn't wanted.

'What's the problem?' said Jude, softening slightly as she noticed the terrified look on the old woman's face.

'I think Bertie and I have just found a dead body.'

24

Jude felt a sickening plunge in her stomach at Janet Timms's words. Surely she was mistaken – a sick attempt at grabbing some attention, perhaps. No, not even Janet would sink quite that low, would she?

'Where?' she asked.

The woman was ashen and trembling like a leaf. Jude could see her fingers clasped so tightly around the Cocker Spaniel's lead that her knuckles had drained of all colour.

'Do you need to sit down?' Jude asked.

'No,' said Janet.

'Are you sure it was a dead body?' asked Lucy.

'I'm fairly sure,' she said. 'It certainly looked it.'

'Did you call the police?'

'I *never* bring my phone with me when I go for a walk,' said Janet, as though mobile phones were the very antithesis of a respectable country-woman's exercise.

'Right,' said Jude. 'What exactly did you see?'

'It was Bertie,' said Janet. 'We were walking through the fields when he suddenly took off. He does like to chase the rabbits, so I thought he'd caught the smell of one. But then he ran right into the trees by the pit and he wouldn't come back when I called, which is rather unusual for Bertie, so I followed him in.'

There was a pond in the middle of the small wood, locally known as *the pit*, although Jude knew it as McElligot's Pool, named by Adam after his favourite bedtime story. The trees were old, thick and dark, making the pool well-hidden and a little creepy. Adam had loved it, though, and they'd often taken the dogs down there for a run, but she hadn't been back since he'd died.

'Bertie was barking and barking so I knew there had to be something very wrong,' Janet continued. 'He's such a good animal really so when he barks to tell me I should be paying attention, I go and see what he wants to show me.'

'And,' said Jude, trying hard not to show her impatience, 'what exactly did you find?'

'There was an arm,' said Janet. 'Or at least I think it was an arm.'

'You think?' Lucy repeated.

'Yes,' said Janet. 'It looked very much like an arm to me, with a bit of the shoulder showing too. But it was hidden in the reeds and it's quite dark in there.'

'Lucy,' said Jude. 'Why don't you and Sebbie go and drop the eggs off whilst I go and take a look with Janet?'

It was a quick push through the trees to the pit where, although it was dark, the centre of the pond glinted as the sun broke through the gap in the tree canopy. It was no wonder Adam had believed the pool to be full of magic when he was a child.

'Where did you see it?' she asked.

Janet moved around the edge of the pool, pushing her way through the undergrowth and weeds.

'It was somewhere around there.'

Jude stared into the dark green of the water. The surrounding trees were casting so many shadows that it was difficult to make out what was what. A fallen branch poked out of the water and for a moment it did look rather arm-like.

'Could that have been it?' she asked, hoping fervently that Janet Timms had been mistaken.

'No,' said Janet. 'I think it was further around there.'

Jude peered into the water but she couldn't see anything that looked like a body.

'Perhaps you imagined it?'

'Hmm,' said Janet. 'I was so sure.'

The two women walked the full circumference of the pool, just to double check, whilst the dogs chased each other excitedly through the trees, disappearing from sight and then flying out of the undergrowth from a completely different direction.

Jude felt herself relax a little. The lighting was very strange by the pool in the dark copse. It was very possible, probable even, that Janet had been mistaken in what she'd seen.

'Do you think it might have been one of those branches you saw after all?' she suggested.

Janet sighed. 'Maybe,' she said. 'I think perhaps I'm a little more affected than I thought I was by poor Sarah's death. I'm seeing bodies everywhere now.'

Jude noticed then that the dogs had gone quiet. The running and chasing had stopped and they were both down at the water's edge. Bertie had his spaniel nose pointing down at the water and Pip was pawing at something with her front foot. Every hair on the back of Jude's neck crackled with dread as she glimpsed something that looked nothing like a branch.

'What is it, Pip?' she said, skirting the edge of the pool to where the dogs were paying very close attention to the water.

An arm had made its presence known in a place where Jude was sure it hadn't been when they'd looked just a few minutes before. She stepped forward and stared into the water, a little part of her hopeful that perhaps the light was still playing tricks and making things appear that weren't really there at all. But when Pip's interference rippled the water, which pushed the possible arm a little closer to the bank, the motion rotated it slightly, causing what was unmistakably a shoulder to bob to the surface.

Jude and Janet watched in horror as the shoulder caught under the root of tree, making it wrench backwards just enough for a head to be revealed.

* * *

For the second time in little over a week, police cars came haring down Croft Bank towards Malvern End. And for the second time in little over a week, a body was zipped into a black bag and sent off in the back of an ambulance.

This time, the team was led by Detective Inspector Harrison Peters. DS Binnie Khatri was involved in the investigation but it was DI Peters who spoke to Jude and Janet in the first instance and it was he who told Jude that her presence would be required down at the police station. It was her decision, he told her. But her assistance in the matter would be greatly appreciated.

It was also DI Peters who led the interview. When Jude had discovered Sarah's body, she hadn't been officially interviewed at the station but to have been involved in the finding of a second body, and on her farm at that, well, that was different. And the circumstances were different too. She could tell from the initial questions asked by the DI that they were already treating this death as far more suspicious than that of Sarah Lloyd.

'You didn't call us as soon as Mrs Timms alerted you to the fact she'd discovered a body,' DI Peters said. 'Can you tell me why?'

To Jude, the question sounded like an accusation. Was she now a suspect in a murder enquiry?

'Janet wasn't sure what she'd seen,' she said. 'She asked me to go and have a look with her and I didn't think you'd have been too pleased if we'd called you out all for a broken branch.'

'Quite,' said the DI. 'And you have no idea who it could be?'

'I didn't see the face,' said Jude. 'It was still submerged when we called you.'

'I see,' he said as he leant back in his chair and laced his fingers over his substantial girth. 'It's been quite the week for you, hasn't it?'

'It has,' said Jude.

He had no idea just how much of a week it had been.

'Two suspicious deaths on your farm.'

'I thought you decided Sarah's death wasn't suspicious,' she said, unable to stop herself.

'Everything certainly pointed that way, initially,' said the DI. 'But the new evidence, some diary pages and a list of words from a game, which I believe you had a hand in uncovering, they might change things.'

'Might?' said Jude. 'They *do* change things. Sarah didn't kill herself and, now another body has turned up, you have to see that.'

'I'm not at liberty to discuss the case of Sarah Lloyd's death with you,' said DI Peters. 'But rest assured we take every suspicious death very seriously.'

The look he gave her made Jude feel again as though she was a suspect, but by that point, DI Peters had got everything he needed from her.

'Please do let us know if you think of anything else that might be useful,' he said. 'We'll be in touch.'

'So that's it?'

'For now,' said DI Peters. 'But we'd very much appreciate it if you didn't plan any trips away for the time being as we may well have further questions for you as the investigation progresses.'

'Someone killed Sarah,' said Jude. 'I know it.'

'Thank you for your time, Miss Gray,' said the DI, his dismissiveness needling her.

'Mrs,' said Jude.

'Pardon?'

'It's *Mrs* Gray.'

25

DS Binnie Khatri came round the following day, accompanied by a uniformed officer who sat and made notes as she talked. Binnie asked mundane questions about the discovery of both bodies, all of which had been covered before either by her or DI Peters.

'Howell,' she said to the uniformed officer after a while. 'Could you go to the car and get my bag out, please?'

'Yes, ma'am,' said the officer, who reminded Jude of a baby rabbit, all big eyes and a jumpy disposition with just a little covering of downy fluff on his face.

'Right,' said Binnie as soon as he left. 'I hid my bag under the driver's seat so it'll take him a little while to find it. He won't come back until he has, bless him, which gives us a little bit of time. Anything I need to know?'

'No,' said Jude. 'Nothing that you don't already.'

'You found the body?'

'No,' said Jude. 'Technically that was Janet Timms.'

'Ah, yes, the village busybody.' Binnie grinned.

'Do you know anything?' asked Lucy.

'Looks like murder,' said Binnie. 'There are very clear signs of blunt force trauma to the face. Nasty mess.'

Jude shivered reflexively and she saw Lucy do the same.

'Do they know who it is yet?' Jude asked.

'Not yet,' said Binnie. 'The face is badly swollen from being immersed in water for so long. It'll make identifying them pretty difficult. Forensics will need some time and we're going through missing person records for the area, looking for potential matches.'

'Is the DI taking Sarah's death more seriously now?' Jude asked. 'It was hard to tell when he interviewed me.'

'He's not budging on the suicide verdict and he wants me to put the case on the back burner to concentrate on this new body.'

'So, it's still down to us then?'

'For now, at least,' said Binnie. 'Don't worry, though. I'll keep my ears open and let you know if anything changes.'

'Did you get anything from the pictures we found on the laptop?' Lucy asked.

'Nothing yet,' said Binnie. 'I've given copies to a friend of mine. But they're looking at them out of hours so it will take a bit of time.'

'Good to have friends in the right places,' said Jude.

Binnie smiled. 'My Amma always says be kind and helpful where you can, and others will be so in return.'

'Smart woman,' said Lucy.

'I've been thinking about the laptop,' said Jude. 'Shouldn't we hand it in? The photos are hard to argue with and surely they're further proof that Sarah was in danger.'

'I've been thinking about that too,' said Binnie. 'If we hand it in, it will be difficult for me to get access to it as it's more likely to be used for the investigations into the local robberies. But if you have a memory stick, we could transfer all the files over.'

'I don't have one,' said Jude. 'Sorry.'

'Not to worry,' said Binnie. 'I'll bring one round. Now, just quickly before Howell comes back, I did find something else that might interest you. I did a little background check on Crystal-May-Rose Bradfield.'

'Oh, yes?'

'She was prosecuted for grievous bodily harm around five years ago. Sounds like a nasty incident at a club in Worcester on a night out. Had a row with a man she was dating and ended up smashing him over the head with a bottle. They were picking shards of glass out of his scalp in A&E for two hours.'

'Crikey!' Jude could imagine Crystal-May-Rose getting a little feisty, but this was another level of violence. It didn't quite match the velvet-voiced therapist who had almost made her fall asleep on her massage table. 'I'm surprised she managed to get a job at the spa with that sort of record.'

'She was never convicted,' said Binnie. 'She claimed it was self-defence and the jury went her way. Not guilty so no record.'

'Still wouldn't look good at work if they found out,' said Lucy. 'I can imagine she would have wanted to keep it quiet, whatever the official verdict.'

'And that's not the only time she's been in court,' Binnie continued. 'She was arrested for dealing in stolen goods a couple of years ago over in Hereford. Again, she was never convicted so it wouldn't show up on her criminal record.'

There was a knock on the door and Lucy got up to let Officer Howell in.

'Sorry, ma'am,' he said. 'It had fallen down and slid under the front seat.' He passed Binnie's bag over. 'Here you go.'

'Thanks,' said Binnie. She took a pack of tissues from it and wiped her nose. 'I think we're all done here. Unless you've got any questions?'

Jude and Lucy stood up with the DS.

'I've got your number if I think of anything else,' said Jude.

* * *

That afternoon, Jude decided to bite the bullet and pay Nate Sanchez a visit. She'd been putting it off as she fully expected a cold reception, possibly even an angry one, but if she was going to do Sarah justice in her investigation then she couldn't avoid Nate any longer. He lived in a beautiful, expensive Victorian town house, the address of which was given to her by DS Khatri.

The driveway was weed-free and the flowerbeds surrounding it immaculately kept. Jude felt her Land Rover couldn't have looked more out of place in the otherwise perfect surroundings.

She felt nervous pulling up, having no idea what sort of reception she'd get from him. The door was painted in a shiny black gloss with a brass knocker hanging nobly from the central panel. Jude lifted it and gave three sharp raps then took a step back.

The clear sound of footsteps was followed by the door opening halfway and a tired and unshaven Nate glared out at her. He looked awful. His olive skin had given way to a sickly yellowish green and his hair looked greasy and unbrushed. His eyes were hollow and deeply troubled.

'Yes?' he said.

'Hi, Nate,' she said. 'I just wanted to come and say how sorry I was and to see how you're doing.'

Nate looked confused, as though a gesture of kindness was the last thing he'd expected from Jude.

'I'm all right, thanks,' he said, shortly.

'Can I come in?'

He stepped forward and pulled the door ajar behind him.

'Sorry,' he said. 'What is it you want?'

Jude was taken aback by his bluntness.

'I really just wanted to check up on you,' she said. 'Sarah was my best friend and I know how much she loved you. I think she'd want us to get along now.'

Nate stared at her as though she was talking a foreign language and he was doing his best to translate it as she went.

'She'd definitely have wanted me to come and see if you were all right.'

Nate still said nothing. His dark eyes flicked across her face, trying to read her, the intensity of his gaze unsettling. Jude had hoped for a conversation – she'd thought maybe there would even be the chance to have a subtle look around his home – but there was a wall he was hiding behind, impenetrable and firm.

'I just wanted to say sorry,' she fumbled. 'That's all.'

Before she embarrassed herself any further, she backed off and jumped into the Land Rover, did a messy three-point turn in the driveway, almost ploughing through an immaculate camelia bush, and drove off.

'Well, that went very well,' she said to herself, thumping her hand in frustration on the steering wheel.

If Binnie wasn't allowed to visit again in an official capacity – and Nate was certainly not open to having an informal chat with Jude – then how else were they going to scout him out? She toyed with the idea of channelling Binnie's gumption and breaking in to have a look around but she wasn't sure she had the stomach for such espionage.

Still, if needs must then maybe she didn't really have a choice.

* * *

As Jude was leaving to meet Ben later that evening, Noah turned up at the farmhouse looking unusually tidy in a pair of jeans and funky graphic T-shirt.

'I wondered if you and Lucy wanted some company this evening,' he said, waving a bottle of wine and what looked like a jar of homemade piccalilli at her.

He caught her slight hesitation and his face flushed salmon pink.

'Sorry,' he said, shuffling awkwardly. 'I shouldn't have just turned up. You'll be busy, I'm sure.'

'No,' said Jude. 'It's really nice of you to come. It's only that I'm about to head off to meet Ben at The Lamb.'

Just then, Lucy appeared in the kitchen behind her.

'I thought I heard your voice,' she said, smiling at Noah. 'Ooh, are you off somewhere nice? You look very dapper.'

'Nope, not going anywhere,' he said. 'Just came to drop this off for you.'

He passed her the wine bottle.

'How lovely,' she said, reading the label. 'If you're not heading out then do you want to come and share a glass with me whilst my big sister buggers off to the pub?'

'I don't have to go,' said Jude.

She felt awful. Lucy had opened up to her about Paul, the custody battle and the awfulness of their father, all of which meant she needed Jude's attention and support. Janet Timms and the body from the pit had taken that attention away and then, to top things off, Ben had sent a message saying he needed to speak to her urgently.

'Don't worry,' said Lucy. 'Noah and I will be absolutely fine.'

'Well,' he said. 'If you don't mind the company.'

'Nonsense,' said Lucy. 'I'd love it. I was about to cook a gourmet feast of baked beans and ham on toast with a side portion of frozen peas. You'd be very welcome to a plate.'

Noah held up the piccalilli.

'This might be just the right thing then,' he said.

26

As Jude pulled into the car park of The Lamb, her phone rang. She looked at the name on the screen and her skin bristled with anger.

'Dad,' she said. 'What do you want?'

'Have you seen her?'

'I assume you're talking about your other daughter,' she said. 'You know, the one you are currently trying to throw under a bus.'

'Oh, don't be so dramatic, Judith. Is she with you?'

'No. She isn't. But I have spoken to her and she told me what you did. How could you? It's absolutely disgusting.'

She couldn't keep the utter loathing from her voice.

'Judith!' said her father. 'Don't talk to me in that way, I'm doing what's right. Paul is Sebbie's father and he wants to be part of his life. It's Lucy who's being irresponsible. That girl is impossible, always has been – it was no real surprise when she got herself into trouble. At least Paul is willing to take her on.'

Jude listened with total incredulity and when she spoke, her teeth were clamped together in rage.

'Paul is an arse,' she said. 'He abandoned Sebbie and Lucy, and treated her appallingly. And yet you want him to play a part in her life?'

'There are two sides to every story,' he said. 'And a child needs a strong father figure.'

'No,' said Jude. 'A child needs parents they can look up to and trust, and neither Paul nor you fit that mould.'

She cut the call off and took several deep breaths to steady herself, vowing to make the evening short so she could get back to Lucy as soon as possible.

As usual, Jude was the first to arrive at the pub.

'Evening, my love,' said Barbara. 'Ben reserved a table for you. It's that one over by the window.'

'Thanks,' said Jude, looking over to the table Barbara was indicating, glad that it was slightly tucked away from the ears of the rest of the pub.

She ordered herself half a pint of Dorothy Goodbody and took it over to the table indicated by Barbara. It was set for three and Jude sincerely hoped the third place was for Charlie. If it wasn't then the only other option was that Tilda, the bee-sting queen, was going to be joining them – something Jude wasn't the least bit in the mood for. She thought of Lucy and Noah back at the farm enjoying beans on toast and a glass of wine and it was very tempting to jump in the Land Rover and head back to join them.

When Charlie walked into the bar, Jude breathed a sigh of relief. She waved him over and then cursed under her breath when she spotted Ben, with Tilda, right behind him.

'Hello, darling girl,' said Ben, wrapping his arms around Jude and kissing her on both cheeks. 'How are you bearing up?'

'Not too bad,' she said, noting the bristle of his un-shaven face as it brushed against the skin of her cheek. 'Just keeping my fingers crossed there isn't a third body hidden somewhere on the farm.'

Ben smiled at her attempt at humour, but Tilda wasn't as amused.

'I don't think I'd be quite so blasé about it if it were me,' she said. 'I mean the police must be all over you now, aren't they?'

'Don't worry about me,' said Jude, before turning her attention back to Ben, who looked even worse than he had the last time she'd seen him.

'What about you?' she said. 'You look like you haven't slept since you got back from Marrakesh.'

'He hasn't,' said Tilda. 'It's been a bloody nightmare. Last night I made him sleep in the spare room, he was so tiresome.'

'Drinks, I think,' said Ben.

'Gin and tonic,' Tilda said.

'Anyone else?' Ben turned to Charlie and then to her. 'You all right, Jude?'

'Driving,' she said, pointing to her half pint.

'I'll give you a hand,' said Charlie.

Jude hoped Barbara would be quick with their drinks as even just a few minutes in Tilda's company on her own was too much.

'I'm not supposed to be here,' Tilda said, sitting down opposite. 'It's usually my Pilates night, over in Colwall Village Hall. Lady called Julia Patron, I don't know if you've heard of her. She moved here from somewhere in Bucks and she's the only person around who gives me a good stretch and truly knows the technique properly.'

Jude highly doubted that was true, but she nodded anyway.

'What happened?' she asked. 'How come you didn't go?'

'Bloody annoying actually.' Tilda sighed. 'Her daughter's ill apparently. Vomiting or something equally revolting. She only gave us an hour's warning which was a real nuisance as I was already in my yoga pants ready to go.'

'Oh, that is selfish,' Jude said.

Tilda narrowed her eyes, trying to work out if Jude was teasing. Jude held her gaze as she sipped her beer. Then the boys returned and the conversation moved on. Charlie wanted to know everything about the body in the pit. Jude told them as much as she dared without hinting at the fact she had an inside source of information. She would tell the boys about Binnie when the time was right, but not in front of Tilda who was, to all intents and purposes, a stranger.

Ted brought over three plates of scampi and chips, the best in the county according to almost everyone in the village, and a lasagne for Tilda.

'Cheers, Ted,' said Charlie.

'I asked for a salad, not peas,' said Tilda, pushing the lasagne away.

'Tell you what,' said Ted. 'You keep the peas and I'll bring you a side salad with all the extra fancy bits, on the house.'

'Well, it's not on the house if I asked for it in the first place and you messed up the order.'

Jude cringed at her rudeness and Ben shrugged an apology at Ted.

Ted's thrice-cooked chips were pure perfection, crisp and golden on the outside, fluffy inside. The scampi came in big chunks which Jude dipped into Ted's own tartar sauce.

'What did you want to talk about then?' Charlie asked with his usual bluntness as they tucked into their food.

Ben glanced sideways at his new wife before turning back to his friends.

'Oh, nothing in particular,' he said. 'Just thought it would be nice to see you both.'

Jude caught something in his voice, letting her know without any doubt that he was lying. He'd asked them to the pub for a purpose and Tilda's presence now made it impossible for him to speak freely. Jude thought he'd probably chosen that day specifically because of her Pilates class and had been scuppered at the last minute.

'I went to see Nate today,' said Jude.

'Really?' said Charlie. 'How was he?'

'Rude. He looked awful too.'

'Bloody should do after the way he treated Sarah,' said Ben. 'Why did you go and see him?'

'I'm not really sure,' said Jude. 'I suppose a part of me wanted to see how he was doing. Anyway, he made it very clear I wasn't welcome, so I left.'

'Probably just as well,' said Charlie, giving her arm a squeeze. 'You need to be looking after yourself right now, not mopping up after everyone else like you always do.'

Jude was surprised at this. Was that how her friends saw her? To her it felt as though it was them who had done much of the mopping, especially after Adam died.

'Talking of which,' said Ben. 'How's it going with your guests? I can imagine it's pretty exhausting having a little one in the house.'

'I thought it would be,' admitted Jude. 'But it's lovely having them, actually. Sebbie is a real distraction and it's nice having a bit of time with my sister. I took her to the spa the other day, because I thought we both deserved a treat, and ended up having a massage from Crystal-May-Rose.'

Jude decided not to mention the fact she'd actually booked an appointment to see her deliberately. Charlie and Ben had both been so adamant that she left things to the police, she didn't feel like having another conversation about her amateur sleuthing endeavours. Especially not in front of Tilda.

'What a name!' said Tilda. 'Who's that?'

'She's a beauty therapist.'

'She went to school with us,' added Ben.

'Goodness,' said Charlie. 'I'm not sure I'd even recognise her now. What was she like?'

'Nice enough,' said Jude. 'Until I mentioned Sarah, that is.'

'You talked to her about Sarah?' Ben looked surprised and annoyed. 'Why the hell would you do that?'

'They worked together,' said Jude. 'And it sort of came up in conversation.'

Charlie rolled his eyes, but Jude ignored it.

'She didn't like Sarah at all, did she?' she said. 'Made it sound as though it was Sarah who'd been the one doing the bullying at school. The way she told it, she had a terrible time and that was why her mother moved her.'

Charlie choked into his pint.

'Utter crap,' Ben said.

'It was the other way around,' Charlie said after he'd composed himself, wiping the beer froth from his mouth. 'Crystal was a total cow to Sarah.'

'Is that what Sarah told you?' asked Tilda.

'It's how it was,' said Ben, sharply.

'Did you actually see it, though? Or were you doing what you always did and just taking her word for it? You all thought she was some kind of angel. It was bad enough when she was alive but quite frankly it's almost too much to stomach now she's dead.'

'Hey,' said Ben, angrily. 'That's enough.'

'I'm sorry,' she carried on regardless. 'But it's true. None of you can see past the girl who was ballsy enough to climb trees and skinny dip in the village pond with you as kids. Oh, yes, she could turn on the charm when she wanted to. If you fitted into her life that was. But if you didn't, if you dared to disagree with her or call her out on some of her bitchier behaviour, my God, she could turn nasty.'

'I said, shut up,' Ben growled.

'Don't talk to me like that,' she shot back. 'Just because you could never see what a two-faced player she was.'

'I think that's pretty unfair,' said Jude, not able to identify with this version of Sarah at all. Sarah had been nothing but kind and instantly friendly to her when Ben had first introduced her to the group. It had been Sarah who'd seen a potential match between Jude and Adam, and had encouraged them to go on their first date. Jude had watched her gentleness and patience with Granny Margot. Not just Margot either but all members of the village community. Hell, she'd even been generous with her time when it came to her beyond irritating and hopelessly self-centred neighbour, Janet Timms.

'Everyone in the village loved her,' she continued. 'You only had to watch her with them to see why. Sarah was an infinitely caring and generous person.'

Tilda tossed her a disparaging look, telling Jude in no uncertain way that she thought she was utterly wrong and naively blinkered, just like the boys.

'I think it's time to go,' Tilda said. 'Ben?'

Jude looked at him, willing him to defy his wife and tell her to go home without him.

For a moment, he stared at her, his eyes full of rage but then, with a clearly embarrassed mutter of apology, avoiding eye contact with them both, he stood up and followed her out of the pub. Jude watched them go with a frustrated feeling of anger. She didn't like the way her friend had somehow allowed himself to be changed from the care-free, fun-loving, sometimes-a-little-too-confident man she'd met at university, to this submissive shell, trapped in a marriage with Cruella de Vil's less nice sister.

'What the hell is her problem?' she said. 'And why in God's name did he marry her? She's a bloody nightmare.'

Charlie just shrugged.

'Aren't you worried about him?' Jude asked. 'He looks dreadful.'

'He's a big boy,' said Charlie. 'He made his own decisions and he must've had his reasons. You can't fix everyone, Jude.'

'No,' she said. She didn't need Charlie to tell her that.

27

Jude passed Noah on her way back to the farm. He was almost back at the pink house, with Floss at his side, and when she stopped and wound the window down, she saw he was wearing a fairly sizeable smile.

'Nice evening?' she asked.

'Yep,' he said. 'Young Sebbie was teaching me the actions to some of his favourite songs. I think we may have a new recruit for our barn discoes. How about you?'

'Not so much,' she admitted. 'But don't worry about me. I'm glad you had fun. See you in the morning.'

Noah raised his hand to wish her a good night and Jude carried on up to the farm.

Sebbie was fast asleep and Lucy was already in her pyjamas. Quick work, seeing as Noah had only just left, which made Jude immediately suspicious.

'Noah was in a very good mood,' she said. 'Any reason why that might be?'

'We had a nice evening,' said Lucy. 'If you're not-so-subtly asking if I shagged him then please don't. I get enough of that from Dad.'

Jude felt instantly regretful.

'Oh, Lou-Lou,' she said. 'I'm sorry. I didn't mean...'

'It doesn't matter,' said Lucy.

'Actually, it does,' said Jude. 'It's been utter chaos around here and I haven't been able to give you the support you came here for. Midnight feast time?'

Lucy laughed. 'It's not even ten yet.'

'When did that ever stop us? I'll go and get my pyjamas on and you find some suitable snacks.'

Despite their mutual tiredness, Jude and Lucy stayed up late that night, talking about everything that was on their minds. They sat at either end of the big sofa, toes to toes, sharing a pile of blankets, a bowl of popcorn and a bottle of wine.

Jude listened as her sister told her just how difficult she'd found the past few years and, in return, she talked about Adam and Sarah, about her grief and her helplessness. She opened up to Lucy in a way she had never been able to do with anyone else. Not properly. There were tears, promises and resolutions from both women and, eventually, they climbed the stairs to bed. Jude was just switching the light off when Lucy appeared in her doorway.

'Can I sleep in here tonight?' she whispered.

In that instant, Jude was transported back to her childhood, those nights when they'd been under the same roof and Lucy always tried to sneak into her bed. Their father and Lucy's mother had forbidden it, but it hadn't stopped them. Lucy would tiptoe in when her parents had gone to bed and snuggle up under the duvet with her. Jude would whisper stories, and they'd stifle giggles as they shared a packet of strawberry bootlaces. Spending the majority of her days as an only child, at home with a mother who struggled with life, Jude had always loved the closeness she shared with Lucy.

That night, they didn't snuggle up as they had as children, but Jude felt her sister's warm presence next to her and it somehow made her feel stronger. That night, Jude Gray slept well.

* * *

The chickens were particularly fruitful the next morning and Jude, with the able help of Sebbie, filled both baskets, having to go back to the house for a third.

'Shall we drop some eggs round at the pink house?' Jude asked.

'Yes,' said Sebbie earnestly. 'Noah?'

'That's right,' said Jude. 'That's where Noah lives.'

Jude wasn't expecting Noah to be in when they called round but, as she lifted out half a dozen eggs to set in the egg box he always left in the porch for this reason, she heard whistling coming from round the back. If Jude had thought of leaving him to his private morning jollity, Sebbie had other ideas.

'Noah,' he called, impressively loudly for one so small. 'Where are oo?'

The whistling stopped and Noah came around the side of the house holding a bowl full of fresh purple broccoli heads.

'Well, hello, young 'un,' he said, greeting Sebbie before he said good morning to Jude.

'Eggs,' said Sebbie, pointing to the box in the porch.

'My word,' said Noah. 'That's mighty kind of you. Here, I was just in my veg patch getting some purple sprouting. Plenty spare so it seems a fair swap if you take some back for your supper.'

He passed the bowl to Sebbie, who looked delighted with the gift.

'Any better this morning?' Noah asked Jude.

'Much,' she said. 'Thanks for the broccoli.'

'Look,' said Noah, awkwardly shuffling and avoiding Jude's eyes. 'I know it's not my place to butt in where I might not be wanted but I heard something a while back that wasn't meant for my ears, and I've been wondering whether to tell you.'

Jude's senses prickled. This was very unlike Noah, who hated gossip of any sort.

'Go on,' she said.

'I would have kept it to myself, you understand, in normal circumstances but then I was talking to Lucy last night and it made me think.'

'What is it?'

'It was around a week or so before poor Sarah, you know,' he said, still not able to look directly at her as he spoke. 'I was up in the top field when I heard her and that Nate coming up the path next to the field. They couldn't see me with the hedge in the way and I couldn't see them either. I could hear them, though, be hard pushed not to, they were talking that loud.'

'What were they talking about?'

Noah coughed and Jude saw his cheeks pinken a little.

'He'd seen her with Charlie,' he said.

It was obvious that there was more to this statement than it held at face value, but Noah seemed reluctant to spell it out.

'Seen them doing what?' Jude prompted.

'You know...'

'No,' said Jude. 'I don't.'

'In a *compromised* state together.' Noah blushed deeply.

'Are you talking about having sex?'

'That's it.'

'No,' she said. 'No way! You must have misheard.'

She hadn't quite come to terms with the idea of Sarah having an affair, but the idea that it may have been with Charlie was a step too far.

Noah shook his head.

''Fraid not,' he said. 'By the time they came level with me, they were both yelling pretty loud. He was mad at her, said he'd seen them at her cottage.'

'He was paranoid,' said Jude. 'And jealous of Charlie for some reason. It was all rubbish. There was never anything other than friendship between those two.'

'Not quite true, as it happens,' said Noah. 'She didn't deny it, just got very weepy and told him it had only happened that one time and that it was a big mistake.'

Jude's already topsy-turvy world began to tilt again, throwing her even more off balance.

'I can't believe it,' she said. 'Charlie and Sarah?'

'Like I said, I wouldn't have mentioned it. None of my business really. But then Lucy said that you and that policewoman were trying to find out what happened and you thought Nate was being a bit shifty. I thought I'd tell you and then you know.'

'Lucy told you that?' she asked with a spark of indignation. It wasn't up to Lucy to tell whoever she wanted about their investigation. This wasn't just some bit of exciting gossip to take her mind off her own problems. This was real and serious with equally real and serious consequences if the wrong people found out what they were doing.

'We had a bit of a chat last night whilst you were out.'

'It wasn't really her business to tell you,' said Jude, hearing the stiffness in her own voice. 'Please don't tell anyone else.'

Noah looked affronted.

'Jude,' he said. 'I would hope you'd know me better than that.'

She relaxed. Of course she did. She'd trusted Noah more times than she could remember and she knew he was the epitome of discretion.

'Sorry,' she said. 'I'm just a bit jumpy at the moment. What with everything that's happened.'

'Well, I'm here for you if you need anything,' he said. 'Especially broccoli.'

He smiled unexpectedly and nodded to the grass a little way behind Jude. She followed his gaze and found Sebbie, sitting with his legs out straight in front of him, guzzling the raw broccoli as though it was manna from heaven.

'Don't worry,' said Noah. 'Plenty more where that came from.'

Jude took Sebbie back to the house where Lucy had set the table for breakfast.

'Ah, there you are,' she said. 'I thought the chickens must have eaten you.'

She scooped Sebbie up and kissed him all over his head and face until he squawked in annoyance and wriggled to be put down.

'We stopped off at Noah's to drop some eggs off,' said Jude. 'He said you might have mentioned our investigation to him.'

Lucy looked a little awkward.

'I didn't intend to,' she said. 'It's just he's a really good listener.'

Any anger Jude had initially felt had dissipated on her way back to the farm and anyway, Lucy was right, Noah was a good listener.

'You haven't mentioned it to anyone else?' she said. 'Not Charlie, for example, when he took you out on the boat?'

Lucy crossed her two index fingers over her lips.

'Not a word,' she said.

'Noah just told me he heard Nate and Sarah arguing up in the fields a while back,' she said. 'He thinks Sarah was having an affair with Charlie.'

'Charlie? If that's true, why was she using the initial N?'

'She wouldn't have,' said Jude. 'Noah must have got it wrong.'

'Unless she had a nickname for him...'

'I don't think she did,' said Jude. 'She called Ben Ivy, and Adam was always Apple...' She pointed to where her Adam's apple would have been if she'd had one. 'But I only ever remember her calling Charlie by his real name.'

'Can you ask him?'

'I guess so. I need to call Ben first, though. I'm sure there was something he wanted to talk about yesterday but couldn't because Tilda was there.'

She looked at her watch and saw that there was still time to catch him before school started, so she took her chance and dialled his number.

'Hi, Jude,' he said. 'What's up?'

'I just wanted to check up on you,' Jude said.

'Why?'

'Something isn't right,' she said. 'I only have to look at you to see it. I know you say it's down to a lack of sleep and I know you miss Sarah but that's not all, is it?'

'Jude, I'm not sure what you want me to say.'

'Whatever it was you wanted to tell Charlie and me at the pub yesterday,' Jude said. 'Because neither of us bought the bullshit about just wanting to meet up with friends.'

'It's not a great time, Jude,' said Ben. 'I've got to get to work.'

'Why don't you come round after school today?' she suggested. 'Have a proper chat?'

'I can't,' he said. 'I've got a stack of marking.'

Jude definitely felt as though she was receiving the fob off.

'Fine,' she said. 'Just promise me you'll do two things?'

'What?'

'Look after yourself better and talk to Charlie and me very

soon. It's what Sarah should have done. Who knows, she might still be with us if she had.'

'I'm not going to end up like that,' said Ben. 'I promise. I really am just exhausted and done in, what with the wedding and then Sarah. It's been high on the stress scale all around recently, hasn't it?'

This was a fact Jude couldn't argue with. Instead, she blew him a kiss down the phone and told him to be in touch soon.

*   *   *

With the sprayer prepped for the early flowering rapeseed, Jude climbed up into the cab of the John Deere. Once she'd explained how slowly the tractor would be going, how safe they'd be in the cab and how the air conditioning would keep the totally organic spray outside, Jude was surprised to see how quickly Lucy agreed to it. An overexcited Sebbie was passed up to her before Lucy climbed in after, pulling the door shut and testing it to make sure it wasn't about to spring open again.

'Dactor,' said Sebbie, bouncing on Lucy's knee in excitement.

'Ready to go?' said Jude.

Jude drove out into the sea of bright green leaves and stems with a good scattering of mustard-yellow flowers, the first of the season, just showing themselves. She paused to drop the spraying arms.

'Look,' she said to Sebbie who turned to watch the long arms hinge down.

'Press this button for me,' she said, which Sebbie did, starting the sprayers. 'Brilliant, now don't push any other buttons until I tell you.'

Lucy crossed her arms over the boy like a human seatbelt.

'It's much quieter in here than I thought,' she said.

'Not a bad bit of kit,' said Jude proudly. 'I'll take you out in Maz, the old Massey, one day. Now she's a little bit different to this.'

As she took the tractor carefully across the field, Jude looked sideways at her sister and nephew. Both were gazing out of the window in wonder and it made Jude bubble inside with a mix of love and pride.

Whilst Sebbie remained totally transfixed on what was happening outside with the sprayer head, the novelty waned for Lucy and her concentration moved on to talk of the investigation.

'The more I think of it, the more I'm certain that CB, who *must* be Crystal-May-Rose, by the way, is mixed up with Les Turner somehow,' she said.

'I agree,' said Jude. 'It's all too much of a coincidence. Her being arrested for dealing with stolen goods and then Sarah uncovering the stash house which, if we read Sarah's Lexigle clues properly, has to be something to do with Les Turner.'

'Do you think they're in business together?'

'Wouldn't be the daftest suggestion,' said Jude. 'And it would also explain why she might want to take the diary if she stumbled across it in the spa.'

'Then we've got the mystery of N, who may or may not be Charlie.'

'Not,' said Jude decisively.

Lucy sat in thought for little while, allowing Jude to do the same.

'I take it you haven't heard anything else from Binnie yet about the other body?'

'Nothing,' said Jude.

As though she'd been listening in to their conversation, DS Khatri's name flashed up on the screen, Jude's phone starting to ring at that very moment.

'Hi,' Binnie said when Lucy answered it and flicked it to

speaker for Jude to hear. 'I haven't got long but I thought you'd like to know they've identified the man from the pit. Raoul Toussaint, a known criminal from Birmingham with a list of convictions as long as your arm. Really nasty piece of work, he's done it all and get this, he was on the watch list from the team investigating the organised crime ring my DI is trying to crack.'

'What was he doing in Malvern End?' Jude asked.

'No idea,' said Binnie. 'I've got to go but I'll let you know if I find anything else.'

The line went dead and the two sisters looked at each other.

'Bloody hell,' said Lucy.

'My thoughts exactly,' said Jude.

28

Back at the house, Jude tried calling Crystal-May-Rose again but the receptionist told her that Crystal was in the middle of a treatment.

'I can get her to give you a ring back?' she offered.

'Don't worry,' said Jude. 'I'll catch her after work. What time does she finish today?'

'Five o'clock.'

'Bingo,' Jude said, turning to Lucy. 'I think I'll pay our CB a little visit when she finishes work. Do you mind if I also go and see Granny Margot?'

'Course not,' said Lucy. 'We could come with you if you like?'

'Do you know what? I think Margot would love that.'

* * *

Jude, it turned out, was absolutely right about Granny Margot, whose face lit up like a child on Christmas morning when she saw her three guests. The afternoon had clouded over and March drizzle had taken a firm hold on the county. Margot was playing

Scrabble with another resident of the retirement home, but she quickly excused herself and shakily got to her legs with the help of a walking frame.

'Sorry to disturb you,' said Jude.

'Not a bit. Frida isn't quite the Scrabble player she used to be. It's getting embarrassing how easily I win these days.'

She looked back at her Scrabble mate, who'd clearly heard and wasn't impressed by the comment.

'Come on,' said Granny Margot. 'Let's go and sit over there where we've got a bit more space to spread out. Now, Lucy, my dear, when was the last time we saw each other? Certainly not since the arrival of this handsome boy.'

Lucy beamed at the compliment and put a hand out to help guide Margot into a high-backed chair. Lucy had trained as a nurse and had always taken the responsibilities of her job very seriously, saying that the mental health of her patients was every bit as important as their physical symptoms. She'd often talked about the patients on the care of the elderly ward with such tenderness, and Jude knew she missed it greatly, but Sebbie's place in her life made shift work difficult, so she'd had to give up nursing to work as a cleaner instead.

Margot rooted in the basket of her walking frame and found a bag of fudge squares. She took one out, undressed it from its cellophane wrapper and passed it to Sebbie, who was only too pleased to take a bite.

'Now then,' said Margot. 'Tell me everything. I want to know about the farm and the lambs. Has this little chap been on a tractor? Is the rapeseed out yet? I do so love seeing the first yellow fields of the season.'

Jude and Lucy did as Margot asked and she listened in captivation as they told her about the comings and goings of the village she'd grown up in and the countryside that was a part of her bones. Sebbie behaved immaculately, sitting still for a change and chipping in when asked about his penchant for raw broccoli and his first trip on a tractor. Every time he started to wriggle or squirm, Margot passed him another square of fudge and it didn't escape Jude's notice that Lucy said nothing. It was just as well Noah had plenty of purple sprouting broccoli because Jude had the feeling Lucy might be putting Sebbie on a strict diet of veggies for the rest of the week.

'And the boys,' Margot asked. 'How are they?'

'They miss Sarah,' said Jude. 'Both of them, but Ben particularly seems to have taken it really badly. He looks quite ill.'

'He was always more delicate than the other two,' said Margot. 'Charlie and your Adam. Shame, though, what with him being freshly married. Do you like her? The new wife, I mean. Sarah wasn't very sure of her.'

'She's an acquired taste,' said Jude tactfully.

'And you haven't yet acquired it?' Margot's eyes sparkled.

'Nothing gets past you.' Jude smiled.

'Did Sarah have any nicknames for Charlie that you know of?' Lucy asked. 'We know about Ivy and Apple but what about Charlie?'

'No.' Granny Margot shrugged. 'Funny, isn't it? She might have, at one time, but it obviously didn't stick like the other two for some reason.'

'Can you have a think?' asked Lucy. 'Maybe something that started with N?'

Granny Margot looked a little confused. Jude thought that Lucy had pushed too hard.

'Don't worry,' she said quickly. 'It doesn't matter.'

'It obviously does, or you wouldn't have asked.'

'It's just that Sarah met up with someone with that initial and we know it wasn't Nate,' said Lucy. 'We're trying to figure out who it could be and we wondered if it could have been a nickname she used for Charlie.'

'Why don't you ask him?'

Jude had absolutely no intention of giving Granny Margot even the tiniest hint that Sarah had been having an affair, so she brushed it off quickly.

'I will,' she said.

'And what of our little investigation?' Margot asked, lowering her voice. 'The police tell me nothing. I suppose they think I'm in here because my wits are going, not my body.'

Jude paused for a moment, thinking about just how much to reveal. She opted for a diluted version of the truth, telling her about the stolen diary and the trip to the spa to see Crystal-May-Rose, but missing out the pathology conclusion of suicide being the most plausible cause of death. She avoided any more talk of Sarah's debts and Margot didn't ask. There seemed little point in worrying her with sketchy half details of what they'd found on Sarah's laptop, but she did show her the photos she'd printed out.

'Do you recognise either of these people?' she asked.

Granny Margot took the glasses she kept on a crocheted cord around her neck and slipped them onto her nose to take a careful look.

'I'm afraid I don't,' she said. 'Are they important?'

'I don't know,' said Jude. 'I think Sarah found something out about them but we haven't really got much else to go on.'

Granny Margot stared at the photos again.

'No,' she said, taking off her glasses and letting them hang from their cord. 'I've never seen either of them.'

Margot suddenly leant forward and took both of Jude's hands tightly. Her forehead was a map of deep wrinkles and her eyes were full of torment.

'She needs a good send-off,' she said. 'Our darling girl. I can't stand the thought of her still being stuck in some big fridge some-where. She needs to be laid to rest properly on the hills, near the spot I sprinkled the ashes of her mother.'

Jude squeezed Margot's hands and felt her own eyes start to tear up – the pain of this amazing old woman who'd been forced to bear the grief of losing a child not once, but twice.

'It's going to be a while before they release her,' Jude said. 'But, when they do, we'll plan a proper goodbye, together. I promise.'

Margot gave a thin smile and closed her eyes for just a moment. When she opened them again, she was almost back to her sparkling self. She called Sebbie over and Lucy helped him up to sit on the old woman's knee where she told him a wonderful story full of folklore and fairies. Her sharp imagination and clever wit were enough to keep even the wriggliest of two-year-olds entranced.

'Well now,' Gerwain said, walking in. 'You're popular this morning, Margot. How lovely to see you all.'

He smiled at Jude warmly. 'How are those dancing feet?'

'AWOL since the wedding I'm afraid,' she replied.

'That's a shame. It's time for armchair yoga in here now so I'm afraid we're going to have to clear the day room so Rog can set up.'

'Good-o,' said Margot. 'Rog is very good at yoga. Incredibly stretchy. You should stay and have a go.'

'You'd be very welcome,' said Gerwain. 'All of you, I mean.'

Jude smiled. 'Thanks, but we'd better be getting off. I'll come back soon, Margot.'

She gave the old woman a kiss on both cheeks, taking in the scent of roses and talc.

'And you, young man?' Margot asked Sebbie. 'Will you come and see old Granny Margot soon too?'

'I'll make sure of it,' said Lucy.

* * *

When they left the retirement home, the sun was already starting to slip behind the west side of the hills. Jude looked at her phone.

'Crystal will be leaving work fairly soon,' she said. 'We'd better go.'

She pulled into a space in the spa car park with a good view of the main door, switched the engine off and undid her seatbelt.

'You'd probably be best to stay in the car with Sebbie,' she said. 'I don't know what Crystal will have to say but she's not going to be in a good mood and I get the feeling that, under all that calm crap, she's actually pretty feisty.'

'She's been arrested for GBH and handling stolen goods,' said Lucy. 'I think your deduction might be spot on, Sherlock!'

Sebbie wasn't altogether happy being stuck in his car seat. He arched his back and grumbled to be let out until, eventually, Lucy gave in and pulled his pushchair from the boot of the car.

'We'll wander over to the shops,' she said. 'I could do with buying some teething powders for him anyway. Call me when you're done.'

In the end, Jude was so busy helping Lucy strap the toddler into his pushchair that she almost missed Crystal when she came out. She was already heading to her car when Jude spotted her.

She ran over, less poised than she'd imagined being.

'Crystal,' she said, reaching her just as Crystal blipped the lock of her Mini. 'Could we have a word?'

'Oh.' Crystal opened the back door and threw her bag onto the seat. 'It's you. Sorry, I'm late for something.'

'I just need a couple of minutes,' said Jude. 'I wanted to ask you some questions about Sarah.'

Crystal slammed the back door and stared at Jude.

'I've got nothing to say. I'm sorry for your loss but like I said, I have to be somewhere.'

She opened the driver's door and put one leg in.

'I know about the charges,' Jude blurted out. 'The GBH and the stolen goods.'

Crystal froze for a second. Half in and half out of the car.

'She told you then?' she said. 'I wondered if she had.'

So, Jude's suspicion had been right: Sarah *had* known about the charges.

'Let me guess, you're going to have a pop at blackmailing me too? Well, you can go to hell. I've had enough. If you really want to tell my boss what you know then go ahead. I was cleared of those charges and I've been through enough already because of them. Did Sarah tell you I was forced into it because I fell in love with the wrong man? Instead of the police helping me, they arrested me.'

'No, I...' said Jude, stumbling over her words. 'I didn't know, I'm sorry.'

'Do what you like,' said Crystal. 'I can't keep running.'

Before Jude could do or say anything else, Crystal slammed the door and reversed from her parking space at great speed. Jude stepped quickly out of the way to allow the Mini to disappear from the car park.

For a moment she stared after it, in a state of mild stupor. The Sarah she'd known wouldn't have stooped as low as blackmail, no matter how bad things got, so Crystal must have got the wrong end of the stick. Either that or she was lying through her teeth – but for what reason? Yet again, Jude felt herself sliding further from the truth, feeling the hugeness of the things she didn't understand. Not just about the blurry facts surrounding Sarah's death, but about Sarah herself too.

* * *

Back at the farm, with Sebbie well fed, bathed and safely tucked up in bed, Jude and Lucy looked at the two printed photos again. Jude stared hard at the close-up of the woman. Her face was definitely familiar, but it was still a little like grasping for the wisps of a lost dream; the more Jude tried to place her, the more the woman's identity bobbed away. What if she was wrong about Crystal-May-Rose and this woman was actually CB?

'Why can't I remember who she is?' she said in frustration.

'Don't beat yourself up,' said Lucy. 'Let's put these away and have a poke around on the internet for any inspiration on those last Lexigle words.'

'You go ahead,' said Jude, getting up. 'I can't think any more about Father, Grange or bloody Barley. Every time I look online, I just end up in a whirlpool of nonsense.'

As she filled the Belfast sink with hot water and a squeeze of washing-up liquid, Jude thought how strange it was that millions of people all over the world had become obsessed with solving daily word puzzles that her friend had helped put together. She hoped that this knowledge had brought Sarah a certain amount of pride and happiness in her otherwise troubled last few months. And then she thought of Crystal-May-Rose and realised that pride was almost certainly *not* something Sarah would have been feeling if she really had stooped as low as blackmail. And if she *had* been capable of blackmailing Crystal-May-Rose, then there was the awful possibility that she may also have tried the more dangerous game of blackmailing Les Turner.

29

DS Binnie Khatri was at the farm before breakfast the next morning.

'I'm sorry it's so early,' she said. 'I thought I'd drop in on my way to work and I somehow knew you'd be up.'

Jude was indeed up. She'd risen with the larks and the lambs, had already carried out her early morning jobs and was back in the kitchen with Pancake, who was bleating gently for the bottle Jude had started to prepare for her. The lamb clearly loved company and had become so affectionate that Jude decided to bring her inside for her morning feed. Noah had warned Jude about getting too close, but there was something about the tenacity and life-joy in the little bundle that gave her a heady intoxication she could only imagine was akin to a maternal instinct.

'I'm glad you called by,' Jude said. 'I was going to call you today anyway.'

'You have something?'

'Here,' she said, passing Pancake's bottle to the surprised DS. 'You finish this off and I'll stick the kettle on.'

Binnie bent down to offer the bottle to Pancake, who grasped it so tightly between her teeth that Binnie almost dropped it. She adjusted her position, squatting down to the lamb's height, and stroked her soft fleece as Pancake guzzled hungrily.

'I went back to see Crystal-May-Rose yesterday,' said Jude. 'She told me that Sarah had been trying to blackmail her. I knew Sarah and I know that, if this is true, she'd have had to be completely at rock bottom and terrified of what would happen if she didn't find the money. It also made me think about your theory that the Lexigle clues may have been set as a blackmail tool for Les Turner.'

'If that's right then Sarah was definitely treading on thin ice.'

Binnie shifted Pancake's bottle into her other hand so she could reach into her bag and pull out a piece of paper.

'Look,' she said, handing it over. 'Recognise him?'

Jude looked at the mug shot.

'It's the man from the photos Sarah took,' she said, recognising him instantly.

'Yes,' said Binnie. 'That's Raoul Toussaint, the body from the pit and part of the organised crime group my boss is investigating. So, if Les Turner *is* involved in the stolen goods, then there's a chance that he's also involved in the OCG that Raoul was part of.'

Jude swallowed hard. 'And that would make him even more dangerous than we thought.'

Sebbie was highly indignant when he came into the kitchen and found someone else feeding Pancake, a role he clearly thought should be solely his. The indignation was soon replaced by delight as the lamb drained the last few drops of milk and turned to see Sebbie. She bleated an excited greeting and skittered across the flagstones to nudge the boy in the stomach, before peeing on the floor.

'Canpake, no!' said Sebbie, his face a picture of horror. 'No pee on floor. Canpake need potty.'

At the exact moment he ran over to pick up his potty from the corner, Lucy walked in with an armful of laundry destined for the utility room. She took one look at the small boy waving his potty at a lamb who was skipping about in front of the Detective Sergeant, a puddle on the floor between them that could only either have come from sheep or boy, and she let out a groan.

'I swear my life just gets more surreal every day!'

Jude grabbed an old towel and mopped up the puddle whilst Lucy put on a load of washing.

Binnie thought tea would be a good idea, so she took the whistling kettle off the hot Aga plate and made a large pot. She also took the bread, ready in the toasting grills, and put it under the lid of the hot plates before getting out milk and mugs.

'Thank you,' said Jude, adding plates, knives and butter to the kitchen table and sweeping the rest of the detritus to one side. 'You must think this place is a permanent nut house.'

'No,' said Binnie. 'In fact, I think it's a lovely, warm place to be.'

Jude noted a pensive tone to Binnie's words and, when she looked, she saw that her facial expression matched. It made Jude wonder about the private life of the DS. Jude realised she knew nothing about this woman who'd become tangled in her life but she didn't like to pry.

'Well, you are welcome here any time you like,' she found herself saying. 'If you can cope with this level of chaos on a Wednesday morning and still think it's a lovely place to be then you are definitely my kind of person.'

Around the breakfast table, the three women talked, putting together everything they'd learnt between them, whilst at their feet, a toddler, a collie-cross and a lamb played on the floor. The more they talked, the more the links between Les Turner, Raoul Toussaint, Crystal-May-Rose, the stolen goods and the organised crime group became less theory and more fact in their minds. The only thing they were lacking was concrete evidence – evidence which they hoped the three remaining Lexigle clues might help uncover, if they were ever able to figure them out.

'I think it's time I took this to my boss,' said Binnie. 'Now that this thing has escalated, potentially giving an insight into the OCG case, I have no choice.'

'Will you get into trouble?' said Jude.

'The only thing that's really going to get me into hot water is the laptop. I shouldn't have it in the first place and I definitely should have handed it in straight away. What I've done counts as withholding evidence.'

'What *we've* done,' corrected Jude. 'We did this together and I won't let you take the rap.'

'What if it was anonymously handed in?' Lucy suggested. 'Perhaps with a typed note saying exactly what to look for in the files?'

'Not a bad plan,' said Binnie. 'It could be left for my attention which would also explain why my fingerprints would be all over it. And it would make sense that Jude's were also there, as Sarah's best friend.'

'I haven't touched it,' said Lucy. 'So there shouldn't be any of mine there.'

'This could work,' said Jude.

Binnie's phone rang.

'Good morning, sir,' she said. 'Yes, sorry. I'm on my way now.'

Ending the call, she stood up apologetically.

'That was my boss,' she said. 'I'm late. I'd better go.'

'What shall I do with the laptop?' Jude asked.

'Keep it here for today. There's CCTV everywhere at the station so I'll come and get it after work and take it in tomorrow. I'll say it was dropped off on my doorstep.'

She took a USB memory stick from her bag and put it on the table.

'I brought this for you,' she said. 'I still think it would be helpful for us to have a copy of the files for ourselves.'

* * *

With the kitchen to herself, Jude digested the latest developments. The clear link between Raoul, the body from the pit, and Sarah's investigations into the room of stolen goods was pointing them into ever murkier water. Jude took the laptop from the cupboard where she'd been hiding it and put it on the kitchen table. She switched it on and waited until it fired up so she could push the memory stick into the port on the computer.

When she searched for the corresponding drive on the file menu, it wasn't listed.

'Damnit,' said Jude, pulling the memory stick out of the port and blowing into the end. She put it in for another go. The computer still didn't register it and, when Jude gave it a wiggle to see if that would change anything, the end snapped off inside the machine.

'Bollocks,' she cursed.

She peered into the port. Perhaps she might be able to get purchase on the broken end if she was careful with a pair of tweezers. There were some in the drawer of the dresser, kept there for the removal of splinters – just one of the hazards of working on the land. The book Sarah had been reading was still in there too, looking sorry and unloved, so Jude took it out and looked at the front cover: a pastel mix of blue sea, yellow sand and a pink and green parasol with a pair of tanned legs sticking out of the bottom. She sighed and put it on the table, wondering if she'd ever get around to reading it.

The tweezers were just the thing and it took seconds for the broken piece of memory stick to be extracted from the laptop.

She'd have to get another from somewhere before Binnie came back but it wasn't the sort of thing that Mrs James would sell in the village shop.

A knock on the old front door surprised her as everyone she knew just came straight round to the kitchen entrance that led in from the yard. Nobody ever went to the bother of walking along the little overgrown lane, which split the garden from the orchard, and then up the lavender-lined path so they could use the front door.

She went to answer it and was even more surprised to see Nate Sanchez on the other side.

30

Jude's initial thought was to turn Nate away. She went to close the door on him, but he put a hand out to stop her.

'I don't deserve your time,' he said awkwardly. 'But if you've got ten minutes, could I come in?'

Jude wanted to say no, he couldn't, but Nate's expression made her think again. There was something she recognised behind the dark, bloodshot eyes. It was something that she knew so very well herself. His were the eyes of someone racked with the same raw grief and agony she'd seen in the mirror after Adam died. Her suffering was reflected back at her in the way Nate's eyes showed a heart broken from the pain of losing someone you loved.

'My sister and her child are inside,' she said. 'Perhaps we can go down to the orchard and talk there instead.'

Nate's face remained tense as he nodded.

Jude pushed her feet into a pair of slip-on garden shoes from the porch and called back into the house to tell Lucy where she was going.

'Noah will be in the lambing shed if you need anything,' she

added. It didn't hurt to let Nate know there was help on hand if
things got tricky between them. The memory of the bruise on
Sarah's head came into her mind and she gritted her teeth. She'd
perhaps seen another layer to Nate, but she still didn't trust him
and she definitely didn't like him.

The orchard was at its most beautiful in the spring. Most of the
trees were apple, with a smattering of pears on one side, and a row
of cherries on the other. The blossom was just starting to show,
pale pink of the apple trees in the middle, bordered by dark cerise
of the cherries. The orchard would be at its very best in another
few weeks: the white blossom of the pear trees would need a little
more time in the sun before it started to make its appearance.

Spring had always been Adam's favourite time, despite the
busyness of the lambing season. They'd had picnics under the
blossom trees when the weather was nice enough and they'd
giggled when the wind blew and the petals fell like great gusts of
confetti into their metal tumblers of cider.

As Jude led Nate down to the orchard, she found herself
talking to Adam in her head, wishing yet again that he was there
with her, taking the reins for the difficult conversation ahead and
setting everyone at ease with his lazy smile and gentle coun-
tenance.

'Please shut the gate behind you,' she said. 'The chickens are
free-range but only within the orchard.'

'Thank you for seeing me,' said Nate, closing the gate and refit-
ting the piece of baling twine over the post to secure it. 'I know I
was rude when you came to visit me. I was just surprised to see you
and I didn't really want to talk to anyone.'

'And now you do?'

'I'm not sure,' Nate said. 'But I did want to come and apologise.'

'Well, if you're not sure about talking, then we'd better find something else to do. We're a working farm.' She gestured around her. 'And there's always plenty of work.'

She walked through the trees to the side of the orchard that housed the chicken coops. Noah had already been out that morning to let the hens out for the day. She opened the door of a small shed and passed out a basket to Nate. She then took a second basket and the two went through the coops, one by one, retrieving the fresh eggs from the hatches at the back. Nate was quiet but intent as he filled his basket and Jude heard him speaking gently to some of the bolder hens who came over to check out the newbie on their patch. She listened as he thanked them for the eggs and complimented them on a good job.

'You have a way with them,' she said, noticing how he'd softened in their company.

'They seem very small for chickens,' he said.

'They're bantam hens,' she explained. 'It's a small breed but they do lay the most wonderful eggs. You should take some back with you. I promise you'll be a bantam convert.'

Once all the eggs had been collected, Jude sat on a bench under an apple tree and gestured for Nate to join her. She realised that she too had softened a little as she'd watched him with the hens. Perhaps it was, as Lucy had suggested, a case of dreadful shyness that gave him such a prickly edge. But the way he'd used Sarah's word games and not given her a share of the profits still very much bothered her, as did the bruise and Sarah's caginess when Jude had pointed it out.

'Did you love Sarah?' she asked.

Nate looked taken aback at the abruptness of the question and Jude didn't think he was going to answer. A spider was busy spinning a new web in the arm of the bench next to him and Nate watched the arachnid's endeavours intently for a moment or two.

'Sorry,' she said. 'I didn't mean to be rude. I just don't know you and yet you were such an important part of my best friend's life. I suppose I'm just trying to fill the gaps.'

'That's my fault,' he said, still watching the spider's progress. 'Sarah wanted me to get to know you all. She asked me so many times to come out with you but I found it all a bit daunting. You're all so close and I was the outsider. It was hard to know what to say and I'm not really very good with people.' He looked at her then. 'Never have been. But Sarah was different. She understood me and was patient and kind, and yes, I loved her. I loved her very, very much indeed.'

The revelation seemed to take a lot out of Nate and he broke eye contact immediately to stare at something that was supposedly exceedingly interesting by his feet. He seemed genuine enough, Jude thought. Either that or he was a very good actor. She still had plenty of questions, though.

'How did Sarah bruise her face?' she said, attempting to ask the question without accusation but she could feel it drip from her words as obviously as if she'd asked him outright if he'd been the one to deliver the punishing blow.

Bizarrely, Nate didn't seem to notice.

'She hit it on a shelf,' he said. 'I think she was doing some housework or something like that. Why do you ask?'

This was not the story Sarah had told her, yet Jude found she believed Nate. He just didn't seem like the sort of person who could trip lies off so easily and so convincingly. He was a blunderer, someone who found communication tricky.

'Just gap filling,' said Jude. 'Why didn't you help Sarah repay her debts?'

Nate looked up, horrified.

'I didn't know about them,' he said. 'Not until the police told me. She asked me for some money and it will always be my saddest regret that I didn't give it to her.'

'She asked you for help?' Jude stood up in horror. 'She came to you asking for money that you owed her because, let's face it, without Sarah there would have been no Lexigle in the first place, and you said no?'

Jude could feel her whole body shaking with rage. Seventy thousand would have hardly made a dent in the sum she knew Nate had received when Lexigle sold. It had been bad enough that he hadn't volunteered to give Sarah her share, but for her to have asked for it outright and for him to turn her down – that was beyond anything she'd believed possible from him.

Nate shrank into the bench.

'Believe me, I know that,' he said. 'But it wasn't that simple. The money wasn't really there to give her.'

'I can't imagine money was ever much of an issue to you,' spat Jude.

'It didn't make us anything at the beginning,' said Nate. 'But then it snowballed really quickly and the offers of sponsorship and sales started to come in.'

'So why the hell didn't you share that with Sarah?'

Nate picked a twig up off the ground and started to snap it into ever smaller pieces, still whilst avoiding eye contact.

'We talked about it when we first realised there was money to be made,' he said. 'But we both agreed that we wanted to use Lexigle for good. The only luxuries I bought when I sold Lexigle were the house, which I really hoped to share with Sarah one day, and an engagement ring that I never got to give her.'

Jude didn't allow herself to soften at this.

'The money you made from Lexigle would have stretched further than a house and a ring,' she said.

'I don't know if Sarah ever told you about my sister? She lives in Argentina and found herself stuck in a very dangerous marriage.'

Jude nodded. 'I know.'

'A lot of the money was sent over to enable her to get out. I bought her a house and set up trust funds for my nieces to give them better opportunities in life. I saw what poverty had done for my parents and for my sister and I wanted to make a difference to them.'

'And it's great that you could,' said Jude. 'But are you really telling me that there was nothing left for Sarah?'

'Two point eight million pounds doesn't actually stretch all that far once you've bought two houses,' Nate said. 'But yes, there was some money left and if she'd told me about her debts then of course I would have given her everything she needed. But she didn't. She didn't say what she wanted the money for and, when I asked, she just backtracked and said that it didn't matter. Every day I wake up wishing for the opportunity to go back and just give her the money, no questions asked.'

He appeared to be genuine in his grief and his remorse for everything that had happened, and Jude bought it. Or at least she was pretty sure she did.

'You said she stopped writing clues for Lexigle months ago when she got her promotion,' she said. 'Why did she start again?'

'I didn't know she'd told you she had,' said Nate. 'She asked me to keep it a secret. It was strange, really – she was very specific in that she wanted to write just two weeks' worth of clues and they had to come out in a certain order on certain days. It was a bit tricky to clear it with the new owners but we're still in the handover phase so I could make it happen.'

Jude didn't think that was strange at all. In fact, Nate Sanchez had just confirmed exactly what she'd expected about Sarah's fourteen carefully chosen words.

The bang of the orchard gate made Jude look up to see Noah striding through the grass towards them.

'Everything all right?' he asked. 'Lucy said you'd come in here.'

Nate's face closed down again as though shutters had been pulled across.

'Yes, thanks,' she said. 'This is Nate, Sarah's boyfriend.'

'I know,' said Noah, frostily.

'We were just having a chat,' she said, not wanting Nate to clam up altogether now that she felt as though she'd had a bit of a breakthrough. 'Lucy's in the house if you want to have a cuppa with her and Sebbie. I'll come and find you when we're finished.'

Noah didn't look too happy about leaving her in Nate's company but he picked up the baskets of eggs and took them with him back up to the house.

'Sorry about that,' she said. 'He has a tendency to get protective of me since my husband died.'

'I'm glad you have someone like that in your life,' said Nate. 'I really mustn't take any more of your time up, though. I just wanted to come and apologise and, well, I have now.'

'No need to go,' said Jude. 'There were things I wanted to ask you.'

'Another time.' He stood up. The slight opening Jude had witnessed had gone and he was yet again the tight-lipped, difficult version of himself. There was little point in pursuing things further. But she couldn't unsee what she'd noticed – this different Nate who'd come to her, talked about Sarah with tenderness and care. And she believed him: about the bruise, his family in Argentina, the money and his love for Sarah. The fact that he'd planned to marry Sarah and for them to live together in the house on Avenue Road also made her question what he actually knew of Sarah's affair and if he'd forgiven anything he'd stumbled upon.

Nate started to make his way through the track at the bottom of the garden, heading back to his car, but Jude stopped him.

'You must take some eggs with you, remember,' she said. 'We'll go through the house and I'll box some up.'

Lucy, Sebbie and Noah were in the kitchen when they walked in and Noah glowered at Nate, who shifted uneasily under his scrutiny. Lucy held out her hand and introduced herself but Nate was still the awkward, slightly acidic man. He thanked Jude curtly for the eggs and then left to escape back to his car for a desperate getaway.

'I see what you mean,' said Lucy. 'What an unpalatable guy.'

'Don't know what Sarah ever saw in him,' said Noah.

'Actually,' said Jude, 'I think I do.'

It surprised Jude as much as Noah but she really had seen a very different side to Nate that morning.

Noah remained in a bad mood for the rest of the morning.

When Jude went out to give him a flask of tea, she found him stomping around the empty barn, sweeping out all the old bedding and piling it up to be taken to the muck heap.

'You should have said you were doing that today,' she said. 'I'll give you a hand.'

'Don't worry,' said Noah. 'I'm almost done.'

'Well, at least come in for some lunch with me and Lucy when you're finished.'

'I'm going to be busy out here for a while yet.'

'Sebbie will be disappointed,' she said. 'He's been busy making fairy cakes with Lucy and I know he'd want you to sample them.'

Noah thawed a little at this and promised to join them in the kitchen when he'd finished loading up the trailer with the muck.

Sebbie was ready for him with a little cake covered in yellow icing and decorated with a slice of slightly squashed strawberry. Noah took it with the appropriate amount of appreciative noises but Jude could tell he was still out of sorts. She wasn't sure if it was because of Nate's visit to the farm or the fact that she had changed her view of him. Either way, he was a bundle of barely subdued fury.

When Pancake, who was back in the farmhouse for her second bottle of the day, deposited a little pile of lamb droppings on the floor, Noah lost it.

'What's that lamb still doing in your kitchen?' he bellowed. 'I told you it's bad news to pet a lamb. They're not s'posed to be indoor animals and you're doing her no favours.'

'Hey,' said Jude, putting a hand on his sleeve. 'What's going on with you?'

He held her gaze for a second but then shrugged her hand off and stomped to the door.

'I'll be up in the top field if you need me,' he said before leaving.

'What was that all about?' Lucy asked when the door shut behind him.

'I've no idea. He's no fan of Nate but even so, I've never seen him behave like that.'

Lucy didn't respond as she'd spotted Sarah's paperback on the table. 'Any good?'

'I don't know. I found it at Sarah's cottage and it just looked so sorry for itself with the bookmark sticking out halfway – I thought I should bring it back here.'

'I didn't know you were so sentimental.'

'I'm not usually. And I don't get to read anything these days anyway.'

'How about we just take the bookmark out and give it to the charity shop? Take the guilt away.'

Lucy turned the book on its side and fanned the pages to let the Botticelli cherubs fall onto the table. But the bookmark wasn't the only thing that fell out. Two pieces of paper, folded in half, fluttered down and landed on top of a small smudge of jam that had been missed when they'd tidied up the breakfast things.

Jude picked them up and unfolded the first. On it was a list, written in Sarah's distinctive handwriting.

Extra shifts at work – Not enough
Ask N – wish I hadn't
Scratch cards – lost another £20 SHIT!
Sell cottage – GM said no and I can't ask again
Sell Mum's jewellery – £600 made FFS
Get money from CMR – can't do it. She's got enough going on
Ask LT – use pictures as leverage? Ask N what he thinks first

'What is it?' Lucy asked.

Jude passed the piece of paper over to her sister. The reality of Sarah's plight, so starkly set out in this list of money-making schemes and where they'd got her, made Jude immeasurably sad. And the last idea, confronting Les Turner directly, was frightening given all that she now knew. Had she asked N for help in this decision as the note suggested? And more importantly, who was this N who'd been so important to Sarah that she felt she could ask for their advice rather than one of her closest friends?

'Right,' said Lucy. 'Well, at least we know she didn't take any money from Crystal-May-Rose, so that's something. Although it does mean we're back to square one when it comes to looking for CB because Crystal can't be both CMR *and* CB.'

Jude sighed. 'I suppose not,' she said.

'What's the other bit of paper?' Lucy asked.

Jude unfolded it and saw more of Sarah's writing, slightly less messy this time, as though she was attempting a more formal style.

It was the beginning of a letter. Sarah had only got as far as writing the first line before she'd either been disturbed or changed her mind. But one line was all it took for Jude's world to once again be turned on its head.

> *To whom it may concern,*
>
> *I, Sarah Margot Lloyd, of Malvern End WR13 5KT, would like to confess to the murder of Raoul Toussaint.*

31

Jude could feel any of the colour she had in her cheeks pack its bags and leave, threatening to take her vision with it. She grabbed the back of the closest chair to steady herself until her head cleared enough for her to sit down.

'Bloody hell,' said Lucy. 'Sarah killed Raoul?'

Jude shook her head in disbelief. 'That can't be right.'

'Pass it to me,' said Lucy.

Jude handed the letter over.

'She can't have,' Lucy continued. 'Not on her own, anyway. There's no way someone like Sarah would have been able to get a body into the middle of a wood. If she did kill him then she certainly had help.'

It felt as though someone had sucked Jude's mind out of her, jumbled it up and blown it back in. Never in her life had things made so little sense. Snippets of half thoughts floated around but she could catch nothing.

'Do you think this N character knew about Les Turner too?' she asked.

'Looks like they might have,' said Lucy. 'Which makes me

wonder if they could be the person who helped Sarah get rid of the body?'

She picked up Sarah's pitiful list again and inspected it carefully.

'No,' said Lucy. 'Do you know what, I don't think it is an N. There's a split between the first line, making it look more like two letters. Look.'

She passed it back to Jude, who forced herself to look again. Sarah's writing was dreadful at the best of times but her hand must have been shaking as she'd written this. Jude didn't want to read the words a second time but she focused on the N that Lucy had pointed out. She was right. It was two letters, not one. IV. Did that mean they'd been looking at this wrong the whole time? Searching for the mysterious N who'd been so present and vital in Sarah's diary, the one she had almost certainly been having an affair with?

'I can't think,' said Jude. 'It doesn't make any more sense now than it did when it was an N. I don't know anyone with those initials.'

'Ian?' suggested Lucy. 'Isabel, Imogen, Irene, Iman?'

'No,' said Jude as she tried to rack her brain. 'Nothing.'

'They're not common letters for names,' said Lucy. 'IV. Not many names starting with an I. Isaac?'

'Wait,' said Jude. Somewhere in her mind a horrifying penny was dropping.

'What? Isaac?'

'No,' she said. 'I don't think it's someone's initials. I think it's a nickname. IV. *Ivy*. It's what she used to call Ben.'

'Surely not.'

Jude wished she was wrong but she had a dreadful sense that she'd just stumbled upon a very key piece of this rotten puzzle. Sarah had always loved Ben. It had been such a surprise to everyone who knew them that it hadn't been her walking down the

aisle at his side. If she was going to have an affair with anyone then
it could only really have been Ben and the fact that Noah had
heard Nate and Sarah talking about a fling with Charlie must have
been either a mistake on Noah's part, or a mistake on Nate's part;
he had often got the two boys muddled up.

There was no version of a parallel world where Jude could
imagine either of her friends killing in cold blood. But what if
Raoul had come round and threatened Sarah? If he was working
for Les Turner then this was more than likely, but would she have
used whatever force was needed to stop him? If she had, then Ben
would be the obvious person for her to turn to. But why did they
then get rid of the body if it was self-defence?

Jude couldn't wait any more for answers.

* * *

Ben was at home when she went round to confront him about
Sarah's diary. He was alone, which was a blessing, as the conversation Jude needed to have with him was not one she would have
been able to have in front of Tilda.

'Hey, Jude,' he said when he opened the door. 'How did you
know I was home?'

It was a Wednesday, Jude thought. Of course – Ben should be
teaching.

'I didn't,' she said. 'Are you ill?'

'Something like that,' he said. 'Come in.'

Jude remembered how proud he'd been when he'd taken
possession of the keys to this house, the little 1980s two-up two-
down in a cul-de-sac at the edge of the village. It had been soon
after he'd completed his newly qualified year at the local primary
school. When he threw a housewarming party, the place was
stuffed full of people wishing him well. She'd been there with

Adam, newly married and completely in love. And all the times she'd been there since, celebrating birthdays, sharing takeaways, impromptu evenings watching a film with bowls of popcorn balanced on their knees. Sometimes just the two of them, but more often than not with Adam, Charlie and Sarah. The ghosts of all those happy times played with her as she followed him into the now empty sitting room.

'Are you here to check up on me again?' he asked. 'I told you, I'm all right. Just taking a couple of days out of the classroom to get my head in gear.'

Jude shook her head and took a seat at one end of the sofa, whilst Ben perched at the other end.

'What's happened to us?' she said, aching for the past – the happy group of friends who'd so often filled this very room.

'What do you mean?'

Suddenly, everything felt too much. All the secrets and hidden clues. The things she knew, the things she didn't and, worst of all, the things she wished she hadn't uncovered.

Just by looking at Ben she was certain she was right. N was IV and Ivy was Ben. His gaunt face told her. His wary eyes and haggard forehead. His once naturally well-built frame, now bent and crestfallen.

This was not the look of someone grieving lost friends, this was someone who was carrying a far greater weight than grief alone. This was someone shouldering guilt. A guilt that had ground him down until he was a shell of the person she'd known not that long ago.

Jude had gone there to ask questions and find answers.

'Were you having an affair with Sarah?' she asked bluntly.

For a moment, she thought he would deny it, but he didn't.

'You took her away for her birthday when Nate went off to see his sister, didn't you?' she pressed.

'How did you find out?'

'So, it's true then?'

He nodded.

Jude had to work very hard to keep a lid on her frustration. Her previously neat world full of friendships she'd thought of as uncomplicated had actually been stuffed full of lies.

'Why did you marry Tilda?' she asked. 'You and Sarah were obviously still in love, why the hell didn't you two stay together instead?'

'Money,' said Ben simply. 'I had none and Tilda's family has loads. Don't look at me like that, Jude. I had a taste of what it was like to be facing bankruptcy and losing everything and I didn't ever want to get in that position again.'

'What do you mean, bankruptcy? When?'

'It started when I made a bad investment decision. I had bad advice and poured all my savings into a business that went under within four months. I lost everything.'

Another time, Jude would have felt sorry for him, but she had no space for sympathy now.

'Go on,' she said.

'I needed a loan and I found Les Turner online.'

'Les Turner?' she said incredulously. 'The same guy who shafted Sarah?'

'For me, Les was a shovel that dug me out of a hole. He gave me a low interest rate and plenty of time to pay him back. When I couldn't manage, he offered to call the debt off if I did a bit of work for him.'

'What sort of work?' Jude thought of the photos on Sarah's laptop of the room full of stolen goods. What had Ben got himself tangled up in?

'Nothing much. Just a few deliveries here and there. Mostly in Worcester and a couple in Birmingham. It wasn't a lot, but he said it was enough to call it quits and he was happy to forget the rest of the money.'

There was no doubt whatsoever in Jude's mind that the deliveries Ben had been asked to make were the movement of stolen property. What else would have made someone as ruthless as Les Turner happy to drop the debt?

'Then I met Tilda and she was clearly desperate to get married so I thought it might be a good idea and I proposed.'

'But you kept Sarah as a bit of a hobby, for old times' sake,' Jude hissed, still not able to equate this version of Ben to the friend she thought she'd known for all those years.

'I loved her,' said Ben. 'And I was selfish. I didn't see myself staying with Tilda for very long, and I don't think she'll stick around anyway when she finally realises that I could never leave Malvern End.'

Jude rubbed hard at her temples, wondering how this selfish, blinkered man could be the same generous, funny man she'd met at university.

'Ben,' she asked. 'How did Sarah get tangled up with Les Turner?'

He didn't answer. His body started rocking gently as he turned his face away from her.

'Do you know anything about Raoul Toussaint?' she asked.

There was still no answer, but the rocking stopped and Ben's body stiffened.

'Ben?' shouted Jude. 'What the hell happened?'

He looked up at last, his eyes dry but red-rimmed.

'Oh, fuck,' he said. 'I messed up so badly, Jude. So, so badly.'

'Then let's start putting this right,' she said. 'Tell me everything you know.'

For a moment, Ben stared up at his bookshelf, where a picture of the five friends stood, taken at Jude and Adam's wedding. Eventually he spoke.

'I found out about Sarah's gambling problem and I thought Les could do the same for her as he'd done for me.'

'You sent her to the loan shark?'

Ben winced at the memory.

'Yes, but there's no way I would have done that if I'd have known the sort of trouble she'd get into.'

'Just how much trouble was that?' Jude asked. 'Did Raoul come round?'

Ben nodded.

'Was that when you killed him?'

'No!' said Ben. 'I wasn't even there. She told me about it a couple of days later when I went to see her and asked her why she was so agitated and frightened. It was awful, Jude, she wouldn't stop shaking and I had no idea how to comfort her.'

He stopped talking but Jude needed to know everything. Now that the floodgates had opened, she had to get answers.

'Did you help her move the body?' she asked. 'Did you throw it into the pit?'

'No. She'd already done it and I couldn't blame her, even though she didn't mean to hurt him. He'd been so brutal, taking things from her – precious things that held very little real value, like some of the jewellery from Granny Margot. Sarah tried to stop him but he shoved her so hard she fell and knocked her head on the side of the table.'

'That's how she got the bruise we saw at the wedding? The one you said you thought Nate had given her?'

'It was easier to let you think that,' said Ben. 'And it doesn't change the fact that he was still a dick to Sarah.'

'I can't believe you lied to us all.'

'I promised Sarah I wouldn't say anything. That's when she did it.'

'What?' whispered Jude.

'She picked up the rolling pin from the kitchen table and she cracked him round the face with it. Hard.'

'Bloody hell.' Without her brain wanting it to, the image of Sarah wielding the rolling pin flooded her mind.

'He fell and never got up.'

'Why didn't she call the police?' Jude asked. 'Surely it was an act of self-defence? He was in Sarah's home and that whopping bruise on her head would have shown he'd already been violent.'

Ben was fiddling nervously with the skin around his fingers.

'I don't know,' he said. 'I suppose she was frightened. I wish I'd made her, though. I should have realised how much danger she was in and I should have done more to help her instead of carrying on getting sucked into the plans for that ridiculous charade of a wedding. I don't think I will ever stop feeling guilty about this, Jude.'

Jude didn't answer. She was too busy wondering how much more the world was going to throw at her and what it might reveal about the once close circle of friends. Five people with the world at their feet, ripped apart with now just scraggy remnants of the force they used to be remaining. Adam and Sarah, already gone, and now Ben. Jude knew he would never recover from this.

Jude had, up until this point, still been sure that Sarah wouldn't have killed herself. Despite the overwhelming evidence, she'd thought there was more to it, that someone else had put Sarah in the tree. But suddenly everything she thought she knew about Sarah had changed.

'What are you going to do?' Ben asked.

She looked at her broken friend and her heart wept. It was no wonder he looked so terrible. She wanted to put her arms around him and try to melt the years away, take them back to their uni days when they had nothing more to worry about than final dissertations and looking for NQT teaching positions.

'I'm not going to do anything,' she said.

'You're not?'

'No,' said Jude. 'You are. You know you have to tell the police everything that happened. Not just because it's your moral duty to do so but because you owe it to everyone who loved Sarah and needs answers. You owe it to Sarah and you owe it to yourself to help the police make these vital connections to bring Les Turner to justice. Tell them about the loans, tell them about what jobs you were asked to do for him, and tell them about Raoul. Do you really think you'll ever be able to find any sort of happiness until you do?'

Ben looked like a young boy. Frightened. Out of his depth yet perhaps a little relieved to pass over his guilty secret and let someone else make the decisions. He said nothing but Jude saw him make the tiniest of nods.

'I don't blame you,' she said. 'For what it's worth. There are far darker forces in this whole shitty situation and you and Sarah just got sucked in when you were at your most vulnerable. Sarah wouldn't blame you either. I'm sure of that.'

Internally, she wasn't sure, though. She wasn't sure of anything to do with Sarah now, but she knew it was what Ben needed to hear.

'Thank you,' he whispered. 'And you're right. I'll go to the police today.'

'Ask to speak to DS Binita Khatri,' said Jude. 'Tell her everything.'

'I will.' He paused. 'There are a couple of people I need to see before I go, though. I want to have the chance to tell Charlie myself and I need to do the right thing and break things off with Tilda.'

Jude imagined how those conversations would pan out and a

huge part of her wanted to find a way of cushioning her friend. But this was his mess and he had to face up to the terrible reality of it in order to have a chance of moving forward.

'Just make sure you do it by the end of the day,' she said. 'Or I'll have to do it myself.'

32

The conversation with Ben had drained any reserves Jude had been clinging onto and as she drove back into the farmyard she felt utterly spent. She sat still for a moment, her head resting on the steering wheel.

'What do I do?' she said aloud. 'Adam, help me. What do I do now?'

The house appeared to be empty when she went in, so she threw her bag onto the table and poured herself a glass of water, which she drank in one go with a couple of paracetamol. Propping herself up on the handrail of the Aga, she allowed the warmth to seep through her. She felt rough, really rough, so she pushed her thumbs into the dips of her temples, giving them a hard rub to try to shift some of the tension that had been building up.

Then she heard the sound of the door into the garden open and Lucy's voice, raised in anger. Jude went to see what the matter was and found her on the phone, pacing across the room.

'Yes?' Lucy said. 'Well, in that case I don't think we will ever have anything more to say to one another.'

With a growl, she flung the mobile phone onto the sofa.

'Who was that?' Jude asked.

'Eurgh!' Lucy exclaimed. 'That was our wonderful father. He called and I decided I couldn't avoid him any longer. Big mistake.'

'Oh, Lou-Lou.' Jude instantly pushed all other worries aside to focus on the needs of her sister. 'What did he say?'

'The usual,' said Lucy. 'You know the sort of thing. What a slut I am, how much I've disappointed him, how I'm being irresponsible by not allowing my son's father to see him, how I'm ruining Sebbie's life. You get the gist.'

Jude bristled with pure anger.

'You are not to listen,' she said. 'You don't need to listen to anything he has to say from now on. If he calls again, you just ignore him. Do you hear me?'

'Yes,' said Lucy.

'Does he know where you are?'

'No. That's part of the reason he's so pissed off. He hates the fact I'm finding my independence and he's playing no part in it at all.'

'Good. Let's keep it this way,' said Jude. 'I've been thinking. Is there any reason why you should go back to Maidenhead?'

'What?' said Lucy. 'Now?'

'No.' Jude was realising with utter clarity what she wanted more than anything. 'I'm thinking about the longer term. Would you ever move away altogether?'

'Where?'

'How about here?' she said. 'With me.'

Lucy looked a little taken aback by the suggestion and Jude felt immediately as though she'd said the wrong thing.

'Just an idea,' she flustered. 'Silly, really. I've just loved having you and Sebbie to stay...'

'And we'd love to stay for a while yet, if that's okay,' said Lucy. 'I just can't think much past the next month, or week even. I've taken extended leave from work, but I'll have to go back at some point. The money my mum left me is almost gone and there's no way I'd ask Dad for anything.'

'Of course,' said Jude. 'The offer will always be there.'

'And I love you for it. But I also know you're going through your own kind of hell at the moment and I want to make sure that you know I'm here for you too, if you want to talk. Whatever it is you want to talk about.'

'Thanks,' said Jude.

'Except politics.' Lucy smiled. 'You know I hate politics.'

Jude smiled back.

'Where's Sebbie?' she asked.

'He's down in the orchard with Noah. They're busy working on a surprise for you. I left them to it take the call from Dad, but I said I'd go back when I was finished. Want to come?'

The two sisters pulled on wellies, linked arms and set off down the garden path with Pip trying hard to walk between them, finally giving up when she realised there was no space and walking next to Jude instead.

'How did it go with Ben?' Lucy asked as they walked.

'He didn't help Sarah with the body,' said Jude. 'Although he did know about it. He's been a total idiot but I feel really sorry for him. He was in love with Sarah right up to the end and only married Tilda for her money.'

Lucy looked understandably shocked by this.

'Long story for another time,' she said. 'Today, Ben is going to the police to tell them everything he knows and I am going to stop digging now. I don't think I want to uncover anything else.'

'But what about Sarah?' said Lucy. 'Aren't we going to try and find out what the deal is with Les Turner?'

'I don't think so,' said Jude. 'I was so sure Sarah wouldn't have killed herself that I wanted to find out who had. But now things are different. Now we know everything that she was carrying on her shoulders; maybe it isn't so surprising that she wanted to end it all.'

'What about the shoes, though, and the post box?' said Lucy. 'Those things still don't add up. And what about the pictures she took? She was onto something for sure. Don't you want to see this through?'

Jude stopped at the gate to the orchard.

'Look where Sarah's investigations got her,' she said. 'What if Les Turner found out what she was up to and sent Raoul round to stop her? I don't want to bring that kind of trouble to the farm. Especially not with you and Sebbie here. No, as far as I'm concerned, it's time to move on now.'

Lucy shivered at the mention of Sebbie and the possibility that he might be in danger. Jude knew she was right: she shouldn't carry on probing into the toxic underworld they'd found themselves on the edge of. Their part in this investigation was now over and it was time to start looking to the future.

In the orchard, they followed the sound of banging and found Noah and Sebbie on the opposite side to the chicken coops, under the pear trees. They were busy putting together some sort of wooden hut and Floss was lying on the grass next to them, alert in her capacity as chief watchdog.

'Hello, boys,' said Lucy. 'Look who I've brought to see what's going on.'

'Jude,' said Noah. 'I'm sorry about this morning. Someone rubbed me up the wrong way and I let it bother me. Shouldn't have taken it out on you.'

'Don't worry,' said Jude. 'We're all running on jitters at the moment. What's the deal with the hut?'

'Ah,' he replied. 'This here is part of my apology.'

'Do you usually say sorry with a small wooden building?'

'It's not the hut so much as what's going inside it,' he said. 'Pass me that last bit of roofing and then I'll show you.'

Jude passed over the sheet of corrugated aluminium and Noah hammered it into place. They all stepped back to admire the little hut, made, by the looks of it, from a load of old forklift truck pallets. Sebbie ran in and out of the opening, which was the perfect height for a two-year-old.

'Good job, young Sebbie,' said Noah. 'But this hut isn't for you. Come on, follow me.'

Noah led the little party out of the orchard and down the track that ran along the bottom of the farmhouse garden. It came out onto the main drive opposite the pink house where Noah opened a side gate to let them into the garden. A familiar fleecy bundle came bounding over to greet them, her tail shivering with the pure joy of seeing her favourite people.

'Canpake!' said Sebbie, holding a chubby hand out to the bouncing lamb.

'The hut's for her?' asked Jude.

'Not just for her,' said Noah. 'Sheep are social animals, this 'un particularly, I think we can say. If you're hell bent on keeping this lamb of yours then she'll be needing company.'

He pointed to the back of the garden where a small goat with the most beautiful caramel-coloured coat was watching the scene a little nervously.

'That's Gertie,' Noah continued. 'She's a Golden Guernsey. Mike Norris is breeding a small tribe over at Park Farm the other side of Ledbury. I knew he had a good kidding season in December so I gave him a ring and he was happy to let me have this one to help keep the grass down for the hens. Thought she might be good company for that lamb of yours too.'

Jude felt a sudden rush of affection for the gentle shepherd. He had such a caring nature and she was lucky to have him on the farm. The horrendous revelations of the morning clashed with the thoughtfulness of Noah's gift and Jude couldn't help throwing herself at him and giving him a big hug of gratitude. Not just for the beautiful goat, but for understanding that the kind thought was exactly what she needed.

It was a happy procession that made its way back to the orchard. Sebbie led the way with Pancake skipping loyally along at his side. Jude went next, with Gertie the goat tied loosely to a piece of baling twine. Noah and Lucy brought up the rear, Pip and Floss circled the group, rounding them up and keeping the odd flock together.

They stayed in the orchard for a little while, watching the two new inmates get to know each other and their surroundings. Some of the braver bantams flocked around to see what was going on but soon retreated back to their side of the orchard when Pancake and Gertie bleated at them.

A shrill whistle cut through the air, causing both dogs to prick their ears up. Pip was quick to show her excitement and ran to the gate where she sat expectantly, waiting for someone to open it for her.

'That'll be Charlie,' said Jude. 'If he can't find me, he usually whistles for Pip.'

She opened the orchard gate and Pip flew through it. Charlie crouched down when he saw her rushing over the grass and caught the black and white whirlwind as she barrelled into him.

Jude turned to Noah. 'Want to come inside for a cuppa?'

He looked up towards Charlie and shook his head.

'You're all right,' he said. 'I've got a few finishing touches to make sure the shelter is safe and then I'll get some water and food sorted for these two.'

'Thank you,' she said, squeezing his hand. 'For everything.'

He whistled for Floss and then went back into the orchard to finish up.

'This is a nice surprise,' said Jude, when she met Charlie by the garden gate.

'I had a few hours off work and thought I'd come and see how you're doing,' he explained.

Charlie linked arms with her and they followed Lucy, who was halfway up the garden path, chasing a runaway Sebbie.

'So?' Charlie asked.

'So, what?'

'So, how *are* you doing?'

'Been better,' she said. 'What about you?'

'Oh, you know.'

Jude didn't know because she wasn't sure whether or not Ben had had a chance to talk to him yet.

'Have you had lunch?' Charlie asked. 'I've brought a picnic. Nothing fancy really, just a few things from the supermarket. I thought you might like to share it with me?'

'Have you seen Ben today?' Jude asked.

'No. Should I have?'

Jude knew how important it was for Ben to be the one to tell Charlie what had happened, so she said nothing about the terrible discovery she'd made that morning.

'No,' was all she said. 'But I know he's looking for you.'

'Anything in particular?'

'Why don't you send him a text, tell him you're here?'

'What's going on?' said Charlie, suspicion written all over his face.

'Just text him,' she said.

The farm might be just the place for the two men to have their awful conversation, Jude thought. Neutral ground with plenty of space and no chance of any of the village gossipmongers eavesdropping. It would also give Jude the chance to talk to Ben again before he went to the police. She was already regretting the frostiness of the last visit and she wanted him to know he wasn't alone.

'Okay,' said Charlie, pulling his phone out and tapping a message. 'Now what about this picnic of ours? We could wrap up warm and put a rug on the grass, or we could just eat it inside if you'd rather.'

Jude hugged his arm a little tighter. 'Out here would be really nice. I think the rain's coming back in tomorrow so let's make the most of today whilst we have it.'

There were two hessian bags full of food waiting in the kitchen, which Charlie retrieved whilst Jude dug around in the aptly named *clutter cupboard* at the back of the utility room for a couple of old blankets.

Sebbie was already trussed up in his warmest clothes after his adventure in the orchard and was a more than willing helper when it came to carrying four plastic plates outside for the food.

'This is very lovely of you,' said Lucy.

'You haven't seen what I've brought yet,' Charlie replied. 'You might absolutely hate my taste in food and end up going hungry.'

It was apparent that there was no danger of that. Charlie had bought so much food they could have fed several Duke of Edinburgh explorers should they have chosen that moment to orienteer through the farm.

As soon as the blankets were spread out underneath the budding sumac tree, Lucy, Sebbie and Charlie tucked in hungrily, but Jude found she had very little appetite. She knew Ben would be looking for Charlie and here they were having a picnic in the garden as though nothing was wrong.

33

Once everyone had eaten all they wanted, Charlie went over to the shed at the side of the garden that had once been the chicken coop. It had been turned into a general store when Adam's father had first moved the hens out into the orchard and it was a treasure trove of assorted junk. Charlie knew exactly what he was looking for and he was soon back, pulling a wonderful wooden contraption with large pram wheels and a long piece of rope attached to the front.

'The old soap box,' he said proudly. 'Adam, me and the others spent hours making this. We did have two but the other one met a rather sticky end that involved Adam, a tree and an emergency trip to A&E.'

'That sounds about right,' said Jude.

'We had some fun with this old girl, though,' Charlie said, patting the back of the wooden box affectionately. 'Building her, racing her and fixing her up again. This one's Barbara.'

He pointed to the faded name painted proudly across the side of the box.

'Her sister was Hannah, God rest her soul. We thought we were so clever, naming them after the best cartoon company of all. Wasn't until years later that we realised *Scooby-Doo* wasn't made by two women called Hannah and Barbara.'

Sebbie's interest was piqued and he tried to climb inside.

'No, Sebbie,' said Lucy. 'It isn't for you.'

'Well, it's definitely not for me,' said Charlie. 'I thought Sebbie might like a spin around the garden.'

Lucy hesitated.

'I promise to keep away from hills and trees. He'll be totally safe, we won't even leave the garden.'

Lucy could hardly argue with that, so Sebbie was allowed to clamber up into the box where Charlie positioned him on what looked like an old canoe seat. He gripped the sides of the box tightly and Charlie set off slowly around the garden, bumping him over the tussocky lawn as Sebbie shrieked with excitement.

Lucy and Jude watched them.

'You're lucky,' Lucy said. 'Sorry, I know life's been a bit shit to you.'

Jude raised her eyebrows.

'Okay, a lot shit,' she conceded. 'But you've still got some amazing people in your life including two lovely men who would clearly do anything for you.'

Jude watched Charlie pulling Sebbie around the rockery and under the ancient yew tree before looping back in front of the house to head for the rose garden. She thought about Noah and the effort he'd gone to, buying her such a beautiful goat and making a shelter so that Pancake would have somewhere to live. Lucy was right. If it wasn't for the pair of them, she was sure she'd have gone to pieces totally.

After another few laps of the garden, Lucy decided it was time to take Sebbie inside for a much-needed afternoon nap. Charlie and Jude gathered up the rest of the food and packed it into the bags to take back into the kitchen.

'Has Ben replied yet?' Jude asked.

Charlie looked at his phone.

'Ah, yes. He says he's going to be a little while, but he'll meet me at my house later.'

'Right,' said Jude, with a mixture of relief and anxiety.

'Are you going to tell me what's going on?' Charlie asked as he dumped a bag on the kitchen counter.

Jude shook her head. 'I can't,' she said. 'But can I ask you something else?'

'Okay,' said Charlie, drawing out the word in slow suspicion. 'Should I be worried?'

'It might sound weird, but did you and Sarah ever sleep together?'

Charlie gave an explosive laugh.

'Good God, no,' he said. 'It would have been like sleeping with my sister.'

Jude felt a flush of relief; Noah had definitely been mistaken. 'That's what I thought.'

'What made you ask?'

'Just something I heard.'

'Oh, Jude. You should know not to listen to the Malvern End gossip. Now, I must use your facilities before I head off.'

The sound of a car pulling up outside made Jude look out of the kitchen window. DS Binnie Khatri waved at her.

Jude realised that she'd come to collect the laptop but, with everything that had happened that morning, she had completely forgotten about it. She really hoped Charlie hadn't seen the laptop because, if he knew she'd been searching through it, then he'd just start nagging her again to stop interfering in police work. She went to grab it from the table, hoping to be able to pass it over to Binnie before Charlie came back from the loo, but it wasn't anywhere to be seen.

Lucy came in as Jude was going through the piles of paper and the rest of the bumf that constantly cluttered the table.

'I've just put Sebbie down,' she said. 'What are you doing?'

'Did you move the laptop?'

'Sarah's?' Lucy asked. 'No, why?'

'Because it's not here. Can you let Binnie in? She's just pulled up.'

Whilst Lucy went to the door, Jude looked in the dresser in case it had been tidied away in there somehow.

Binnie stood in the doorway. 'I won't stop,' she said. 'I've just come for the laptop.'

'I can't find it,' said Jude, feeling a panicky heat spread through her. 'It was here, exactly where I left it this morning.'

Charlie came in, still zipping up his fly.

'Hello,' he said to Binnie. 'Any news?'

'No,' said Jude, quickly. 'I asked her to come and see me because I had a laptop I needed to give her.'

'A laptop? Why?'

'It was Sarah's,' said Jude. 'Someone left it on my doorstep anonymously and I called DS Khatri because I thought it might be useful but now I can't find it.'

Charlie looked confused. 'Someone left Sarah's laptop on your doorstep?'

'Yes.' She knew it sounded far-fetched but the fewer people who knew about Binnie's illegal escapades the better. Charlie had already made his feelings about the investigation and hiding of evidence known when he'd taken the suicide note to the police. There was a small part of Jude that wondered whether, if he were to find out about Binnie's breaking and entering, he'd insist on telling the DI in charge of the case.

'It was there when I went out this morning and I put it on the table, right here.'

'Who's been in the kitchen since you last saw it?' Binnie asked.

'Us, obviously,' said Jude. 'Noah maybe, Nate Sanchez when he came round this morning...'

'Nate Sanchez?' said Binnie in surprise.

'Yes. But he was only in the kitchen for a minute or so whilst I boxed some eggs up for him. It's a long story. He came round to talk to me about Sarah, which was actually a really interesting conversation and I got the feeling he really did love her, you know.'

'Bollocks,' said Charlie. 'You can be soft, Jude. I can't believe you had him in your house.'

Jude glared at him. 'Like I said, it was only for a minute and I was there the whole time.'

'But he could have seen the laptop,' said Binnie.

'Yes,' Jude acknowledged.

'Is there any way he could have come back later to take it?'

'Jude leaves the door unlocked all the time,' said Lucy. 'I keep telling her it's not safe but she doesn't listen.'

'I live on a working farm.' Jude felt like she was a naughty teenager whose actions were under sudden scrutiny. 'I'm forever coming in and out of the house. It would be a right pain to have to keep locking and unlocking the front door.'

'Maybe,' said Binnie. 'But I would advise it's a pain worth bothering with.'

'So basically, anyone could have come in and taken the laptop,' said Charlie.

'I suppose so,' said Jude miserably.

'I'm really sorry, I'm going to have to head back to work,' Charlie said. 'But I'll be back later to check your door so please make sure you lock it from now on!'

Once he'd gone, Jude apologised again to Binnie. First the

diary, and now the computer. She couldn't believe she'd been responsible for losing pretty much all the vital evidence they'd collected.

'It was still on the table from this morning when I tried to copy the files,' said Jude.

'You *tried* to copy them,' said Lucy.

'The memory stick broke. I meant to get another one but then Nate came round. Shit.'

'Well, I guess that's that then,' said Binnie.

'I've still got the printed copies of the photos. Would they be any good?'

'Better than nothing,' said Binnie. 'Although I don't know how we'd explain to the DI how your fingerprints ended up all over them.'

As it happened, this wasn't a problem they needed to worry about as, when Jude went to her bag to retrieve the pictures, she found that a bottle of hand sanitiser had leaked all over them, causing the ink to run.

Jude held them up. 'Not much use now.'

Binnie looked downcast and Jude felt terrible. The DS had stuck her neck on the line to help them with the investigation and Jude had really messed things up. On top of that, she was sitting on a vital piece of information she knew she should have told Binnie straight away. But she'd promised to give Ben until the end of the day to do things his way and she would stick to her promise.

'I did find this,' she said, handing over Sarah's list. 'I'm not sure if it's much use other than telling us that Crystal-May-Rose is not CB after all.'

'So, what does that leave us with?' Lucy said. 'Three words that we have no idea what they mean. Father, Grange and Barley. Not a lot to go on, is it?'

'I wouldn't blame you if you gave up on us,' Jude said to Binnie.
'I don't want you to risk your job any more than you already have.'

'It's not my job I'm worried about,' she replied.

Jude felt an icy tickle somewhere at the base of her spine.

'What do you mean?'

'Isn't it obvious? Someone knows we had the laptop. The
laptop that was supposed to be at Les Turner's house, until it was
stolen. And that means someone is on to us.'

34

When Charlie went back to the farm that evening as promised, he found that the door to the kitchen was not just locked but double bolted.

'I'm not staying,' he said to Jude. 'Just wanted to check you were taking your safety a little more carefully.'

'How did it go with Ben?' Jude asked. She'd been on tenter-hooks waiting to hear from either Charlie or Ben, imagining the conversation they were having.

'I haven't seen him yet,' said Charlie.

'What?'

'I got called into work for an emergency I couldn't get out of. I phoned him to say I'd be late and he suggested we left it until tomorrow morning. Said he had something planned with Tilda this evening. Whatever he wants to talk to me about doesn't sound quite as important as you're making it out to be. Can't you just tell me what's on your mind?'

'No,' said Jude. 'Just call me when you've spoken to him.'

'All right. Lock up again behind me and go and get some sleep.'

Jude relocked the door then took her phone out.

What's going on Ben? You said you'd do it today.

There was a short break before a reply from Ben lit up the screen.

I know. Just wanted one more evening with Tilda to tell her properly.
Hope you understand.
First thing in the morning,
I promise, Ben x

Jude felt desolate. Her friend had made some momentous mistakes, there was no denying that. But there was also no denying the fact that he was paying heavily for them. He'd been a total fool, but he wasn't evil. Jude refused to even toy with that idea and she ached for him and the life that had become his because of his terrible decisions.

It's the right thing to do. You're not on your own. Charlie and I will always stick by you so just get it over with so we can all move on together. J xxx

There was another pause and Jude could see that Ben was crafting his answer.

Jude, I'm sorry I messed up so badly. I wish things were different. Whatever happens I want you to know that I love you and I miss what we all had. xxx

* * *

Jude slept fitfully. By 6 a.m. she'd started to get cabin fever, so she got up. There were no teabags in the caddy and it definitely wasn't a morning for peppermint or chamomile so she nipped down to the pink house to ask Noah for a couple. There was no sign of him, which wasn't unusual at that time in the morning as he liked to get a good start on the farm jobs.

Oddly, though, Jude could hear Floss barking inside. It was unlike Noah to go out without his sidekick so maybe he was trying to have a bit of a lie-in after all. The village shop opened at seven, so Jude decided to take a walk over the fields and get there for when Mrs James unlocked for the morning customers. She reached the shop ten minutes before it was due to open, but when Mrs James saw her standing outside, she waved her in.

'How are you now, Jude?' she asked. Her eyes were sympathetic but Jude knew her ears were gossip-ready.

'Not so good today actually, Mrs James.'

'Oh dear, I'm sorry to hear that.'

'Yes,' said Jude. 'I've run out of teabags, which is never a good thing in my eyes.'

Mrs James chuckled. 'A girl after my own heart. Grab a box. Do you have enough milk now?'

'Milk I do have.'

She went over to the counter to pay for her teabags and there she saw a pile of newspapers lying bound on the floor ready to be sent out for distribution. On the top was a bundle of *Malvern Gazette*s. The front page caught Jude's eye.

'Oh yes,' said Mrs James, noticing her pick up a copy as she rang the teabags up on the till. 'More robberies. Terrible, isn't it? Eastnor Castle this time.'

PRICELESS PAINTING NABBED FROM CASTLE IN DARING RAID
ACCOMPLICE CAUGHT ON CCTV

But it wasn't the headline that stuck out to Jude, nor the picture of the landscape painting that had been stolen. It was the grainy CCTV image of the woman setting fire to the stolen car that had been used in the robbery. Jude recognised her instantly as the same woman Sarah had taken photos of.

'I'll take a copy please,' she said, paying for the newspaper and the teabags.

She read the opening paragraph with shock – the cocky audacity of the two men in overalls and caps who'd walked into the castle in broad daylight, telling the guide on duty they were there to collect a painting for cleaning. She was so busy reading about how they waved a fake piece of paperwork at the guide before waltzing off with the prized masterpiece that she didn't see Tilda coming the other way and bumped straight into her.

'Oh, gosh,' Jude said. 'I'm so sorry.'

She wasn't Tilda's biggest fan by any stretch of the imagination but she had enough empathy and compassion to realise she'd be suffering greatly from Ben's confession the night before.

'How are you?' Jude asked.

'Pissed off, if you must know,' said Tilda. 'Ben's gone AWOL. I don't suppose he was with you last night?'

Jude felt the now familiar feeling of dread start to rear its ugly head again.

'No. He said he was taking you out for the evening. Didn't you go?'

'First I've heard of it. Mind you, it isn't exactly a new thing, is it? I mean him telling you and your friends things before he bothers to let me in on the secret.'

'Don't be too harsh on him,' said Jude. 'He knows he did a bloody stupid thing but at least he's putting it right now.'

'How? It's too late for that. Harpesdene won't offer him another chance now he's turned it down. And it would have been the perfect job for him.'

'Sorry, what are you talking about?'

'Harpesdene College in Hampshire. They offered him a job in the prep school a couple of weeks before we got married. I set up the interview for him as one of my oldest friends is married to the head. Ben said he was still waiting to hear back from them and then I find out from Harvey that they offered him the position and he turned it down. Isn't that what you're talking about?'

Jude felt like a sheep who'd got stuck on her back and couldn't find a way to get up again. Everything was confusing and wrong.

'Sorry,' she said. 'I need to get back to the farm.'

She left Tilda muttering something under her breath and marched up past Sarah's cottage, onto the track that led back to the top field and into the farm. As soon as she was back inside, she called Charlie. He didn't answer the first time and Jude knew he'd still be in bed, but she didn't care. She redialled and this time he picked up, sounding half asleep still.

'Jude?' he said. 'It's really early. What's the matter?'

'Have you seen Ben yet?' she asked.

'Not that again.'

'He's gone AWOL,' Jude continued. And then, bit by bit, she told him everything, finishing off with the news that she'd bumped into Tilda, who hadn't seen Ben since lunch time the day before.

'Shit,' said Charlie. 'Do you think he's done a bunk?'

'Looks like it. Silly, silly man. I'm going to have to call the police.'

'Of course you do,' said Charlie. 'Give me twenty minutes to get some clothes on and I'll be round.'

Jude called Binnie and told her everything she'd already told Charlie. If there was any hint of annoyance from the DS that Jude had failed to tell her all of this the day before, then Binnie showed no sign of it.

'I'll have to inform the DI,' she said. 'I have no choice. We'll be round soon.'

* * *

Detective Inspector Peters accompanied DS Khatri to Malvern Farm and listened as Jude explained, for the third time that morning, everything she knew about Ben, Sarah and Raoul, as well as giving him Sarah's confessional note.

'I'm interested to know why you kept this information from the police, Mrs Gray,' said the Detective Inspector.

'Ben is a close friend. He was my husband's *best* friend,' said Jude. 'He made some stupid mistakes, but he wanted the chance to set things right himself and I thought he deserved that much.'

'And you think he's innocent in all of this?' DI Peters asked.

'Obviously not totally innocent. He should have come forward with the information he had about Raoul's murder. And his ethics around marriage are definitely questionable.'

'So the question I ask myself is,' said DI Peters, 'why has this innocent man scarpered? Could there be something else you aren't telling us?'

'Like what?'

'Like how he may in fact have been involved in the dumping of Raoul Toussaint's body in the pit? Perhaps even involved in his murder?'

'No,' said Jude, pushing away the niggling doubt that she herself had had.

'What sort of person would you say Miss Lloyd was, physically I mean?' the DI asked.

'She liked to run and she watched what she ate.'

'You said in an earlier interview that you'd noticed how thin she'd become.'

Jude nodded. 'She had.'

'So, tell me, Mrs Gray,' the DI continued. 'How would you suggest a woman of Miss Lloyd's stature would be able to drag the body of a man weighing somewhere between eighty and ninety kilograms through the village of Malvern End, up your driveway and through the woods before dumping it in the pit, all on her own?'

'I don't know,' said Jude quietly.

'No, Mrs Gray,' said DI Peters. 'Nor do I.'

He let the thought hang in the air for a little while before he spoke again.

'Is there anything else you'd like to share with us today?'

Jude thought about the laptop for a few moments. It had gone missing again so she wondered if there was much point in mentioning it, but there seemed no reason to hide it now either. There was no chance of the DI finding a link between the laptop and Binnie now and she didn't want any more secrets.

'I saw Sarah's laptop,' she said. 'Someone dropped it off on my doorstep yesterday.'

'Just like that?' asked the DI. 'And I don't suppose you saw who it was?'

'No,' Jude fibbed. 'It was there when I opened the door to bring the milk in.'

'Again, I wonder why you didn't call myself or DS Khatri straight away with this information. It seems to be a bit of a pattern with you. Never mind, if you could hand it over, we'll get forensics and IT to take a look.'

'That's just it,' said Jude. 'I can't.'

'You can't?' said the DI, both eyebrows raised.

'Someone stole it.'

'Right.' He took a moment to scrutinise Jude's face in a way that made her feel extremely uncomfortable. As though he was able to see to the very heart of her lie. 'So let me get this absolutely straight. Someone dropped Sarah Lloyd's laptop off on your doorstep but, before you had a chance to hand it in for investigation, someone else stole it again?'

'Yes,' said Jude. 'But I did have a quick look beforehand.'

'Of course you did. Which means I could have you arrested for tampering with evidence.'

Jude faltered.

'Let's just get on with this, shall we?' said the DI. 'What is it that you saw?'

Jude explained about the pictures and the connection she'd made with the woman from the CCTV footage linked to the robbery at Eastnor Castle.

'Interesting,' said DI Peters. 'Do you have any idea how such photos may have ended up on Sarah Lloyd's laptop?'

'No,' said Jude. 'I'm afraid I don't.'

'Well, if the laptop happens to be dropped off on your doorstep again, I'd very much appreciate a phone call straight away if it isn't too much trouble. Now, if there's nothing else you want to share with us?'

'Nothing else,' said Jude.

'Right,' said DI Peters. 'Well, in that case, I'll be sending in a team to do another search of Miss Lloyd's house as well as Benjamin Wilkinson's house and we'll see if we can't track this fugitive down. DS Khatri?'

'Yes, sir,' said Binnie, giving Jude a small smile of camaraderie before following her boss to the door.

'Oh, and Mrs Gray,' said DI Peters, 'if there is anything else you think we should know, then please do tell us. *Immediately*. Or I may be forced to arrest you for perverting the course of justice.'

* * *

Lucy had taken Sebbie to the Splash swimming pool at Jude's suggestion. The atmosphere at the farm was tense and unhealthy for a little one and Jude needed some head space. The promised rain had come and was battering the ground, making it also a bad day to be outside.

Jude, however, needed to be out. She couldn't stand being cooped up, just waiting for something else to happen. There was still no sign of Noah. The tractors and quad were all in their shed, so she walked down to the pink house to see if he was home. Floss was still inside and barked again when Jude knocked so, this time, she pushed the door open and went into his kitchen.

'What's up, Floss?' Jude said, rubbing the collie between the ears. 'Noah hasn't left you alone, has he?'

She called out his name and then knocked on the door of his bedroom. There was no answer so she opened the door. Being there in Noah's most intimate space felt like an intrusion so she only glanced inside enough to make sure he wasn't there before closing the door again.

'Don't need any more missing people today,' she said to Floss. 'Come on, you come back to the farmhouse with me. You can keep Pip company whilst I try and figure out what the hell to do next.'

Jude found a pad of Post-it Notes and a pen on the side and scribbled a quick note to Noah, telling him where she'd taken Floss. Then she opened the door and stepped back out into the rain. Floss didn't wait to be called; she was off like a rocket into the woods beside the pink house.

'Floss!' Jude called. 'Come on, girl, not today.'

She peered into the rain-drenched trees, looking for any sign of the sheepdog.

'Floss,' she called again. 'Come.'

Jude noticed a strange flattening of the undergrowth that led into the woods. It matched the path that Floss had taken, but the broken foliage and snapped twigs were far too destructive to have been made by a dog. It was as though something large had been dragged through the trees and, with a horrific feeling of déjà vu, Jude followed the flattened path. Before she'd even got to the end of it, she already guessed there was going to be another body there. She just didn't know whose it would be.

35

Ben looked surprisingly peaceful, lying cradled on a bed of leaf mulch. If it wasn't for the enormous crack along the side of his head, and the large blood stain that had soaked into his T-shirt, Jude might have thought he was just sleeping. She knelt next to him, her hands shaking as she called the emergency services.

She stayed with the body, waiting for the ambulance and police to arrive. A blanket of numbness cloaked her, smothering any feelings that may have tried to surface as she sat, shivering in the rain until she heard the sirens coming up the drive.

'And then there were two,' Jude whispered.

The numbness didn't leave her as she was put into a police car, and it remained as she sat through another interview, answering the DI's questions as though a robot had taken over.

Binnie drove her home afterwards and, although Jude was aware of Binnie talking, she wasn't able to listen to a word, far less join in. Back at the farm, she found Floss sitting in the yard.

'Come on,' she said, opening the kitchen door.

Floss whined but followed Jude into the house. Noises from the playroom told her that Lucy and Sebbie were home, but she wasn't ready to talk to anyone else. She crept up the stairs, hoping the creaks of the old wood wouldn't alert them to her return.

In her bedroom, Jude took one of Adam's old fisherman's jumpers from his chest of drawers. She'd cleared a lot of his stuff out but she couldn't bring herself to get rid of everything. She pulled the thick woollen jumper over her head and drank in the scent of the lamb's wool. The jumper was baggy and the arms a good few inches too long for Jude, giving her the feeling that it was embracing her. She wrapped her arms around her chest and walked to the window from which she had the perfect view of the west profile of the hills. Unlike in story books, the weather did not match her mood. She was a tempest of emotion but the earlier rain had cleared completely and the sky was blue and cloudless, the fresh spring growth a Day-Glo green.

Jude felt a growing anger and resentment at the hand that she'd been played. Not just her but Adam, Sarah, Ben, Charlie and even Lucy too, when it came to the men in her life. The cocktail of anger and frustration grew and bubbled until it was too big for her to keep inside. She opened her mouth and let out a guttural moan that came from somewhere deep down, a moan that wouldn't stop until there wasn't a scrap of air left in her lungs. Then she held her breath, focusing on the throbbing in her ears.

'Judy!' said Lucy, rushing over to her sister. 'What is it?'

Jude gasped and her head cleared as oxygen flooded her system again. She turned to Lucy and fell into her arms.

* * *

Tea, Jude mused a short time later as she sat in the kitchen cradling a large mug, really was a super drug. The reality was more likely that it was because of the care and attention of someone else, someone who loved her unconditionally. Lucy had sat with her on the bed for a while, neither of them saying anything. Then she'd led Jude downstairs and made a cup of tea. The long sleeves of Adam's jumper acted as insulation, allowing Jude to wrap her hands around the soothing warmth of the mug straight away.

'Sorry about that,' she said. 'I think I may have broken up there.'

'It's about time,' said Lucy. 'You know you don't always have to be Superwoman, don't you?'

'Ben's dead,' said Jude, shivering despite the warm mug in her hands.

'I know,' said Lucy. 'I had to get through the police blockade when I got back from the swimming pool. Then Binnie came to ask me some questions.'

'I found Floss out in the yard,' Jude said. 'Have you seen Noah at all?'

'No. Floss was out there when we got back so I thought Noah wasn't too far away. The police were round here asking about him too so maybe he's helping them with some questions.'

'You're probably right,' said Jude.

Jude wanted to crawl under a large blanket and stay there for at least a few days, just to make sure there was no chance she'd stumble across anything else that would push her right over the edge. But Jude was a farmer and that meant there were certain things she needed to attend to.

'Do you think Sebbie would like some fresh air now that the sun's out?' she asked. 'Pancake and Gertie will need feeding. So will the chickens. I didn't collect the eggs this morning either so we'd better do that too.'

'I'm sure he'd love to,' said Lucy. 'We'll all go.'

From the orchard, the noise and activity of the police investigation could be clearly heard coming from the other side of the drive.

Lucy kept up a steady stream of chatter to try to keep Jude's focus off what was happening. It didn't work.

Gertie the goat trotted over to greet them but Jude ignored her. She'd already mixed the lamb's bottle and she left it with Sebbie and Lucy, whilst she went to the shed and scooped out a bowl of pellet feed. By the time she'd got back to the shelter to put it safely out of any further rain, Pancake had already finished her milk and Sebbie was giggling as Gertie nibbled the corner of his coat.

The chickens were next to deal with, but Jude was not concentrating. She managed to drop two eggs and tip over a feeding station before she began cursing and taking her anger out on the job at hand. If Sebbie hadn't been there, she would almost certainly have chucked the entire basket of eggs across the orchard before dissolving in a heap on the floor. But Jude didn't have that luxury.

Left foot, right foot, left foot, right foot, she told herself.

'Aundy Chewdy,' Sebbie said when he caught her dropping a third egg on the floor and it smashed into a sticky puddle. 'Don't do dat.'

'I know,' Jude said. 'Silly Aunty Judy. Let's get these back to the house and you can box them up for me.'

Floss was lying by the kitchen door with her head on the mat, looking thoroughly dejected.

'Come on,' said Jude. 'I don't fancy another trip to your house at the moment, but you can come with me up to the grazing fields and see if Noah's fed the flock.'

As soon as she opened the door, Floss ran out and made a beeline for the storeroom next to the house, where she scratched at the door before turning back to Jude and whining.

'What is it?' She went over to the door with a large lump of trepidation in her chest. Dogs had led her to two bodies recently. Surely this couldn't be happening again?

She opened the door nervously but there was nothing in the storeroom other than the jumble of brooms, old grain sacks, ladders and various other clobber that had no place elsewhere. Floss ran inside and sniffed around every corner of the room, her nose working overtime as she carefully examined the nooks and crannies.

'Come on,' said Jude. 'I could do without that sort of behaviour today.'

She left the storeroom and whistled for Floss to follow her. Then she crossed the yard to the big machinery barn where she pulled the trailer over to the quad and hitched it up in preparation for taking fresh forage up to the field. Before she could finish the job, Binnie joined her.

'Hello, Jude,' she said gently. 'Can I have a moment?'

'Is there any news? Do they have any idea who did this to Ben?'

'Perhaps we should go inside,' said Binnie.

'Just tell me,' said Jude, her nerves raw.

'Okay,' said Binnie. Her voice was calming but Jude could tell from the look on her face that she was not here to deliver good news. 'They found the murder weapon thrown into the under-growth not far from the body. It's not certain yet – forensics will need to match it to the wound – but we think that's just a formality as it matches in every other way.'

'Right...'

'It's a shepherd's crook, Jude,' said Binnie. 'And I'm afraid it looks like the one I've seen Noah with.'

'But it can't be Noah's. He's the last person on earth who'd do something like that. And he had absolutely no motive. He and Ben always got on really well.'

'It's not just the crook,' said Binnie. 'We did a search of the house and found Sarah's laptop in his bedroom.'

'No,' said Jude. This was too much. It was ridiculous on every level that the police were even pointing a finger at Noah. There had to be a reason why the laptop was in his cottage.

'And there was evidence of a fire in the grate that we believe to contain the remains of Sarah's diary.'

Jude shook her head. 'It can't be Noah,' she said. 'You've met him. He's the gentlest person anyone could come across. Besides, he's been here on the farm with me most hours of the day. When would he have time to get mixed up in the sort of things we're looking at? Especially during lambing season?'

'I'm afraid it isn't looking good for him,' said Binnie.

'What does he say? I assume you've had him in custody all day. Although it might have been nice if someone had let me know.'

'No,' said Binnie. 'We've been trying to track him down but he's proving quite elusive so far.'

Jude struggled to believe what she was hearing. Was she really that bad a judge of character? She'd got Sarah and Ben wrong, not believing for a moment that either of them could have been capable of the things they ended up doing. And now Noah too?

'What now?' she asked.

'We really need to speak to Noah,' said Binnie. 'If you do hear from him, don't keep it from me. In the end you won't be doing him any favours.'

Jude nodded. She knew that Binnie was hinting at how she had kept all she knew about Ben from the DS – and he'd ended up with his head caved in.

'I will,' she said. 'He's left Floss behind, so he won't be gone for long.'

'I don't like you being here on your own,' said Binnie. 'Out in the middle of nowhere with all this stuff going on around you. Is there somewhere else you can stay, just for a little while?'

Jude stood up. 'This isn't just my home,' she said. 'This place is my life and I need to be here if it's going to survive. Without Noah,

I'm going to have to do twice the work to make sure my animals thrive.'

'Fine,' she said. 'Just promise me you'll lock up properly and call if you're worried about anything at all.'

Jude noticed a real look of concern on Binnie's kind face.

'Thank you,' she said. 'I will.'

Binnie laid her hand over Jude's. 'I'm so sorry,' she said.

'So am I,' Jude replied.

36

The rest of the day passed in a haze of absence. Jude was aware that life was going on around her but she felt as though she was playing no real part in it. Lucy and Sebbie occupied themselves in the playroom and out in the garden. At some point, Charlie came round and at another, a police officer knocked on the door to ask again if she had heard anything from Noah. Jude was vaguely aware of the phone ringing and Binnie telling her that Sarah's laptop had been wiped and cleaned of prints but that the tech team were looking to see what could be recovered. Nothing really mattered, though. Her body was still functioning but her mind had gone into its own mini-lockdown.

It was the same numb haze that took Jude down to the orchard to give Pancake her milk and put the hens away for the night, then out on the quad for the final check of the fields.

When she got back to the farm, Charlie was still there. He and Lucy were looking pretty cosy together on the sofa with a bottle of wine, whilst Sebbie sat on a cushion on the floor watching cartoons with Pip and Floss lying next to him. In another, fairer world, this could be the perfect scene of a happy family life.

Lucy sprang up when Jude came in.

'Can I get you a glass of wine?' she asked. 'Charlie and I were thinking of making cheese on toast. Would you like some?'

'No, thanks. I'm just going to go to bed.'

Still on auto-pilot, she went upstairs, swapped her clothes for pyjamas and brushed her teeth. She didn't have the energy for a proper shower so she gave herself a quick flannel wash to take off the day's muck. If only it could be so easy to strip back the thicker layer of muck that clung to her insides.

She popped a couple of over-the-counter sleeping tablets. She'd wake up with a thick head in the morning, but it was better than the sleepless night that awaited her if she didn't take them. Then she put Adam's fisherman's jumper back on, crawled under the duvet and waited for the tablets to kick in.

* * *

When Jude woke up, the numbness had gone, uncovering the intense pain that had been buried the day before. But pain was not a stranger to Jude Gray and she'd developed ways of dealing with it. Busyness was the key to getting on with life and she knew that the days were going to be very busy for a while to come.

Charlie was on the sofa when she came downstairs. Unshaven and very rough.

'You slept over?' she asked.

'I wanted to check you were all okay,' he said. 'And to make sure you'd locked the doors properly, of course.'

'Of course,' said Jude.

Charlie's eyes were bloodshot and his skin sallow. He looked as broken as she felt.

'Just us two now,' he said, his voice cracking.

Jude wanted to hug him, to allow them both to spill their grief, but she knew that would lead to tears, and tears would hinder her attack of the day.

'I'm not going anywhere,' she said.

'Nor me.'

'Right,' said Jude, forcing a hardness that she did not feel. 'Tea and toast then.'

Lucy joined them as the pot was filled and the toast taken from the grilling plates. She was already dressed in a pair of jeans and an old flannel shirt.

'Why are you wearing one of my work shirts?' said Jude.

'I've got your jeans on too,' she replied, proudly. 'I don't want to spoil my own clothes whilst I'm helping out today.'

'You want to help on the farm?'

'You said yourself you're going to be up against it with Noah missing so put me to task, boss!'

'Me too,' said Charlie. 'I'm sure I can take the day off work today and I think I can remember some of what Adam and his dad taught me about sheep farming.'

Sometimes it's kindness that triggers the biggest reaction to pain or grief. And the love and support of her sister and her friend proved to be just that trigger. The tears came then and Jude was soon wrapped up in a three-way hug that gave her the strength she needed to keep going.

Over breakfast, Jude set about making a list of jobs that needed to be tackled that day. Charlie had driven the quad bike many times before, so she charged him with the field rounds.

'I'll show you where the pellets are and help you load the trailer. The feeding stations are obvious and then you need to drive round, looking out for anything that doesn't seem right. Any lameness, sheep on their backs, particularly large clots of muck around their bums.'

'Got it,' said Charlie. 'Check sheep's bums. Anything else?'

'Whilst you're up there, could you do a quick border check to make sure there aren't any new holes in the hedges and fencing? Don't want to lose any. Once one finds a way out, they all start to follow.'

'Will do,' said Charlie.

'Do you want Sebbie and me to do the orchard?' said Lucy. 'I think I can remember what we did yesterday.'

Jude smiled gratefully, silently marvelling at how this total townie had started to embrace the country life and was stepping up to do things she'd have run a mile from not that long ago.

'That would be brilliant. Just make sure you shut the orchard gate properly before you open the doors of the coops.'

The new arrangement wasn't sustainable, but it would get them through the next few days at least.

Frank had been round in a complete state when he'd discovered what had happened. Like Jude, he was certain that Noah had nothing to do with the awfulness of the murders on Malvern Farm and was just as worried as Jude about where his son was. He was also concerned about the strain Noah's disappearance would have on Jude and the flock so he promised to send word out amongst the other local farms, letting them know she needed temporary labour. How temporary, she didn't know. That depended totally on where Noah was and what exactly he'd got himself caught up in.

* * *

There was still a strong police presence around the pink house and the patch of woodland next to it. Jude avoided that area and kept herself busy in the sheds. She knew that the few sheep remaining were ready to be moved out to pasture, but she couldn't handle Floss and wasn't sure how to get them up to the field without her so it would just have to wait.

Instead, she decided to take down the remainder of the now empty individual lambing pens and build a second large pen to move the sheep into to allow her to clean out the one they were currently inhabiting. It wasn't ideal but it was the best solution she had and she took some solace from having Charlie's soothing presence, helping without the need for small talk that neither of them were capable of.

Whilst they were busy, Lucy made a hearty lunch of thick vegetable soup and potato wedges.

'Where do you suppose Noah's disappeared off to?' Charlie asked. 'He was always a weird one but I'm not sure I'd have pegged him as a murderer.'

Jude had been doing a noble job of tricking her spent mind into not thinking about the myriad of awful things it kept trying to focus on. She winced as Charlie pulled them straight back into the spotlight.

'No,' said Lucy. 'Nor would I. He seemed so gentle.'

'Gentle?' said Charlie. 'That's not a word I'd have chosen for Noah Grange. Not the boy I remember from school who'd pick all the legs off daddy longlegs and burn ladybirds with a magnifying glass.'

Jude started at the name Charlie had used.

'Noah's surname isn't Grange,' she said. 'It's Harrow, Noah Harrow.'

'Not when he was at school,' said Charlie. 'Back then he was Grange but then his dad left and his mum re-married. He took his stepdad's surname.'

'He used to be called Grange?' said Lucy.

Jude knew her sister had made the same connection as she had. Grange was one of the last three words from the Lexigle list, those that they'd yet to assign a meaning to. But Jude didn't want to think about it.

'Right,' she said. 'I've got a barn to muck out.'

'I'll give you a hand,' said Lucy. 'If you wouldn't mind watching Sebbie for me, Charlie?'

'Happy to,' he replied. 'Although I do feel as though I've got the easiest part of this particular deal. Are you sure you wouldn't rather I do the shit shovelling?'

'Shit shulling,' said Sebbie. 'Shit shulling.'

Lucy rolled her eyes. 'That child has learnt far too many new words since coming here. If you can manage a couple of hours without teaching him any more then I'm happy to shift the muck.'

Jude was keen to put her head down and get on with clearing the barn, but Lucy wanted to dissect this new piece of information Charlie had inadvertently fed them.

'Grange?' she said. 'Would Sarah have known?'

'Yes,' said Jude, with certainty. 'She knew him as a child, they went to the same school. If he was Noah Grange as a child, then of course Sarah would have known.'

She sat down on a hay bale and blew a big lungful of air out through pursed lips.

'Look,' said Lucy. 'I know it's not something you want to think about but perhaps we need to face the facts. His crook was used to kill Ben, and Sarah's things were found in his cottage. His surname was used by Sarah in the clues she set.'

'Stop,' said Jude. 'I know. I know all of this but that's it for me. I told you, no more clues, no more digging. It's gone far too far and it's got too dangerous.'

'But...' Lucy began.

'No,' said Jude. 'Charlie's right. This has to be left to the police. Now are you going to help me clear up in here, or not?'

'Fine,' said Lucy. 'What do you want me to do?'

Jude offered Lucy the choice of broom or shovel and Lucy chose the latter. Jude swept the carpet of hay and sheep muck into piles by the door of the barn, and then Lucy shovelled them into the quad's trailer. The atmosphere was strained and a million miles away from the barn disco she and Noah had shared just a week or so earlier when they'd cleared the other half of the shed, but Jude couldn't think like that. She couldn't allow herself to wallow in such pointlessness so she concentrated on sweeping up, using old distraction techniques that had worked in the past, such as describing to herself what she was doing in the minutest of detail to absorb her mind and keep it away from the reality of the things she didn't want to think of.

After a while, Jude took a moment to watch her sister, who'd rolled up her sleeves and was showing an impressive strength and drive as she shovelled load after load. It didn't seem to bother her at all that stray blobs of dung were sticking to her jeans and wellies.

'What?' Lucy asked, catching Jude watching. 'Am I not doing it right?'

Jude felt a warm rush for her ruddy-cheeked sister whose usually neat hair was trying hard to escape from its band.

'I just never thought I'd see you shovelling shit!'

Lucy pulled a face. Then she drew the shovel back and flung its contents at her. Clods of saturated straw hit Jude in the stomach and tumbled down, falling into her wellies as it went.

'You didn't just do that! Right. That, little sister, is war.'

Jude had no shovel but she was used to being covered in muck, so she bent down and scooped up a pile, walking towards her sister with revenge on her mind. Lucy screamed as Jude took aim and turned as the muck hit her squarely on the back.

In that moment, the girls reverted to their childhood selves as, for a few sweet minutes, the rest of the world disappeared and they became totally absorbed in their efforts to out-muck each other. Shrieks, yelps and laughter filled the shed, accompanied by barking as the two dogs joined in the excitement. When Lucy skidded on a wet patch and fell backwards, landing with a crack on her behind, Jude ran over.

'I think we might have got a bit out of control,' she said. 'Are you okay?'

'Help me up,' said Lucy, holding out her hand.

Jude took it, instantly realising her mistake when Lucy yanked it hard and Jude fell forwards into the muck heap. Lucy roared with laughter and Jude couldn't help joining in. They sat next to each other, surrounded by filth, bits of hay in their hair and sticking out of their clothing.

'What would Dad say if he could see us now?' Lucy giggled.

'Bollocks to him.'

'Bollocks to all of them,' Lucy agreed.

When Jude and Lucy walked into the farmhouse with smiles on their faces, arm in arm, covered in muck and smelling like sheep, Charlie raised an eyebrow.

'What happened?' he said.

'I won!' said Lucy.

37

It was late in the afternoon and Jude had thought they were pretty much done for the day, when a tractor turned up in the yard with a trailer full of hay bales.

'Bugger,' she said. 'I'd forgotten these would be arriving today.'

'Where do you want this lot?' shouted the driver.

'In the back barn. Round the side of that one. I'll meet you there.'

'Need a hand?' said Charlie.

'I'd love one,' she replied, relieved again to have her friend there.

Charlie and Jude followed the tractor to where the driver had pulled up by the entrance of the hay barn and was already throwing bales down off the tractor.

'We need to start stacking,' she said. 'Watch your back.'

It was hard work picking up the bales, each one weighing in at about fifteen kilograms. Whilst the driver threw them down, Jude and Charlie lugged them over to the back of the barn and stacked them up, carefully positioning them to be as stable as possible, until the stack was as high as they could manage, then they moved on to the next row and then the next until half of the bales were stacked.

Jude signalled to the driver.

'We need to go up a level,' she said. 'I'll have to go and set the elevator up. It's round the side, can you back the trailer up, please?'

'Most farmers have their kit set up before I arrive, love,' said the man.

Jude bristled. She was fairly used to the chauvinistic ways of some people in her industry but it still very much annoyed her. She clenched her teeth against any retorts that were fighting to get out and walked round the side of the barn to where a metal contraption sloped against the side of the barn. Its top edge was hooked over the lip of an opening three-quarters of the way up the wall.

Jude took the waterproof cover off the motor and oiled the chains that would drag the bales up the conveyor. She plugged it into the outdoor socket and was relieved when it sprang into life as the trailer was backed up by its grumpy driver.

'Are you happy to stack them?' Jude asked. 'If we load the elevator?'

The man gave an irritated sigh.

'Get a move on then,' he said.

Charlie climbed into the trailer and threw the bales down to Jude, who loaded them on the elevator. Each bale was then taken up to the opening in the barn where it dropped through, ready to be stacked.

They loaded the last bale just as dusk was setting in and Jude went round to tell the man they'd finished and to thank him for his help, unwillingly as it had been given. When she went into the barn, though, she was not happy.

'You haven't stacked them right,' she said.

'Typical woman,' grumbled the man. 'Never happy.'

Jude's hackles went up and she felt her fingernails biting into the palms of her hands.

'These bales aren't safe,' she said. 'Look, the ones at the top are already teetering.'

The man wasn't even the tiniest bit interested in what Jude had to say. He was already climbing back into the tractor's cab. Jude kicked the closest bale in anger.

'Leave it, Jude,' said Charlie. 'Nothing we can do now. Let's go and find something to eat. It's been a busy day.'

'He would never have done that if Noah had been here,' she said. Then she realised how that sounded.

'Sorry,' she said. 'You've been brilliant today. I really couldn't have managed without you. And you're right. There's nothing we can do about it right now and I'm bloody knackered. Let's go in.'

* * *

Charlie left the following morning after helping out with the field checks. He apologised profusely for having to leave but he couldn't take any more time off work as all hands were needed.

When Lucy asked what she could do, Jude suggested she take Sebbie out for the day. A quick look on the internet showed that Sudeley Castle was open.

'It's a bit of a trek but Sebbie would love it. The grounds are beautiful and there's a fantastic playground too,' said Jude.

'Are you sure you'll be okay?' Lucy asked, her eyes full of worry and compassion.

'It's fine,' said Jude. 'I'm going to be snowed under anyway.'

Half an hour later, Sebbie was bundled into the car and Jude waved them off down the driveway, which was now mercifully clear of police, although the yellow tape remained. Floss went down to the pink house and sniffed hopefully around the garden gate. She gave one sharp bark and Jude sighed.

'Sorry, Flossie,' she said. 'He's not there. You'll have to stick with us for now.'

She whistled and Floss came back to her dolefully. Back in the yard, she went to the storeroom again and scratched at the door.

'What is it about this room?' Jude said. 'I told you there was nothing in there. You even looked yourself.'

Floss barked, making Jude wonder all the more. She opened the door again and the sheepdog ran straight in, her nose once more on high alert as she did the same routine of sniffing every inch. Jude was about to whistle for her to come out so she could close the store up again but then she thought she saw a little movement behind one of the shelving units.

'Hello?' she called into the dark.

Floss saw the movement too and bounded over to the shelves, barking when she got there. An enormous rat tore out of the shadows and Jude yelped, jumping backwards as it shot past her and across the yard. Rats were pretty commonplace on farms, but Jude still didn't like them and this one was particularly huge.

'Floss!' she said. 'Enough. Let's go.'

The house felt incredibly quiet when Jude went back in. She filled the dogs' bowls with food and topped up their water before making herself a large mug of tea.

Jude hated paperwork. Really hated it, which was probably why there was such a mountain waiting for her when she went into the office.

She picked up the pile of unopened envelopes and leafed through before throwing them defiantly back onto the desk. She knew they needed dealing with but she couldn't have been less in the mood. Instead, she took her phone out and scrolled through to a file she'd made of some of her favourite photos of her and Adam.

Holidays were a rare luxury for farmers, she'd soon realised, but they'd managed to get away for a few weekends here and there. And they'd made the most of every single hour each time. There were pictures of them walking on a beach in Devon, through the busy streets of London and in the hills of the Peak District.

The memories were both happy and painful and she used her fingers to zoom in on Adam's face. Tanned from the hot summer outside, his freckles standing out like a map of the stars and his eyes crinkling with their usual love of life.

She kissed her finger and laid it on the screen.

'I miss you, darling boy,' she whispered.

The slightest movement of her finger caused the photo to disappear from the screen, taking her back to the photo album choices. She was about to switch the phone off and try to turn her attention to the paperwork when she saw the front image on her WhatsApp album. It was the one Sarah had sent her of the two of them at Ben's wedding. Jude touched the image and it filled the screen. She looked at Sarah's smiling face, now seeing the fear behind her tired eyes. How could she have been so blind not to see it more at the time?

She swiped sideways and the other photo Sarah had sent from the wedding popped onto the screen. It was the photo of Jude looking like a shocked scarecrow, taken in error when Sarah had tried to use her phone camera as a mirror. Jude looked at the woman in the photo. She'd thought she had problems then: cold legs, an unshifting farm smell that she was pretty sure had only been made worse when mixed with Sarah's strong perfume, and a field full of ewes who still had to be helped through the birthing process. If only that was the extent of her problems now.

Jude was about to put her phone down when she caught sight of the woman sitting two rows behind them – the bright fuchsia pink of her jacket standing out and making her instantly recognisable as poor Charlie's disastrous date. He'd been up at the front of the church during the wedding as Ben's right-hand man and Jude hadn't noticed his abandoned date sitting behind them. She squinted at the woman's slightly blurry face and felt sorry for Charlie. He was such a warm-hearted person and it was a huge shame that he seemed to mess up so horrifically whenever there was a woman involved. He'd clearly played things really badly with this particular one for her to deliver such a whopper of a slap in public but then, Jude thought, even in its blurry form, this face was already looking pissed off.

Jude zoomed in on the woman with interest and then felt her blood chill as a sudden recognition hit her. She pushed her chair back and went into the kitchen where the *Malvern Gazette* from a couple of days ago was still on the table.

She held the picture on her phone next to the CCTV still of the woman who'd been involved in the robbery of the Eastnor Castle painting, the same woman who'd been in the photos on Sarah's computer. There was no doubt in Jude's mind that they were the same person. What she couldn't understand was what this woman had been doing at the wedding with Charlie.

She leant back on the dresser and put the newspaper down on it, forgetting the framed photo of the gang at their school ball. It fell sideways and crashed to the floor with a shatter, sending shards of glass across the flagstones.

'Bugger.'

She rescued the photo which she put on the table, then she fetched the dustpan and brush from the clutter cupboard and swept up the broken glass. She threw the frame in the bin, along with the contents of the dustpan, before hoovering up any last crumbs of glass that were just waiting to do a mischief to a toddler's foot or dog's paw.

The mess tidied away, Jude picked up the photo and looked at the broken group of friends, focusing on each one at a time before turning it over. There, scribbled on the back in Sarah's scruffy writing, was the inscription.

Me, Apple, Ivy and Charlie Barley at the school leaving ball.

Every follicle on Jude's body prickled as she read it a second time. She'd known about Sarah's childhood nicknames for Adam and Ben, Apple and Ivy, but this was the first time she'd seen Charlie referred to by his nickname.

Charlie Barley.

The fact that Charlie was now a fit for the elusive CB was something that Jude could hardly bear to consider. And there was something else. Barley was the penultimate unsolved Lexigle word. As much as Jude didn't want to link Charlie to this whole dangerous tangle, she knew she had no choice but to confront the facts.

38

Jude was desperate for someone to talk to but she'd run out of people she could trust. Two of her friends were dead, she had absolutely no idea where Noah had disappeared to, and now she had so many questions about Charlie.

She tried Binnie's phone but there was no answer.

And then it hit her. There was one person who might have answers – some at least. Someone who had watched all of those involved grow up and might be able to shed a little light on how all of this slotted together.

* * *

Granny Margot was in the middle of a round of bingo when Jude arrived.

'Hello, sweetheart,' she said. 'What a lovely surprise. Here, take a dibber and you can help me mark the numbers off.'

Jude was desperate to talk to Margot but she did as she was told. As they played, she wasn't in any way helpful as Granny Margot got to the numbers quickly, dibbing them out with her marker before Jude even spotted them. After about ten minutes, the game came to an end when a lady with long plaited grey hair shouted, 'House!'

'Ooh, that Gurinder is good,' Margot said in admiration. 'I've not beaten her once. Now then, let's find somewhere to have a chat, shall we? I think the day room is booked for karaoke next and, trust me, that is not something you want to be anywhere near. They do have the mic on a very low volume, due to the havoc it plays on some of the hearing aids. But even so...'

She pulled a face that demonstrated exactly what she thought of the singing skills of her fellow residents.

'How about I ask about some tea, and we go out to the gazebo? It's far enough away down the garden to be clear of the singers.'

Margot flagged down one of the carers and sweet talked her into doing exactly what she asked. Jude fetched Margot's woollen coat from the back of her bedroom door and helped her into it before they followed a paved path down to the wooden gazebo at the very bottom of the garden. The carer was just behind with cushions for the plastic chairs as well as a blanket for Margot to put over her knees.

'I'll be back with some tea in a minute. We've got some lemon drizzle in too if you'd like some.'

'Thank you, Shona,' said Margot. 'You're an angel.'

The young carer smiled and left them to it.

'Now then,' said Margot. 'Have you come with an update?'

'I've come with a puzzle.'

'Then I'm the right person for the job,' said Margot. 'Go on.'

'Have you heard of the name Les Turner?' Jude asked.

'Yes, I have. And it's funny you should ask because Sarah was talking about him only a few weeks ago. He used to come to the village when my Lizzie was a teenager. She didn't like him at all, thought he was trouble. But he hung out rather a lot with Nessa Watson, that's Charlie's mum.'

'Really?'

'Oh, yes,' said Margot. 'They were quite the couple for a while. Went drinking at The Lamb a lot, although I could never see what she liked about him. He was pretty rude and boy did he like to pick an argument. Maybe she wanted a bit of a bad boy in her life? Some do, you know.'

'You're right,' said Jude. 'Do you know how they met?'

'Now that's a question. It was such a long time ago, but I think it might have been something to do with the Young Farmers' Club. Les's parents owned a farm somewhere in Herefordshire, near Ledbury, I think. Grange Farm, it was called.'

The word jumped out at Jude as though Granny Margot had shouted it loudly in her ear.

'Are you sure it was called Grange Farm?'

'I am. I remember because it was in the news maybe ten years ago now or longer. Really sad story. It burnt down, you see, and Mr and Mrs Turner were inside when it happened. She died and he had what they call life-changing injuries.'

'Goodness,' said Jude, rubbing at her goose-bumped arms. 'How horrid.'

'It was.'

As Shona returned to set out two cups of tea and two slices of cake in the table, the three elusive Lexigle words spun through Jude's mind like a fruit machine, slotting into place in a row that seemed like it could only point in one direction.

BARLEY, GRANGE, FATHER.

'Do you think there's any chance Les Turner could be Charlie's father?' Jude asked in trepidation.

'I have to say I do,' said Margot. 'As did a lot of the gossips at the time. Although I'll say to you what I said to Sarah. Don't go mentioning any of this to Charlie as he certainly doesn't know of the rumours.'

And there it was, the final piece of the puzzle moving into place to paint a hideous picture. Jude desperately hoped she was wrong and yet she didn't see how she could be this time. Unlike with Noah, where nothing made sense, with Charlie she could see it clearly. Sarah had found out that Les was Charlie's father and that he'd been using his parents' old home, Grange Farm, as a base for his stolen goods. She must have gone there to see what else she could uncover, perhaps in the hope of finding something to hold over Les but almost certainly biting off more than she could chew. And then what? Perhaps Raoul had been sent round to teach her a lesson and she was too scared to go to the police so she left a trail of clues on Lexigle instead. What about Ben? Did he know too much about all of this to be a threat? Had it been one of Les Turner's men who had killed him? Maybe even Les himself. And Charlie? Granny Margot seemed to think that he didn't know about the possibility of Les Turner being his father, but what if Les knew about him? Did that place him in danger?

There were so many questions and yet it was starting to feel as though she was so close to touching the answers.

And then she thought of Noah. Dependable, kind, constant. There wasn't anyone on the planet that Jude trusted more, so how had he got so tangled up in it all? But what if he hadn't? What if poor Noah was nothing more than a scapegoat, easy to frame? The evidence had all been very easily got – *too* easily perhaps. Would a real murderer be slack enough to leave the weapon so close to the body? A weapon that was so recognisable too? Her shepherd was a thorough, tidy person. If he'd taken Sarah's diary then he'd have made sure the whole thing was burnt properly; there would certainly have been no remains handily left for the police to find. Ditto with the laptop.

Jude needed to keep a clear head. If Noah wasn't involved, then where was he and who had framed him?

'Thank you, Margot,' she said, getting up and kissing her on the cheek.

'You're not going already, are you? You haven't touched your lemon drizzle.'

'I'll come back and see you again very soon,' she said. 'But there's something I need to do.'

Jude sat in her car on the road outside the retirement home. A quick internet search for *Grange Farm fire Herefordshire* turned up several articles about Mr and Mrs Turner. Granny Margot's sharp mind had remembered everything just as it was. The farm had been set in land not far from Ledbury and had burnt exactly as Margot had said. The photos showed a shell of a farmhouse, only the outbuildings still standing. According to the internet, it had been a fault in the wiring and a lack of fire alarms that had caused the catastrophic and total ruin of the farm.

Jude searched for its location on the satellite map and found it virtually hidden in the surrounding countryside. She zoomed in onto the blackened wreck of the building, still untouched after all these years. The house was obviously deserted, but there must have been someone there at some point when the satellite image was captured because there was a car parked outside. A white 4x4 with a red roof.

'Les Turner,' said Jude. 'Gotcha.'

39

DS Binnie Khatri didn't answer her phone when Jude called and she didn't leave a message.

Jude remembered none of the journey as she drove back over the hills to Malvern End. She pulled up outside Charlie's house and knocked on the door. When there was no answer, she let herself through the gate and into the back garden. She peered through the windows but there was no sign of him.

'He'll be out at work at this time, my dear,' said Janet Timms, when Jude walked back onto the street. 'He is a mysterious one, isn't he? I have no idea what line of work he's in. Do you?'

'Of course I do,' said Jude, climbing angrily back into the Land Rover and slamming the door behind her.

Jude was fired up and ready for answers. She realised that, despite all she'd said to Lucy, she did need closure. She needed to find out for certain what had tied each of her best friends to the repulsive Les Turner. But even more importantly, she needed to find out what had happened to Noah and she couldn't help feeling that there was a clock ticking.

She punched the address for Grange Farm into her phone. It was about a seven-mile journey, roughly sixteen minutes away.

Before Jude set off, she redialled Binnie's number and put the phone on speaker. It went straight to answerphone as she had been expecting.

'Hi, Binnie,' said Jude, leaving a message. 'There's a place called Grange Farm near Ledbury which burnt down several years ago. It used to belong to Les Turner's parents and I think he's using it as his storage or processing place or whatever. The closest village is called Little Havington. Anyway, I'm heading over there now. I know you won't be happy, but I think they've framed Noah. I think he might be in danger so I have to go and see if I can help him.'

The words *if they haven't already killed him* sat in her mouth but Jude refused to voice them.

She clicked the red off-button and switched back to the satnav app.

The road that led up to Grange Farm was so completely overgrown that Jude's Land Rover rubbed the hedges on both sides. She didn't fancy announcing her arrival so, when she could see the farmhouse approaching, she pulled into the entrance of a field, turning the car so it was pointing away from the house and reversing back so that it was almost totally hidden from the road by a row of trees.

Jude zipped the car key into her jacket pocket. Then she switched her phone to silent and slipped that in the other pocket. Sticking close to the trees that lined the road, she made her way towards the farm. The road turned into a track and Jude realised that this was indeed the perfect hideaway for criminals as nobody would ever have reason to head this way, leaving them in peace to do whatever it was they needed to do. There was clearly only one way into and out of the farm and Jude was already grateful for her forethought in turning the car; it might be easier if she needed a speedy getaway.

The driveway opened out into a yard around the same size as Malvern Farm's but there were no other similarities between the two. Close up, the burnt remnants of the house looked even more harrowing than it had in the newspaper pictures. The top floor was missing entirely, just one heavily blackened wall showing how tall the house had once stood. Weeds and even small tree saplings had embraced the opportunity to reclaim the land and were sprouting from every corner of the ruins as well as in the many cracks of the concrete yard. It looked a little like the film set of a thriller and it gave Jude the chills.

On the opposite side of the yard stood a row of barns. Mostly empty except for the odd rusting oil can and broken bits of old farm machinery – Jude imagined anything worth selling had gone years ago. Beyond the house stood the outbuildings they'd seen in the photos Sarah had taken. She looked around but she couldn't see any cars. She wondered if she was alone on the farm. It was definitely quiet enough.

Still with high levels of caution, Jude crossed the yard and went over to the outbuildings. The windows were all covered with thick black material, making it impossible to see what was inside, possibly added after they found Sarah taking photos. She edged carefully around the building and tried the door which was, unsurprisingly, locked. The next building was also locked but here, someone had been a little slacker with the window coverings and there was a small gap in the fabric. A quick peek through the gap was all it took for Jude to know that she had been absolutely right. A skylight lit the room, which was just as it had been in the photos, piled with stolen goods ranging from electronics to silverware, bikes to jewellery. The bronze busts were missing, obviously moved on since the photos had been taken, but Jude could see a large flat package near the side of the room, covered in a blanket. She wondered if that was the Eastnor Castle painting.

She took her phone from her pocket and cursed under her breath when she saw the battery warning light flashing. She took a couple of photos and just managed to send them to Binnie before the battery died altogether. Jude prayed that Binnie would pick both these and her earlier voicemail up quickly.

It was strange how the absence of a phone connection suddenly made Jude feel even more alone. She thought about cutting her losses, playing it safe and going back to her car. Surely the police would have enough now to bring Les Turner in? But then she thought of Noah. She'd lost two friends already and she didn't want to lose any more. There was no doubt in her mind that Les Turner had framed Noah for Ben's murder and it was likely he'd try to make sure Noah didn't return to defend the charges.

There was a third, smaller building and Jude made her way over to that. Again, the door was locked and the windows were covered. Before Jude could think of what her next move should be, she heard the sound of a vehicle coming up the drive. She pushed herself back into the undergrowth behind the office and waited.

She peeked out as much as she dared and watched Les Turner's striking 4x4 pull up on the concrete of the yard. Les got out, accompanied by the brunette from Sarah's pictures: Charlie's wedding date.

Jude wondered how much Charlie had known about her. Had their meeting been a coincidence or a deliberate set-up by Les? Did Charlie already know that Les could be his father? But, if that was the case, he would have recognised his father's name when he found out about Sarah's involvement with him – so why hadn't he stepped up then? Jude tried to swallow down her misgivings; she needed to deal with things one at a time and concentrate on what was happening right now. She pulled back further, feeling the breath chill in her chest, and made sure she was completely out of sight, listening as they walked towards her.

'Here, Anya,' said Les. 'You unlock the office. I need to get something from the storeroom first.'

Jude listened to the jangle of a bunch of keys and then the sound of a door opening. With her eyesight limited, she was suddenly so much more aware of her hearing and recognised the sound of a chair being scraped along the floor on the other side of the thin corrugated metal wall.

Heavy footsteps told her that Les Turner was walking back to join the brunette in the office building and then the door was shut. She moved as close to the metal wall as she dared in order to listen to what was happening on the other side.

'This is my last job for you,' said the woman, speaking with an accent that Jude couldn't place. 'I didn't sign up for this.'

'Quit your whining,' said Les. 'I've told you before, you're welcome to bugger off. Go to the police for all I care. Let's see how far you get when they find out you don't even have the right paperwork to be in this country. They'll have you shipped back off to wherever it is you're from pretty bloody fast.'

'This isn't right,' said Anya. 'Too many people have been killed.'

'Yeah, well, your choice, sweetheart. You're getting to be a bit of a liability, to be honest. First bailing on the wedding when you had the perfect way in to case the castle before sending the lads in. Then being stupid enough to get caught on camera torching the car.'

So that had been their game. Playing with Charlie in order to get an invitation to the wedding. Poor, gullible Charlie. It probably wouldn't have taken much flirting for her to get his attention and he'd been told by Tilda that he had to have a date so it would all have been pretty easy.

There were sounds of movement then from inside. Jude shifted her weight, trying to untangle her leg from a patch of brambles that were clinging to her jeans. She tugged a little too hard and stumbled sideways, falling against the side of the building with a thud that seemed to magnify a hundred times in her ears.

'What was that?' said Les. 'Go and look.'

Jude's heart raced. She looked around but there was nowhere for her to go. She couldn't move any further into the undergrowth, which only left her with one option. As the door opened, Jude flung herself hard at it, knocking the woman over in surprise.

'Oi!' shouted Les Turner in fury. 'Come back here.'

But Jude was not about to listen to him. She was already off, running as fast as she was able to across the yard and was halfway down the drive, almost back at her Land Rover when she heard an engine start behind her. The wheels of Les's 4x4 skidded on the concrete as he spun it round and then he was after her. Jude undid the zip of her pocket and felt around inside for her car key, blipping the lock in preparation to jump in. She was only metres away when someone stepped out from the trees into her path.

'Charlie!' she said.

'Hello, Jude,' he replied.

Then he caught the back of her head and smashed it against the side of her car.

40

Jude hit the ground with a thud that knocked the breath from her body. She was still conscious but shaken and very wobbly as she tried to get up.

'Charlie, no,' she pleaded as Les's car screeched to a halt next to them. 'Don't do this.'

'Hold her,' said Les, jumping from the driving seat.

Jude saw that Les was pulling on a pair of surgical gloves and she wriggled frantically as Charlie stepped forward and wrapped her in his arms, forcing her hands behind her back.

'Oh, Jude,' he whispered into her ear. 'Why did you have to interfere?'

She wriggled and tried to kick out but she was weak from the fall and Charlie's arms were strong. He was easily able to hold her as Les tied her wrists with something soft before ripping some tape from a roll to secure it in place.

'Get her into the car,' said Les. 'Then take her back to her farm. Make sure she has some sort of accident and for God's sake get rid of the tape. The rag I've put under it will make sure there's no marks or tape residue for the post-mortem to find. A little trick of the trade there for you.'

Jude tried to swallow her fear at the mention of post-mortems. This was Charlie. There was no way he'd do what Les was asking him to.

'Can't you do it here?' Charlie asked.

The fear pushed up further into her mouth. This wasn't Charlie talking; he must have a plan of some sort. And yet, deep down, Jude now knew that he was in this whole sickening drama up to his eyeballs.

'I don't want any of that happening on my patch,' said Les. 'You know that. Just make sure it looks like an accident.'

Jude didn't struggle as Charlie pushed her up into the passenger seat of her Land Rover. The way she saw it, she had two options. She could try to spend the journey talking Charlie out of this. They'd shared so much together, a past that was full of happy memories – surely she still had a decent chance of talking some sense into him. Or she could cause a fuss by the side of the road, hoping to bide enough time for Binnie to send a rescue party out for her. But Jude didn't even know if Binnie had got her voicemail and the photos she'd sent. If she was still busy with interviews, it could be hours before she checked her phone. And what would Charlie have done to her in that time?

Charlie leant over to buckle her seatbelt.

'Safety first,' he said, before climbing up into the driving seat and starting the engine. 'I wish you hadn't come here,' he said as he drove off. 'When I saw your car, I knew you'd worked everything out.'

He let out a deep groan.

'Why did you all have to stick your noses in? First Sarah, then Ben, now you.'

'Do you know who killed Ben?' she asked.

'I had to,' said Charlie. 'Just like I had to kill Sarah. They left me no choice. You have to understand that.'

For a moment, Jude couldn't understand what she'd just heard. Her head throbbed from the pain of the impact and she wondered if her brain was playing tricks on her.

'You didn't kill Sarah,' she said. 'You can't have.'

'Sarah was drunk that night,' he said. 'I hated it when she got herself in that state. It didn't suit her. I got the taxi driver to drop us both off at her cottage to make sure she was safe, just like I told you. I meant to leave her but all of a sudden, she decided she wanted to talk.'

Jude kept very quiet, not wanting to hear the truth she'd been striving so long to find but unable to do anything to stop it from coming.

'She wanted to go to the police about killing Raoul.'

'You knew about that?'

'Of course I did,' said Charlie. 'You didn't think Sarah really killed him and chucked him in the pit on her own, did you? She did hit him pretty hard, though. I was waiting outside and heard him go down with a right thump. See, I knew Les had sent him round to put the pressure on but I didn't want that neanderthal, Toussaint, to go too far. I assumed it was Sarah who'd fallen, but no. She came running out of the cottage in a right state so it was a good thing I was there to scoop her up. She was so relieved to see me and told me how he'd been rough with her and she'd been so frightened that she bashed him round the face with a rolling pin. I told her to wait in the garden whilst I went to take a look and she hadn't been kidding. There he was on the kitchen floor with his face caved in and blood everywhere. She didn't kill him but it was obviously important that he didn't live, so another quick crack with the rolling pin and that was that. It was much easier to let Sarah think she'd done it, though. It made her more pliable, and it made her a lot less likely to go to the police.'

Bile began to rise up in Jude's throat and she fought to swallow back the acidity.

'That night she had a proper attack of the guilts and said she was going to the police to tell them everything. I told her that if she did that, she'd be the death of Granny Margot and that sent her mad. She ran out of the cottage, just as she was, still in that furry coat of hers and her high-heeled wedding shoes. So beautiful and feisty and wonderful. Such a waste.'

Charlie made a deep groaning noise at the memory. He looked stricken and bereft. Jude felt a huge wave of fury burst through her.

'Your waste,' she said. 'You killed her. So don't you dare pretend you mourn her now.'

Charlie's eyes took on a deadly anger. Flint-like and dangerous in a way Jude had never seen them before.

'But I do mourn her,' he spat. 'She was my friend and I loved her. I didn't mean to kill her.'

'Then why is she dead?'

'She was wild,' Charlie said. 'Wild and desperate. She ran out into the rain and I followed her, shouting for her to come back, but she wouldn't. She went up the track behind the cottage. Her beautiful hair, wet and straggly, and her make-up running down her face, and she didn't stop until she'd got to the top of the hill.'

By the oak trees in the top field, Jude realised.

'I told her to come back to the cottage so we could talk about it, but she just kept shouting that she'd ruined everything and that she had no options left. Then she climbed up onto the pile of logs under one of the trees and she threw that bloody stupid scarf over a branch. I mean, who needs a scarf that long? It was ridiculous, right?'

Jude said nothing. She was transfixed with horror as he

continued to callously recall the events of the night that he killed another of their group.

'Anyway, then she said that it wasn't just about Raoul but that there were other things she'd done that she didn't know how to fix. Somehow, she'd figured out the truth about my dad, like you've done apparently, and she wanted to tell me all about it too. She thought it was her duty as my friend to tell me that she knew who my dad was and that he was a nasty piece of work. Something to do with spotting Anya at the wedding and thinking that meant Les was coming after me. And that was it. I couldn't trust her because she knew too much. She knew about my dad, she knew about the business and Grange Farm. And she was volatile. But she'd given me the perfect way out. I climbed up on the logs next to her and then it was easy. Poor, silly girl. I grabbed the end of the scarf, looped it around my hand and jumped off the logs, pushing with my foot so that they gave way and rolled out from under her.'

Jude closed her eyes against the treacherous tears that had forced themselves out. Poor, darling Sarah. Flawed, vulnerable, gullible. How frightened she must have been in those last desperate moments.

'You remember how thin she'd got. There was nothing of her. She was so light, it wasn't hard to hold her weight until her legs stopped kicking. The scarf gave way before I did so I just had to tie the remains in the tree to make it look like Sarah had done it all on her own. The rain and mud helped get rid of any evidence I'd ever been there and a quick note to you would confirm Sarah's suicide.'

'That was you,' said Jude, cursing herself for not spotting what was now so bloody obvious. 'Adam told me you always faked the sick notes at school. You were the best at copying anyone's handwriting.'

'And Sarah's was easier than most. So scatty and disorganised.'

Acid turned over and over in Jude's stomach and she had to

swallow to stop it rising up into her mouth. How could this be Adam's Charlie? *Her* Charlie? Their friend and best man at their wedding. Someone who had supported her through so much pain and heart ache and the last of their tight friendship group left. Now a complete stranger and the very reason why the group had been ripped apart.

'But why Ben?' she whispered through a dry mouth and cracking lips. Her tied wrists were aching and her hands were digging painfully into the small of her back. She tried to shift her position to ease the discomfort but it made no difference.

'Ah, Ben,' said Charlie. 'The last of the old gang. I was sad to have to do that. But he was about to blow everything wide open. I'd helped him out before, although he didn't realise it. He had no idea of the connection I had with my father when he told me about his own debts. I'd only just discovered myself who Les Turner was then. Les had found out about me and paid me a visit, wanting to build some sort of relationship. I talked to him about Ben's little predicament and we came up with a deal. He'd let Ben have a low-interest loan with no consequences on two conditions. First that Ben never found out about our connection, and secondly that I went to work for him. So, I did.'

Charlie looked at Jude as though expecting to see some sort of recognition of his selflessness. He didn't find it.

'How was I to know the silly bugger would recommend Les to Sarah? I'd have done the same for her too if she'd only come and asked me for help. If either of them had come to me at the beginning, none of this would have happened. But I couldn't help her because I didn't know about her link with Les until much later and by then she'd already played her stupid games.'

He stopped talking and stared at the road ahead of him.

They drove in silence for a bit. Jude hadn't seen Binnie or any other police cars passing them and she wondered if it all might be too late. It was certainly too late to wish she'd played her hand differently. But then it always was.

Jude knew they were getting close to Malvern End and she would soon be forced to face whatever Charlie had in mind for her next. She knew there was nobody at the farm so it would just be the two of them when they got there. Just her and the man who'd already killed two of his so-called best friends and who would clearly not worry about adding a third to his blood list.

Lucy and Sebbie would be gone for hours still, Sudeley Castle was a fair way and they'd taken a picnic with them. The thought of her small family filled Jude with more anger. The two people more precious in her life than anything else and she'd allowed a murderer to sleep under the same roof as them. Jude knew she had to stay alive for them, to protect them from people like Charlie, Sebbie's father, even her own dad. She needed to do whatever it took to survive.

'It must have been difficult for you,' she said, swallowing her anger and trying hard to win his trust.

'It was,' he said, pulling into the village 'First Sarah and then Ben. She'd told him about Raoul, although she'd obviously kept my name out of it, which was absolutely typical of her. Always looking out for her friends. Anyway, Ben suddenly had an attack of conscience and decided he needed to come clean about everything but he wanted me to hear it from him first, as the poor sod was worried how I'd take it. Of course, I couldn't let him go to the police. He was about to give them a concrete link between Raoul Toussaint and my father. You understand?'

Jude didn't understand. She didn't understand anything of what was happening but she nodded anyway, trying to keep Charlie on side as much as was possible.

'Killing Ben was easy. He was so trusting and submissive. It was almost as though he'd had enough of life anyway and I was doing him a favour. Getting rid of the body was slightly more of a problem but then I had one trump card already. And then you handed me another.'

'I did?' Jude was keen to keep him talking whilst her frantic mind whistled through all the possible options she had for getting out of this mess.

'You did. Or at least whoever gave you that laptop did.'

Charlie stopped then, his crazed eyes flicking over Jude's face.

'Oh,' he said, his face splitting into a maniacal grin. 'Oh, bravo, Jude. I see it now. It wasn't someone else who stole the laptop from Les's house, was it? It was you. Bloody hell, you really are gutsier than I thought. I was wondering how you managed to find Grange Farm. I'm impressed.'

They were in Malvern End now, driving past the village shop and on past The Lamb. If anyone saw them, they'd just assume Charlie and Jude had been out on a trip somewhere. Two old friends together.

'Yes,' she said, hoping that her false confession might stop Charlie looking further afield for an accomplice. Whatever happened to her, she wanted Binnie kept out of it. 'I knew Les was involved, I just needed to get proof. But how did the laptop help you get rid of Ben's body?'

'It gave me another way of framing Noah for his murder, along with the diary I had already pinched from your bag when we were at the pub. You see, I already had the crook – I'd taken that earlier in the day when I'd come to the farm to see you. You were busy with that godawful Nate Sanchez but I did bump into Noah. Another person who would have done much better to have kept his nose out. Asking me about Sarah and our one-night stand.'

'You told me you didn't sleep with her,' said Jude.

'I know I did,' said Charlie. 'I knew what you'd think if I told you that I'd taken advantage of her the night Ben told her he couldn't still see her after the wedding. God, imagine what Noah would have said if he'd found out about Ben sleeping with her whenever they had the chance. Such a pious prick, telling me he knew I'd had a hand in her death and he was going to make sure I got what was coming to me. Nobody likes a have-a-go hero, do they?'

They were heading up the drive to Malvern Farm and Jude thought of Noah, faithful and kind, and yet somehow Charlie, the true monster in all of this, had managed to make her think Noah was responsible for killing Ben. As they drove past the pink house, she wished Noah was still inside, or working in one of the sheep sheds. But it had been days since he'd been seen and Jude was fearful that he'd met the same fate as the others. A fate that seemed to be dangerously close for her too.

'Grange?' Jude said. 'That was never Noah's surname, was it?'

'No,' said Charlie. 'That was a little nugget of brilliance to try and get you off my case whilst I tried to make things happen so you'd stop your bloody investigation. You see, I really didn't want it to come to this, Jude. I can't tell you how much I wish we weren't in this position now.'

'They'll find out the truth about Noah soon enough,' said Jude. 'Charlie, please. Why don't you just go to the police now? We could tell them Les killed Raoul and made Sarah think it was her so she killed herself from the guilt. We could also say he killed Ben, then you'd be free from all of this.'

Would he see through her lies? Jude didn't know but it was a risk she had to take if she was going to survive.

Charlie ignored her and carried on as though she hadn't uttered a word.

'I didn't know how I was going to use the crook. Plant it some-where strategic to get him implicated in something juicy, a robbery perhaps or maybe even the organised crime group. I just wanted him to be so busy defending himself that he would stop bothering me for a while. And then poor Ben came round to tell me he was about to shoot his mouth off to the police about Raoul and Les and suddenly I had the perfect way of killing two birds – with one shepherd's crook.'

As Jude looked at this man she no longer recognised, she felt sick to the core. How could she have been so wrong about him? How could they all have been so blinkered? Sarah, Ben, Adam and her. They'd all loved Charlie and now he was picking them off, one by one. She was extraordinarily glad that Adam wasn't here to see it.

She wriggled her wrists inside their binding, but they held tight.

41

Charlie got out of the car and walked around to open the passenger door. Jude climbed down, finding her legs to be wobbly and heavy. The bash on her forehead was throbbing like a trooper and the effort of moving made her feel light-headed.

'No sign of that wonderful sister of yours,' said Charlie. 'Is she out?'

'I've no idea,' said Jude.

'Her car's missing, so I think we're safe. But we'd better make this quick, just in case she comes back and catches us at it, so to speak. I thought the hay barn would be a good place, don't you? We're out of sight if anyone does happen to turn up at the wrong time and I know how precarious those bales can be if not stacked properly. Come on, let's get this over with.'

He guided Jude towards the barn behind the big lambing sheds. Charlie was right, it was the perfect place for doing things you didn't want others to see. Adam and Jude had discovered this very early in their relationship, when his parents still lived on the farm and the young couple wanted somewhere to sneak off to.

'You don't have to do this,' Jude pleaded. 'I know you, Charlie. I know this isn't you.'

'It *wasn't* me, no,' snapped Charlie. 'Not the old Charlie, the one who always accepted his lot in life. The prick who worked all hours in a crap job and barely brought in enough money to go to the pub for a pint at the end of the week. Who watched his mum and his best friend wither away in front of him within six months of each other and couldn't do anything to stop it. They led good lives, Jude, and look where it got them. But then Les turned up and showed me what else I could be. I don't have to stay here in this claustrophobic place. We've just bought into a new venture that will make us enough money to choose our destinies and I've got my eye on a place in Mexico, where the sun always shines.'

'The organised crime group,' said Jude. 'So, you *are* involved.'

'Bravo again,' said Charlie. 'Spot on. And why not? Someone's going to do it, may as well be us. It's far more lucrative than robbery and it's a lot less work. Raoul gave us the introduction and we just had to raise enough money to buy our way in. The last job we did, stolen to order, will give us the stash we need to be taken seriously.'

Jude couldn't believe what she was hearing. She thought she'd been let down by Sarah and Ben. That their actions had taken away all she'd held precious about their friendships, turning them into strangers. But this? What Charlie was doing was on a completely different plane. Sarah and Ben had been stupid. They'd got caught up in something without meaning to and they'd both paid the ultimate price for their shockingly poor decisions. Charlie had walked into his part of this story with his eyes wide open. Money was the driver and it appeared he was prepared to go to any lengths to get as much of it as possible.

'What would Adam say?' Jude asked quietly.

Charlie spun round and pushed her up against the side of the hay barn.

'Adam isn't here,' he snarled. 'Adam left us all to deal with life in our own ways, just like Mum. You chose this—' He waved his hand around the barn. '—and I chose my own path. Now let's get this over with.'

Charlie pushed Jude roughly into the middle of the barn where he held her arms tightly behind her back and surveyed the hay from the new delivery, piled high, the top tiers teetering from the poor stacking.

'I reckon there's a fair few tonnes up there,' he said. 'I don't think anyone would survive if that lot fell on top of them, do you? I think we'll get you up high on the bale elevator and then push you off first. Hopefully that will make it quicker for you too. I'll take off your wrist bindings before I push the bales onto you.'

Jude stared at the ground, only half listening. The crack on her forehead was pulsing and her eyes were starting to swim again. She felt a sudden intense rush of heat flood her body, making the follicles of her armpits prickle. Charlie's voice became thick and muffled as though she'd covered her ears with a pillow. Jude knew she was about to faint, and she knew that this would only make things easier for Charlie to finish the job.

She put her head down and concentrated hard on breathing. Deep breaths. She needed to stay breathing for herself and she needed to breathe for Lucy and for Sebbie and for Noah because she was the only person who could help any of them.

She felt Charlie's arm around her, supporting her in the way a friend might do.

'Oh dear,' he said. 'Did I bash you a little harder than I meant? Breathe deep. I'm going to need you to help me.'

As quickly as it had descended, the threat of a faint passed. Jude's head still throbbed and ached but the fog had gone and her eyesight had cleared. She kept her head down, though, and tried to act as though she was still close to passing out, letting her legs go heavy so that Charlie had to support her weight.

She knew she'd only get one shot at this and she had to make it count. From somewhere deep inside her, a hidden reserve of energy coiled itself in Jude's shaking legs and she pushed backwards with everything she had, swinging her shoulders around to release herself from her captor with enough force to knock him sideways.

Then Jude ran, her heart roaring and her head pounding. She headed for the door but wasn't even halfway there when she felt a huge shove in the centre of her back that sent her sprawling forwards onto the ground. It was a relatively soft landing, the ground of the barn covered in a thick layer of hay. Jude scrambled up onto her knees, but another shove sent her flying into the hay once more.

'Stop making this harder,' Charlie yelled at her. 'You know it has to happen. It has to be this way.'

Suddenly Charlie was on her back. Jude cried out in desperation before she felt her head pushed forward, down into the carpet of hay.

Her mouth filled with the dusty dried grass. It was up her nose and she couldn't breathe. She kicked out urgently but he was so strong. Jude felt the muscles of her face straining and her lungs screaming as she choked on the hay and tried desperately to pull in enough air to survive.

And then, just at the point she'd almost reconciled herself to her fate, there was an enormous *clang* and Jude felt Charlie's weight fall from her.

New hands were on her then. Gentle hands that rolled her over and wiped the mess from her face so she could breathe, before helping her to sit up and cutting the tape from her wrists.

For a few minutes, all she could do was clutch at her chest as she coughed up lungfuls of hay dust and spat out a revolting mix of mucus and bits of dried grass.

When her breathing steadied and she knew for certain she was going to survive, she looked up into the face of her rescuer.

'I hit him with the shit shovel.' Noah smiled.

42

The following evening, Jude sat on the sofa in front of the log burner at Malvern Farm, wrapped in Adam's dressing gown with a towel around her hair. Her nose and throat were on fire, as though she'd inhaled a thousand tiny razor blades, but the doctor at the hospital had told her that she'd be fine. Her head still pounded but she'd been given a few days' worth of strong painkillers to take home and they were keeping the worst of the pain at bay.

The ache inside her, though, would take a lot more than a few pills to start healing.

DS Binnie Khatri, Lucy and Noah sat with Jude, forming a solid ring of support around her. Pip hadn't left her side since she'd returned from the hospital. Even when she'd gone up to soak in the bath Lucy had run, Pip sat at the bottom of the stairs and didn't move until she'd come back down.

'How are you feeling?' Lucy asked.

'Been better. But could be worse.' She looked over at Noah. 'Thanks for not leaving us.'

'As if I would,' he said.

'Noah's been a total hero,' said Lucy. 'All this time we thought he'd done a runner, and he was hiding out on the farm. He was the only one who knew Charlie was no good.'

Jude stared at Lucy and then at Noah.

'How?' she said. 'How could you possibly know that?'

'It was the morning I bought Gertie for you,' he said. 'Charlie came round to the farm when you were busy with that Nate. He was so cocky and I'm afraid I got a bit cross. I told him what I thought of him messing about with Sarah and he told me that I was jealous of him because he could have anyone he wanted.'

Noah stared deep into the flames of the log burner.

'Then he told me that you were next on his list and that he'd probably have his way with Lucy too. Made me pretty mad, it did, but I didn't know how to tell you.'

Jude remembered that day and how angry Noah had been. She'd assumed it had been Nate's presence on the farm that had rattled him but now she saw differently.

'I'd seen other stuff too. I'd seen him in the farmhouse, poking around in the office. He said he was just looking for something you'd asked him to fetch, but I didn't buy it. I told him I didn't trust him and that I had my eye on him but he just said that if it came down to it, he'd just tell you I'd been mistaken and you'd believe him.'

'Oh, Noah,' said Jude. 'That's why he took your crook and tried to frame you for Ben's murder. He wanted you out of the picture.'

Noah nodded. 'I knew it as soon as I saw him dragging the body into the woods that afternoon. He'd taken my crook, I was sure of that, but I had no proof of any of it. I feared I would be taken in for questioning at the very least, and I suspected that he'd do a good enough job of laying traps to make sure I was out of the way for a while. I knew he was capable of anything and I didn't want to leave you on the farm without me, not even for one night with him out there.'

'So, he hid in the coal store,' said Lucy. 'Isn't that just like something out of a Brontë novel?'

'But we don't have a coal store,' said Jude.

'The farm used to,' said Noah. 'The entrance was in the floor of the storeroom at the side of the house.'

That was why Floss had been so interested in that space. It wasn't the rats she was after, it was her master.

'It has a second entrance at the back of the utility room,' said Lucy. 'Sealed up now but still thin enough for Noah to hear through perfectly so he knew what was going on in the house.'

'Really?' said Jude.

Noah nodded and got up to poke the fire and add another log.

'Idea was, the coal man would tip the coal down into the store to limit the amount of dust, then it could be accessed from the house,' he explained.

Jude shook her head. Even the farmhouse itself had been keeping secrets from her.

'How did you know it was there? I had no idea.'

'I did some work on the store with Adam's father before you lived here,' Noah said. 'He showed me then how it worked. It wasn't ideal but it was the only way I had of keeping out of sight but still looking out for you.'

'You can't have lived under the floor of the storeroom all that time?'

'It was only a few days, really. I took myself out at night to get some fresh air and a bite to eat. Had to nip out in the day once or twice too, when nature called. Thought I'd been caught once but I got away with it.'

'Thank goodness you did,' said Binnie. 'And thank goodness you noticed that Jude didn't go back into the farmhouse when you heard the car return, and went looking for her.'

Noah sucked in through his teeth and then took a deep drink

from his glass of cider. Jude looked at the gentle shepherd and felt an eternity of gratitude that this man was a part of her life. She noticed the way Lucy was also gazing at him and thought that her sister echoed her feelings.

'Something's been bothering me,' said Jude. 'Noah, when did you see Charlie dragging Ben's body into the woods? What time of day?'

'I suppose it was about five. Just starting to get dark. Why?'

'I had a conversation with Ben by text,' she said, taking her phone out and searching for it. 'There, look. It was around nine that evening.'

'We found Ben's phone in Charlie's coat pocket,' said Binnie. 'It was him who sent those messages. I suppose to stop you going to look for him.'

Jude read the last message with fresh tears in her eyes.

Jude, I'm so sorry I messed up so badly. I wish things were different. Whatever happens I want you to know that I love you and I miss what we all had. xxx

Charlie had even stolen that from her.

He'd come to check on them that night, pretending to make sure they were locked in and safe, all the time knowing Ben was lying dead just a few hundred metres away. Had he already killed him when they'd sat together sharing a picnic in the garden? Oh, God, had Ben's body been in the boot of his car then? There were some things she supposed she'd never know.

A murmur from the baby monitor drew Jude's attention to the little screen showing an image of her nephew, bundled up in his travel cot, flat on his back with two balled-up fists on the mattress by his head. The perfect picture of innocence.

For a while, they all sat in silence, each deep in their own thoughts. Thoughts that were only broken when the doorbell rang.

'That'll be the pizzas,' said Binnie. 'They're on DI Peters. He had a good day today, got a big breakthrough in the OCG investigation thanks to your tip-off about Les Turner. When I told him I was bringing you back from the hospital this afternoon, he gave me fifty quid and told me to get something nice for your dinner to say thank you.'

'You believed me and stuck by us when he didn't,' said Jude. 'I'm not sure I'll ever truly understand why you did, but I want you to know how grateful I am for everything you've done.'

The DS raised a hand to silence any further gratitude.

'I'm just glad we got there,' she said.

Noah went to the door to fetch the pizzas and Binnie told Jude and Lucy about how easy Les Turner had been to break. Thanks to Jude's message and the photos, a team of squad cars had been sent to Grange Farm not long after Charlie had driven Jude off in the Land Rover. Les had nowhere to escape and was caught up to his eyeballs in a paper trail that connected him to a plethora of robberies as well as hinting at an involvement in the organised crime ring. Quite the catch for an ambitious DI.

'It didn't take much for Les Turner to cave,' said Binnie. 'Turned out to be a very willing grass if it meant landing himself a shorter sentence. He handed over the details of everyone he knew to be involved, including the top three cheeses of the OCG. The drug squad went to three different addresses early this morning and busted the lot of them, seizing several millions of pounds' worth of class A drugs. Needless to say, the DI is reaping the praise and he's even willing to overlook some of the slightly more shadowy aspects of your investigation – and even my possible involvement in it.'

This was very good news. Even with a shortened sentence, Les

Turner would be in prison for a very long time – Jude was sure of that. She was also fairly sure that if word got around that he was a grass he would not be well received amongst his fellow inmates.

'What about Charlie?' Jude asked. 'What will happen to him?'

Binnie and Lucy exchanged glances. Lucy took hold of Jude's hand and gave it a tight squeeze.

'He's being held in custody,' said Binnie. 'There'll be no hope for bail and with all the evidence stacked against him, he will be locked up for a very, very long time.'

Despite everything he'd become, everything he'd done and everything he'd tried to do, Jude's heart still ached. It ached for the friend she'd thought she had but who she realised had never really existed. She ached from the loss of all her friends and she ached most of all from the loss of her husband to share the pain with.

'I'll be back in a minute,' she said. 'I need to get something from the kitchen.'

With a heart so heavy she feared it might never heal, Jude picked up the photograph of the four friends from the dresser. She stroked the faces of each one before turning it over.

Me, Apple, Ivy and Charlie Barley at the school leaving ball.

Jude gave the photo one kiss, then she walked back into the sitting room, opened the door of the wood burner and placed the photo onto the flames where it began to curl and blacken. She watched as the faces of the people she had loved so fiercely were consumed by the flames until they had disappeared altogether.

'And then there were none,' she whispered.

43

Jude Gray filled two flasks with orange squash and added a generous handful of ice cubes to each. The farm was in for a busy day.

'Come on, Sebbie,' she called. 'Noah will be waiting for us.'

Lucy insisted on pulling a jumper over her son's head, despite the fact that the mid-summer sun was already heating the day up and it was only going to get hotter. Sebbie stretched up to hold hands with both his mother and his favourite aunt. With Pip in the lead, the little party walked over the yard to the lambing shed, which had been transformed into the shearing shed the day before.

'Morning, all,' said Noah. 'Ready for the big day?'

'Oddly, yes!' said Jude. 'I think I actually am.'

It had been a difficult few months, but Jude had found solace and strength in her new unlikely tribe. Once they'd finally been able to bury Sarah and Ben, it felt as though she could somehow move forward and rebuild her life again. Lucy had decided to stay on and had thrown herself into the running of the farm in a way that Jude recognised from her own early days of learning the ropes with Adam. Although Granny Margot had offered Lucy the use of Sarah's old cottage, Lucy had declined, choosing instead to move the rest of her belongings into Jude's house. Both women had let their father know that he had no place in their lives, at least for the time being. And he'd stopped trying to contact either of them.

'If you're all set then,' said Noah, 'I'll take Floss up to the field and get the first load in.'

Rick, the shearer, had been the previous afternoon and set up his equipment ready for an early start. The lambing shed now had a fenced-off channel that led from the large back doors up to the shearing station. Jude and Lucy took Sebbie through the lambing shed and out the other side. The fenced channel continued across to the bottom field, where it fanned out to create a funnel.

Jude always loved watching the way Noah and Floss could control the flock. With a few whistled commands and some simple directive calls, Floss tore around the field, then was perfectly still with her ears pricked, waiting for the next instruction. This carried on until, within just a few minutes, a group of around thirty sheep had been sectioned off from the flock and were herded into the wide mouth of the funnel.

'Now watch them, Sebbie,' said Jude. 'Look, they all come walking through here and end up in a nice, neat line in the shed, waiting for their hair cuts.'

'Shall we go and watch them?' said Lucy.

'There's no watching, I'm afraid,' said Jude. 'It'll be all hands on deck until we're done.'

A production line of individual jobs ensured that the morning ran smoothly. Rick would expertly shear a sheep, then Noah would move the freshly shorn animal to the big barn next door, allowing Rick to crack on with the next customer. Jude took the fleece and pulled any large clods of muck off before folding the sides in and rolling it up tightly. Then it was down to Lucy to put the fleeces into the enormous bags ready to be taken to the British Wool depot for grading. The farm would get paid according to the quality and weight of the wool and, if they were lucky, they might just make enough money to cover the cost of hiring a professional shearer. It wasn't a money maker by any stretch of the imagination, but it was essential work in order to keep the flock healthy and comfortable during the summer months.

The shed was noisy as the lambs, who weren't impressed at being split from their mothers, called out urgently from the big barn where they were waiting.

By midday, they were all exhausted, hot and sticky. Jude's knees and back were aching from kneeling down, but she felt happier than she had in a while. She took Sebbie over to the sink and rubbed soap into his hands.

'No, Aundy Chewdy. No wash.'

'No wash, no lunch,' said Jude. 'And if you don't eat your lunch then you can't have any Tony's chocolate.'

'I do want a Tony clocklet,' said Sebbie.

'Then let's get those hands clean, shall we?'

As the shearing team sat on hay bales, eating their packed lunches and chatting about the luck of the dry weather and the speed they were getting through the flock, Jude heard a car arrive in the yard.

DS Binnie Khatri joined them in the barn, wearing a pair of jeans, cut off at the knees, and an old T-shirt. Binnie had been a regular visitor to the farm since the terrible events of the spring. At first to check up on Jude and make sure she was coping with the awfulness of what had happened, but a strong friendship had quickly developed and they often shared a meal, a movie or a chat.

'You look ready to work,' said Jude.

'Well, you said it would be busy today, so I thought I'd come and see if you needed a hand.'

'Dangerous that,' said Lucy. 'Once she gets you here, it's very difficult to leave!'

'Rubbish,' said Jude, nudging her sister's arm so that she spilled the water from her camping mug down her top. 'You can leave any time you choose.'

'I think we'll stay,' said Lucy. 'After all, you couldn't do without us.'

Binnie sat down on the bale next to Jude.

'How's it going?' she asked.

'Rick is officially amazing,' said Jude.

'Not sure about that,' said Rick. 'It's a good team here. We've got through around seventy sheep or so, I'd say. Should make a hundred and fifty by the end of the day.'

'At this rate we'll be done by the end of the week,' said Jude. 'Which makes you amazing in my eyes.'

'And you thought of giving all this up,' said Lucy.

'I did,' said Jude.

It had all seemed so pointless without her husband and her friends around her. But Lucy, Noah, Binnie, Granny Margot and little Sebbie had gradually shown her that there was still plenty of life left to live and that life was on the farm, doing what she loved.

'But there's nothing like the smell of a sheep barn in the middle of summer to make a girl change her mind,' she said.

Jude looked at Binnie. If it hadn't been for her diligence and tenacity, there was a good chance they'd never have got to the bottom of the tangle that had become of her friends' lives.

'It was never just about Sarah, was it?' Jude said gently.

'What?' asked Binnie.

'You don't have to say,' said Jude. 'Not if you don't want to. I just keep getting the feeling that there's something else you aren't telling me. Something else to do with that case you worked on in Birmingham.'

Binnie sighed. 'You're a good detective, Jude,' she said. 'Nothing much gets past you.'

A dark shadow passed across Binnie's face again, her previously buoyant mood shifting visibly.

'Sorry,' said Jude. 'I shouldn't have asked. Forget I did?'

'No,' said Binnie. 'It's fine, I'd have told you anyway. Everything about that case was true. The apparent suicide, the girl Ashani who'd been harassed and terrified by her stalker, the second murder that he was convicted of. But I left out something. I didn't tell you that I wasn't allowed to work on that second case, on Bhavra's case. I was too close to it, you see.'

She stopped and Jude looked into her friend's haunted eyes, seeing the truth.

'She was your sister,' she said. 'Bhavra was your sister, wasn't she?'

'She was.' Binnie gave Jude a watery smile.

Jude leant across and gave her a fierce hug. This tenacious, courageous, incredible woman who had shown up in Jude's life as it had been crumbling around her, who came with her own baggage and who had kept the worst of her pain from Jude. The pain of shouldering that guilt all this time, telling herself that if she'd done things differently then perhaps she could have saved her sister from the hands of a monster.

'It wasn't your fault,' Jude said gently.

'Come on,' said Binnie, pulling away and rubbing her eyes on the edge of her T-shirt. 'I was promised there'd be takeaway this evening if we got enough work done today, and I'm here to earn my lamb biryani!'

* * *

After lunch, Lucy took Sebbie in for a rest and Binnie took over her job of bagging up the fleeces.

'Thanks for putting us in touch with Katie Sullivan,' said Jude. 'She's been absolutely amazing.'

'I knew she would be,' said Binnie. 'She's one of my oldest friends and the best family lawyer in the Midlands. How's it all going for Lucy?'

'She's had the initial hearing and now we're just waiting. Paul hasn't tried to come and see her and Sebbie, which makes me wonder how much he actually wants to have to do with his son and how much is just a power game. Katie thinks we've got a really strong case, but it'll be nice to have it out of the way so that we can put it all behind us.'

Binnie put her arm around Jude.

'And you?' she said. 'Are you starting to put things behind you?'

Jude considered the question. She had deep scars from everything that had happened, and they might never truly heal. But she had so much to be thankful for in her life and she fully planned on living that life and running Malvern Farm in a way Adam would have been proud of.

'Yes,' said Jude. 'I believe I am.'

ACKNOWLEDGMENTS

There are so many people who have helped make this book into the thing that it is and who deserve my huge and heartfelt thanks. Starting with my wonderful agent, Amanda Preston. Having you on my side is like being cared for by the very best shepherdess. I knew I was in a safe pair of hands when you took me on and will be forever grateful for your encouragement and belief.

Thank you to my amazing editor, Emily Yau. I am so glad you chose to champion me, Jude and the farm, bringing us safely into the world and watching as we take our first steps into new pastures.

To Amanda, Nia, Marcela, Claire and the entire Boldwood team, what a fantastic book flock to have found myself part of. Such an exciting and fresh publishing house and unbelievably welcoming.

Tim, Nick and Chase on Yew Tree Farm – Thank you for giving me a real insight into your working lives, in the rain, the wind and even a little bit of sunshine. I learnt a lot about lambing, the real issues that affect farmers, and also how many different ways there are to get rid of a body on a farm!

Thank you to *Farmers Weekly* for the constant stream of information via webinars and podcasts, and to *The Farmers Guardian* for my weekly dip into the world of agriculture. To the awe-inspiring Emma Gray, thanks for keeping me entertained with your real shepherdess stories and for unknowingly being my muse for Jude. Maybe one day I'll make it to watch you in the field.

As always, a massive thank you to the incredible writing community that have always been such a vital source of support. My fabulous crit group, Donna, Clare, Meredith and Fi and to the Arvon girls, Jo, Nikki and Sarah who brainstormed early chapters and ideas with me in Glasgow. A special thank you to my crime writing posse, the Furies, who make my life of crime so much sweeter for their constant banter, book talk and advice. Ewe girls rock!!

Thank you Alex at Four Bears Books in Caversham for being such a fantastic cheerleader and for reading an early draft of Malvern Farm, and to everyone who keeps the marvellous Malvern Book Cooperative running. Please support our local indie bookshops!

Elane and Sarah at I Am In Print – you wonderful pair. I don't know how you do it, such a huge support to the writing community and ALWAYS with big smiles and endless kindness. Thank you.

Thank you to Jenny Parrott for the early advice and manuscript feedback and to the brilliant folk at Write Magic for the boot camps and sprints that helped me get this thing written. To all my friends who have become would-be-killers as soon as murder is mentioned and have armed me with so many new ideas. Especially Lindsey for the astonishingly enthusiastic brainstorming over tapas, Kajsa for all the hot-tub inspiration, and Claire for just being totally brilliant and always you.

Love and thanks to Mum and Dad for giving me a childhood full of adventure, nature, farms and stories, and to Jon and Nick for sharing the fun. So many of the happiest parts of this book were born from my memories of life on Bank Farm and in West Malvern – but thankfully, not the murders!

Thank you also to the Wests who welcomed me onto the farm and into the family all those decades ago.

And to Will, Lily, Jemima and Pippi dog, whom I love even more than a whole field of new lambs in the spring sunshine. You are my world and I am forever grateful.

ABOUT THE AUTHOR

Kate Wells is the author of a number of well-reviewed books for children, and is now writing cosy crime set in the Malvern hills, inspired by the farm where she grew up.

Sign up to Kate Wells' mailing list for news, competitions and updates on future books.

Visit Kate's website: www.katepoels.co.uk

Follow Kate on social media:

 twitter.com/KatePoels
 facebook.com/KatePoelsWest
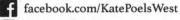 instagram.com/KatePoelsWrites
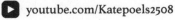 youtube.com/Katepoels2508

Poison
& Pens

POISON & PENS IS THE HOME OF
COZY MYSTERIES SO POUR YOURSELF
A CUP OF TEA & GET SLEUTHING!

DISCOVER PAGE-TURNING NOVELS FROM
YOUR FAVOURITE AUTHORS &
MEET NEW FRIENDS

JOIN OUR
FACEBOOK GROUP

BIT.LYPOISONANDPENSFB

SIGN UP TO OUR
NEWSLETTER

BIT.LY/POISONANDPENSNEWS

Boldwood

Boldwood Books is an award-winning
fiction publishing company seeking
out the best stories from
around the world.

Find out more at
www.boldwoodbooks.com

Join our reader community
for brilliant books,
competitions and offers!

Follow us
#BoldBookClub

Sign up to our weekly
deals newsletter

https://bit.ly/BoldwoodBNewsletter

Milton Keynes UK
Ingram Content Group UK Ltd.
UKHW041850231023
431205UK00004B/114